Columbia&Britannia

An Alternate History

Columbia & Britannia

An Alternate History

Edited by

Adam Chamberlain & Brian A. Dixon

Fourth Horseman Press

Columbia & Britannia
Edited by Adam Chamberlain & Brian A. Dixon
Published by Fourth Horseman Press

First Edition, October 2009

Printed in the United States of America

All Materials Copyright © by the Individual Authors

"Christmas for King George" (Pg. 393) by Brian Coppola

Figures 2A–7 (Pgs. 384-91) by Joe Tangari

Cover Artwork: "Columbia & Britannia" by Cyril Van Der Haegen

ISBN: 978-0-615-33327-4

Fourth Horseman Press
http://www.fourthhorsemanpress.com/

Table of Contents

Intolerable Acts   17
Brian A. Dixon

Total Emancipation   39
Joe Tangari

The Thunderbird   77
Mark Beech

All the Jungle is Thine   105
C. Mitchell O'Neal

Here Grow No Flowers   139
Alexander Zelenyj

Flag Day   193
Adam Chamberlain

The Sun Yet Sets   227
Joe Tangari

The Last Day of the Old World   253
Brian A. Dixon

The Twelfth Man   275
Adam Chamberlain

Appendix A   315
    Timeline

Appendix B   331
    Biographies

Appendix C   345
    List of British Monarchs

Appendix D   347
    List of Prime Ministers

Appendix E   351
    Letters & Documents

Appendix F   383
    Maps & Diagrams

If buttercups buzz'd
after the bee;
If boats were on land,
churches on sea;
If ponies rode men
and grass ate the cow;
If cats should be chased
into holes by the mouse;
If mamas sold their babies
to gypsies for half a crown;
If summer were spring
and the other way round,
Then all the world
would be upside down.

—English Nursery Rhyme

Intolerable Acts
by Brian A. Dixon

14 February 1776
Richmond, Virginia

When I arrived at the home of my love on the eve of St Valentine's Day I found the Baroness in the parlour, a printed pamphlet in her hand.

To one side of her stood an unfinished portraiture, nearly as tall as she was, commissioned weeks earlier. I had enjoyed observing its progress during my regular visits, for although aspects of the familiar countenance and delicate dress of that painted lady had yet to be crafted, it captured all that was stunning about Susanna and the sight of it regularly returned me to the moment I first beheld her.

I understood, when my marvelling eyes had first beheld the Baroness Susanna Arrieta Aguirre de Córdoba of Spain, with her raven-hued hair and porcelain countenance, that hers was a beauty capable of delivering a man to astonishing heights of joy or boundless depths of misery. Her glorious eyes, with their thick lashes and nobly arched brows, would have been able to command a man to fight or to die for her. Men so often regard such beauty as delicate, fragile. They forget the true and dangerous power of such things. 'Twas a consideration I too had long failed to recall.

She was poring over a pamphlet beside her portraiture, standing in the small circle of dim light cast by a candelabrum, and so intent was she in her private study that she failed to take notice of my presence in the parlour. I stood in the doorway and watched her a moment, to observe her elegant features in that warm, golden light. She seemed, though, not as a woman but as a mischievous child looking over some stolen trinket, her posture betraying a guilty conscience.

'What have you got there, my love?' I asked her pleasantly.

Susanna's reaction was immediate and drastic. When she turned to face me the pamphlet was gone, discarded to the table behind her, thrown down on its face as if it were nothing more than a bit of paper to be used for the fireplace. 'Simeon, you startled me!' she breathed, a quivering hand held tight over her fluttering heart.

I went to her at once and aimed to embrace her, though she took a step back at my advance and refused to meet my gaze. 'Look at you,' I said. 'You're positively shaking. Are you not glad to see me?'

'No, Simeon.' A moment later she was weeping, her bright brown eyes brimming over with tears that soon pitter-pattered to the carpeting below. 'No, no, 'tis—' She stopped herself and turned her head away.

She was a witty woman, bright and well-spoken. Her tongue was as sharp as her mind and the two of us had spent many an evening engaged in playful repartee. Truly, such nights had lent momentum to our impetuous love affair. It was not like her to be without words and it disturbed me to see her weeping and stuttering so. 'I don't understand,' I remarked.

'How could you understand? Oh, Simeon. My poor, poor Simeon.' She kissed me then on the cheek, but briefly, and I felt a cool tear pass from her cheek to mine. It was the saddest kiss she had ever granted. 'You are so good to me. You take such care of me these past months. You are a loving man. But love renders you so blind, and I am happy to maintain that blindness. How can it be, that I must wound you at such a time as this?'

Susanna had backed to the table now and I could see her delicate fingers playing behind her back upon the cover of the secret manuscript she had clutched so desperately. My curiosity would not be denied. 'What is this?' I demanded, moving to one side. She gasped and vainly tried to hold me back but I soon held the slender volume in my hands. 'What message hath left you so distraught? I will not stand for this, my love. Tell me what has devastated you so!'

I soon had my answer.

The pamphlet was crisp and new, its pages sturdy. One could smell the black printer's ink fresh upon its pages. It was a thin volume, no more than fifty pages, and cleanly presented. The cover told that it had come from Philadelphia and that the price of its insight was one shilling. My gaze was first drawn to a quotation the cover page bore, attributed to 'Thomson': *'Man knows no Master save creating Heaven, or those whom choice and common Good ordain.'*

My memory thus kindled, I could not halt the wave of horror the came over me as I mouthed the words of that volume's title page. *'COMMON SENSE; addressed to the inhabitants of British North America on the following interesting subjects: of the Origin and Design of Government in general, with concise Remarks on the English Constitution; of Monarchy and Hereditary Succession; of the Columbia Compromise; of the present ability of America, with some miscellaneous Reflections.'*

Though the incendiary tract did not bear the name of an author—it was a political statement delivered in cowardly anonymity—the discussions I have held in the Virginia legislature had made the man's name known to me. 'Susanna!' I nearly cried, and almost immediately I cast the pamphlet down as she had. 'Do you wish to return to England and hang at the Tower of London, Thomas Paine himself by your side? Do you wish to be branded a traitor to the King's rule in his American provinces?'

'No! Please, Simeon.'

My voice crackled with anger and fear, I could not help it. If my tone then frightened her it was for the better. With these writings the woman I loved had brought great danger into her home, and she knew it was a matter a man in my position could not ignore.

Susanna Arrieta Aguirre de Córdoba was a woman of great wealth. She had been born the daughter of an influential Spanish baron and here, in the British territories of North America, there were vast tracts of land bound to her family name. Though it was in her interest to oversee this inherited acreage, as her father and all other heirs had passed, I had convinced myself that it was those affecting, poetic words that had flowed from mine own pen that had brought her to these shores. So long had British North

America struggled to find its place beneath the Crown; truly, 'twas only the stability brought by the admission of the Colonies into Parliament that had even allowed for the Baroness's safe living on North American soil, that had convinced me we could have a life together in the colony that had long been my home.

The work of a revolutionary like Paine threatened all that America had achieved and, what is more, its presence in this home threatened the very life of my Spanish Baroness. 'Do you not recall the January burnings in Baltimore, when boxes of this blasphemy were set ablaze on the green? The smoke was seen from four counties hence, and you well know the fate of the men found distributing those wares. I have told you myself, and I have signed such warrants with mine own hand!'

'I know it,' she cried out, but her tears had since stopped flowing and I soon witnessed the familiar hardening of her features as scorn took hold. 'I know it. Stop, Simeon. Please, stop.'

'Who has provided you with this printed poison? Tell me.'

The parlour fell silent about us. I watched in the flickering candlelight as the tears dried upon Susanna's face and she stared at me, her bosom still rising and falling with a terrifying and unhealthy quickness. I then came to understand that, dreadful though the discovery of that forbidden text was, the most terrible secret of this night had yet to be revealed. I felt the weight of personal threat settle about my shoulders in the silence that followed.

Another moment passed before I stepped forward, and I could feel her quickened breath upon my face in the chilled parlour. 'Do not protect the name any longer,' I demanded. 'Say it.'

'You do not understand, Simeon,' she said most sorrowfully, and again she avoided my gaze. 'This book—and all the others that are now hidden in the storerooms behind this house—they come with papers bearing your name!'

I nearly gasped. Comprehension eluded me. '*My* name?'

'They come addressed to you, my love, but I know you did not order them. You speak of the burnings, the warrants you signed, and I know you did not send for them.'

'Where are they now, these papers?' I asked her.

'I burn them in the fireplace as soon as they are delivered. The crates of books are stored, but those papers I destroy. I wish it were not this way, but I know why they've come, Simeon. These shipments bring trouble to you, and they bring trouble for me. They signal the approach of an Englishman.'

Though I was frightened to know it, I asked her, 'What man?'

She breathed deeply and closed her eyes to say it. 'Edward Loomis.'

Truly, the very sound of it brought to mind images too painful for me to bear. Know that his was a name I had hoped never to hear again; his was a name that had burned so long in my memory, with hatred and jealousy the likes of which I have never experienced before or since. Loomis, Member of Parliament, the lauded gentleman that had tasted the lips of my love long before I had placed my own claim on them. Loomis, the pompous monster that treated her with all the tenderness of a knave, who once neglected her wants and her various needs.

She had loved him, during her time in London. She had spent more than five years in his company, sharing his time. Then she left it all behind for her properties in the new provinces and the promise of new love in American lands. 'Twas the carelessness of Edward Loomis, the inferiority of his love, that had spawned a space in Susanna's heart for a gentle man like me.

But the heart of that Spanish lady of beauty and power had never completely been mine to claim. Though Thomson would insist that man knows no master save creating Heaven, 'twas the aching of mine own heart that had rendered me a slave to my love in spite of Susanna's duplicitous nature. She had left Loomis in London but he held her heart captive still.

'Edward, he comes to Virginia,' Susanna warned, and though I would listen closely for it there was no hint of apology in her voice. 'He is here tomorrow. I swear unto you, I did not know of it. The shipment of pamphlets, they arrive this very afternoon along with trunks of his belongings. I know that he is responsible for sending them. He comes here to be with me, and the supplies shew that he plans to stay with me for some time.'

'He comes,' I moaned, 'and you would let him come.'

'Please, Simeon,' she said. It was not a plea, it was a command. Her voice had taken on a familiar severity. 'Do not make this any more difficult.'

I could not keep the defeat from my voice. 'How long have I been a fool, Susanna? Have you always been in contact with him, since the day you left London to make your way to Richmond? Have you sent letters of longing across the Atlantic to him? Or was it he that longed, and wrote, and pleaded?'

'It matters not,' she said.

'It matters not?' I shouted. 'You have loved him, and I have ignored it. I felt this love would fade with him so far away, with more than an ocean's breadth between your two hearts. Now, you have opened your home to him and, whether you intend it or not, you betray not only me but this kingdom as well!'

Susanna's expression had undergone a familiar transformation. Gone were the quivering breath and tear-filled eyes of a woman frightened; her lips were pressed tightly together and her dark eyebrows dove over accusing eyes. She looked on me with all the grace and charm of an injured rattlesnake. 'Judge me not, Simeon Trask,' she all but shouted, 'and neither cross me. I have loved you deeply, you cannot deny. Though you act the part when you preach in the House of Burgesses, you are no saint, and I am no sinner!'

'Have you been robbed of choice, woman? What prompts you to halve your heart so?'

'Force my hand and you will not relish the results,' Susanna snapped. Then her voice softened to a near whisper as her eyes fluttered and she seemed to grow faint. She continued, 'Do not ask me to choose. I lost a father in the Seven Years' War, a mother to plague. I lost a brother. You would have me now choose, to pluck one man from my life? And if you were that man? I look upon you both, I read your letters of passion and love, and I see before me two paths that reach to distant horizons. No one can tell me where they lead, to fortune or ruin. No one can tell me what fate holds for Trask or for Loomis. How am I to script a history? How can I choose?'

'You have brought this upon yourself, Susanna,' I told her, and it was true. 'You have split your being between these paths. 'Tis unnatural. Now, the consequences are inescapable.'

She would not hear it. 'You must leave, Simeon,' she commanded. 'You must not be here when he arrives. I care for you, for what happens to you, and I do not wish to learn what Edward intends for you. Go, go to your home. I write to you when it is safe. You two cannot meet; those twin paths must never entwine. Heed my words, and do not cross me! Leave!'

'Edward Loomis comes to America,' I breathed, and now it was I that felt my heart as it pounded with fear and fury. I shook my head at her. 'So, it shall be finished. Hear me, Susanna, this will find its end. I'll not leave you now; I'll not leave this house. Loomis comes, and I shall be here when he does.'

My stubborn stand declared, Susanna abandoned her pleas. She stormed away with such speed and force that the whipping of her dress put out the centremost light on the candelabrum.

I waited a moment before following Susanna out of the room and then made my way through the manor's front door and onto the porch. Night had long since fallen and there was no Moon in evidence. It was a dark and foreboding eventide. A veritable trap had been laid at this familiar homestead and I was still uncertain of its true design and complexity. I knew not what trials awaited me on the other side of night but I knew well enough to be prepared. 'Waller!' I called out in the direction of the stables, for I knew the lad that served as my coachman would not be far. He was undoubtedly still tending to the horses following our arrival.

'Twas a mere moment before I heard his fast footfalls upon the frosty ground. ''Tis cold tonight, sir!' he exclaimed when he appeared before me at the manor's door.

'Yes,' I said solemnly, 'and I fear I must ask you to abandon the comforts of your bed. Something comes, and we two must act swiftly. I want you to take one of the horses and ride. You are to ride into the city. 'Tis urgent that you make haste.' Then, as he listened intently and the smile faded from his young face, I gave Waller my very specific instructions for the day that lay ahead.

Although the Baroness retired early that evening, our arguments ended, and with the brutal inevitability of this particular St Valentine's Day looming before us, I remained in the study, careless on this occasion of any perceived impropriety. With the study's door locked tightly behind me and its key safely upon the desk I sat in private and examined the filth-covered pages of Thomas Paine's *Common Sense*. The words did nothing but inflame my contempt. 'Tis impossible to calculate the potential destruction inherent to the distribution of such a text. The storerooms of the Baroness's estate held enough books to taint a thousand minds, literature waiting to spread its ignorance and fear. The Columbia Compromise promised harmony and the provinces have declared their loyalty to Great Britain, but that safe unity is only as stable as the citizenry on which 'tis built.

I have always trusted in the American people but they are a mass easily swayed. Paine would push them toward revolution. Imagine! A hundred-thousand angry men, stubbornly unwilling to pay their taxes, inflamed by the sophistry of a wicked tongue. Imagine British citizens in Virginia or Maryland senselessly revolting against the Crown, after all that has been accomplished, after all that has been forged in the courthouses of the Colonies and the hallowed halls of Parliament. Truly, I could not bring my mind to conceive of such a thing! 'Twas the mere implication of it, not the chill February night air, which then prompted me to shiver. Whatever Loomis's devious intent, I could not allow those crates of *Common Sense* to see distribution. They would burn by my hand, this I vowed. I fell into sleep that night with righteous fury in my heart and the name of my rival upon my lips.

Edward Loomis arrived with the punctuality of a man accustomed to attending the House of Commons, his boots sounding upon the steps of the Baroness de Córdoba's manor at one o'clock on February the fourteenth. The commotion outside the home was considerable—Loomis had with him a veritable entourage, consisting of at least half a dozen horses and two wagons full to brimming with crates undoubtedly carrying more of his incendiary contraband.

'Baroness!' he called upon entering, an unbridled

enthusiasm in his deep voice, and though I knew this was his first visit to her Virginian home, he tromped down the hall as if he were in ownership of the manor. 'Baroness?'

Susanna did not answer; she was undoubtedly hiding from the forthcoming clash that would surely encompass her home. Fate had brought her lovers face to face and this was a prospect that both shamed and frightened her. I was not sure whether that beautiful Spanish lady I so loved was a devil, a fool, or merely a coward, but she stood aside and let destiny take its course.

I waited for him in the parlour, sat in shadows beside a smouldering morning fire, watching the embers burn on the stones, able to identify with the sort of heat that burns so furiously from within it makes the whole being glow. I was smouldering myself in that cushioned chair, and though I felt my eyes must be burning brightly with my rage, still Loomis did not see me when he first entered. His attentions were at once drawn to that magnificent unfinished portraiture that lay against the wall beside the room's only window and he strode toward it. He looked first, with relish and a sickening savouring, upon the visage of my love. 'Twas then that I had my first glimpse of the man.

'Baroness, your portrait; 'tis magnificent!' he called.

He was older than I, if not by many years, tall, dark-haired, with a strong chin and an even stronger brow. He wore a coat of richly coloured green emblazoned with buttons of bronze, and though he stood proudly and with an aristocratic air, there was a smallness to the size and placement of his eyes that, to my mind, caused him to resemble a certain rodent as much as any Member of Parliament. Those eyes, they were too close to one another for him to be mistaken for an honest man. One could discern from listening to his voice and seeing him walk that the arrogance he displayed upon entering this Virginian manor was a defining quality.

After watching him a moment I spoke with a level voice and declared my presence. 'It is indeed quite stunning, Mr Loomis,' I said of the portraiture, 'though unfinished. In this 'tis true to that from which it draws inspiration.'

He whirled on his feet, coat trailing behind him, and found

me in my place by the fireside. His eyes were instantly accusatory. It was an expression I did not hesitate to return. 'You,' he said, a bit startled, and then drew himself up to his full height before asking, 'Who are you? Where is the Baroness de Córdoba?'

I sighed and shook my head, doing my best to maintain assumed tranquillity for as long as it would last. Here was a man, rash and impetuous, abandoning political responsibilities and traversing whole oceans selfishly and on a whim. 'Twas my duty— my destiny!—to behave as his opposite. I had to keep my head. 'If she hath sense, will that she has been driven away by the presumptuousness of your arrival and by the indisputable danger of those materials you bring with you in your wake. Alas, my faith in the Baroness's powers of rationality is not strong this day. I would not fear. She has not been known to hold her tongue for long; she will no doubt soon emerge, though not before you have explained yourself to me.'

Loomis was furious now and his beady eyes narrowed still further as he stepped toward my chair and repeated his earlier demand, though I was certain he now knew who comfortably occupied this seat by the Baroness's fire. I was, after all, unquestionably his reason for travelling to British North America. 'Who are you?'

'I am Simeon Trask, of the Virginia House of Burgesses, and you now know the face which represents that familiar name.'

'Trask,' he breathed, and those sharp eyes soon glimmered with the light of recognition as his snarl seemed to change itself to a sinister smile. 'You are Trask. Trask the lawyer, Trask the letter-writer, Trask the lover.'

Though there was admittedly some satisfaction to be gained in facing my rival at long last, I could not return the man's Devilish grin. I glowered at him. 'I am. Please,' I said, gesturing with forced civility to the chair that sat opposite the fireplace. 'Sit.'

That smile on his face, though it lasted only the briefest moment, was unsettling. I felt, from the start of our conversation, as I had upon first hearing of the man's imminent arrival upon Virginian shores. I was as an invader in my own land, as an intruder in the halls of a home I knew as well as mine own. I was the petty American lawyer facing the imposing arrogance and assumed right of a well-known English statesman, the humbled prey trapped before a sly and self-satisfied fox. Despite the trembling of my spirit and the anger in my heart, I forced control and feigned civility still. I would not give way. 'You are greatly displaced from your constituency, Mr Loomis. I trust the journey was not too gruelling. Tell me, what brings you to His Majesty's Colonies?'

In an instant that predatory smile was gone, replaced once more by a snarl that seemed to suit his face. 'You know well what brings me to the Colonies, Trask, and you possess either bravery in dangerous quantities or ignorance in great abundance to greet me here in the halls of the Baroness's home.'

'Surely, such a meeting—dare I say *confrontation*—was inevitable the moment you made plans to cross the ocean that both the Lord Almighty and the Baroness de Córdoba have used to keep us separate, Mr Loomis? Need I remind you that you are the stranger here in Richmond, and I am very much at home?' Indeed, I said those words to reassure mine own self as much as convince the man.

'You invited your confrontation on the day that you invited the Baroness to these shores, Trask. 'Twas a mistake. If I do not belong here, neither does she, and know now that I intend to bring her with me when I depart.'

I nodded solemnly at this, and I then knew that nothing of what had been shared between Susanna and I was sacred and secure. The man was aware of my many letters to her, he may have read them himself, and was as a result no doubt aware of the depths of my reckless passions for this woman. Whatever her rationale, Susanna had not kept our correspondence as secret as I and her reason for coming to American soil was known.

Truly, if ever I had thought to have been in her confidence, if ever I had thought to have held some part of her that was for me and me alone, I was a full-hearted but empty-headed fool.

'So you have come here, so selfishly, and you plan to take her away. I know, as does Susanna, that this is not the full extent of your despicable design.' The civility had now bled from my voice, and I reached within my coat for that copy of Paine's political poison that I had earlier discovered. I threw it at him then, as much to be rid of it as to reveal the extent of my knowledge, and the fluttering pages nearly caught Loomis on the exaggerated cleft of his chin. 'You would so threaten the life of every man, woman, and child in these provinces? Nay, you would so threaten the safety of the one woman you profess to care for above all others? Your shipment has arrived from its Philadelphia publishers, my name upon the forged papers, and Susanna was the first to be touched by this poison! How dare you, sir!'

Loomis reached for the pamphlet as it fell to his lap and nearly tore its title page as he hastily brought it up before his face. 'I need not lecture you on the illegality of those pages you hold in your hand,' I told him then. 'What does a Member of Parliament need with crate after crate of *Common Sense*?'

Loomis carefully placed the now-tattered pamphlet on the table by his side and looked back across the tense space between us with an anger tempered by his smugness. 'You have no conception of those things of which you speak, Trask. You hurl books without pausing to consider their words; you hurl words without pondering their meanings. 'Tis not hard to fathom why the Colonies are in such a state, with men like you in position to guide them. You were right; clearly, I am far from English shores.'

His condescension for the provinces was clear and I found it despicable. 'Do not forget that you stand now on British shores, and 'tis the words of radicals like Paine that will lead to the ruin of the realm. You would have Susanna tied to such a work? You would have her harbour materials you know to be so dangerous, so wicked, so illegal?'

'The Baroness knows nothing of this,' Loomis said coldly. 'She cannot grasp the significance of these happenings, nor is she required to. It is not her name that will prove of importance to the authorities.'

I wondered then where Susanna had hidden herself away and whether or not she was listening to her lovers debate their right to possess her as if they were entrenched in political rebutting. 'I say again, explain yourself, sir!' I shouted, unable to keep the shock from my voice. 'Perhaps you would comment on the significance of these events for a man who does comprehend the danger of what you have undertaken.'

'I do not intend to explain myself to a man like you, Trask, a simpleton and blackguard. When I leave these shores I shall be done with you, and so shall Susanna. As I understand it, it is your name that can be tied to these materials you consider to be so dangerous. According to the delivery papers, you are the radical responsible for this act of sedition. You are not a worthy man in any respect, and Paine's so-called "common sense" will help to prove that, I shall see to it.'

'This is treason!' I cried, and surely the whole of the house must have heard me. I cared not who heard me. 'Yours, not mine! You would risk thine own safety and that of Susanna simply to see me destroyed? Have you gone mad? Have you lost all perspective?'

'Have you lost all decency?' Loomis bellowed, and he was the first to rise from the comfort of his chair. When he next spoke through gritted teeth his voice was a harsh and accusatory whisper. 'You dream of representing this province in Parliament, of one day taking that allotted seat from the likes of Ferry or Harper. I know it. It is troubling enough to see your lot filing into the House of Commons, to see Bostonians and Carolinians standing alongside Britons of true standing, playing at politics as if they have the right to chart the course of England's history. I shudder at the thought of seeing you beside me in the House of Commons. It repulses me! And damn the cursed Columbia Compromise! What you have done to Susanna is beyond all indecency. You, who have tainted a glorious woman. Trask the trickster, Trask the tempter, Trask the thief! You, an American, have dared court a woman far beyond your station. You have stolen her away from me and brought her, a lady of such beauty, grace, and honour, to this wilderness!'

'She is a woman,' I told him, rising from my own chair to face him. 'That is all. A woman of great beauty, yes. A woman of wit, yes. A woman of power. But the cause for such recklessness? The cause for such great risk, all to accomplish an elaborate scheme of personal revenge?'

Loomis snorted and looked away. I pressed on. 'My G–d!

What are you doing here, Edward? I have studied my history. When Prime Minister Pitt so nobly endeavoured to induct the Colonies into Parliament you stood beside him yourself and cast your vote in favour of that plan, in favour of a future for Britain and America greater than that they could ever hold separately. You betray yourself when you damn the Compromise. You helped to bring this union into being. You knew it was right, and though you complain of American inferiority you know they have their place and that they boast strengths and resources all their own. And yet you travel across the Atlantic to insult me, to slander me with false accusations and to use tracts of unspeakable threat as the tool of your revenge. What do you presume will become of your deleterious contraband, this "common sense", once you have destroyed my reputation? Will it be forgotten? Will it be scattered? Will it reach American readers and into American minds? Explain your plan. You would risk an empire out of your jealousy? You would tear Britain in twain to put a Virginian lawmaker in his place?'

I paused to breathe deeply and move back from the man as it was then that my fury was tempered by something much like pity. Here before me was a man so consumed by the fires of hate that I myself had felt burning so hotly within, a man so warped by jealousy and discontent, that his very purpose in life had been taken from him and had been perverted by his mind. Once a proud politician, a man who still carried such pride in his posture and his walk, Edward Loomis was now nothing more than a madman raving feverishly of revenge. 'You *have* lost your senses,' I breathed, almost whispered. 'Can you not hear yourself? Madness. You speak such madness.'

'Do not speak to me of madness,' Loomis snarled.

''Tis a sort of madness,' I heard a melodic voice declare and I turned to find Susanna had rushed to my side. Her beauteous features were now twisted by her emotions and she looked up at me with red and inflamed eyes.

'Baroness!' Loomis cried.

'End this,' she said, tugging insistently at the sleeve of my coat, her lips brushing my neck desperately. 'You have both gone mad. Leave us, Simeon. Let me alone to talk with Edward, let me reason with him. I love him as I love you! Go now and leave us. It was not meant to be this way. You were never meant to know!'

I turned on her then and raised my voice to her. '*I* was never meant to *know*? I was *meant* to sit in shadows, to keep myself hidden, to keep myself blind? I was *meant* to share your heart with this madman?'

The shouting that had filled the parlour for many minutes was now accompanied by a rising commotion as many other men and women, house servants, had followed Susanna to the parlour and crowded the doorways to catch a glimpse of us. Neatly clad attendants, undoubtedly in the service of Loomis, stood in the doorway behind him.

'I will not leave,' I stubbornly told Susanna, 'until *you* have ended this.'

''Tis not the Baroness's duty, Trask. A woman may have started this,' Loomis declared, and there was a new tone of clarity to his voice that instantly chilled me, 'but she shall not bring it to an end. You have tainted the reputation of a Spanish Baroness and, hear me now, you have insulted my honour. We shall settle this as men!'

When I turned to face him once more, Edward Loomis had moved to the parlour's crowded doorway and stood beside one of his menservants, and in his hands he held a case of dark mahogany with a baize interior of red as bright as blood. 'They were the first items packed for the cross-Atlantic voyage,' he explained calmly, 'and they have remained with me every step of the journey. I have heard enough of your words, Trask. If you love this woman, as do I, then it is time that we settled the affair. I demand it, and you will comply.'

Nestled within this case were two duelling pistols.

They were beautiful flintlock guns, long and sleek, crafted from perfectly polished silver and finely smoothed walnut, with chequered grips. There in their case, looking as identical twins bearing grace but also lethality, they seemed the perfect solution. The American lawyer and the English statesman would end this unnatural romance with symmetry, as it had begun. Despite

Loomis's arrogance and perceived self-import, we would face each other as equal men with equal arms and a decision would be made for the indecisive Baroness de Córdoba.

Susanna, a new look of horror warping her once gentle features, still clutched desperately at my coat sleeve and I had to wrench my arm from her gasp to be rid of her. Though I had come to feel the smallest pang of pity for that maddened man before me, my counterpart and rival, I could not help but think that the Baroness was deserving of these horrors and perhaps a bit more. This conflict was of her own design and making and it was now her fate to harvest the fruit of the poisonous tree she had long ago planted. I stepped away from her, stood before Loomis and gestured boldly for the foyer.

Though it was mid-February and very much still winter in the counties of Virginia, we emerged from the manor to face a beautiful day. Grey clouds were aloft but the sun was shining and the sky was marked by patches of brilliant blue. The ground was soft and muddy beneath our boots as we marched into the yard. The air was crisp and I knew this: 'twas too good a day to die, and certainly too good a day to die for a woman who knew nothing of true Love.

Edward Loomis, with his black gloves and twin duelling pistols, paused as he neared the centre of the yard to reflect back upon the sizable crowd that was gathering on the steps of Susanna's home. It seemed the whole of the household had overheard our most vocal debate and now, with the promise of blood and lethal spectacle, these witnesses were unabashed in their interest. I saw maids and stewards, cooks and scullions. More to my interests, however, to one side of the vast manor I spied my own coachman standing beside a pair of horses with familiar saddlebags; Waller had returned at last from the city of Richmond.

As I looked back to my rival I saw he was extending his opened case toward me. The choice was mine to make. But where Susanna would undoubtedly freeze, faced with a split decision of immeasurable consequence, I did not hesitate to take the topmost of those two handsome pistols by its handle and find comfort with its grip. 'Call forth your second,' Loomis demanded.

It was then I paused, seeming to look over the barrel of my pistol, and considered the mass of men standing before the manor. My coachman had returned from Richmond, but had he been able to fulfil my instructions? 'Waller,' I called out. 'My coachman, he shall be my second.'

The young man scurried across the yard and Loomis, looking him over, seemed to nod with approval. 'Dickens, my assistant. Come forth!' Loomis commanded, and a young lad far better dressed than my own, the same manservant that had brought forth the case of duelling pistols, made his way through the crowd.

Slowly and with deliberation, I took a position several yards from my opponent as I fitted my gloves. When Waller reached my side I carefully placed the pistol in his hands such that he could attest to the weapon's fairness. 'I leave your side for a night and look what you find your way into!' he said to me, both nervous and excited. 'It seems a fine pistol to me, sir, but I cannot say I am an expert in such things. An afternoon duel, it's all very arresting! What's this all about, then?'

'You have returned from Richmond,' I whispered to him, ignoring the question. 'Quietly, tell me you were able to carry out my instructions.'

The young coachman could not keep a smile from spreading betwixt his boyish cheeks. His voice came out a conspiratorial hiss as he tapped a finger upon his nose. 'You just give the signal. That is, unless—you aren't going to let that British ass shoot you dead, are you, Simeon?'

'Mind your tongue, lad,' I said, 'and keep those eyes and ears of yours open.'

The pistol returned to my hand, Waller made his hasty retreat. Loomis's man, Dickens, had also finished his examination and moved to a safe distance.

I looked upon the crowd of servants that had gathered to watch me die and I saw Susanna standing among them, her eyes now dried and her countenance as cold and hard as stone. It occurred to me that some part of her might relish the prospect that this duel would absolve her of all personal responsibility in deciding our conflict. I hefted the weight of the pistol in my gloved hand and, as if some Heavenly insight had come upon me, I no longer felt as a member of the House of Burgesses facing his rival in a duel; I felt as if some great and blessed broadsword had been placed into my gauntlet and that I stood upon a thunderous battlefield, the fate of England and its future Empire before me. Truly, as I looked upon the contemptible Edward Loomis, I understood that I was not fighting for that Spanish Baroness whom I once had called mine. I was not fighting for any mortal woman. I was fighting for Lady Britannia and the future of my kingdom.

We came together once more, he and I, and stood back to back. I could feel his coat brushing against mine and, though it may have been in my thoughts alone, I could feel the heat of the man mingling with my own. 'When next I see your face,' Loomis growled, 'it shall have the look of death upon it. Then we shall see if you can answer for those crates of *Common Sense* delivered in your name.'

I did not give him the satisfaction of my reply.

The paces were torturous. With each step I felt certain I would feel the hot bite of Loomis's bullet in my back. He wore the face and the costume of a gentleman well but my brief meeting with the man had proven to me that he was mad and without honour, more a blackguard than ever I could be. I was, in fact, quite surprised to reach that tenth and final pace without hearing the premature report of his pistol.

When I turned I saw the fanning of his green coat as he turned to face me. I could almost feel his small, sharp eyes upon me, pricking at my head. I held my pistol before me, watched him over the tip of the barrel, and braced myself. I knew he would fire first.

I did not have long to wait.

The sounding of that silver trigger mechanism was a loud, sharp clack that echoed across the space between Loomis and the crowd and the spectators reacted at once, flinching, some ducking, holding their hands over their heads and their faces. I thought I heard Susanna let out a low moan. An instant later and that echoing clack was drowned out by the explosion from the mouth of

Loomis's pistol.

Susanna spoke of divergent paths that lead to a distant horizon, of fate and destiny and myriad potentialities for glory or doom. She spoke of facing one's future without choice. Truly, it is not hard to fathom that at that precise instant in history something as minute as the cool February wind blowing upon my cheek from the west or the sinking of my boot in that shifting Virginia mud had the potential to change my life forever. When a bullet slices through the air towards a man he sees those phantom paths flickering in gun smoke before him. There is hope, there is chance and there is death.

I watched the weapon fire, watched the smoke obscure my opponent's face, and then, it was as if he had reached out and cuffed me with all his strength. The small, round bullet struck my shoulder with such force that it sent me back another two paces and nearly knocked me from my feet. I sucked hard at the chill February air and, for dignity's sake, kept my back straight despite the searing in my flesh. Several women in the crowd cried out as if in pain upon seeing me shot. Susanna, I noticed, did not.

And so, with a deliberation far more brutal than that my rival had shewn me, I lifted my pistol once more and, as a scarlet stream spouted fresh from my wounded shoulder, I took aim. The bluish smoke obscuring Edward Loomis soon cleared with the aid of a gentle winter breeze and I saw him, his proud profile raised high in the air as he watched me take aim. He was afraid and I was glad for it. I am a lawmaker, not a soldier, but never before or since have I so wanted to act as an instrument of death. I spoke softly to myself before squeezing the pistol. 'For all that is England.'

I fired.

When the smoke obscuring my stinging eyes had cleared I was feeling the first wave of faintness and I knew that the blood spilling forth from the place of Loomis's misdirected bullet might be draining my very life. I stood my ground, strained my eyes and I saw him standing unmoved at the place of his tenth pace, his chin still raised pompously, though I was glad to note that there was no smugness on his disproportioned face. The report of my own pistol had removed any expression from his vile visage.

I do not know how closely the bullet passed Edward Loomis by but I do know that, though I was wounded, my aim was true. Undoubtedly that pistol ball still lies lodged in one of the white ash trees that stand in the crowded wood before the manor house that once belonged to Baroness Susanna Arrieta Aguirre de Córdoba of Spain.

The look of disbelief on Loomis's face grew stronger with every wavering stride I took toward him in the aftermath of our duel. 'I have wounded you,' he observed once I had nearly reached him, seemingly unable to take his eyes from my blood-stained coat. 'But you missed!'

'No,' I told him quietly. 'I did not miss.'

I turned slowly to the manor house to see that my coachman was still waiting, standing by those horses that bore the distinctive gear of the Virginia regulars. The crowd waited still. 'Waller!' I cried with all the strength I could muster, then allowed myself a cough. 'Bring them out! Bring them out.'

Though it may be hard to imagine, I have never felt more satisfaction than I did as I stood in that soft, late winter mud, clutching a shattered shoulder with a bloodied hand, and watched as no less than six soldiers emerged from behind the manor to join my coachman in making his way to my side. When I made my announcement it was loud and clear, such that all of the soldiers and scullions and stewards and stablemen in attendance would have the resolution they both thirsted for and deserved. 'Edward Loomis, of Bedfordshire, of the House of Commons, is to be taken into arrest for acts of High Treason committed against his Crown and Country!'

The Virginia regulars were quick to take their prompt; they knew me and they knew their duty. Two of the soldiers took Loomis by the arms and soon the arrogance of his posture no longer seemed to suit him so very well. 'Men, you will find the stables behind the house contain Mr Loomis's wagons and supplies,' I explained. 'They will need to be confiscated, and I do not want them opened until they have been delivered with him to the authorities in Richmond. There is no need for this man's madness nor his poisonous pamphlets to touch any more lives.'

Young Waller beamed, never more proud, and he looked upon Loomis with bold contempt now that the angry Englishman was well restrained. Two other soldiers began to make their way to the stables and I sent the lad along with them.

'Edward, you shall not die today,' I told him, and I dropped his well-kept duelling pistol into the mud by my side. 'Neither shall you die tomorrow. You will be brought to your home and tried for these crimes and, if I can claim that Virginian House of Commons seat, I hope to be in London on the day that you are hanged at the Tower.'

The din rising from the crowd of observers before the Baroness's manor house grew louder as I shambled my way toward them, two Virginia regulars standing close behind me. Susanna watched as I came, cold eyes looking to my bleeding, tired form, and she must have understood something of what was to come. The fateful conflict she had constructed with her own reckless heart was brought to its end, though not in the manner she may have expected.

I did not look upon her smooth, pale face as I gave the regulars their final order, nor did I stand close enough to feel her breath or smell her night-black hair. I did not want to see the emotion in her dangerously beautiful eyes, not then, not ever again. 'The Baroness Susanna Arrieta Aguirre de Córdoba is also to be taken into custody, under charges of Treason,' I told the two remaining regulars. 'You will find offending documents in her home. On the road to Richmond she is to be kept separate from Loomis at all times.'

She screamed my name as they took her away, as full of scorn and selfish spite as she had ever been, but still I would not look upon her. I did not want to see that angry face of hers; 'twas not the face I had loved. Truly, I had loved her, and I have long since kept that unfinished portraiture of the Baroness hidden in my home, a reminder of the beauty that nearly brought me to my end, as evocative as the scar that mars my left shoulder.

Though she was imprisoned in Richmond, to this day I do not know what became of the Baroness de Córdoba in the years that followed. I do know that on St Valentine's Day in 1776, though my heart was broken, I was blessed by creating Heaven with the courage and the conviction to recognize choice and the common good—to, above all else, ensure the strength and prosperity of my beloved British North America.

Total Emancipation
by Joe Tangari

23 November 1834
Newfound Gap, Appalachia Territory

No matter how I tried, I couldn't clean the blood from under my fingernails. I scrubbed them in the creek water and scraped under the nails with a knife until my own fresh, red blood mingled with the dried, brown stains.

Steven and Fortune sat on a rock ten or so yards away, dangling lines into the rushing water. We all thought that with luck, we might share a dinner better than Royal Army rations that evening.

'Solomon!' cried Fortune. 'Come here!'

I stared at my unwashable hands for a moment longer and rose to join them.

'Here,' Fortune said, handing me the end of a line. 'Fish for a while. It will take your mind off it.'

I nodded and took the line. 'It's not the first time, you know, that I've had my brother's blood on my hands,' I said, wiping away the crust of unused tears. 'I always tended his wounds when he was whipped back home. I never suspected that I might see his blood again so soon after we were freed.' A brief tug on the line quickly passed and it drifted in the current, casting a small ripple downstream. Somewhere, I knew that this creek fed the Little Tennessee River, but it was hard to imagine that looking at the narrow rush of water in front of us. I wondered if any fish lived there at all. My stomach rumbled at the thought and I felt exhaustion creeping over me.

After a brief silence, Steven attempted to comfort me. 'It's the way of God,' he said, his eyes locked on the point where his line entered the water.

'Yes, I suppose it is.'

'I don't believe it is,' Fortune offered from over our shoulders. 'I don't believe God would free this man only to take his life months later.'

Now Steven looked away from his line. 'It is God's plan who lives or dies, Fortune,' he said.

'Is that so?'

'This is what Sosimas says.'

Fortune kicked a small stone into the creek. 'And I suppose Sosimas knows everything.'

'He knows more than we do. He can read and write.' Steven looked at me, then craned his head toward Fortune. 'Do you think it's a comfort to Solomon to hear that his brother died in battle and God was not there to govern it?'

'Solomon himself can read, Steven—he was a house slave and was taught. Other men in our regiment read quite well. What of them? Will you ask them to tell you about God as well?'

Steven's wide nostrils flared. 'It's not the same, Fortune. Sosimas has studied the Bible—the true Bible, from Ethiopia, and—'

'Please,' I interrupted. 'Don't fight like this. My brother is dead, so let him lie. You are my brother now, Steven. You're my brother, too, Fortune. Sosimas is my brother. Even Sergeant Clark is my brother. We're all brothers here. Let's not forget that.'

Fortune sat down on the rock. 'I 'spose you're right. Any tugs on the line?'

'Nothing that keeps tugging.'

Fortune gazed up at the slowly darkening sky and cursed just above his breath. 'The sun is almost down, brothers.' He let the word hang for a moment on the cool creek air. 'We should get back to camp.'

✻　　✻　　✻

A chill shivered its way up my spine and I moved closer to the dying fire. November nights were colder in Appalachia than they had been back home in Nelsonville. I was still at the fire because I was too exhausted to sleep.

'Frightfully cold, isn't it?'

Sosimas startled me when he posed the question from behind.

'Yes. It doesn't get like this in Florida.'

'We're not built for this,' said Sosimas as he stepped closer to the fire. 'We're Africans. We're built for the sun and the heat.'

I shoved my hands in my armpits and clenched my teeth to keep them from chattering. 'Am I really an African, though? I've never even been there. I was born in Nelsonville, and so were my mother and father.'

Sosimas tugged his red topcoat tighter around his neck and moved his eyes from the flagging flames to me. 'You must realise, Solomon, that we are Africans and we always will be. We in this unit are a small piece of Africa in America. Even after slavery, we're not allowed to be Britons.'

I didn't know how to answer this assertion. To me, Africa was more an idea than a place. Still, it was an idea warmer than Appalachia.

'Solomon,' asked Sosimas, his voice softening, 'are you well? I know you lost your brother in the battle this morning.'

'I'm as well as one might expect. It's not only my loss. We lost twelve men out of twenty, with another who will likely die on a surgeon's table. And now we have these new men, sleeping in the tents of our fallen.'

'The new men in the squad went through the same thing we did today. They also lost half their numbers. Two of them are all that remains of a third squad. I suppose it seems the natural thing to our commanders to throw us in together.'

Sosimas stepped closer to the fire, jabbing at the glowing ashes around the edge with a long, knotted stick. His words, and the choices made by our commanders, exposed an unsettling truth. The outcome of this desperate fight against the upstart rebels of the South—fighting sparked by abolition—did not seem so certain. I could see in the firelight that Sosimas's topcoat was fraying where the sleeve met the shoulder. The dying logs pulsated with red heat.

'Colonel Harrington calls this morning a great victory over

the militias,' I said, watching the sparks rise and die as Sosimas turned over a glowing log, 'but it doesn't feel as though anything has been won.' I had developed a habit of running my thoughts by Sosimas like this, because he always had a way of exposing the reasoning behind my feelings in a way I was never adept at expressing.

'Nothing has,' he agreed. 'We're still in the same place we were three days ago. Still lost in the mountains, for all purposes. The Georgians and the Carolinians will only fight us somewhere else in a few days. Perhaps next time there will be Virginians or Floridians with them. And Colonel Harrington'—Sosimas spit into the fire—'will send us in front of the cannons and rifles again to be cut to ribbons. His tactics will murder the lot of us before long.'

I hugged my arms closer to my body and considered that I should go to my tent, if only for the relative warmth. 'I think it's time to retire, Sosimas. We're supposed to march tomorrow. It'll be a long day.'

'There is a mass tomorrow morning to pray for the fallen. Will you be there?' He looked me in the eye then, his bulging whites leaping from his dark features in the firelight.

I nodded.

'Before daybreak. Some of the new men may come. I'll see you then, Solomon.'

'Where will we march to tomorrow, Sosimas?'

'Only God knows.' Sosimas turned to go, then paused and said over his shoulder, 'God and Colonel Harrington.'

The first thing I saw the next morning was my own breath, swirling through the darkness overhead. What light there was shone dimly from a lantern hanging in the centre of the tent. I fought my way through stiff resistance from every muscle to an upright position, attempting to ignore the damp coldness of my clothes and blanket.

Howell Garvey was already up, looking at the pages of his Bible under the lantern. He couldn't read it but spent hours leafing through it, running his hands over the rough pages, trying to feel the meaning of the characters.

'Mornin', Private Smith,' he said, smiling as I shook the sleep from my eyes and rose. He pronounced my last name 'Smiff'. 'You goin' t'hear Sosimas?'

'I am. Shall we go together?'

Howell closed his Bible and carefully placed it back in his carrying pouch. 'Yass. I think we should.'

Howell was new to our regiment—he was one of fewer than a hundred reinforcements who had arrived two weeks earlier during a brief stay on the outskirts of Asheville—and had been rushed to the field with little of the intense language training that the Royal Army dictated for all of its American recruits, and especially us former slaves. We were drilled in the King's English nearly as hard we were drilled for combat. While I was raised in close proximity to proper grammar, syntax and enunciation as a house slave, it still struck me oddly to hear men like Steven and Fortune contorting their words to comply with it, with the occasional slide back to plantation dialect. Howell, though, sounded natural and easy-going to the point where he made it sound as if the language drills were a mistake.

The newest reinforcements could also be easily identified by their faces, as they still bore a modicum of the fat that the rest of us had slowly lost to our rations and marches. The hollowness hadn't yet made it to his eyes, and there were no depressions at his temples where the blood would pulse visibly.

We slipped out of the tent and crept quietly to the supply wagon Sosimas had turned into his makeshift Ethiopic church— Lieutenant Colwell, our squad's commanding officer, tacitly allowed our masses, such as they were, in spite of Colonel Harrington's direct orders prohibiting non-Anglican church activities.

Corporal Kwame Zulu stood guard outside the wagon and greeted us with a silent nod. The serenity of his expression belied the bayonet he always carried just inside his coat, 'should the need arise,' he always said. We saluted him casually, but once inside we knew his rank would become meaningless. Howell stepped up into the wagon while I stopped to take one last shivering look at the light creeping over the hills to the east.

Seven men were huddled within the wagon when I entered, and Sosimas sat at the front. Kwame followed me inside and the congregation was complete. Nearly half the men of the squad were present, including three new squad members I didn't yet know. A fourth man, David, had been added to our ranks only days ago and I'd barely had more than a few words with him to that point. I sandwiched myself between Howell and Steven, hoping some of their warmth would transfer, but I could barely feel them through my thick Royal Army coat.

'This morning,' Sosimas began, placing his elbows on his knees so that his long, square frame leaned into the centre of the group. 'We have much to discuss.' He put his Bible aside and studied the faces of the men. Keeping his voice low, he continued, 'First, a moment of silence for the men lost yesterday, including Solomon's brother, Andrew.'

We bowed our heads. I tried to clear my mind, to pray, to focus on God, but my mind allowed only thoughts of my brother, his dying instant and the flash of smoke that took him instead of me because I was on the left and he on the right. The thoughts were duller, unable by then to bring more tears. I ran my thumbs over my fingertips, knowing the blood was gone yet feeling it there between the scabs I'd made the previous day at the creek.

It occurred to me at that moment how large a swath something as small as a bullet could cut through the world, how an inch of altered aim spares the one and not the other. If the man who fired Andrew's fatal shot had lingered a moment longer on the trigger, we may have gathered in that wagon to mourn Sosimas, and our church may have been at an end.

Sosimas stood, head bent to avoid the cold cover of the wagon, and began his sermon.

'African brothers, welcome. Welcome to our new friends, Carter, Cassius and Youssou. My name is Sosimas Negus and I am a free man. Do not for one second believe, however, that I became a free man last year when the British crown recognised my freedom. No,'—he held up a long, scolding finger—'I was born a free man, because I was free in my mind. I lived with the whip and the cudgel, and men owned my labour and my body, but they never owned my soul.

'What you must do, brothers, is make a pact with yourself this morning, and every morning, to let no man own your soul. Now, I understand that this is tough, tougher now perhaps than it was in the days of slavery, because everywhere we are confronted with physical freedom, which in truth is the illusion of freedom. Colonel Harrington tells us daily how free we are and how we should be thankful to His Majesty the King for that freedom. Rubbish!' He clenched his fist and the veins bulged on the back of his hand. 'They deserve our spite for making us slaves in the first place.'

Sosimas raised his voice slightly on this last thought and continued after a weighty pause.

'To become truly free, you must emancipate yourself from mental slavery. This is the belief that you are less than someone else by virtue of the colour of your skin. God did not make you this way.' He picked up his Bible and held it out for the group to see. 'This book is the word of God, and in it, He offers no opinion on what the colour of your skin means for your station in life.'

He held out his hands. 'This army is merely a new slavery. Each day drill, drill, learn to speak like the man who owns the property you are not allowed to buy, fall in, fall out, fall down, go on kill, go on die. You cannot leave until your time is through and they will tell you when it is through. And while we are here, our women are back in our towns living the same way they've always lived.'

The words of Sosimas chased away the ghost of my brother, however briefly, and I was glad to listen.

Sosimas took a seat at the front of the wagon and swept his eyes across us in the lantern light. He dropped his shoulders and became more casual. 'When I was born, a name was given to me by my parents. They named me James McAlmont. McAlmont was the name of the man who kept them as slaves. I taught myself to read and write by stealing books from the McAlmont family library.' He laughed, and the men in the wagon smiled. One of the new men—

Cassius—let out a small noise of assent.

'I was never freed by the Royal Army. I escaped from the plantation when I was fifteen years old or perhaps a bit older. I heard they were planning to sell me to a man in Maryland. Culloden, Georgia, was the only place in the world that I knew and I was afraid to go north. Mr McAlmont—I never knew his first name—had always said that people in the North were much harsher than those in the South.

'When I fled into the woods I discovered that the white criminals who lived their lives on the run were more willing to accept my humanity than their supposedly more refined counterparts. Five years ago in Hampton Roads, Virginia, I met a black man named Segun, who was born in Ghana and kidnapped by Europeans, taken from his wife, children and the village his ancestors had lived in. Segun was a man of great wisdom, though his difficult life had deprived him of the opportunity to learn reading and writing.'

Sosimas's teeth briefly shone through his lips as they parted in a small smile, and he continued, 'So shrewd was Segun that he learned to speak English in the months after he was sold to a Georgian man named Davis entirely without help, but he kept this to himself. Thinking him dumb, his master and other whites spoke without reservation in his presence. By eavesdropping, he learned when best to make his escape and seized his first opportunity. A façade of ignorance was the key to his freedom, and this is the greatest lesson he taught me: when you are confronted with a prejudice, you must use your enemy's assumptions against him. If he thinks you a simpleton, be the simpleton until his back is turned, and outfox him while his guard is lowered.'

Sosimas slammed a fist into his open palm. 'Segun took me in and told me about his life in Africa. He helped me avoid capture and a return to a life of forced bondage. I came to trust him and thought of him as a brother. Though he couldn't read himself, he procured books for me, which I read aloud to him. And he gave me this.' Sosimas held up his Bible and then placed it on his knee. 'The Bible of St Sosimas. The white people have their Bibles of King James and Erasmus.' He tapped the Bible on his knee with a finger.

'This Bible is ours. The Ethiopic Bible.

'Segun told me it had come to him from a real Ethiopian he met in Philadelphia. This Ethiopian was nobody's slave, but a dignitary of the Emperor—the dignitary had translated it into English himself. At the time, the idea of a man so fluent in two languages as to be able to translate this book from one language to another was nearly beyond belief for me. It was then that I knew I must change my name. Sosimas after the saint, Negus after the king of Ethiopia, where Sosimas was from.'

I knew all about Ethiopia. Sosimas had told me many times and seemed to be going back over it for the benefit of the three new men. Sosimas directed his words to them.

'Brothers, Ethiopia is a real African empire, as grand as Britain and more ancient than any of the nations of Europe. The only white men to be seen are the ambassadors from Russia, France and England.' Sosimas looked around at his parishioners. The new men seemed interested in what he had to say, elbowing each other and nodding.

'Whites don't like to mention Ethiopia,' Sosimas said, 'because the notion of Africans in power frightens them. During my time in Boston, I read every tiny mention I could find of it in the library, but there was so little, and the wilful ignorance of whites was evident in much of it.'

'What do you mean by wilful ignorance?' asked David as Sosimas paused.

'It is the practice of many white men,' answered Sosimas, 'not all, but many, to form in their minds a picture of an African, and then to treat Africans in accordance with this picture. The reason for this is clear: to see the African's true nature as a thinking man would make it impossible to keep him as a beast of burden.

'Men tell themselves things they wish to hear, and not only white men. We do it to ourselves as well. For instance, an African in this army, in the absence of a truer freedom, might convince himself that he is no longer a slave, all the while following the orders given to him by his new masters without so much as a thought to the similarities between his prior condition and his current one.'

Sosimas looked around at the men, settling his eyes on Kwame.

'This is an interesting subject, but we've other things to discuss this morning. Kwame,' he said, 'has heard we are not marching as planned today.'

The big corporal rubbed his hands together and nodded. 'The white English captain of C Company told all of his American lieutenants to see that the men in the company received heavy rations and plenty of sleep, because he expected another fight today. The retreat of the militias was false, according to him, and they've taken up a new position. I was told this morning by one of the black sergeants when I met him at the latrine by chance. Apparently, C Company's commander cares more for his men than D Company's, because we had a meagre dinner last night.'

'Colonel Harrington does not care for any man in any company in his whole regiment,' said Steven, 'A, B, C, D Company... It hardly matters. We are all thrown on the field to clear the way for his British cavalry. This army is a shambles walking in circles in the mountains. Our company used to have nine squads and now there are three. He thinks the success he had twenty years ago in Libya means he will be successful today.'

Light was beginning to creep in from outside. Sosimas stood and placed his hand on Steven's shoulder. 'This is all true, of course, and it is why we must take matters a little more into our own hands if the problem is to be solved. When Harrington sends us against the guns, we'll do whatever it takes to survive.'

An uncomfortable silence descended within the trailer, and incredulous expressions crossed the faces of the new men. Finally, Youssou spoke, his voice aquiver with questions and apparent fear. 'We'll be shot if we disobey orders,' he said, leaning forward and looking up to Sosimas.

This was true, more or less, though as Sosimas was fond of pointing out, it's the man who gets caught who gets shot. Still, I felt Steven and Howell shift uncomfortably next to me, and it briefly felt as though Sosimas had untethered us from his words with this suggestion. No longer in his thrall, the men, new and old, began to murmur quietly to themselves.

Kwame brought things back to order: 'We'll also be shot obeying orders, if the past predicts the future. But what to do differently? Sergeant Clark will certainly report us if we leave the line. That rat would bleach the black from his skin if he could.'

I usually kept quiet during the meetings but felt I had to speak. 'I agree that the colonel disregards us and uses poor tactics, but how are we to use our own tactics? We don't even know where we'll be in the line or what the battle will be like. How many men will we face? In what sort of position?'

'They're good points,' said Sosimas. 'We must do something differently, however. I'm afraid we'll need to improvise when the opportunity presents itself. When I was in Boston, I read a great deal of history, and a pattern emerged in my readings about war. He who innovates and adjusts the most quickly wins the most as well. There was an ancient nation called Parthia—it is called Persia today—whose warriors won battles by appearing to retreat on their horses and then firing arrows over their shoulders at the pursuing enemy. They were intelligent enough to learn that when an enemy thinks he's beaten you, he becomes overconfident and may well sow his own destruction. Our enemies already think of us as less brave, less cunning and less human than they are. That is the advantage we must seize, if we can.'

'Sir, may I?' asked Howell.

'Speak, Howell,' said Sosimas. 'We are all equals in this wagon. Even a corporal like Kwame. Please do not call me sir.'

Howell's face registered some confusion at this, but he went ahead. 'I jus' wondered 'bout th' others in the squad. We's jus' nine. There's 'leven mo' men.'

'They can follow who they like,' said Sosimas.

A pang of doubt stabbed me as I considered what Sosimas was saying. It seemed as though he was simply trying to make us feel as though we possessed a small amount of control. Nine men could hardly turn a battle, could they?

Reveille sounded sharply from across the camp, ending our debate. We surreptitiously left the wagon one by one or in pairs. Bile hung around the back of my throat, but I didn't have to throw up—I wasn't sure if it was the prospect of another battle so soon or the gut-clenching cold that turned my insides.

Andrew and I had been so happy to be in the Royal Army. We were treated and fed well and reminded of our freedom at every turn. In retrospect, we had no choice; from the day of emancipation, we were bodies at the King's behest. The queerness of instant liberty is a feeling one could never forget if one were to live for a thousand years. It is terrifying and exhilarating, happiness tempered by the realisation that you're unfamiliar with the world. I remember the haste of the Royal Army officer who delivered the news.

His horse restlessly clomped its hooves below him as he read the proclamation without dismounting: 'By order of Parliament, all enslaved peoples of His Majesty's Realm are hereby released from servitude. As of the first of August, eighteen hundred and thirty-three, no man shall have ownership nor exert dominion over another man.' The officer looked at us as though expecting us to do something, but how does one react to such news? It was impossible for us to move, much less perform an act of gratitude. 'You are free now,' he said, and he rode off.

The following day, Royal Army men arrived in town, signing up every newly freed black man who could be found. We were told constantly of the prestige of serving in the Royal Army, the King's army, as opposed to one of the many locally controlled Continental militias. Now we were fighting the militias of the Southern colonies and it seemed the prestige of the Royal Army wasn't enough to win a decisive victory or even fight a battle without needless sacrifice. If he who innovates most succeeds most, then it seemed our enemy's more fluid tactics were bound to seal our defeat. My brother's excitement had faded long before his death, and mine along with it. Sosimas gave our disillusionment a voice.

I doubt whether the Royal Army would have maintained its lustre in my mind even had my freedom felt real. Colonel Harrington had led this army for five months through Appalachia, losing men in droves with nothing to show for it. There were Cherokee mercenaries in the army who were paid handsomely to fight, and yet we, the backbone of this army, received nothing for our trouble but bad rations. Several men of the squad, myself included, had taken to placing a piece of hardtack beneath our uniforms in the place where our hearts beat, in the hope that it might spare us from death via a single well-placed shot.

Steven and Howell chatted softly close behind me. Steven touched my shoulder and asked what I thought Sosimas meant when he talked of doing what it takes to survive in the field.

'I've no idea. I think it doesn't mean much, all things considered. But it feels good to talk about it.'

Fortune was on mess duty that morning and greeted the three of us as we approached the already roaring fire. 'You've been listening to Sosimas this morning, I imagine,' he said as he doled out portions of something like soup.

'We have,' Steven said quickly with a hint of pride in his voice.

Fortune changed the subject as quickly as he had brought it up. 'There's word going around that the Carolinians and some other militiamen are just over that hill.' He pointed behind us. 'Lieutenant Cowell will be here soon.'

'I'm tired of fighting,' I said. 'I'm tired of the Royal Army. Let the British do their own fighting. I suppose we'll be sent straight at a cannon today.' I cut myself short as Fortune nodded toward something behind me and turned to see Sergeant Clark approaching.

We saluted him half-heartedly, and he returned the gesture. 'Good morning, men,' he said, indicating with a flourish of his index finger that he was trying to get to the meal Fortune was serving.

'How does the morning find you, Sergeant Clark?' Fortune asked as he spooned out a portion.

'Splendid, splendid,' he replied and, turning to the rest of us with his face screwed up in puzzlement, asked, 'Have any of you heard of a religion called Islam?'

We shook our heads.

Sergeant Clark nodded and stirred his bowl. 'Apparently, it's becoming very popular in the Royal Army. There are some men in C Company who say they practise it.' He shrugged. 'Seems strange to me. And I don't think the colonel would approve.'

No one else said anything. The colonel had proscribed all religions other than the Anglican Church. Strictly speaking, the Anglican Church was the only legal church in North America, but it wasn't enforceable at all. I had been brought up with it and so was able to convince anyone who asked that I was a good, law-abiding worshipper, but Sosimas's services had more fire and were more interesting, ranging far from endless readings from the Bible and talk of God's grace and punishment. They were conversations and debates where the rules and protocols of the Royal Army melted away to expose the real, thinking men we were.

'What is it you think Colonel Harrington would disapprove of, Sergeant Clark?' asked Sosimas, who had just arrived. He saluted the sergeant.

Sergeant Clark paused for a moment, staring at Sosimas, then swallowed. 'We were talking about Islam,' he said, pointing at the rest of us with his spoon. 'I was saying that Colonel Harrington had banned everything but the Anglican Church, but that men in C Company were still calling themselves Muslims.'

'I can't speak for Muslims,' said Sosimas, 'but I know there are Muslims in Africa, and I think these men are simply trying to connect with their African-ness through it. What does the Anglican Church offer them but white men's words?' Sosimas stepped toward Fortune with his bowl at the ready, and Fortune silently filled it.

'This may be true,' said Sergeant Clark, 'but this is the Royal Army. There are rules here, and if we don't live by the rules people can die.'

'People seem to do a great deal of that anyway,' snapped Sosimas.

Sergeant Clark spooned a piece of dirt out of his bowl and flung it to the ground. 'Sosimas,' he said, 'what is Africa? Is it a magic land? It is unlikely that even your parents' parents ever saw it. You do a great deal of complaining, and not once have I heard gratitude in your voice. These men you fight for are the men who freed you.'

'What is there to be grateful for? These same people who

freed us are the ones who put us in chains originally.'

'They provide for us.'

'They provide opportunities to die. They provide opportunities to advance to your rank and no further. They provide food that is just good enough to make us sick. If we don't die in battle, walking like asses straight toward guns, we're just as likely to be struck down by illness.'

'Enough!' said Sergeant Clark. 'I order you to stop talking like this.' He straightened his coat and looked around at the rest of us, including some of the new men who had come to gawk at the exchange. 'Get ready for Lieutenant Colwell. He will be here soon.'

No one moved immediately.

'Well, get going!' Sergeant Clark flailed at us, spilling from his bowl.

In many ways, I pitied Sergeant Clark. He wished so badly to be liked by both the men above him and the men below him, but he could never gain the good graces of both parties at once. The men mostly saw him as a man striving to be something he could never be: white. He was truly proud to have attained the highest rank a man with his skin could hold, and as a former house servant myself, I could sympathise with the coldness he automatically received from many former field workers. There was a general suspicion that we who worked in the homes of the slavers were on the wrong side, or had made a deal, and gaining the trust of others was not easy.

I think he chose to ignore the continued iniquity of our situation and focus on the opportunity, where others, including myself, could never accept anything less than total equality and freedom. My brother perhaps put it best a few days before his death: 'Sergeant Clark is the carefree man I wish I could be but cannot allow myself to become.'

The squad slowly pulled itself together as the shadows grew shorter, making more show of tidying the camp than they did actual clean up. The motley assemblage hastily threw itself into crooked lines when the lieutenant arrived, and if when at attention your back was supposed to be as straight as a board, most of us were probably only halfway to standing at attention. Half the men had been added the previous night in a quick ceremony conducted by Captain Armstrong, D Company's commander. Even the three new men in Sosimas's congregation seemed unfamiliar to me.

Lieutenant Colwell came by on foot several minutes after his usual time. He put us at ease and most men barely had to move.

'Men, I'll make this brief,' he said, saluting. 'We'll not be on the march today. The force we fought yesterday has taken up a new position in a line of trees just beyond that hill.' He nodded toward the hill Fortune had earlier indicated. 'Sergeant Clark, you're to have the men ready to move to their positions in one hour.'

Sergeant Clark, still stiff as a board, saluted. 'Yes, sir.'

'Sergeant, I also need one man from your squad to assist me briefly in retrieving four muskets from the quartermaster to replace the ones broken in the battle yesterday morning.'

I was standing closest to Sergeant Clark, and he nudged me forward. 'Solomon will help you,' he said.

'Good. That is all this morning. I shall see you all shortly. Solomon, come with me.' Lieutenant Colwell dropped his shoulders and stroked his fingers lightly upon his beard as he took one last survey of our sorry state.

Sergeant Clark shouted for the squad to fall out and I ran to catch up with Lieutenant Colwell, who was already on his way.

'Good morning, Private,' said Lieutenant Colwell. He walked with purpose, but his pace was unhurried. Exhaustion showed in and below his eyes.

'Good morning, sir,' I replied as I fell in step with him.

'Thank you for helping. Under usual circumstances, the quartermaster would bring new weapons to us,' he said, half to himself. 'But these are no usual circumstances. The quartermaster has no men working for him. This army is losing its structure. We've lost so many men and so much materiel that even basic operations are stretched to the brink.'

I wondered how much I could say in this situation. An abolitionist in Ontario before emancipation, Lieutenant Colwell was always kind and gracious toward us. As an American, he also saw the injustice at work in the Royal Army, unable as he was to rise above the rank of captain without transferring to the less prestigious Continental Army.

As we wove through a maze of white tents to the wagon path that cut through the centre of camp, he continued. 'Were you aware, Solomon, that over two hundred men deserted this army four days ago?'

'No, sir.'

'It's true. I was only told today, as it happens. The colonel thinks he's keeping morale high by keeping these things to himself. He also thinks we scored a victory yesterday in that mess of a morning skirmish, but all we've done is delay the full battle to today and ceded a well-placed ridge to the enemy.'

'I lost my brother in the battle yesterday, sir. It's difficult for me to think of it as a victory.'

He thought about this for a moment. 'Aye, as I suppose it would be,' he said, staring at the wagon ruts below his feet. Then he looked directly at me. 'I'm sorry for your loss.'

'It wasn't you who gave our orders.' I stopped short of criticising the captain or the colonel directly.

'True, but I do feel responsible for the men who march behind me. I've seen so many of them die.' His eyes were back on the wagon ruts.

I tried to look only forward and keep my head high. 'Many are injured as well.'

'Injury is the same as death in this army. The men who enter that hospital tent'—he pointed toward it as we walked down the wagon path—'rarely emerge alive. We've no way to treat them.' There was despair in his voice, as there was in the voice of nearly every man I spoke to. Only in Colonel Harrington and his staff was there a lack of it. Even Sergeant Clark's speech was tinged with sadness and frustration at times.

The camp was huge, but by this point our army was not. When we had settled in this valley a week before, every tent in the regiment's possession was erected, in spite of the fact that there were not nearly enough men to fill them. Though they were made for eight men, most had only four occupants and some were entirely empty, there for show. Surely the rebels we were fighting weren't so stupid as to believe we were as numerous as the camp made us look?

We reached the quartermaster's lodging and Lieutenant Colwell explained our needs. The man stroked his beard as he looked over a pile of rifles, then selected four. I took two of them.

'I certainly hope these shoot better than they look,' said Lieutenant Colwell as he eyed the rifles he was carrying. The quartermaster just grunted and sneezed.

I looked down at the two guns I had taken. One had an elaborate wooden inlay on the stock with a message that read, 'A man lives until he dies. South Carolina will live forever.' The message ran below a carving of the harbour at Charleston, where I had been briefly when we were first deployed.

'Sir,' I asked the lieutenant as we retraced our steps on our return, 'if we beat them today, will this expedition end? It is hard to imagine staying in these hills much longer without reinforcements.'

Lieutenant Colwell's eyes had a distant look to them, as though he was somewhere else in his mind. 'Who knows what tomorrow brings, soldier?'

We walked on for a few moments before he continued, sounding more engaged this time. 'We may return to Asheville for a time. It would be the wise move. This rebellion can't last forever, though sometimes it seems as though it may. I do long for Ontario, though. I've no idea when I'll see it next.'

Back in my squad's camp, Lieutenant Colwell issued the new weapons to four of the new men, but I managed to trade my own rifle for the one with the inlay. I don't know why, but it struck me that there was a certain power to facing the enemy with a gun personalised by one of his own.

There was little more to do and we fell into the waiting game of soldiers. Some men grimly pitted their head lice against each other in battles to the death on the small pieces of paper that wrapped our hardtack rations, some stared at the fire, others at the hill that supposedly hid the enemy.

Sergeant Clark apparently sensed our anxiety and tried to cheer us. 'No worries, men. Colonel Harrington will tell us what to do.'

❋   ❋   ❋

As I readied myself for battle, placing the customary hardtack over my heart and filling my cartridges with gunpowder while sitting on a log outside my tent, I was joined by Sosimas. At first, we worked in silence, but as it became clear we were alone, Sosimas began to speak.

'Are you frightened?' he asked me.

I shook my head and dropped another finished cartridge in my belt pouch. 'It's no good to be frightened,' I said. 'What happens will happen.'

'True...' he said, pulling his hand inside his sleeve and running the cuff over the exposed portion of his rifle barrel, '...to a point.'

I didn't get what he was saying. 'What do you mean "to a point"?'

'Well, it's true that a man's will only takes him to a certain point. That's where God takes over. No one else can control the flight of a bullet. He set down the rules that make it fly as it does. But!' He stopped fiddling with his rifle. 'A man can choose when he fires it. A man can choose his path through a field, his route up a hill.'

'Is this what you were talking about this morning?'

'The essence is the same.' He resumed rubbing his gun down with his sleeve. 'Can I be candid?'

'Of course.'

'I don't believe we are fated to anything. The more I consider it, the more clear it becomes to me that God's plan is not a script or a pre-determination of every moment in a man's life as it is a process He set in motion when He created the world.' Sosimas put down his gun and began to inspect the cartridges he had made, talking as though in a trance. 'It seems a bit silly, doesn't it, to write a script and then play it out if there is no audience. So why write a script, then?'

He paused as though waiting for an answer, though I wasn't sure if he wanted me to respond or if he was attempting to find the answer himself. This was a strange line of thought to me, one Sosimas had never mentioned to me or our group before.

'Do not misunderstand me, Solomon,' he continued when I failed to speak. 'I do not contradict anything I've said about the constant presence of God in all things at all times, but I see the horror of our lives now and our lives before this and I wonder how that presence could possibly be a guiding hand.'

I was alarmed less by the substance of what Sosimas was saying than by the strangeness of his cadence and tone; this was uncertainty in the voice of a man I considered my true leader. I wondered if the fatigue of war might be weighing upon him more heavily than he showed to others. 'I apologise, Sosimas,' I said, 'but I am afraid I don't understand what you're saying, or why you are saying it to me.'

Sosimas met my eyes with his own, and the depth there was too intense for me. I looked back toward my pouch of cartridges.

'I say this to you, Solomon, because I respect your mind. Not to say I don't respect the minds of the other men, but I see you as exceptional. I think you, too, are a philosopher, though you may not call yourself that. More than a man of God, I am a philosopher. A philosopher's ideas must change as he changes or he ceases to be a philosopher and becomes an ideologue, a prisoner of ideas. A slave to ideas, if you like.

'When I was in Boston, I spent nearly every waking hour reading. Plays, political treatises, poems, philosophical works, different translations of the Bible, banned books, whatever I could get into my hands. There is a French philosopher I read called René Descartes who posits that God set the world in motion and then removed His hands, allowing things to go on from there without His guidance. When I first read it, I dismissed the notion as preposterous, but it stayed in my mind. Europeans are a strange lot in that they are capable of unspeakable barbarity, but their ideas can have amazing power. As I've considered my beliefs during this horrible journey they call an expedition, I can never escape this idea. All my readings and meditations bring back to this conclusion that while God may receive you into His hands after your death, His hands are not the instrument of your death.'

He let that sit for a moment, and I knew it would soon be

time to end the discussion and march. I shuffled the questions in my head and arrived at the one that seemed most important: 'What does this mean for your teachings?'

'Nothing in the short term. It would hurt the men at a time when unity is paramount. Religion, in many ways, is the way to interest the men, whose whole philosophy has been rooted in the church their whole lives. There are other ideas beyond religion that can be reached once you have the audience. Most would not belong to a discussion group, but would belong to a congregation. I believe the Bible of St Sosimas is truly ours, but I also believe it is not all we have.

'When this is all over, I want to spend time in contemplation and to produce a book of my own, one that builds a bridge from the Ethiopic Bible to the world we live in today. I need to see how possible it is to return to Africa. I need time to read more, explore my beliefs and bring my ideas to a state of order.' He was counting his cartridges over and over with his fingers as he spoke.

'If God is truly a spectator and not an active participant, how does one explain Jesus or the Exodus or the Flood?'

He thought for a moment and lifted his rifle with both hands, weighing it in his grip. 'Some circumstances are extraordinary. Consider the birth of Christ—it is the hand of God setting events in motion, seeing how we will react. The resurrection could well be the very last act of God on this Earth to this point. And as I've said before, some stories are meant to teach.'

The bugle rang out, calling us to the line, and we gathered our things.

Sosimas offered a final thought as we made our way to the staging area: 'The English philosopher John Locke wrote that when a man finds himself in a position of slavery, it is his prerogative to rebel. Something to consider as we follow the colonel today.'

❋ ❋ ❋

As noon approached, the twenty men of our squad stood in three rows, staring across a winter-browned meadow at a tree line we knew concealed enemy soldiers. A split-rail fence cut through the centre of the meadow, reaching nearly to its far end, well to the right of where we would soon be marching. Lieutenant Colwell, who had three squads under his command, made his way back and forth up the line, attempting to reassure us.

'Colonel Harrington has informed me,' he said to our squad, 'that it's an even fight, with about two thousand men on each side.'

We looked at each other nervously. An even number of men only benefits the defenders, I considered, and I knew the others were thinking it as well, especially the men in Sosimas's congregation. Our squad was the very last unit on Harrington's right flank. Beyond us was open country, and I thought I might simply walk away into it, into the hills, perhaps on to some port and to Ethiopia from there. I wondered how many days such a trip might take.

Men around me flinched as the sound of cannon began somewhere behind us and to the left. Puffs of smoke and dirt curled skyward at the edge of the tree line on the opposite rise. Moments later, the cannon were answered and shouts rose from the centre of the line, far to the left. Lieutenant Colwell ran up to the front of the squad and shouted to us. 'We have our orders from the Colonel.' He sounded almost mournful as he continued. 'We're to march across the field and engage the enemy's left flank. Your sergeant will give the command.'

The lieutenant ran back toward his other squads as artillery fire rang out through the gentle valley. Sergeant Clark gave the commands to check rifles and fix bayonets. As I fixed my bayonet, I considered this new rifle. It had a heavy stock, framed with metal, and it felt substantial in my hands. Once the enemy was reached, it would be more useful as a club than a firearm, and I found myself wishing for a knife or an officer's sword.

Through the men in front of me, I drank in the land before us. The enemy was on high ground and appeared to have the benefit of a stone wall to hide behind. The small valley sloped downward to the left and I was grateful that our squad had less climbing to do than any other for once. Of course it was open ground all the way, and it seemed impossible to make the distance alive.

Before I could consider it any further, we were marching forward. Sosimas was to my right, with Howell, Steven and Kwame in front and Fortune behind in the third row. I could make out the form of Lieutenant Cowell leading his squads, the only white man I could lay eyes on at that point. I knew there were many more white men in the trees ahead.

About fifty yards to the right, the meadow was swallowed by trees, and the dark forest looked inviting, more so as the enemy's guns drew closer. We received the first musket volley minutes after beginning to move forward, but it mostly fell short and to our left. A few men in the next squad fell and Sosimas began shouting. 'The trees! The trees! Go to the trees!'

He pointed to the right and broke formation, running full tilt toward the forest. Other men became confused, watching him run.

Sergeant Clark, who was ahead of us, noticed and called for us to remain together, but it was no use. Howell, Steven and several others had already broken formation, and I charged after them, followed by others. By the time we reached the trees, it seemed the entire squad had run from the line. Sergeant Clark had followed. As he puffed his way into the squad, which squatted on the ground within the tree line, he screamed at us.

'We will be killed for this!' He looked at Sosimas. 'You coward! Why are you running? You cannot simply leave the line!' He slackened a bit and leaned against a tree. He was older and heavier than the rest of us. 'We'll be shot, all of us.'

'We are not leaving the battle,' Sosimas said, rising from his crouch. 'Follow me!'

Our choices were clear: follow Sosimas or keep running from the battle. To a man, we chose the former. Our view of the field was obscured by a rise, and we followed the crackle of gunfire through tangled underbrush up a steep slope until we could see men in front of us, facing away toward the field.

'He's led us behind them!' Steven said as the men of the squad, and a few who had joined us from the next squad, lined up together behind the cover of the rise. Though still in the woods, beyond the backs of a thin line of militia fighters in front of us I could see the meadow, where the men of the other squads were moving forward, taking fire. I felt the morning's queasiness coming back to me knowing what they were suffering as we left the field.

Following Sosimas's commands, we advanced in tight formation, crested the rise and advanced down the opposite slope toward the tree line, rifles ready, closing within mere yards of the rebels before firing. Men fell all before us with the volley, and survivors whirled to face the surprise attack coming from behind them. Their faces were streaked with terror and I ran unthinking into them, swinging the intricately decorated butt of the rifle into the chin of a man who had fallen. He crumpled and I stabbed his staggering neighbour with my bayonet. I tried to run on but couldn't pull it from his body as he sagged to the ground. I had no ball in the chamber and twisted my weapon as he screamed in agony.

His screaming quieted as I pulled, and I swear I could hear his breathing over all other sounds at that moment, quickening and then stopping. His left hand clutched the breast of his uniform, which bore the seal of South Carolina. He was looking away from me, his head at a queer angle, mouth agape as if registering silent horror at the turn of the battle. Finally free, I followed his empty gaze to the few rebel soldiers who had survived our assault. They were falling one by one in the field as they abandoned the tree line.

A handful who held their positions fared little better as we fell upon them with bayonets and rifle butts. Men further down the enemy line turned toward us and began to fire. Grabbing whatever cover was available—trees, rocks, the bodies of enemy soldiers, a pile of enemy gear—we reloaded frantically for a scattered return volley. We were spread apart by this point, though, and each man resorted to firing individually. The only advantage to this was that we also presented a terrible target.

I still had a good view of the field and could see Lieutenant Colwell's remaining men nearing the tree line just ahead of my position. We ran forward to meet them as they breached the enemy line, and the white militiamen ran for their lives. I swung my rifle at any man who moved and the red of my coat deepened with the blows. My mind went blank and my limbs were numb, as though acting on their own volition. The trees blurred as I ran after the enemy's collapsing line, my comrades around me, a streak of red illuminating the dark of the forest.

I became aware that the man running to my right was Steven and froze when I saw the figure jerk backward and tumble to the ground. Slipping on the thick cover of dry leaves, I fell beside him. My head rang from hitting the ground, and in the haze of gun smoke swirling through the trees overhead, I could see trails carved by bullets as they passed above me. I wanted to leave my body and join them. A wail of pain from Steven shook me back into the moment. He clutched his side just below his left armpit and gasped for air between cries. I crawled to him.

'I'm dead, Solomon, I'm dead!' Steven shouted. I placed my hand on the wound and pressed as hard as I could, but blood flowed over my fingers and mingled with the leaves. I kept pressing, trying to push the life back into him, remembering my brother and the way his blood had washed over me in the grass. My mind was awakening in the midst of a battle and I thought I might stay there, next to Steven, until it was over, holding his life in. There were few living men around us now, and they joined in a choir of groans that filled in the strange, smoky silence that had gripped this part of the forest.

Steven had grown quieter but still he repeated the words, 'I'm dead, Solomon.' His breathing was sharp and his gaze fixed on the naked branches above him so intently that I reflexively looked up, half expecting to see an angel or God Himself. When I turned back to him, the life was gone from his face. I pulled my hands from his wound, covered in the stuff of his life. The blood was so dark, especially on the lighter skin of my palm.

The sweat was cooling on my forehead. I tried to will myself back to the battle but, as if in a dream, my legs wouldn't respond. I searched deep within for hate or some other emotional fuel to propel me further, but all I found was sorrow. I grabbed the stock of my rifle, but it slipped from my blood-drenched grip. I scraped my hands across the leaves, smearing them brown. The blood was growing ropey, and I quite suddenly noticed the noise of battle again as I laid my hand on the carved stock. I forced myself to rise, wiped aside my tears and chased the snapping of muskets.

✻   ✻   ✻

The taste of acid in my mouth was as persistent as my brother's blood the day before. I had drained a full canteen and still failed to chase it. In the hours after the brief engagement with the enemy I had stumbled through the carnage trying not to vomit, but I'd given in and let it come as I watched fellow Royal Army soldiers—one a former slave, the other a Cherokee mercenary—take the valuables from the body of an enemy soldier whose legs were gone. The legs, they weren't even nearby. It was simply as though he had vanished from the knees down.

The white officers stood and watched. There was a feeling after a battle—whether it was won or lost—unlike any other. The silence was deeper, and I never knew what to do with myself but to try not to hear the pleas of the wounded or look at the dead. There were times when it was unavoidable, the rare occasions when we buried our fallen on the day following a battle. We were too often in retreat to inter them with consistency.

I wandered the edge of the forest, tripping over the barrel of a smashed enemy cannon, the wheels of its caisson split and charred. I found Steven just yards away and could hardly bear to look at him as I covered him with leaves and sticks. Returning to the cannon, I pulled a singed scrap of the South Carolinian flag from beneath one of the wheels. I returned to Steven and covered his head and chest with it. I tried to think of a prayer Sosimas might say at this point but was left at a loss.

Returning back across the field in a soldier's post-battle daze, I found Howell. We made our way back the mile or so to camp bruised and exhausted as the shadows grew long. Kwame had already returned and sat by a new fire with a piece of white cloth tied around part of his head. Blood had soaked through it in a long, fuzzy line.

'We smashed them today,' the corporal said as we crashed

down on whatever objects made the most convenient seats. 'Thanks to Sosimas. Did you see their terror when they turned to find us behind them?' He curled his fist ever so slightly, but his hand quickly went limp again in his lap.

I couldn't drum up any exultation, though it was clear that our feigned retreat had caused the enemy's left flank to fail and made it easier for the other squads to advance. I tried to ignore the taste of acid, and it slowly dawned on me how sore my ankle was after the fall next to Steven. Howell idly wondered aloud how many of the men we had killed that day had owned slaves. Answering his own question, he imagined they all had—they must have. Why would they be fighting otherwise?

'Steven is dead, Kwame.' I said to break the silence that followed. 'I was with him when he died. Tomorrow, he'll be put in a hole with all the other men, just like my brother. If he's lucky.'

Silence engulfed us as the night advanced. Members of the squad trickled into camp, seventeen in all, and nearly twice as many as from the old squad after the previous day's battle. Aside from Steven, two men were missing: Sergeant Clark and Sosimas.

I forced down my rations, threw them back up and retired to my tent. The four cots were empty. Steven's few possessions lay where he had left them and I forced my eyes elsewhere. Howell's bed was neat and Fortune's looked recently slept in. Fortune and I hadn't spoken since the morning and though I desperately craved solitude, I felt I should find him and talk, as he had also been close to Steven.

I was walking to the fire when Fortune found me.

'Solomon!' Fortune's voice was low.

I stopped and searched out his features in the dark. The nearest fire was behind him, and I could catch a glint off his temple but I couldn't see his eyes or mouth.

We groped for words and Fortune found them first: 'I heard of Steven's death. You were there?'

'I was.' Sadness I hadn't yet had time for welled within me.

Fortune didn't respond, and as we stood quietly we began to shiver. 'Solomon,' Fortune finally said, 'why did Sosimas run today? Did he say it would happen?'

Fortune wasn't a part of Sosimas's congregation, but he knew the gist of the sermons from what I, Steven and Howell had told him.

'Not precisely,' I said. 'He talked about Colonel Harrington's tactics killing us, but I didn't know he would make his own tactics in the middle of battle. I just followed because it seemed like a better idea than walking into the guns.'

'Me too.' He turned his head, and I caught a flash of his eyes, wide in the darkness, as though viewing something awful.

'It was a good idea. I think we won the battle because of it. They thought we had run away,' I said. My legs felt weak and I longed to sit, but we were standing far from any suitable seat.

'It could have caused a disaster,' Fortune said. 'If other men from other squads had followed... It was reckless. Only luck prevented it. And we will be luckier still if we are not punished for it. Colonel Harrington has had men whipped for much less than disobeying orders on a battlefield.'

I shuddered from a mix of cold and the thought of a lashing. I had never felt a whip on my back—my brother had always taken the punishment at home. He would sometimes lie to keep me safe and in the good graces of the family and other house staff. 'Let's go to the fire,' I said. 'I'm beginning to lose feeling in my feet.'

The men of the squad huddled in clumps around the blaze, some speaking quietly, others simply seeking warmth. It was only minutes but it seemed an eternity to the point when Lieutenant Colwell dragged himself into our camp. We saluted nervously, and a few men who were sitting rose to attention, but several didn't bother.

'Please stand for the lieutenant,' ordered Kwame, and the men reluctantly complied.

Lieutenant Colwell swept his eyes across us. 'At ease,' he said and stepped closer to the fire. 'I don't know where to begin.'

The men were silent. Most looked toward the ground.

Lieutenant Colwell straightened his back and addressed us more authoritatively. 'Colonel Harrington wants to have you all hanged for mutiny. A small part of me wants to allow it. I could very well have been killed out in that field while you, all of you, ran to the woods. I'm frankly surprised any of you are in camp. You'd have been as well advised to leave entirely.'

Kwame spoke up. 'Sir, do you have news of Sergeant Clark or Private Negus?'

'Sergeant Clark and the private are with the colonel. Private Negus is under arrest, and Sergeant Clark is his accuser. Private Negus claims that running from the field was his idea and that the rest of you had no choice in the matter.'

'It's true that it was his idea, sir,' said Kwame, 'but it was our choice to follow him.'

Men shifted where they stood as Kwame said this.

'Choose your words carefully, Corporal. You very nearly brought an entire army with you,' said Lieutenant Colwell. 'It seems, though, to have had an effect on the outcome.' He stared into the fire for a moment before going on. 'I know this is hard for you men, and there is little love lost between the colonel and myself, but orders on the battlefield are to be followed, even if they're poor orders. If more men had run to the woods, it could have been catastrophic.'

A few men wrinkled their brows at this word, apparently unsure of its meaning, but the implication was enough to get the point across. I knew the word from my childhood—it was a favourite of the master of our house.

'I've spoken with Colonel Harrington at length about the situation. He hasn't yet agreed not to punish the men of this unit, but he has agreed that only one of you will die for your actions. That is Private Negus. He will be whipped tomorrow at dawn and then shot, and all men of this unit will be present, per the colonel's orders.'

Kwame stepped toward Lieutenant Colwell as the other men moved closer together. 'Sir, with respect,' he said, 'you are a kind commander, and the men admire you, but this can't be allowed. Sosimas—Private Negus—lead us to victory and away from certain death. We've lost Private Steven Jackson, and as much as we mourn his loss, to lose but one man in such a battle... It's unthinkable with the orders the colonel gives.

'Sir, in the Royal Army a black man can be no more than a sergeant. Never have we ever been in control of our destiny, and our lot in the King's army is no better. Mutiny is the only manner through which we can gain control.'

Lieutenant Colwell pulled his fingers across his moustache and raised his voice now. 'Corporal, I understand you concerns. As a native-born American, I can rise no higher than lieutenant in the Royal Army, even as a white man. I'd have to transfer to a Continental Army unit to rise higher. However, at this point, you should feel lucky to be free and alive. There's nothing I can do to stop this, but I will tell you one thing, and listen carefully.'

He held up a finger, as if to give every man something to focus on while he spoke.

'I am under orders to have my other squads guard this unit in the night and escort you tomorrow while the colonel decides your cases. I have not passed this order on to my other men. We are at the very edge of the camp. You should understand what this means.'

The men looked at each other.

'When you leave,' Lieutenant Colwell said, turning to go, 'head west. And stay north. You'll be safe in Cherokee country, but until you cross the Mississippi River into the Spanish Cession, everywhere else will be dangerous. I've no idea how you'll cross the river, but once you have, go north. If you end up in Texas or even near it, you could pay with your freedom or your lives. Texas still practices slavery and sponsors those men we fought today. You will not be welcome there.'

Before any of us could reply, the lieutenant was off into the ink of night. Murmurs spread quickly. The men new to the squad huddled together. Kwame, Howell, David, Carter, Cassius and I—nearly all of Sosimas's congregation—gathered away from the fire and Fortune joined us.

Cassius's language training abandoned him, exposing his Caribbean past as a rage no one present had yet seen or even imagined possible rose in him. 'We canno' allow dis! We mus' go, but Sosimas... I ain't gon' leave him!'

Fortune cut in. 'We have no choice. We leave, we leave

now, and we forget him. If it wasn't for him, we would not even be discussing this.'

'You never even listened to the man,' said Kwame. 'If it wasn't for him, many of us would not even be here to discuss it.'

'What of it? Will you die trying to free Sosimas? You don't even know where he is.'

David, whom I had rarely heard speak, chimed in. 'We should kill Colonel Harrington. He deserves it, always sitting back there on his horse while we march into bullets.'

I quieted everyone with a hiss. 'Calm down. We must consider this. What does killing the colonel accomplish?'

'It saves the men we leave behind from his tactics,' offered one of the new voices, but I couldn't see who in the night.

'And who is to say that an even worse man will not be put in his place?' asked Fortune. 'Remember that when General Hawkins was killed in his tent it was Colonel Harrington who rose to his command and led us to ruin in these mountains.'

No one had a reply. There were many times when I wondered if Fortune was not the smartest man in the entire unit. Kwame called the other group of men over.

'Will you help us free Sosimas?' he asked them.

None seemed interested. They had decided to leave together as soon as they could gather provisions.

'You see?' said Fortune. 'They are leaving now, as we should.'

'Go with them, then,' said Kwame.

'Solomon,' said Fortune, looking at me. 'This is madness. Come with me.'

I looked at Fortune in the distant fire light. A sliver of moon had risen low in the sky, filling in the details of his face. I decided then that Sosimas couldn't be left behind. 'I won't, Fortune. Sosimas deserves to be rescued.'

Fortune's shoulders slumped and he backed away. 'I am going to our tent, and I will gather together what I can carry.' He paused and looked toward the row of five tents the squad was quartered in. 'I will gather enough for each of you—food, clothing, weapons. I'll wait for you until the first light shows over the hills, but no longer.' With that, he ran to our tent.

The rest of us stood attempting to devise a plan. 'We must be silent,' said Kwame. 'Sosimas must be under guard, and we may have to... We should be armed, but with knives only.'

'We're not issued knives,' I said. 'Bayonets, though. It will be clumsy, but it will have to do.' We each retired to our respective quarters to retrieve a bayonet. Even in the low moon and firelight, I could see that mine was still caked with blood. We met back at the fire to determine how to find Sosimas. It was clear it wouldn't be simple.

We knew the location of the colonel's quarters and the nearby stump where we had been forced to watch the lashing of a soldier accused of stealing supplies two days earlier. It made sense to begin there, and we agreed that two small groups were less likely to cause a stir than one large group. Howell, Kwame and I would stay together, while David would lead the other two men. We would search for Sosimas until the moon reached its apex over the hills to the south, and if this met with no success would return to the squad's small encampment to change the plan.

David and his charges immediately disappeared into the woods, but Howell stopped us before we could follow.

''Fore we go,' said Howell to Kwame, 'd'you think I could get an African name, like you, Kwame? I's named Howell for the family of the missus and Garvey fo' the name o' the massuh, and I's right tired of it after hearin' Sosimas.'

Kwame thought, then smiled. 'Of course, Howell.' He placed a hand on Howell's shoulder. 'You will be...'—he drew out the last word while considering it—'...Ife Asante. Ife was the name of my grandfather's father. And Asante for the people who once ruled an empire in the desert.'

Howell ran the name over his tongue. 'Ife Asante. Ife Asante.' The second time it had more force.

'Ife Asante,' Kwame repeated. 'Now, let's be off.'

We could see the other men of the squad departing westward in the dim moonlight as we lit out for the opposite end of the encampment, just inside the tree line on the edge of camp where the chance of being seen was low. In the cold night, the trees looked as tired of war as were we. The white of the tents in the camp seemed to glow under the moon despite the tarnish on the cloth. I knew there would be pickets and probably patrols in the woods but couldn't be sure where. We took each step with immense caution.

As we approached the area of Colonel Harrington's quarters, a large fire cast a dim orange glow over everything. We retreated to the woods and spied on the scene from the shelter of brush and the nude, orange-lit trees. Colonel Harrington sat close to the blaze, holding his shako in his lap, officers spread around him in chairs. Four Cherokee mercenaries stood behind them, rifles at the ready.

It didn't appear to be worth making our presence here known. We silently agreed to move on and search for Sosimas. Moving as quietly as possible along the edge of the camp, we could see men lingering around cooking fires through the dead spaces between tents. Snatches of conversation drifted on the moonlight and Kwame led us into the camp, whispering that Sosimas was unlikely to be held somewhere near the edge. As we moved quickly through shadows, I fought away the thought of tripping and falling on my own bayonet.

This is hopeless, I thought as we made our way between rows of white canvas tents. Even if we do find him, what are the chances we can free him without calling attention to ourselves? My ankle ached more with every inch the moon rose in the sky.

Kwame paused in front of me where the rows of tents terminated at the wagon path. The sound of a man snoring wheezed softly from the tent to our left. Kwame and I took turns peeking out into the wagon path. At one end, the colonel's fire burned, framed by figures and the walls of tents. A few men walked alone on the path.

Kwame looked to the moon and backtracked, leading us through the narrow space between a few tents. Conversations were dwindling, but I could hear two men urgently discussing a comrade. 'Where was he from? Can we write to his family?' one asked, to which the other could only reply, 'I don't know. He had come to us in Charleston only days ago and I diddin' know his whole name.'

We followed Kwame as he wove between tents, stepping lightly, until we arrived in a clearing near the hospital tent which emanated moans and soft prayers. The glow of Colonel Harrington's fire formed a hellish halo around it. The voices of officers were faintly audible and then, just above them, the unmistakable baritone of Sosimas. 'I would not stop you from praying if you were about to die,' he was saying.

A chill ran through me and we moved toward the tent his voice had most likely come from. Through the canvas of the tent two plots removed from the hospital and in full view of the men around the fire, we heard him softly speaking in prayer, keeping his voice loud enough for the guards to hear. At the front corners of the tent, the forms of two guards—one clearly white, the other black—stood erect, staring toward the colonel and his inner circle.

We crouched, paralysed, behind the tent. What could we do in full view of the colonel, those Cherokee soldiers and the other officers? Were there others in the woods? I focused on the low drone of Sosimas, trying to parse his barely audible prayer through the canvas. I hoped that some small part of it would follow Steven's soul and fill the void I had left earlier.

The colonel's voice boomed through the night. 'They don't fight a proper war, do they, these Carolinians and Georgians. It reminds me of my time in Tripoli in 1818, when we fought the Berbers and took the coast to protect our trade routes. There was no discipline in the enemy ranks.' There was a heavy pause. 'Rather like some of ours, I'm afraid to say.'

An unknown officer's voice responded: 'That will be seen to tomorrow, sir.'

'I was just a lieutenant back then, like you,' Harrington continued, addressing someone none of us could see. 'But even then I could see that you had to have discipline. I took a Berber fort with fewer men than I have at my disposal today. I made captain for that, you know. I replaced my own commander, who was killed that same day, God rest his soul. It started me on the road to where I am today.'

Wandering around in the woods waiting to die, I thought,

wishing I had the luxury of replying.

'Anyone can shoot from behind a rock, but it's an open fight that reveals the real score,' the Colonel went on. 'Those men today nearly unravelled my whole army. Unconscionably small thing, this army. I don't know how they expect us to win with so few men, especially these negroes, who don't appreciate the value of good learning and discipline. Or the freedom we've given them, for that matter.'

In the tent, Sosimas broke his prayer and raised his voice. 'You've given us nothing, you old buffoon. It was you who took freedom from us in the first place. Merely returning it and re-enslaving us in your army does us no favours.'

Colonel Harrington laughed. 'You see what I mean, gentlemen? No respect for authority.' The colonel's voice grew louder as he said it. I bit my lower lip at the sound of canvas rustling. 'I should hold my tongue if I were you,' the colonel continued, apparently still speaking to Sosimas.

'Why should I hold it? I'm to be murdered on your orders by a man who thinks too highly of himself. What have I to lose?'

'You'll be executed for mutiny,' the colonel's voice said quickly and angrily, and the sound of canvas slapping against canvas filled the air.

'This is the fifth time you've sentenced me to die,' Sosimas called after the colonel. 'Four times in battle and now this. Tell me, is it a coincidence that every time you've ascended in rank, the man in front of you died to clear the way?'

The sound of moving canvas again and another officer spoke. 'That's enough from you,' he said, and I gritted my teeth at the dull sound of fist on flesh. I imagined that the officer beating Sosimas would hear my heart if I let it beat too loudly against the wall of the tent.

Howell, crouching on the ground at the rear corner of the tent, waved me over. The white officer no longer stood at the front of the tent. It occurred to me that he must be the one inside. At the other corner of the tent, the other guard was still at his post, and beyond him I glimpsed several officers paying respect to Colonel Harrington. I held my breath and tried to shut out the noise within the tent. It was then that I realised how starkly visible we must have been against the white of the tent in the moonlight.

I signalled Howell and Kwame to lie on the ground, and we watched without so much as a twitch as three officers—captains, by their insignia—trudged past on the wagon path.

'Not talking now, eh?' The officer in the tent could be heard dusting himself off. I again peeked around the corner of the tent at the black guard, who may have been a statue for all he moved. Kwame moved behind the next tent to have his own view of the same narrow alley as me. The Cherokee mercenaries were still at the ready, but only Colonel Harrington and three of his aides remained at the fire. My blood froze as something snapped behind me.

I turned to see Howell hastily backing away from the other corner of the tent, but a shout from the direction of the fire recaptured my attention. Looking again down the alley I saw a blur of red by the fire as the aides, the colonel and the mercenaries struggled. Out of the corner of my eye, I saw Kwame spring up and lunge across my back. As I tumbled forward to make way for him, I turned to see a white officer take Kwame's bayonet in the throat as Howell struck from below.

This was the moment. I plunged my still-stained bayonet through the canvas and tore a hole in the side of Sosimas's holding tent. The black guard turned and clearly saw me cutting the fabric but simply turned back as though he'd seen nothing. Once in the tent, my vision failed and I groped for Sosimas in the dark. 'Sosimas! It's me, Solomon!'

'I'm tied,' came a feeble reply from just ahead in the darkness.

My hands found Sosimas and I felt my way down his awkwardly bent arm to a thick, knotted rope. Feeling past the knot, I cut with my bayonet as quickly as I could. Shouting could be heard from around the fire and a shot was fired, followed by three more. Finally, the rope was severed, and I pulled Sosimas through the hole in the tent. The black guard had run to the fracas by the fire, and I could make out Colonel Harrington moving erratically, hands on his gut, a deep crimson gash on his neck. One of the new men from the congregation—I thought Cassius was his name—swung his bayonet wildly in the centre of the melee, and at least one of the aides appeared to have been shot.

Sosimas was crawling out of the tent and I wondered if we should join the struggle or retreat. Cassius was shot twice as I helped Sosimas to his feet, and we watched as he made a dying lunge for the staggering colonel, pushing him into the fire. Colonel Harrington did not move after hitting the fire and his aides rushed to pull him from it, still aflame, and limp as wet cloth.

The mercenaries stood above a man I discerned was David, who struggled against them, slashing with his bayonet. He caught one of them in the thigh just as another brought the butt of a musket squarely down on his forehead.

Around the back of the tent, the white officer was dead and once Sosimas had fully discarded the rope, we ran at top speed to the edge of the camp and the woods. The camp was alive with voices and men could be seen streaming toward the colonel's fire. Only we moved in the opposite direction. Back at our camp, Fortune was the only soul remaining, and he waited in our tent with supplies at the ready.

'Where are the others?' he asked.

'Dead,' Kwame explained. 'As is Colonel Harrington. They killed him. We have Sosimas.' I wondered about Carter, as I'd caught no glimpse of him in the skirmish by the fire.

Outside the tent, we gathered ourselves and prepared to leave. In the fading light of our dying cooking fire, Sosimas's face looked like the back of a whipped man. His lips were swollen and wet, and his left eye could open only half way.

'Thank you, brothers,' he said, his speech slurred through gaps in his teeth and his puffed lips. 'I only wish no one had died coming to my aid.'

'They were brave,' said Kwame. 'They knew they would be killed cutting down Colonel Harrington and still went through with it. And they succeeded. Solomon saw with his own eyes.'

I nodded.

'We must be going,' Fortune reminded us, hefting his pack and raising his musket. 'Sosimas, your Bible is in your pack.'

The moon was near its apex. We had no notion of what lay ahead. We simply pointed ourselves to the west and marched into the woods, moving as quickly as the moonlight allowed.

The shouts of men faded behind us as we climbed a hill that seemed to rise forever, and when I looked back over my shoulder I caught a pinpoint of flame in the valley through the naked branches.

So this is it. Total emancipation. I felt sick with the thought of the dead and terrified at the thought of running and alive with the thought of the future. I looked at my friends and wondered what new life we'd be able to build. There would be no return to servitude.

We faced west and marched on.

The Thunderbird
by Mark Beech

From the journal of
William Charles Lumsden,
7th Viscount of Balmedie

Wednesday 25 April 1888

We resolved to leave Gateway City with still no word from Rutherford.

Chaos had broken out at the railway station. I was standing with the trunks watching Khaled toe and elbow a path through the torrent of American Ladies and Gentlemen: nut planters, landlords, war profiteers. Their haughty expressions bobbed about like balloons amidst the patterns of their two seasons old English fashions. How I detest them and all their *faux*-Victorian pretensions. With every ounce of my will I had to stop myself bellowing out to my valet, 'For heaven's sake man, use your fists!' I was certain then that no force on Earth was going to keep me in Gateway for another afternoon.

'It's no good,' Khaled was at last able to tell me, in breathless bursts. 'There are no railway trains heading west today. And they say, with all likelihood, there will be none this side of Sunday.'

I was naturally at the point of outrage, but Khaled, ever the master of situations, had a rabbit up his sleeve.

'There is the possibility we will be able to get a steamboat, at least as far as Kiowa or Tribal Council Bluffs. It will, I fear, be slow going, and I cannot speak for the comforts of the journey, but we will certainly be there by Saturday. With luck we will be able to pick up the railway trains from there...'

Later, and in less frenetic surroundings, Khaled told me how, that morning, as he had been waiting at the telegraph offices, a hullabaloo had developed around the arrival of another message. A number of senior employees were called to the machines for verification; voices were raised and exclamations bandied about; a boy was despatched with an envelope. Khaled, whose talent for picking up gossip I have often complimented him upon, eavesdropped as best he could. Through the noise of the locomotives arriving and departing outside, he was only able to pick out a very few and possibly erroneous clews to the business of the message: 'Blackfoot. Dynamited. Third one since January'.

Khaled said he could make nothing of it, but I was moved to agree with him that the upset caused to the railways was possibly in some manner connected with that telegraph. In any event, we were by that time in a cab bound for Dock Street. Even as the first signs of an approaching thunderstorm rumbled and flickered in the west, my mood lightened, and I was perfectly content to put the events of that morning behind me.

By teatime we had secured a place on the middle decks of one of the hulking council-run passenger boats we had so often observed from our rooms at the Royal as they went, sunken low and lurching up the wide Missouri River, laden with emigrant wagons. I had on one occasion commented upon how much these boats had put me in mind of the West Pier at Brighton: all those garishly painted panels and baroque advertisement placards, pinioned and bound with a mass of pig iron girders. Where we were to find ourselves that afternoon, however, upon the decks of one such vessel, with animal muck and river scum swilling about our boot ankles, the English seaside was not immediate in my mind.

I told Khaled to look after the trunks and went off for a while on my own, at length finding an unoccupied place near the aft to smoke my tobacco in relative peace. The rain was lashing down about us; the river was a froth! Night was descending, fast and early. Numbly, I observed the limits of Gateway fading into the obscurity of our smoke trail. What surrounded us now was the preserve of the rich Missouri plantation families: fox and hare hunting country; English gardens and brightly painted boat huts. And I remained numb.

From amid the din of the lower decks, in the shadows that milled about beneath me, the voices of quack doctors and three-card-trick men bewailed their services; some fellows sang in Yiddish, I believe, and I became gradually fixated upon the gruff Irish voice of one with evidently no great talent for confidence trickery busying himself amongst the travellers, attempting to ingratiate himself upon one or another of them.

'Why, can it be, sir? Surely not! How the devil have you been? No, no! Don't tell me! I know! We bought shine from the same boy in Frankfort, is that it?... A joke sir! Merely that! I can clearly see you're a Christian man and wouldn't... Well then, sir, allow me to make it clear that you're more than welcome to KISS MY ARSE, SIR!!'

I burst into laughter. At that moment, the wind blew a violent gust down the deck and almost took my hat off. The sky went up in a blinding flash and it seemed to me as if the heavens themselves were heard to tear into pieces. Were we hit? I looked about myself wildly, I think. My heart was pounding. Was anything amiss? In the gloom of a little alcove just over the way from me, there seemed to stir the forms of several human beings. Instinctively, I moved towards them. Through stone cold expressions they met my approach and stopped me dead in my tracks. Huddled up in blankets and overcoats: they were a family of Red Indians, tired looking and probably sick; nothing really but skin and bone. More shaken than ever, I tipped my hat inelegantly and left them to themselves.

Four months have now passed since first we arrived at New York docks, and in that time I am depressed to think that these unfortunate wretches are my first and only experience of the native people of the Americas.

I have not slept this night, and I shan't sleep. The storm rumbles and flickers ever on. The rain is into everything.

We chug! Westward.

✳   ✳   ✳

Sunday 29 April 1888

My title precedes me, even if my reputation does not. Wherever I travel, I am normally afforded the best rooms in whatever hostelry I take the trouble to properly sign the guest book in, and the best food and even wine, though at often higher than market prices.

It is clear that no one this far west has seen a British newspaper for some very long time, and that that 'Great and Terrible Business' with which the name of the New Hellfire Club gained such immediate infamy in the pages of the London dailies has yet to scandalise the gentle folk of the American colonies.

In the meantime, I am happy to have them bow and scrape about me like sticky fingered snobs on Derby Day. I almost wish I could stay and see their faces pucker in total disgust on the day they see my photograph and behold those lurid headlines. But by God! They should think themselves blessed to have so graciously humiliated themselves before so notorious an English exile. Ha ha!

Council Bluffs was a sure bet! Our rooms at the Herefordshire Inn were as comfortable and spacious as ever we might have hoped. The large bay windows looked out along the riverbank.

A few hundred yards further on, I soon discovered, a garrison of the Queen's Royal Lancers had been recently stationed around the rotting wooden sheds of a disused 'jumping off' point. The place, of course, reeked of Empire. From every balcony, balustrade, beam and finial fluttered or wove the colours of the Union Flag. Morning had risen to find itself ashamed by the almost heavenly glow of the many dozen ornate brass lions and eagles upon display. And at their centre, the righteous figure of Lady Britannia clutched her sword and shield and glared, resolutely, into the heart of the sun.

Remarkably soon after our arrival, a boy cadet had shown up at our door with an invitation to dine with a General Sir Nevill Maskelyne Dudley that Saturday evening. I had no intentions of still being at Council Bluffs on Saturday evening, least of all in the company of a general of the Empire. However, I made a point of not bothering to reply.

In the morning, I had been reading Claudian in a rare state of contentment, when Khaled burst in.

'Sir,' he said breathlessly. 'We have news from Rutherford at last!'

My valet had been at the telegraph offices since sunrise, hoping to intercept something from our architect after weeks of silence. I snatched the transcript from his sweating hand. The house and gardens were coming along splendidly, it informed us plainly. 'But eucalyptus will not take in soil of the Hathaway Valley.'

By this time the railways were running again, and we had intended to catch the noon train to Alliance. In that moment, however, the urgency had gone out of our journey. I was in an excellent mood. I told Khaled to dig out my evening suit. Having eaten nothing but crawfish for a week, there seemed now little harm in delaying our departure for the sake of a decent dinner at the garrison.

I arrived late. Two grinning Bengali servants took me into the General's dining room, where the other guests were already milling about the table, chatting vacuously and putting names to the various stuffed heads that loomed down at us from the walls. They were apparently all military men of rank, barely able to carry themselves, it seemed, beneath the weight of their tassels and brasses and their overstuffed bellies. The General staggered past them to greet me, his face swollen into something like an expression of pride, hemmed between a forest of face-whiskers. He commented blandly upon the weather as he walked me to my seat.

The food was reasonable if unsophisticated: a wild rabbit stew followed by steak with wild onion. For pudding there was hot apple pie.

I was surprised to discover that I was not, after all, the only civilian there present. A young Belgian journalist had also been invited. I could only think it was in the hope he might give mention to the General in his writings. In fact, I discovered, he was on his way north, to write about the beleaguered tribes of the Red Indians.

At this, I told the story of my experiences on the steamboat.

'The tribes of the western plains,' he said in a soft voice, 'believe in a creature called the Thunderbird. This vast and vengeful being creates storm clouds and thunder by the very clapping of its mighty wings. You see?'

A ripple of laughter ran around the table.

He went on: 'They say that any man it lays its eyes upon is stuck down on the spot by a bolt of lightning, or else carried off into the storm...'

The General slammed his fork down on the tabletop.

'This is precisely what I mean,' he said, although it was clear that nobody had any idea what he meant. 'If the Americans had only spent a little more time putting these ludicrous pagan whimsies out of the native's heads—rather than brushing the problem under the carpet, so to speak—they might by now have cultivated a half decent working class instead of just a lot of bad blood.'

Some of the officers muttered agreeably into their puddings.

'What the Americans fail to comprehend,' he went on, 'is that given the choice between becoming an active and valuable part of the greatest empire the world has ever known, or otherwise lolling about in the sun like wogs 'til doomsday, I am in no doubt they would have jumped at the former... They're reasonable human beings, I'm sure.'

He went on for some time in this manner, beating out more than a few quite preposterous solutions to the 'the Red Indian problem' and receiving few challenges from his guests. I glanced from time to time at the Belgian journalist. He smiled benignly throughout.

Ultimately, and despite the General's most enthusiastic efforts, the vast ideological ocean he was attempting to show as existing between Great Britain and this lawless and, to his mind, unpatriotic backwater of the Empire with regard to its native people amounted to little more than a drainage ditch!

It runs, I think, something like this.

The Americans believe that in return for Red Indian hospitality, it is quite reasonable to claim exclusivity to any or more of their most fertile and valuable lands in the name of the colony, depriving them of their heritage and food supplies.

The British, on the other hand, subscribe to a method of forced integration, Christianisation, imperial servitude and death from syphilis. It has worked the world over.

I asked the General whether he was here to help the Americans put things right. He pointed his fork at me and grinned like an imbecile.

By eleven, they were all moving into the billiard room with fat cigars jutting out of their sweaty red faces. I had had my fill. I made a barely observable excuse and left them to it.

The chill night air hit me unexpectedly. I was giddy. I steadied myself against a pillar.

'So tell me, Monsieur Lumsden, is the Hellfire Club going west?'

I blinked dizzily into the shadows. There stood the Belgian journalist, a cigarillo perched delicately between his fingers, looking quite the dandy in the light of the moon.

I must have seemed apprehensive but he laughed out loud and, stepping forward, took up my hand, shaking it enthusiastically.

He explained that between Brugge and America he had spent some time in London—at more or less the same time as I had been making my escape—lobbying for funding. The newspaper offices of the time, he said, were abuzz with the details of my libertine adventures. It was all anyone could talk about!

'Such delicious scandal! I fancy to some—and may I count myself amongst them?—that you are something of an icon, yes?'

This time, *I* laughed.

'Not to anyone at Scotland Yard, I can assure you!' I said.

'Perhaps if you would care to join me at my hotel, I still have a bottle or two of Pernod to my name, and if ever an evening was in need of saving, this was surely it!'

In a sweet perfumed oblivion of that absinthe we spent the remaining night together, lounging drowsily about my rooms.

He took some interest in the designs I had made with Rutherford for our new home in Oregon. Our palace, I told him: our new Pompeii! And it seemed to me that as I spoke it rose up in vistas through the rolling clouds of our absinthe glasses; like Bosch's paradisiacal gardens, it did! And it was a land of the most fabulous beauty and basest perversity. We frolicked there until dawn.

'Watch out for the Thunderbird,' he said before he left.

The railways do not run on Sundays. The soldiers do not drill. I watched from my bay windows the staff officers, sat about their tea caddies combing their moustaches, polishing their boots and shining their brasses. Occasionally they took pot-shots at the water foul, purely out of boredom.

In the afternoon they played cricket out on the prairie. The privates kept score. These bored, wayward-looking youths lounged about in the long grass, tipping their caps and clapping politely whenever an officer was called out. Later still they were allowed beer and sang 'Rule Britannia' for hours at the tops of their voices. Then they got teary over letters from their sweethearts and wandered off into town, looking to get a grope out of the foreign girls.

We leave in the morning.

✳   ✳   ✳

Wednesday 2 May 1888

The towns and villages of eastern Great Plains have the qualities of London junkshops about them. I am told that before the railways came, these busy byways were strewn almost to the horizon with westward-bound wagons and that it was here, during the first hundred miles of their trek, that most travellers found it necessary to abandon their bulkier items of luggage. Whole communities had then grown wealthy out of the trade in salvaged goods. This alien detritus was the closest they would ever come to the wonders of the old world.

Our train had stopped for water in a town called White Hart and I decided to get some air. The station, like so many I have seen, was built out of all proportion to the traffic it receives, no doubt from lithographs of Waterloo or Paddington but with no concept of their scale. The streets and architecture of the houses similarly reveal a sort of fetishism for an idea of Imperial Britain by people who have never been there. A form of bastardised English country farmhouse nestles near a row of Georgian façades there, patched roughly together out of crooked and unsymmetrical planks of whitewashed wood. Overhead, from the confusion of rooftops, towers the ridiculous twin broach spires of their town chapel.

I found my way to a tavern, which hailed itself improbably to be 'The Old Swan'. It was lunchtime; the place was crowded. The locals pushed and jigged about with their pints of ale, kicking up dust, playing Nine Men's Morris and billiards by their own rules. There were pages torn from English picture books tacked on every wall without any obvious theme. In a corner near the bar a troop of old men were gathered about a decrepit upright piano, thumping out strangely inaccurate versions of unfashionable music hall songs: 'Knick Knock Paddywhock' and 'Cheer Up Mother Brown'. Everything gave the impression of hanging crookedly there! I left without ordering any drink.

Back on the railway platform, a man was hawking paperbacks from a barrow. I looked over the muddy colours of their illustrated covers. Tales of the Wild West. Cowpokes and Red Indians.

He seemed to be doing a roaring trade. I even bought one myself.

＊　　＊　　＊

Thursday 3 May 1888

One might imagine that being trapped, as it were, for several hours at a time in one of those cramped and smoky capsules of railway carriages with several similarly dedicated pilgrims, a certain camaraderie would naturally develop. I was learning, however, that very few of these travellers have anything but the most empty-headed 'shoptalk' to their repertoires. Not too many hours into the journey I had already had my fill of the solutions to the problems of prairie irrigation and the fundamentals of the New World Zionist philosophy. I barked to Khaled that I was going to see if I couldn't shove my way to the dining car. I made no apologies to the others.

Hobbling out into the crowded aisle, I became at once aware that some yards further down our carriage, another fellow with, I should imagine, the same look of urgency in his eyes as did I, came clawing his way towards me down the jungle of humanity. He struck me as of an almost comic wretchedness, all ticks and twitches, this greasy brush of hair flopping back and forth over his pinched-up face. He pulled at the collars of the passengers, chattering urgently into their faces. They shoved him away. Now and again he looked anxiously back over his shoulder. (I supposed the ticket collector was somewhere close behind.) When at last we came face to face, he took me awkwardly by both elbows. He grinned and blinked and in a broad Belfast accent, through a belch of the roughest bath-tub whiskey breath, yelped out: 'Can it be, sir? Why yes it is! How the devil have you been then? No, no! Don't tell me! We shot dice with the sailors at Boston Docks! Am I right... No?...' He began to trail off. 'Ah, ballocks to it!'

Evidently, his hustle had borne him little success since Gateway City. I had to bite my tongue to stop from bursting into laughter.

'Boston Docks,' I managed, at last. 'Yes! I expect that was it! Would you care for a drink?'

The fellow looked nervously again over his shoulder, then

nodded enthusiastically.

His name was Michael O'Herlihy. After another drink or two he told me he was heading for the Dakota Territory, to catch up with some old acquaintances even though his money, he said, had gone west some time before him! He proved himself the most gloriously perverse fun, telling the vulgarist jokes and being in turns charming and obnoxious to the English ladies in the dining car.

'So tell me,' he winked to one, 'do you have any Irish in you?...' I shan't go on.

As the train puffed and hissed into the station at Alliance, O'Herlihy looked excitedly out of the window.

'Did you ever hear of the elephants of Alliance?' he asked.

'Elephants?' I laughed, but he was perfectly serious.

I recalled that some months earlier, a tobacconist in New York had told me a story of how, during the '30s, the British army had decided that elephants would the ideal beasts of burden for the untamed new world and had attempted to import a number from the Indian colonies. Only a handful had survived the sea journey, and of those most grew sick and died soon after their arrival from feeding on the American plants. I had sometimes imagined the stiff, moustachioed English officers—pith helmets and all!—riding those sick and emaciated mounts to their deaths under the sun of the open prairies. It was simply too ridiculous.

But what O'Herlihy was proposing was still more ridiculous: that a handful of these beasts had escaped into the wild and had trekked as far as Great Plains! He had been here before, he said. He had seen the evidence.

I laughed freely at him: 'How could anything that big go about unnoticed in America?'

I was nonetheless impressed enough by his unwavering conviction to have found myself, that very evening, forsaking the comforts of the Holborn Inn to go kicking the toes out of my good shoes, following him off into the hills outside the town.

'This is it!' he kept calling back at me. 'I remember this! I remember this ridge, I'm sure!' His voice sounded flatly against the air.

Occasionally he stopped to scratch about in the dirt like a dog.

'What exactly are you after?' I kept asking him. He wouldn't reply.

Before too long, the sun had dug in low over the bluffs, turning them a deep bloody red colour. The wind was up. It was getting chilly. Still, O'Herlihy would not be defeated.

'Look!' he implored. He had uncovered a few blackened and eroded bits of bone. He held them out proudly upon his palm.

'They're ivory,' he said. (I was not convinced.)

'I saw a tusk here once,' he said, 'the size of a man!'

I bit my lip to stop from laughing again. How could anything that big have gone about unnoticed in America?!

O'Herlihy stomped off in a huff. I had already offered to put him up at the Holborn that night. I think he must have stayed in the hills though. Just O'Herlihy and his phantom pachyderms!

Khaled had been waiting for me in my room. He had another telegraph.

'Laurel trees,' it said, 'are not best suited to the Hathaway Valley.'

Are my visions slipping away from me?

❋   ❋   ❋

Saturday 5 May 1888

I was pleased enough to find O'Herlihy blowing smoke rings at the railway station the next morning. We did not speak again of our misadventures in the hills. I told him I should be more than pleased to pay his way as far as Montana, which he naturally accepted.

I would hate anyone to think that this I did out of entirely selfless motivation. (Whatever else I am, I am never selfless!) Besides the obvious relief from the monotony of travel he has provided, either by his encyclopaedic repository of filthy anecdotes or the splenetic abuse he would so often let fly on the other travellers, I have discovered also that those horrendously snobbish innkeepers, who had always swooned so over the mention of my title, tend to offer more reasonable prices with him in tow. They assume, I should think, that no English aristocrat worth more than a few dollars would have allowed himself to become familiar with such a beastly ne'er-do-well. The cost of O'Herlihy's railway fares, and that of his not insubstantial whiskey consumption, in some way manages to balance itself out.

O'Herlihy remains adamant that one day he will pay it all back. Some time into our third day together I was afforded a notion of precisely how he intended to do so.

Some years earlier, it became apparent, he had made this same trip into Montana, but before the railways were running. He had trekked as far west as the Victoria Rock with the three Irish trapper friends, whom he referred to as the Collins Brothers, and claims to have chiselled a particularly obscene depiction of the Queen there in her honour. (Nothing O'Herlihy could say surprised me, though the idea of him ever having had friends gives me cause to wonder!) He told me they had spent a few weeks trying to sell furs in the early springtime and generally making nuisances of themselves on the trails. When that proved unfavourable they had taken up with a company of the North American cavalrymen as buffalo killers and followed them into Dakota Territory. There was good money to be made slaughtering buffalo for the soldiers, O'Herlihy said, but still more running card games and smuggling in whiskey and whores after dark. It was during the early hours of a particularly debauched session that one of the younger soldiers let slip of how they were being recalled north to Fort Lincoln, where General George Armstrong Custer—that perennial thorn in the paw of the Great British lion—was assembling men and wagons for a very special expedition into Red Indian country. The Empire had long since given up concerning itself with the purposes of these covert little American operations. After all, in the past they had rarely offered anything of any significant economical advantages to the Empire (when compared with Africa or India, say). And while the nationalists gained some degree of glory by tales of their figurehead's heroic incursions into savage country, the British were perfectly content to sit and watch in the certainty that sooner or later Custer would overreach himself and come suddenly unstuck at the end of a *tomahawk*.

But for O'Herlihy and the Collins Brothers it was clear that what this young soldier was talking about was no mere squaw hunt! The rumours had been circulating for some time amongst the Americans that there was gold in the Black Hills and, while not a single British person knew anything about it, the Irishmen found themselves at a peculiar advantage. They had, they believed by this time, made themselves indispensable to the American soldiers and in so doing afforded themselves their very own armed escort into *El Dorado*. Gold! Riches!! Even before the night was out they were to their minds men of idle wealth, sitting out their lives on the porches of gleaming white pipedream mansions in states of the sweetest oblivion.

But in the days that followed, as their road wound north to the rendezvous point, they began to concern themselves less about the concealment of their clandestine services to the soldiers. Then, one night, encamped a mere thirty miles from Fort Lincoln, the company captain, stepping out of his tent to take the night air, had practically banged noses with O'Herlihy as he came clambering over the tent-ropes, a half-naked China-girl on each arm and a whiskey bottle in each hand. ('A rare good night's hunting,' he told me.) No one, of course, was likely to step forward in O'Herlihy's defence and, not being one to take his punishments like a Gentleman, he chose instead upon the swift administration of a boot to the captain's privies before gambolling off as fast as his drunken limbs could propel him into the darkness. A single pistol shot was heard, cracking mutely upon the night, but he was already gone.

In the morning, the soldiers had ridden on. His friends, the Collins's, were gone too, having no doubt denied him to save their investments. Kicking over the cold ashes and detritus of the camp he found the same group of Chinese merchants with whose whore-daughters he had previously become acquainted and somehow ended up on the road with them, dealing textiles and fake oriental medicines in the settlements and, when there was nothing else for it, the tattered virtues of their women. Time and again in the weeks that followed, he had attempted to steer their course towards Dakota. But being unwilling to divulge his reasons to the Chinese, they went south instead, and quite soon he had lost the advantage. The gold was no longer a secret. The papers were full of it. The rush was on!

O'Herlihy was, by this time, penniless somewhere in Ozark.

His thoughts of ever catching up with the Collins's went eventually from his mind. Except that two winters ago he had shacked up with a group of itinerant house carpenters who claimed some time previous to have found employment amongst the affluent tenant farmers around the newly tamed Dakota Territory. By some far fetched spiral of logic, filled with almost hermetic details of significance, he had finally convinced himself that one of the wealthy Irish families of whom his hosts spoke were the Collins's, though it made perfect sense to O'Herlihy that they had changed their names.

It had taken him a full year to claw his way back as far as Great Plains, working his passage but more often hustling other travellers.

But what precisely does he want with the Collins's if he finds them? Does he suppose they will welcome him back after all these years? Does he believe they owe him a share of whatever wealth they acquired in his absence? Or will he seek revenge for his abandonment?

That much is O'Herlihy's business.

❋   ❋   ❋

Monday 7 May 1888

For many, Montana represents the end of the civilised world. That is to say it has been, historically, a point at which the evangelical thrust of the Empire has relinquished control to those apparently cruder forces of the American Army. Furthermore, it remains a 'cat's cradle' of innumerable old trails which even in this day and age remain a tangle of the traffic of political, religious and economic refugees from every lesser nation in the world. It is, in short, an unrelenting Babel of languages and exotic customs. We are no longer on British soil.

Our arrival at the town of Greenwater was, however, far from portentous. I had observed O'Herlihy acting nervously all that day, gnawing incessantly at the insides of his cheeks and looking over his shoulders. Things came to a head when we stepped down from the train to be met on the platform by the sight of three finely wrought black coffins and the pitiful figure of old woman in full mourning dress, baying desolately over them. O'Herlihy fell at once into a sort of anguished fit. He took me by the lapels and told me we should not stay in this town. He spat through the gaps in his teeth.

'You're being a bloody fool!' I hissed back. There were no more railway trains before morning, I reminded him, though he would be more than welcome to proceed on foot if it meant that much to him! He hung his head and lurched out into the street with the porters.

We took rooms at the Tarn saloon, and what remained of the afternoon I spent in a state of irritation not only with the ridiculous O'Herlihy, who stayed crouching motionless in the shadows behind my door, but also with Khaled, whom I perceived to be enjoying the high ground over the situation a little too much. I told him to make himself useful and sent him off into the barroom to see whose business he could poke his nose into.

I tried to read my Claudian but nothing would stick. As the first crimson light of evening touched the corners of our windows, I found myself looking out almost enviously over the processions of mule- and ox-drawn wagons in the road below, dusty from the plains, moving up in that slow and laborious fashion as if the weight of the open skies and the length of the day had been too much for them.

The sound of a slamming door somewhere behind me brought me suddenly out of my reverie. A moment later, the figure of O'Herlihy shot out onto the street below, dodging off between the traffic.

I followed him out shortly after but went in the opposite

direction, not precisely sure what I was hoping to find.

The night had opened up wide onto a shining quarter moon, from which it seemed a cruel and biting cold descended. I took out and lit a cigarette and walked into the camp ground. How like Chinese junks the wagons appeared in that light, stacked one after another, pell-mell across their rivers of dust and dirt. All about me hissed and cracked the damp green wood of campfires. Their flames cast uncertainty into the lines of the travellers' faces where they were huddled in the folds of their greatcoats and blankets. The sleepy chatter of numerous nations hung dully on the air. A mule eeyored. A baby cried. A mandolin rattled out a homesick waltz into the night, and the negros hollered in mournful accompaniment.

I found myself, at length, on the edge of a gloomy grove, puffing away dazedly upon my tobacco. Then, through the columns of poplars I became aware of a single wagon whose owners appeared deliberately to have set themselves apart from the rest. I may not have given the matter a second thought were it not for the fact that this wagon had been decorated with such baroque and garish grotesquery that it seemed to me, in the firelight, that its painted whirls of colour spiralled in upon themselves, and the likenesses of what appeared to be beasts of the inferno verily wagged their tails, roared and blinked. However did such a fantastical thing come to be amongst such desperate mundanity? I wondered. And I naturally resolved to meet with its inhabitants.

As I trudged upon the little oasis of their camplight I fancied for a moment my vision had been in some way warped by the residual effects of old Moreau's hashish parties, for sat there at the fire were four figures of the most exquisite and godless perversity I have ever had the pleasure of meeting. Unused to visitors though they were, they welcomed me wholeheartedly.

The leader, I soon discovered, was one Clever Jack, a fellow of barely three feet I should say (though he wore a stovepipe hat of half that height again). His companions, all female, consisted of a bearded lady, a pinhead and a caterpillar girl. He told me, with bored candour, of their failed attempt to jump circuses in New Cambria and how, in the fight that had ensued, Jack had stabbed their ringmaster through the heart. One might not have expected such a conspicuous band of fugitives travelling in so gaudy a vehicle to have got very far without the law catching up with them. But to the contrary, once on the trails their appearances had, if anything, deterred the idly curious (in all but my own case, of course) and the fact is that all anybody really cares about on the trail is minding their own business. 'Everyone's runnin' from somet',' observed Jack, and I was reminded of the old proverb about people whose houses were made of glass not throwing stones.

Jack spoke at great length of their plans to build a ranch somewhere deep in the Rocky Mountains. I listened sleepily for much of the night, dozing, smoking his strong tobacco, watching the campfire sink upon its embers. A poorwill sang us on into the empty hours.

Life for Clever Jack and his companions had been one unrelenting procession of clattering wagon-wheels over dusty roads and white beans eaten out of the same enamelled bowls they used to wash in. They know a life on the road better than anybody. How can they fail in their ambitions?

I pictured them at their mountain home: their herds of cattle grazing contentedly in the paddocks; their topsy-turvy farmhouse they have built and lacquered in carnival paint and all the profoundly hideous beauty of the freakshow. They will have married, polygamously. The pandemonium of the wedding celebrations are echoing out through the foothills and it is a fearful, uneven music of banjo, voice and pipe-organ. Soon, they will have raised children of the most fantastical deformities who will grow strong on red meat and malt, smart and fast as cats. From time to time a stray drover might happen to catch sight of one or another of them, thundering barefoot over rough country after rabbits or lassoing mustang in the valleys. The effect will be terrifying and wondrous to behold. And the drover will hurry on, nervously, unwisely, into the gathering night.

I woke in the chill of the early morning. The cold was deep in my bones, my head was spinning. The campfire smoked lazily. The circus caravan had already gone.

'Stay off the railways,' Clever Jack had told me. An

unpleasant, unfathomable sense of something forgotten gnawed at me. I was afraid.

Upon my return to the Tarn, Khaled greeted me with the news that I had missed a gunfight in the town square that previous night. Three men had had their brains blown out in the street.

He also told me that he believed someone had broken into our rooms that night and had taken a sum of our money.

O'Herlihy had not returned.

✳   ✳   ✳

Wednesday 9 May 1888

Why did we delay at Greenwater? Why? And how different things might otherwise have been.

Yet it seemed as though a rank of storm clouds was running the extent of our horizons that morning. Neither Khaled nor myself had made any attempt to pack our things. Khaled barely spoke. In the afternoon, I found myself meandering near the town square, alone, staring confoundedly over the stable doors of a smithy's cabin, wherein, and through the brownish gloom, the dented remains of a steam tractor were visible, hissing and chuffing, rolling drive belts between a huge pair of bellows. With each gigantic breath the air itself looked to catch light in clouds of vivid orange cinders. What my valet had told me of the events of the previous night had shaken me in a way I cannot easily explain. I found myself pressing him for more details. He had seemed guarded.

'I think you have a fever,' he had told me.

I wandered several times the length of that dreary little town square, which appeared to me hemmed in and bound by the huge, charmless and imposing nail-and-plank façades of provision stations, whore houses, low saloons and so on. There remained no signs of what violence had so recently transpired there. I nonetheless found myself constantly fixating upon a figment of those three wretched corpses sprawled out before me, their limbs in an impossibly clumsy disarray; their skulls burst open like peaches in the dirt. Then a hostelry man would almost knock me over rolling barrels off his cart, or a couple of ladies with parasols and muddy skirts would giggle abruptly into my ear before sauntering off suggestively in the direction of the meeting-house.

Perhaps I *did* have a fever!

I decided to return to the Tarn. I went into the barroom. I stood at the counter, feeling out of breath and with a burning indigestion. Our landlord, of whose name I remain completely ignorant, stepped up out of his cubby-hole.

'Sir,' he said, taking no notice of my grimace. 'You have a message.'

I took the folded scrap of paper from his fingers. It had scribbled upon it: *'It is of the upmost inportance you cume and see mee to day. I am at the old ranch, at the north rige. O'Herlihy.'*

I had barely thought of the Irishman all day, except to suppose that he had already left town with whatever money we had not thought to lock in the Armada Chest that previous night.

I struggled upstairs where I found Khaled just finishing *Asr* prayers. I showed him the note.

'We should not go,' he said instantly.

'Not go?' said I. 'Why on Earth not? Don't you suppose he owes us some explanations?'

'I think, sir, we are better off leaving him where he is.'

He was very probably right, of course. O'Herlihy's charm and usefulness had only gone so far and no further. But Khaled had never really taken to the Irishman, and I was often annoyed to catch a glimpse of a little surreptitious scowl on my valet's lips whenever he was asked to do anything for him. O'Herlihy *did* owe us some answers—that much was true—but also Khaled deserved a dressing down.

'We shall go!' I ordered him. 'Now go and see if you can't hire a couple of horses off the landlord or something.' My stomach was burning up. 'And while you're about it, see if you can find something for my stomach.'

Khaled hovered hesitantly on the balls of his feet, then hurried out without a word. I packed my own rucksack.

By six o'clock, we were in the saddle, heading out of town

through the dried out and abandoned pastureland that was the North Ridge. Amid its lonely, broken matrix of paddocks an echoless quiet swiftly descended upon us, into which the hooting of a goshawk and the grinding, metallic squeals of the buckled windmills played a callow symphony of welcome.

The old ranch came up ahead of us, a cluster of corroded wood cabins and tin lean-tos from which I observed several columns of smoke ascending high into the dimming sky. As we dismounted, a burst of laughter, somehow neither male nor female, hung momentarily on the air before us and then was gone. Two dozen horses poked listlessly about amongst the muck and cattle bones and rusted skeletons of ancient farm-gear that littered the yard. The place stank of cesspools.

I called a feeble 'Hello!' into the air. Khaled watched me silently, though I could see it was only through great effort. I went to the door of the largest cabin and with some difficulty heaved a tin sheet out of the doorframe. 'Hello!' I called again. From within I could hear what I took to be human movement. I ducked through the doorway.

An atmosphere of sweat and burning fish oil bound me to the spot. Shadows encircled me, cast up through the glimmer of a few wick lanterns on a table before me and a sunken grate fire at the other end of the room, about which a sort of leathery looking mosaic of human faces stood out against the gloom.

My mind swam. I called out in a voice that sounded to me preposterous: 'O'Herlihy?' And the trap was sprung.

Gruff exclamations and whispers in various foreign tongues passed between the men at the fireside and ran off into the darkness that surrounded me. There was the flicker of gun metal in the black shapes that now moved in on me from every angle. The insignia of a crescent and cross flashed before my eyes. A hand took me first roughly by the shoulder of my coat, then another clamped around my wrist. I thrashed out instinctively but my legs gave way. I made a kick into the air and the table went crashing over. The lamps clattered across the floor. The oil caught alight. There was a flash and a heart-stopping bang as the lamps ignited. For an instant, I felt my startled assailants loosen their grip on me.

I was able to snatch myself away, making immediately for the door. The next hands I felt around me belonged to my valet as he hauled me out into the open.

'SHOOT LOW!' a voice bellowed from the yard. The crack of gunfire cut across our path.

It seemed that from every one of those ramshackle cabins a furious rush of human figures was emerging. Thoughts of escape slipped rapidly from my mind but Khaled was determined, all but dragging me on.

The woodwork splintered around our ears. A stray bullet thumped into the side of one of the lazy horses as we passed, sending the beast rearing up, squealing and thrashing against the others. In their collective panic they were able to snap their post, going into a stampede across the yard and creating confusion amongst the gunmen. We reached our horses and, clambering up into the saddles, kicked off at a gallop.

In whatever direction we were going, it did not matter. We galloped on! But I was not in the best of health and our shocking encounter had only exasperated my symptoms. With every jolt of our flight it seemed as if the very hooves of the horses were beating at my brains and stomach. I found myself slumped forward in my saddle, the reigns wound tightly around my wrist, and with all my might holding onto my balance. Khaled rode beside me. He could surely see that there was something wrong.

'Just hold on!' he called to me. 'If we can only reach those trees there's a chance...'

A chance? I could see him looking back over his shoulder and, with difficulty, I was able to do the same.

Only a couple of hundred yards behind us, two of the gunmen, clearly having managed to calm their steeds, were fast gaining ground upon us.

We hurtled into the pine wood, the soft ground suddenly silencing the pounding of the horses' hooves so that an eerie hush closed in on our flight. The sun had set early amongst the trees and I quickly lost sight of Khaled in the shadows. Invisible twigs scratched at my face and pulled at my hair. I became dizzy, slipped in my saddle and toppled awkwardly from my horse.

I am not sure if I lost consciousness. Before I could gather my thoughts I was aware of what I initially took to be my own horse snuffling in the pine-needles at my side. Then, however, I realised it was not one but two horses, and as I watched further, the gunmen were dismounting. The first took out his pistol.

'This could have been much easier,' he said breathlessly. (I could not place the accent.) 'Just tell us where the Irishman went...'

He lifted his pistol. At that second, a shot rang out through the trees. The bullet hit home with a thud, cutting a wedge of bone and sinew out of the gunman's side. He fell down like empty clothes. His partner jumped into action, drawing his pistol, but before he had had a chance to raise it there was a second shot, hitting him somewhere in his lower torso. He went double, screaming horribly. A third shot tore off his jawbone, silencing him forever.

I lay in utter, wordless shock. I could see Khaled's outline amongst the trees, the pistol hanging limply from his forefinger. His whole body was twitching.

'Khaled...?'

He ran off.

I raised myself onto shaking legs and followed, walking in the same direction. When I found him some minutes later, he was sitting on the bank of a little stream with his back turned toward me and the pistol still wound around the finger of his hand, which lay, as if no longer a part of his body, on the pebbles by his side.

I sat down next to him. The stars, revealing themselves in ribbons through the amethyst coloured mists of twilight, reflected up at us through the softly trickling water of the stream, so that it appeared as if we were sitting on the rim of an incalculably vast chasm, looking down upon heaven.

It was then, and in a voice that cracked at every word, Khaled told me what had occurred on that previous night in Greenwater.

He had not been there at the gunfight. He was still at the saloon when it happened, boredly striking matches and listening to the drunken chitchat of the local store keepers. Then, the street door had almost flown from its hinges as a mob of the townspeople burst through, sending that sleepy, queasily intoxicated lot into an immediate tumult! They gabbled all at once about gunshots and blood and bodies. Khaled had been practically carried outside in the human rush.

The streets were alive! The town square was packed and in chaos. The town photographer was calling for more lamps to be brought out, and several of the burlier townsmen were employed in trying to prevent the hordes from trampling over the corpses. Details of what precisely had happened were elusive; rumours were rife. Khaled soon became frustrated by the whole business and decided to head back to the Tarn.

As he strolled back through the unlit streets—though it had seemed insignificant enough at the time for him to have quite put it out of his mind until now—he had found himself, on more than one occasion, staring out through the pitch dark nooks of doorways and alleys, unsure whether he could make out faces there, gazing back at him. On the corner before the Tarn someone very real leapt out of the shadows onto him. It was O'Herlihy. There was pure dread in his eyes.

'How?' he muttered. 'How could I have known they had become so many?' He gave a lunatic's stare. Khaled shoved him out of the way. It was only at that moment he noticed that the Irishman was holding a pistol.

'They've followed me since Great Plains!' he wept, waving the thing in front of him. 'They know why I came back...'

With some trepidation, Khaled turned his back and marched indoors, but the Irishman was close behind him, jabbering hysterically at his ear. '...were only supposed to be spies...' he sobbed. '...never our gold...!'

Whatever was his story, Khaled knew for certain that the Irishman had become a liability, just as he had been a liability to the Collins Brothers all those years previous. Outside the door to our rooms he turned suddenly to find him cowering at his heels.

He reached down and twisted the pistol from the Irishman's shivering grip. Then he cracked him across the side of the head with the butt. O'Herlihy stumbled dazedly and fell over, sobbing loudly. Khaled took a wad of banknotes from our chest and held them out in front of O'Herlihy.

'Buy yourself a horse,' he barked. 'Do it tonight! Make certain we never see you again. Do you understand?'

O'Herlihy stared blankly up at him, the tears running down his cheeks. Khaled forced the money into his shirt.

'NOW GET OUT!' he yelled.

And so he had, limping, defeated, back down the steps and out into the night, which was at once so very full of dangerous looking shadows.

Having finished his story, Khaled fell silent, the weight of guilt upon his sunken shoulders. He must surely have suspected O'Herlihy's note of being the work of another, that whoever was actually beckoning us out into the wild meant us harm. But in his mind, that same sense of loyalty which had prompted him to liberate us both from the treachery of the Irishman was just as thoroughly at odds with him ever having to confess his own theft and deception on that previous night.

His debt, nonetheless, I perceived as paid.

The cold was coming in. The trees hissed harshly about us. I took the pistol from my valet's fingers and struggled to my feet, swallowing some amount of pain.

'If we follow the stream,' I said commandingly, 'we can ride all through the night, see? Put some distance between them and us.'

Khaled blinked up at me and gave a feeble smile. 'We can never go back to Greenwater,' he said. It had not needed saying.

The pistol weighed heavily against my side all that night. I later discovered only three of its chambers had been fired. In the half-light of dawn, I traced with my fingers an engraving set upon the grip: a cross and crescent.

✳   ✳   ✳

[Undated]

I had happened upon it, quite by accident, from time to time, in the bargain baskets and mouldering cabinet drawers of junk-antique shops on the streets of Manhattan, whiling the winter afternoons away, pricking my fingers on broken spectacles and old-fashioned dental tools. But the first time I can recall ever having seen the sign of the cross and crescent was as a German silver talisman, nestling in a box of rusted wire wool, outside a shop in Greenwich Village. It had seemed to me so *profoundly* pointless at the time that I simply had to make a fuss of it!

'Tell me sir,' I queried, 'how much for this little thing?'

The old Russian gentleman squinted at me from the doorway.

'This little thing,' he said. I let him take it out of my hand. He waved it in the air in front of my face. 'This little thing!' There was a drawn out silence, then he shook his head and tottered off inside, chuckling to himself.

When I passed the same shop a few days later the talisman was back again, nestling in its box outside.

'I think it's a sort of signal,' I told Khaled. 'If it appears meaningless to *us*, then it isn't *us* it's intended for!'

By that time we had already seen the same design, repeated in a dozen different forms, on a dozen other streets, without explanation. I had very nearly given up on it when one night, as I sat in the plush velvet wallpapered dressing rooms of one of those little music halls off Longacre Square, drinking vermouth with the young theatre gentlemen, I found my enquiries met, not with the usual silence and evasion, but with at first drunken guffaws of laughter, then more eventually the explanation I desired.

'Do you think for a moment,' this young playwright had said, 'that this insignia—whatever you want to call it—has anything at all to do with the city of Manhattan? Oh God, no! It goes a long way deeper than that. All the way to the heart of America. This is a rallying cry, my friend, to all those folk for whom the new world represents a last stand.'

I'm sure I must have looked bemusedly at him. He went on: 'Let me put it this way. The British Empire holds sway over about half the world's population now, and though you'd think that would make for one big, terribly happy fraternity club, there are an awful lot of people—people who didn't ask to join this club in the first place—who take exception to the membership fees. You know the sort of costs I'm talking about here? Cultural suppression. The stripping out of assets and resources. The overthrow of any less patriotic elements of their administrations. An awful lot of very angry people from a great many nations have found their ways onto these shores over the past few decades. Very angry people, you understand? So, while the mighty forces of the American and British armies had their backs turned taking care of the nonexistent Red Indian threat, they decided to get together their own fraternity club. The sort of place where anarchist bombers can share stories with exiled Mesopotamian royalty, and Irish nationalists draw up plans with Crimean Tartars. You see what I'm saying here? You get it now, don't you? This, my friend, this'—he traced the form of a cross and crescent in the thick bluish fog of incense smoke that hung in the air between us—'this is a call to arms! The fuses have been lit!'

Little more was said on the subject, though I remained there until dawn. With the first, pallid beams of sunlight cutting strips out of a shadowy and deserted Broadway, I staggered back to my hotel, squinting into frosted shop windows along the way at the shapes cast up through the gloom within and also at scuffed, faded advertising posters plastering brickwork in alleyways and on the sides of cabmen's shelters. With all the logic of a drunkard I was trying to conceive of a sign running through the very substance of America as rings run through a tree trunk, but really nothing appeared amiss.

Whenever I think of the young playwright now, it is O'Herlihy's face I see: O'Herlihy staring wildly back at me in the way he had when he told me about his bloody elephants! And I find myself wanting to laugh out loud again and yell at him that nothing that big could possibly go unnoticed in America.

I suppose I shall never know what became of the Irishman, though I picture him from time to time as a very shoddy sort of Don Quixote, trampling over the Dakota farmlands in the futile quest for an imagined fortune he has even less claim over than those in whose possession it now lies. If the Collins Brothers are still in the west, which I cannot seriously suppose they are, they will certainly have hidden themselves well enough not to have their old travelling companion lead their debtors to the door!

In any event, our ways have parted, and somewhere still to the west I wonder at the folly of *my* ambitions. Since we no longer risk being seen at the telegraph offices, do Rutherford's messages rebound still, back and forth, east and west, in clicks and whirs, obliviously turning one after the next of my hopes and dreams of earthly paradise into just some wind blasted vision of Oregon marshland, where nothing but brambles and gorse grass will take root?

Whatever the case, we continue our way west on horseback. What other options do we have?

In the town of Eloisa we learnt the news that a train had been derailed somewhere further south. Many people had been killed and injured. A Salvation Army Band was playing 'Jerusalem' in the town square where the crowds were queuing for the newspaper stands, and the heavens opened up on us all. We waited there for nearly an hour, Khaled and I, on a staircase of empty tea chests beneath the canopy of a closed down general store while our horses kicked about in the muddy road. To the west we observed the jagged knife-blade of mountaintops that appeared to us to rise up so far over the curve of the Earth before the great weight of that leaden sky fell against them and they could rise no further. The rain didn't stop.

'We're wasting our time here,' I finally admitted. 'We should ride on further.'

Khaled got to his feet. 'Do you need help?' he asked.

'I think I can manage.'

All the Jungle is Thine
by C. Mitchell O'Neal

15 August 1924
Queens, New York

This is how it all started.

'Froggy. Hey, Froggy! Damnit, Timmy, wake up!'

Carlo's voice sounded far away. Like when we were still kids, and he'd call from the fire escape so I'd open the window and we'd run on the rooftops and play Mowgli and Bagheera. I tried to ignore it. I was sleepy.

'C'mon, Timmy. We're almost there.'

Someone goosed my arm, hard. I cracked open an eye and did my tough look, like the big monkeys at the Brooklyn Zoo.

Carlo was driving the truck. It was still pretty dark. I'd been sleeping. He gave me a grin.

'Don't give me that look, ya big mick! I've been driving all damn night.'

'Sorry, Carly...' I yawned and rubbed my eyes. 'Carly Baggy-pants.'

Carlo smiled. I'd called him that forever, since the time when Bagheera had been too hard to say and he was so skinny his pants would fall down without suspenders. My back hurt because the truck cab was too small for me. I didn't like driving much, but that's all Carlo and I really did these days.

'Where are we?'

'Queens,' he said as he lit up a cigarette while driving with his knees and elbows. Yeah, it looked like Queens. Tenements, clotheslines hanging over the streets like jungle vines, dogs running the empty sidewalks. My uncle Diarmaid had worked at the ash dumps here until he died of the consumption back in ought nine.

105

He'd called it the dustbin of the world. 'We came off the Williamsburgh Bridge half an hour back. We gotta drive through the Exhibition grounds and drop the last of the hootch at Charlie Bursar's over on Main Street. You seen the Exhibition yet, Timmy?'

'Nope.'

'Well, you're gonna love it. Like Coney, but new and shiny.'

'I like Coney. It's not so bad.'

'Who doesn't like Coney? I'm just saying this is something else. Top notch. Pony Tom says they spent over three million pounds on the buildings alone. Took down a whole mess o' tenements and cleared out half the ash dump to make room.'

'That's a lotta money.'

'Sure is, Timmy. A whole lotta money. Think what you and me could do with that much money.'

'Could get my mum her own flat.'

'Could get your fine mum a hundred new flats. Hey, there it is.'

Carlo turned the corner and I almost lost my breath.

The whole world was lit up. A block back it'd been dark still, but here it was like daytime with electric lights and all. Behind the lights, huge buildings of grey stone and white pillars glowed in the colour of the lights. The buildings were like museums or castles or whatever comes bigger than castles. Coloured electric lights hung from every tree and post. A lake spread out in front of the buildings. The light from the lanterns danced on the water. Every which colour you could think of.

'What is it, Carlo?'

'That's it, Timmy. The British Empire Exhibition. That's the Palace of Industry there, and that one farther down the row is the Palace of Engineering. Over there's the Australia Pavilion, and there's South Africa, and there's, well, some place with coconut trees, I guess. All the countries of the Empire are here together. Folks take the train out from Manhattan to see the sights.'

We drove on and Carlo pointed out the buildings, naming 'em off one by one, like right out of one the picture books he used to read to me when we was kids. Places with fancy names like Burma and Ma-la-ya. You could hardly pronounce 'em. Some buildings you could see from the street and others you just saw hints of past the others, far off and mysterious like they were the real far off lands they was from.

'Why is it here, Carlo? Why not in England?'

''Cause we're the best, ain't we, Timmy? America's the best part of the Empire and those pasty Teabags know it! Everybody knows it.'

'Do they?' I asked, but Carlo didn't answer me.

'Wait'll you see this one,' he said instead.

We turned another corner.

'Recognise those flags?'

It was the Hall of America, bigger even than all the rest, the territorial flags flying from tall white walls that towered over the others, and I got kind of choked up when I saw that, how pretty and big it was and how proud. Carlo was right, we were the best.

'Sissy,' Carlo joked and goosed me again in the arm. 'That's nothing though, Froggy. I got a real surprise for you.'

Carlo parked the truck on a side street. There were lots of stores here. A whole line of them running up the street back towards Manhattan.

'This isn't Charlie Bursar's,' I said.

'Nah, but we got a little while 'fore we're due. Let's go for a quick walk.'

The streets were empty this early and Carlo and I walked alone into the Exhibition. He pulled on my coat when I stopped to stare at the glowing lake and hauled me along when I mooned over a giant ball of wool from Australia—taller than three men!

'Alright Timmy, close your eyes.' I did, and Carlo pulled me along by my coat. I chuckled a little. 'Okay, you remember our book, yeah?'

'Course I do, Baggy-pants. I'm Mowgli and you're the great panther.' Carlo'd read me the Empire Stories when we were kids. Parts of it over and over again, if I asked him to. We'd read about Kotick the seal and Red Jacket the Loyal Iroquois. But my favourites were the ones with Mowgli and his animal friends, and his best friend of all was Bagheera the panther, who watched over him day and night.

'Then open your eyes.'

I opened them and my jaw dropped. It was another palace of white stone, like the others, but with white towers coming out of every corner rounded with spiky points, just like the palaces of the rajahs that I'd imagined from the book.

'What do you think, Timmy?'

'It's amazing, Carlo. It's amazing. I never seen anything so amazing.'

We walked up to it and I rubbed the white stone. It was as smooth as glass.

'It's the India Pavilion. Just like the book, Timmy. They got a snake charmer in there pipes up cobras and a mongoose just like Rikki-Tikki-Tavi. If you can't bring the mick to the Empire, bring the Empire to the mick, eh?'

I gaped at Carlo. I felt silly with excitement.

'We can play Mowgli and Bagheera again!'

Carlo laughed.

'Don't you think we're a little old for that?'

I grinned back.

'Can we at least go inside?'

'Not now, Timmy. Maybe after we've done our run. It's not even open now.'

We started to walk back to the truck. Something caught my eye. A group of brown women in colourful skirts and blouses walked towards the India Pavilion in the early light. They looked like Indian princesses and I guess they was going to work. I stopped to stare and one of them looked my way. Her hair was black as raven feathers and her skin was the colour of gingerbread and cream. Her eyes were big as plates and when she smiled my heart near to stopped. She turned to her friends and giggled and then gave me another smile. I felt loopy.

'Froggy!' Carlo called from ahead. 'Let's go!'

I turned to follow Carlo, but not without taking a few more looks at the raven-haired princess.

Back at the truck I noticed a group of hard-looking fellas

gathering across the street in front of a newsstand. They had handwritten signs on fence pickets and funny red and black flags. They were talking in angry voices.

'What do those signs say, Carlo?'

'Workers' rights. Fair pay. The usual baloney. They're union boys, Timmy. Half of them are on the payroll of one of the Families. They stop work just to put the squeeze on businesses. It's a racket.'

'Oh.'

Carlo knew lots. He was smarter than me by a long shot. He'd almost finished secondary school even. He had big plans for the two of us. He was gonna be a player in the Family someday, and he was gonna take me right along with him. 'Only mick in the mafia,' he'd say.

Charlie Bursar's was a speakeasy in the basement of a tobacco store. The real Charlie'd died back in the war, but his kid Davy ran the place and just took up his pop's name. We parked the truck (it was made up to look like a milk truck) in an alley in the back and Carlo knocked on the door while I stood lookout. Charlie-Davy came out and talked to Carlo. He looked nervous. Kept looking up in the air and over his shoulder. I got that itch that I sometimes get, but before I could say anything somebody gave the go ahead and we started offloading barrels and cases down a slide that ran into Charlie's cellar.

The barrels were marked with the Crown in case any liquor agents showed up. I'd never quite figured the whole thing out, though Carlo'd tried to explain it to me a couple times. Near as I could tell, the American Parliament had started prohibition four years ago, meaning as how you couldn't make spirits in the territories, but the Home British had said no, we Americans couldn't prohibit the sale of British liquor in British dominions, which we are. Now you'd think the American anti-saloon folks would give up on this and say, 'Well, somebody's gonna make money off booze, might as well be us,' but no, they was stubborn pur-i-tan-i-cal bastards, according to Carlo. So now, the only liquor you could buy legally was British, and it was damned expensive. Like Carlo said, that wasn't too fair, so folks like him and me made it a business to bring cheaper American spirits to the speakeasies in the city. It was just being fair, said Carlo, but we was careful all the same to make our liquor look Home British.

We were almost done unloading by the time I was done thinking about all this. I remembered the funny feeling I'd had about Charlie-Davy and was about to tell Carlo something when Charlie-Davy hisself invited us down into the cellar for a drink and to settle up. Carlo gave me a grin and headed down and there wasn't much I could do but follow.

The cellar of Charlie Bursar's was dark and musty. When it was busy it was a stand-up-and-dance kinda place. A long bar went around two of the four walls. Not so many chairs. There was a couple doors behind the bar that led to the liquor storerooms and another door in the far wall that probably led upstairs to a secret entrance. Charlie-Davy had us sit down at the bar while he dug through a box of notes that was kept behind the bar. Two of Charlie-Davy's rough boys sat at tables behind us. Carlo put back a shot while I watched the boys.

'I never seen you fellas before,' I said to them. And it was true. I hadn't been at Charlie Bursar's in ages but, like Carlo said, I had a good thing for faces and these boys didn't look quite right.

'Leave 'em alone, Timmy. They's just doing their job,' said Carlo. But I saw that the bigger rough boy was looking nervous. He was patting his pocket like he kept forgetting what was in it and sending hard looks at Charlie-Davy. Charlie-Davy was having the devil's own time trying to get our money out of the box; his hands were practically shakin'. My funny feeling was going crazy and I put a hand on Carlo's shoulder.

'Jesus, Timmy...' he started again, but then he looked up at my face and shut up real quick. Carlo turned around to look at the rough boys. He gave 'em a hard look, and I could tell by the tenseness in his shoulder under my hand that we was in trouble. 'You two aren't the talkative types, are ya?'

The roughs just stared at us. There was the sound of car doors slamming outside in the alley. Rushing footsteps.

'I'm sorry boys,' said Charlie-Davy behind us. 'They said they'd shut me down for good.'

'Merda,' said Carlo, and went for the knife he kept in his boot.

The bigger of the two roughs went for me while the smaller one went for Carlo. I hit the big guy in the jaw before he could get all the way to his feet. He staggered a bit and I kicked him in the chest. That sent him down to the floor. Chairs went flying. I turned to help Carlo and all the doors in the place opened up at once. There was coppers everywhere all of a sudden as well as hard looking men in brown long coats who stayed back as the coppers went in for the tussle.

The rough boy—I guess he was really a copper too—had one hand on Carlo's neck and the other wrestling his knife hand. I jumped forward and put my fist into his kidneys a few times. Then they was all over me, clubbing my knees and head, and the world went dizzy and grey and then black.

✻   ✻   ✻

The Indian princess was running her fingers through my hair. She whispered something in my ear I couldn't understand and then melted into dark smoke. I came to. I was cuffed to a chair, still in the cellar of Charlie Bursar's. Carlo was next to me in another chair. He looked worried.

'You okay, Timmy?' he asked.

I just nodded. My head felt like it was two sizes too big and I had a ringing in one ear that was gonna drive me crazy before long.

A man in a brown coat stood in front of us, packing a pipe. He was short, balding, and had a thick moustache that covered his top lip and most of his bottom one. He had small eyes and big cheeks. He reminded me of a fishmonger or a butcher. I looked around. There was three or four dressed just like him around the room. The coppers were gone.

'So, what's this all about?' Carlo asked. 'Since when is it a crime to sell British booze?'

Brown Coat lit the pipe and raised his eyebrows to Carlo.

'Not British,' he said around the pipe. He had a thick

English accent, a city accent. 'Seal's from a year ago. Maker's mark is a forgery, bad one at that. It's American booze. That's illegal 'ere, ain't it?'

'So why don't you run us in? You ain't coppers, are you?' Carlo asked. That was a good question, I thought, but I kept my mouth shut. It was always better to let Carlo do the talking in a situation like this. He'd always made the decisions for us. I trusted Carlo to get us out of this, just like Bagheera always got Mowgli out of the tough spots.

Brown Coat just puffed and smiled.

'We're coppers. Ain't we, boys?' he said. The other men in the brown coats nodded so small you could barely see it. 'Special Branch.'

'Never heard of ya,' Carlo said.

Brown Coat lit the pipe again. He seemed to be having a hard time getting it going.

''ere's the story, Carlo, and I'll put it to you quick and easy so your thick Irish friend can understand...'

'He's not stupid,' Carlo said.

''ow's that?'

'His name's Timmy and he's not stupid. Don't call him stupid.'

Brown Coat considered that for a while.

'Didn't call 'im stupid. Called 'im thick.'

'Thick's the same as...' Carlo began, but Brown Coat stepped forward and landed his boot right in Carlo's privates. Carlo screamed and thrashed in his chair as Brown Coat ground down, twisting his boot like he was putting out a cigarette. I pulled with all my might on the cuffs but they had me in tight.

'Can you believe it?' Brown Coat said to his crew. 'A wop takes a kick in the jollies to defend a mick's honour. Right strange land, eh?'

I huffed and puffed and gave Brown Coat my big monkey face, but he just smiled underneath his big moustache and gave me a wink. He tried again with the pipe.

'Like I was saying. 'ere's the quick and easy version. 'is Royal 'ighness the Prince of Wales is visiting the Empire

Exhibition today as part of a month-long visitation of the American Dominion. Now the Special Branch—that's us—is responsible for the safety of the Royals while they wave 'ankies at the wogs and all...'

'What the hell does that have to do with us?' Carlo said. He was still panting with the pain of the kick.

Brown Coat leaned down and looked Carlo right in the eyes.

'That's a good question, Carlo. You're smart as a whip, I can see that. But open your gob one more time while I'm speaking and I'll feed you your own ears. Yes?' Carlo nodded slowly. I got a funny feeling in my stomach. I realised Brown Coat scared me. He scared me bad.

Brown Coat smiled again and stood up. I guess he finally gave up on the pipe because he tossed it to one of the other men. 'Goddamnit, Smythe! Would you light that? My leaf is soused.'

Smythe tried to light the pipe. A couple of the other men gathered round to help him. Brown Coat turned back to Carlo and me.

'Do you know what a Catalanist is, Mr Morton?' He was talking to me. I wouldn't have answered even if I had known.

'I know what it is. It's a dago,' said Carlo. 'One of them anarchist types. They kilt the King of Spain.'

'They killed King Alfonso and 'is whole bloody family. Then they killed the rest of the Spanish nobles, then they killed the landowners, then the professors, then for shits and grins they started killing everybody else. Now we've got the whole fucking Iberian Peninsula crapping out anarcho-syndicalists like a Galway prossie craps out Irishmen—no offence, Timmy m'boy. Now bear with me lads, bear with me. 'istory lesson's almost over.

'Now, Carlo, since you've got all the answers, can you tell me who the grandmother was of the King's lovely wife?'

Carlo shook his head no.

'Ah, skipped that day in 'istory of the Empire, eh? Well, I'll tell you. It was our own blessed Queen Regnant Victoria, may she rest in peace.' Brown Coat paused and shook his head sadly. Then he perked up. 'Of course the old sow had so many piglets that 'ardly qualifies as a surprise. You can't take a piss on the continent without some of the spray 'itting some royal or other. But it does constitute a bona fide threat to the crown and that, boys, that makes it my bloody business. The Special Branch's bloody business.'

Brown Coat was pacing now, like a preacher getting worked up for his sermon. I looked at Carlo, who looked at me. His eyes were wide and he mouthed, 'Crazy.' I nodded.

'Now I ask you, lads, what should the good men of the Special Branch do in the face of anarcho-syndicalists and socialists and bloody-fucking Custerites, all standing in line to take a pot shot at any 'ead-of-state who 'appens to set foot in a colony, dominion or territory? Eh? What are we to do?'

Brown Coat spread his hands as if honestly helpless.

'I mean, we can admire the Tsar for 'is spine, can't we? Quite efficient, what 'e did, in a way, and certainly kept the old cock in power. But if *we* shot every poor bastard who ever attended a workers' meeting we'd run out of bullets before we ran out of bastards!'

'Ahh... There we go,' said Smythe from the corner.

The men gathered around the pipe made noises of congratulation to Smythe. He'd gotten the pipe lit. He took a couple more puffs and handed it back to Brown Coat, who took a long puff and then nodded appreciatively to Smythe.

''ere's what I'm saying, boys. We've got to be more creative than that. We've got to go for the 'ead. Just need one bullet for that. See what I mean? Take away the rabble-rousers and the barkers and the others will go back to their jobs and their fine British-made booze.'

'People don't like your booze,' said Carlo.

Brown Coat stopped pacing and stared at him.

'Jesus, Carlo. I don't give two shits about your fuckin' booze problems. I'm talking about the future of your fuckin' country.'

It was quiet for a while. Brown Coat sighed and shook his head like he was real disappointed in Carlo.

'Look, lads.' Brown Coat pulled up a chair and sat as he

talked. 'At noon today, 'is Royal 'ighness will be giving a speech outside the Government Pavilion on the Exhibition grounds. We 'ave it on good intelligence that a march of labourers, unionists and the aforementioned pain-in-my-arse anarcho-syndicalists has been organised to coincide with and disrupt the speech. The march will be led by one John Rutheim. Does that name at least ring a bell?'

'Yeah, I've heard of him,' said Carlo. 'The Family don't like him. He won't play ball on work slowdowns and all that. He hasn't hurt anybody, though, he's just too political.'

''e's too bloody political by 'alf, Carlo! Very good, you're winning some points back. And you know who else doesn't like Mr Rutheim?'

Carlo looked him in the eye.

'Lemme guess. You.'

'Right-o, Carlo. Right-o,' smiled Brown Coat.

'Does he want to kill the Prince?' I asked.

Brown Coat took a long puff on his pipe and then leaned over so that his face was just inches away from mine.

'Timmy lad, 'e wants to kill the whole bloody Empire.'

'I still don't see what this has to do with us,' said Carlo.

Brown Coat looked at him.

''ave you not heard a fucking thing I've said?'

'I heard what you said. I just don't see why you need Timmy and me.'

'Carlo, do you love your country? Do you love your king?'

'Course I do. What kind of question is that?'

Brown Coat took a deep puff.

'The Empire is at a crossroads, boys. Men like Rutheim want to tear down what took a thousand years to build up. I can't let that happen, and I need you to help me. Your king needs you now. The Empire needs you.'

Carlo got real quiet, then his head drooped.

'What?' I asked.

'He wants us to kill this guy, Timmy.'

I went a little cold and clammy. Carlo and me wasn't killers. We was just drivers. Delivery guys. Yeah, I was the muscle, but I'd never killed anybody, just put the squeeze on if someone didn't pay up like they was supposed to.

'What have you got?' Carlo asked.

''ow's that?' Brown Coat replied.

'What have you got on us? I can bet you ain't counting on our love of king and country to whack this guy.'

'Besides sending you to jail for bootlegging?'

'Must be more.'

Brown Coat smiled and then shook his head.

'Your girl, the beautiful Miss Rossi, isn't it? And Timmy's mum. Neither's looking very healthy if you take my meaning.'

Carlo sighed and looked up at the ceiling.

'What does that mean, Carlo?' I asked. 'What does that mean about my mum?'

'It means they'll kill 'em if we don't play ball, Timmy. We gotta kill this guy.'

I had to think about that for a second. Once I had, I put my whole body into getting out of that chair. My face turned red and I made some horrible noises, and I could hear the wood bending and the glue coming apart. The one called Smythe stepped forward and clubbed me in the side of the head with a sap. It was hard enough that the whole chair tipped over and I went down on my side. The world out of that eye went completely white and shimmery.

'Timmy!' I heard Carlo's voice. 'Cut it out, Timmy! They got us. Think about your mum, Timmy.'

I thought about my mum. But I also thought about Smythe, and Brown Coat, and the Special Branch. I thought real hard about all those.

❋　　❋　　❋

A couple hours later Timmy and I were back in the milk truck, driving east. Smythe sat behind us in the little door between the cab and the cargo area in back. He'd changed out of his long coat and into worker's clothes.

We drove across the north edge of the Exhibition grounds. The towers of the India Pavilion peeked over the building tops.

According to Smythe, the worker's march was going to

come down Northern Boulevard and enter the Exhibition grounds where it dead-ended at the park gates. They'd protest for a bit about better treatment for the poor and American independence and then Rutheim was gonna show up, give some big speech along the same lines and lead the marchers into the Exhibition grounds right as the Prince was starting his own speech. Rutheim was holed up in a safe house and wouldn't move until the marchers were almost at the gates. Guess we weren't the first ones looking to kill him. Unfortunately for Rutheim, Brown Coat knew the route Rutheim was taking and when he was supposed to leave. At least that's what Smythe told us.

'Turn in here,' Smythe ordered Carlo. Carlo took a left down a thin alley. 'Park over there behind those dustbins.'

Carlo pulled in the truck and turned it off.

'Here's the way this will go down, boys.' Smythe talked as he checked three pistols he'd been carrying in his coat pockets. I stared at the guns as he fingered them. You never saw a real one. Yeah, maybe at the cinema or in the newsreels, and some of the Family toughs used them but they never carried them, never out in public. But now, now in the daylight seeping in the truck windows, they looked so strange and hard and not right. 'Timmy! Are you listening or not? In about twenty minutes Rutheim and his minders are going to come down that alley. You two will play like you're offloading dairy from the truck. I'll be inside the back. We wait until the group passes by. I come out the truck and am the first one to shoot. Don't shoot before me, you hear?'

We nodded. My palms were sweaty and I was feeling claustrophobic in the tiny cab. The thought of actually killing somebody was making me sick.

'Rutheim will be wearing a suit coat. The others will be in long coats. There'll be four or five of them, and some will be carrying. Rutheim won't. Do not shoot Rutheim. Inspector Hamish wants to talk to him first.'

Hamish. That was Brown Coat's name. I said it over and over again in my head so I wouldn't forget it.

'Are you ready, lads?'

Carlo nodded. So did I, though I wasn't. Smythe handed us

the guns but kept a hold of them for a moment.

'Don't get any funny ideas, boys. I don't make it back and your girl and mum will pay the price. Hamish knows everything about you two: where you live, your work with the mob, the colour of your morning shit. He can squeeze you in a thousand different ways, and he's a ruthless old job. Are we clear?'

Carlo nodded angrily and jerked the gun out of Smythe's hand. I took mine. Carlo checked his over and I copied what he was doing. It was so cold. I hadn't expected that.

Carlo looked at me working with the gun. He looked worried.

'Timmy doesn't have to be here,' he said to Smythe.

'What?' Smythe said.

'You and I can do this just fine. Timmy doesn't have to be here.'

Smythe looked at me and for moment his face went soft. But it was only for a moment.

'This is a nasty business, lads. I don't want to be here anymore than you do... but three guns are always better than two. Sorry.' He melted into the darkness in the back of the truck. 'Remember. I shoot first.'

Carlo and I got out of the truck and opened the back. We took out a few crates and flats to make it look like we were working. Smythe stayed in the dark inside. Rutheim and his men wouldn't see him come out of the back until it was too late. I felt nervous and took a leak against the wall. Carlo came over to me.

'S'gonna be okay, Froggy. You just point and squeeze. Aim for the chest... or the back, depending. It'll all be over in a second.'

'Don't feel right, Carlo.'

'S'not right, Timmy. S'not right. But it's a tough life, eh? You do what you gotta do. For king and country, huh?'

'What does that mean?' I asked. I finished up and put my parts back in my pants.

Carlo looked down and rubbed his shoe in the gravel of the alley.

'Aw, hell, Timmy. I don't know what that means. But this guy, this guy Rutheim, there've been a hundred more like him come before, and a hundred more like him will come after. Killing this guy isn't gonna change nothing, and it might keep some fellas from getting beat down on the picket line.'

I sniffled. I was starting to cry a little. I didn't want to kill nobody.

'Why's it gotta be us, Carlo?'

Carlo stood there behind me, patting my back until I got it together. I looked up at him and he had a funny look. His brow was all crunched up like when he was thinking real hard. He walked over to the back of the truck.

'Why us, Smythe?'

'Shut up, you stupid wop! They're due any second,' came a hiss from the darkness of the truck.

'Nah, I mean, why couldn't you and your Special Branch boys do this business? Seems like old hat for you, plugging guys like Rutheim.'

There was silence inside the truck.

'Just think of your girl and mum, boys. Think of them. Here they come.'

Smythe must have been watching out the front window of the truck. I peeked around the corner and saw a group of men in long coats walking our way.

'Grab a box, Timmy,' Carlo whispered. He was already making like he was working. He picked up a box and crossed the alley and set it by a door. Who knew where the door went but Carlo made it all look real natural, like he wasn't nervous at all. I felt the gun in my pocket. I picked up a box.

One of the men in long coats walked ahead of the others a bit. Carlo tapped his forehead as the man walked by. The tough nodded and gave us a good looking over. I nodded to him, trying to stay real relaxed like Carlo.

The man turned and nodded to his group, then walked on ahead. The main group walked by us. There were four more toughs and a handsome man in a suit in the middle of them toughs. He had a good, full beard and grey at his temples. He had big hands. The man saw me looking and winked. I smiled back despite myself. He seemed like a nice sort.

Smythe came bursting out of the truck and opened fire.

It's hard to remember what happened after that. Two of the men dropped almost at the same time. One had been shot in the back and he clutched at the back of his shoulder like someone with a bad itch. Carlo had pulled out his gun and shot another one of the toughs as the man was going inside his coat, for a gun I guess. The man went down to one knee and tried to get back up. Carlo shot him again. Smythe pushed past me.

'Shoot, you mick bastard!' he yelled. I guess he was yelling at me, but for the life of me I didn't even remember that I had a gun. Smythe shot the last tough right in the face. His brains splattered on the brick wall of the alley.

'Timmy! Behind you!' Carlo yelled.

I turned around. The lead man had run back down the alley. He had pulled a shotgun out of his coat and was bringing it up, looking to shoot me. I danced left as the shotgun went off. Everything went all quiet for a second. I jumped back and grabbed the gun from the man's hands. He was a lot smaller than me and it just came right loose. He had a scared look on his face. I jammed the butt of the shotgun into his gut and he doubled over. Carlo came up behind me. The only sound I could hear was him cocking his pistol. He had tears in his eyes.

'Don't!' Smythe commanded. Carlo hesitated, and Smythe came over and pulled down his arm.

'Why?' Carlo asked. Smythe didn't answer him.

'Run,' he said to the last tough. The man ran, looking back at us in horror, thinking we were gonna shoot him.

'What are you doing?' Carlo yelled. 'He's seen us. He's seen us good. He'll pick us out easy...'

Then Carlo stopped and got real quiet.

'What is it, Carlo?' I asked.

'He's supposed to finger us, isn't he? Supposed to look like the Family took out Rutheim there.'

I'd completely forgotten about Rutheim. He was kneeling in the middle of the dead and dying toughs, holding one man's head in his big hands. He wasn't crying, but he was shaking his head back and forth real slow.

'I didn't want it to be this way,' he whispered.

Smythe looked guilty, then hardened up.

'Sorry, lads. Someone's got to take the fall. Think of your...'

'Don't say it!' Carlo interrupted. 'Just don't say it.'

Smythe walked over to Rutheim and poked him in the shoulder with his gun.

'Let's go, Mr Rutheim. Let's go.'

Rutheim looked up, saw the gun in his face.

'I didn't want this,' he said to Smythe. 'I didn't want anyone to get hurt. We were going to do this peacefully here. Bloodless.'

Smythe pulled a black hood out of his coat. He looked around. Already people were staring in from the ends of the alleys, but no one approached and no coppers had showed up. Maybe Hamish had made sure they wouldn't.

'Nothing's bloodless, chap. Look, I don't have a lot of time, Mr Rutheim. So we can do it the easy way or the hard way. Cooperate, be quick about it, and the hood stays off; you do this like a man, dignified-like. But give me cheek, play it tough or slow me down, and we'll do it the hard way. Gag and hood.'

Smythe pulled Rutheim up, mussing his coat and shirt when he did. Rutheim shook him off.

'I can stand myself, thank you,' he said coldly. 'The truck?'

'The truck.' Smythe nodded.

Rutheim got into the back of the truck. I stood there for a minute, the gun hanging in my hand. Carlo gently pushed me into the back with Rutheim.

'Come on, Froggy. This is almost over. I'll get you out of here, I promise.'

Carlo got in front and started up the truck. The fear and surprise were draining out of me and my hands felt a little numb and noodly. Even though I'd just gone, I had to pee again. Rutheim must have seen something in my face. He watched me close.

'Not your usual line of work this, is it?' he said after a bit.

I didn't know what to say. I looked away.

'It's alright. You didn't shoot anyone yourself. That's good. I fought in the last of the Red Indian Wars. You never get over your first killing. Especially when you're doing someone else's dirty work.'

'I'm sorry,' I whispered. 'They said they'd hurt my mum.'

'Shut up, Timmy!' ordered Smythe. 'You too, Mr Rutheim.'

I shut up, but Rutheim kept looking at me. I felt like he was seeing right through me, like I was about six inches tall. I felt ashamed. Carlo pulled out and we drove down the alley. The back doors of the truck didn't have windows so I couldn't see the dead men, but I could feel the four bodies behind us like lead weights pullin' on me. I felt their pull for the rest of my life.

'Take us back to the pub, Carlo,' said Smythe. He leaned into the cab to direct Carlo. 'And don't draw attention to us. Pretend it's just another bootleg run.'

Carlo huffed from the front seat. The two of them started talking to each other in quiet but angry words. I knew that Carlo was trying to find a way to get us out of this.

I looked back at Rutheim. He was still looking at me. I wanted to say something just to get him to stop looking at me. I noticed a bit of silver at his neck. It was showing through the tussle of his mussed clothes.

'You've got a necklace,' I said.

'This?' He pulled it out. Hanging on a silver chain was a cross laid over a crescent, like the moon. 'It was my father's.'

'What does it mean?' I asked.

'Not much. Not anymore.' He looked at it sadly, then smiled at me. 'Why does your friend call you Froggy? You're a bit big for a frog.'

'When we were kids, we'd play Empire Stories. Carlo'd be Bagheera and I'd be Mowgli, and we'd pretend the city was the jungle.'

Rutheim laughed and shook his head. Smythe scowled back at the two of us, then went back to hissing orders at Carlo.

'Not such a stretch, that,' said Rutheim.

'What?' I didn't understand.

'Nothing.' Rutheim looked at Smythe's turned back and then leaned over to me. 'Do you remember the Law of the Jungle that Bagheera taught Mowgli? The First Law?'

'No,' I said.

'He told Mowgli, "all the jungle is thine, and thou canst kill everything that thou art strong enough to kill," but the great panther forbade him from eating the cattle of men. Do you know why, Timmy?'

I thought about it. I shook my head no.

'Because Bagheera, like the other jungle animals, was afraid of what the men would do if the animals dared to take their cattle. The panther was content to be a prisoner of the jungle, as long as he could pretend to be its king. But make no mistake, he and Mowgli were just prisoners.'

'I'm warning you,' said Smythe coldly from the box he was sitting on, surprising me. But Rutheim kept talking in a low voice, as if Smythe couldn't hear.

'It doesn't have to be this way,' Rutheim continued. 'We don't have to live in the jungle, a puppet parliament that licks the royal boot. The people can make their own choices. Mowgli took fire from the men and brought it back to the jungle to set them all free. We can do the same.'

Rutheim's voice was hypnotic, like Kaa the python's. I found myself trusting him and felt miserable for what we were doing to him.

'They want to shut me up because I speak for the people. They want to keep us in the jungle.'

'It's always been this way,' I whispered. I'd never felt so miserable in my whole life, not even when my da' died at the mills.

'That's it!' Smythe got the hood out of his pocket. He had his pistol in one hand still and he pointed it angrily at Rutheim.

'It's a choice, friend. Like Mowgli's choice. Between tyranny and freedom.' Rutheim spoke quickly. His deep green eyes flashed like there was sparks inside 'em. They were fixed on mine.

'My mum...' I muttered.

'We can save your mum. I can help you save her. What do you think's going to happen to you once I'm dead?'

'Timmy!' yelled Carlo from the front. 'Stop eggin' him on!'

Smythe had the hood out and was advancing on Rutheim.

'It's a choice, Timmy,' Rutheim whispered, and his green

eyes were full of desperation.

And I chose. I'll never quite know why.

Smythe had too many hands full. One on the gun, one on the hood, and both trying to steady himself in the bouncing truck. I grabbed his gun hand and squeezed hard. Something popped and he screamed. The gun fell to the floor.

'Jesus Christ, Timmy!' Carlo yelled. 'What are you doing?'

He hit the brakes. Smythe and I fell forward. I hit an elbow on the floor. Smythe hit his head against the back of the cab. I banged it again for him, hard, for good measure. He went limp.

Carlo looked in back. His eyes went wide.

'Merda, Timmy! Merda!'

'Don't move, friend.' I looked up. Rutheim had Smythe's gun. It was pointed at my face.

'Oh no, Timmy. Oh no,' said Carlo over and over again. He had his face buried in his hands. 'Gina. Your mum. Oh no.'

I just looked at Rutheim. I looked in his green eyes and hoped. He looked at me and then grimaced, like he was hurt or something.

'Sit there.' He waved me over to a box and I sat. He dug the other two guns out of Smythe's coat and put them in his own pockets. Then he sat down on another box and wiped at his forehead with his coat sleeve. 'So hot in here.'

I nodded. Carlo looked at me from the cab but didn't say nothing.

'Okay,' said Rutheim, and he didn't look so grand now, just deflated and relieved. 'Okay, okay. This is a true mess we've arrived at isn't it, Frog Boy?'

I nodded. Hope grew brighter.

'Alright. First things first. Tell me everything about the men who made you do this.'

So I told him about the bootlegging run, and Charlie-Davy, and Hamish of the Special Branch, and the part about Carlo's girl and my mum. All the while Carlo just stared from the front looking really down, and I knew what he was thinking. That Gina was going to die, and my mum too, and it was all my fault. And I wish I could tell him why I did it, but the truth was I didn't know. It just seemed like the right thing to do.

By the time I was all done Rutheim had seemed to have found his nerve again. He had that spark in his green eyes that I had first noticed, and that spark looked angry.

'In all this time, since the La Purga in Spain, I've preached a better way. I've outmanoeuvred party men who I knew would bring revolution and war down upon us. I've sacrificed allies when I had to, even family. Anything to keep control of those who demanded blood. I said there was a better way.'

'Is there?' I asked.

Rutheim looked down at the gun in his hand. His green eyes glistened with moisture.

'I don't know. Maybe not anymore. The way I see it, the only way to save you, and myself, and the movement, is to get rid of Hamish and those like him. Those in power.'

'Kill Hamish?' Carlo said. The surprise of it seemed to have brought him out of his misery.

'Aridjis says that there are no absolute rules of conduct, either in peace or war. Everything depends on circumstances. I think he must have been talking about situations like these.' Rutheim sounded a bit like he was trying to convince himself of the right of it.

'Who the hell is Aridjis?' Carlo whined. But he didn't wait for an answer. 'You gotta be kiddin' me! You don't kill people like Hamish. He works for the tip top. He protects the Royals for Christ's sake! He's untouchable.'

'He's not. He's just used to people like you and I lying down so he can walk on our backs. He'd never see it coming.'

'Oh, he'll see it coming. If we don't have Smythe, if we don't have you, his boys'll plug Timmy and I before we get within fifty feet of him.'

Rutheim looked at him and smiled sadly.

'I will take care of that. Take us back to the alley. All the local police are undoubtedly at the Exhibition grounds, preparing for the demonstration. If we move fast, we can still beat them to the murder scene. Mr Hamish feared I would sow the seeds of discord, but it is he who has reaped the whirlwind.'

✳   ✳   ✳

Forty minutes later I was sweating bullets as Carlo pulled up to Charlie Bursar's. The street was busy with folks walking towards the Exhibition grounds. Carlo pulled into the back, where we had offloaded the hootch before. He looked at me.

'You sure about this, Froggy?'

I nodded, but truth was I didn't know. Things had gotten so complicated.

I looked into the back of the truck. Smythe sat on a box. We'd tied him up and gagged him, and he was still bleeding a little from a cut on his forehead.

'I'll bet you're ready, you Teabag,' said Carlo to Smythe.

The Special Branch man grunted and thrashed but the rope held tight. Carlo reached back and slipped the black hood over Smythe's head. Smythe was now wearing Rutheim's clothes. Next to him was the dead tough from the alley who'd been shot in the face. We'd dressed the stiff in Smythe's clothes. We'd dropped Rutheim off at the Exhibition grounds.

'If this plan was any more complicated we'd need an instruction manual,' said Carlo, then he got out of the truck. I got out with him and we went around back and pulled Smythe out. We left the stiff.

A Special Branch man opened the door to Charlie Bursar's before Carlo could even knock.

He took one look at us and asked, 'Where's Smythe?'

Carlo acted a little panicky. It was really convincing, I thought. Crafty as Bagheera.

'Things went tits up. He's in the truck. He's hurt.'

The Special Branch man threw the door open and ran to the truck. Another pulled us inside and patted us down. He took the guns that Carlo and I had in our pockets. There was Hamish, sitting at a table, puffing away on his pipe. His eyebrows went up when he saw us.

'What 'appened?' he asked stonily.

Carlo did the talking while I sized the place up. There were five of them, including Hamish and the fella who'd gone outside.

Too many. Even in close, with no guns. Too many by far. Rutheim had to come through.

'We got Rutheim,' said Carlo, shaking Smythe's arm as if he was really Rutheim. 'But it went south. They plugged Smythe. He's in the truck. Needs a doctor.'

Each of us tightened our grip on the real Smythe's arm. He let out a moan through the gag and twisted in our grip. I put a fist into his stomach and he doubled over, retching into the gag.

'Feisty bugger,' said Carlo with a grin. He was almost enjoying this. Mowgli and Bagheera running on the rooftops again.

Hamish looked confused.

The Special Branch man from the door came panting back into the room.

'Smythe's dead. His fucking face's been shot off!'

Hamish stood up. He took the pipe out of his mouth and gave us a sour look. His face scrunched up and he fixed one eye on the hooded Smythe.

'Get that 'ood off...' He didn't have a chance to finish. From far away came a huge sound like a bomb going off. I suppose it was a bomb going off. Rutheim and his men were at work.

'Peavey,' Hamish shouted to the door man. 'Get your arse out there. Find out what's going on!'

Peavey ran off again.

'You two sit down!' he ordered me and Carlo. We pulled Smythe into a chair between us and sat down. Another boom went off in the distance. Carlo looked at me but, except for a small grin at the corners of his mouth, his face said nothing.

'Who's on the Royals?' Hamish asked another man.

'Only Carter and Merriweather. Coomey is checking out the train for tomorrow.'

'Jesus and piss, this is a cock up,' spat Hamish.

Peavey came running back in. He was breathing real heavy now.

'Riots... at the Exhibition grounds... can't tell... workers are... rushing the Government Pavilion.'

Hamish rubbed a hand over his face. His eyes had gotten suddenly very red.

'Okay. First priority is the Royals.' He pointed at two of the Special Branch men. 'You two go with Peavey and get to Government 'ouse. Carter and Merriweather will have pulled them inside to a secure room. Get some constables and push the rabble out of there. We'll follow up as soon as we're done 'ere. Go!'

The three Special Branch men bolted out the door, guns already drawn. That left Carlo, Smythe and me with Hamish and just one other tough.

'Now get that fucking 'ood off 'im,' Hamish roared. He'd pulled a gun out of his coat and had it trained on us. I looked at Carlo. I was realising we hadn't figured this part of the plan out very well.

The other Special Branch man advanced on Smythe from the front and tugged loose the ropes holding the hood tight. He was blocking Hamish's view of Smythe as he pulled the hood off. I think maybe that was what gave us any chance at all.

'Bloody hell,' he breathed. The hood was off. Smythe's eyes were burning with anger. He tried to yell through the gag.

Carlo and I reached into Smythe's coat pockets, where we'd hidden the other pistols. We'd gambled the whole thing on the toughs not patting him down and we were right. Shots rang out. I fired into the stomach of the Special Branch man; he went down on his back. Hamish had kicked over a table and was firing away. I ducked right and went under some other tables. Out of the corner of my eye I saw Smythe jerk back. He'd taken a bullet from Hamish.

Next to me, jerking on the floor, was the man I'd shot. I'd shot him and he was gonna die. I wanted to reach out to him and touch his foot or something to say I was sorry, but Hamish was yelling something vicious and I could hear him reloading. I stood up and kicked the nearest table in his direction. It was a clumsy kick, but I'd put a lot into it and the table smacked him in the hip. He cursed and went down, then scrambled on all fours across the room. I moved to chase him but then I saw Carlo.

He was sprawled on his back on a table. Blood was pooling under him, spreading out slowly on the tabletop liked spilled syrup. I ran to him.

'Carly! Carlo! Are you okay?'

His lips moved but nothing came out. His eyes went dull and empty, and I knew I'd lost him.

My Bagheera was gone.

I remembered a boy. A big boy, but always alone. And he couldn't hope to fight off the bullies who always came in packs, like wolves. There were just too many. Then one day, when his face was in the gutter, and the wolves were pounding on his back, and he was thinking he couldn't take it anymore, someone came. A small, quick, black-haired rascal who kicked and punched and took a beating to help the big boy. And when the wolves were gone, he'd put out his hand and said, 'You're going about this all wrong, Irish. You wanna beat those guys, we gotta stick together.'

And I took his hand, and we were gonna live forever.

'Your wop friend's dead, Timmy.' Hamish was there in front of me, the pistol in his hand. He smiled an ugly smile. 'Jesus, what a cock up you two turned out to be. I want a simple killing, and what do I get? A med-case and a mick, running bootleg and fucking up my life. Only in this fucking country, right? Only in this country. With your Custerites and your provinces'-rights buggers, and your cross-and-crescent arseholes. It's like 'erding fucking cats over 'ere. I won't even ask what you did with Rutheim. I guess that's 'im setting off the fireworks. Bloody fucking anarcho-syndicalists. Jews, the lot of them, you know? Dago-bloody-Jews.'

He shook his head and spread his hands out wide.

'What were you really thinking you'd accomplish with all this?'

He waited for an answer. I didn't know. I closed Carlo's eyes, thinking that that was a fine last thing to do. I felt so empty, so alone; even that was an effort.

Another bomb went off, close this time. The building rocked, just a little bit, but I guess it was enough.

I heard the shot and felt a horrid stinging in my shoulder, like I'd been burned with a hot poker. I looked at my shoulder. It was nothing but dirty white shirt for a moment, and then in the next second I was bleeding red all over myself and a fire of pain had come to life inside me. The red of the blood was like a spark.

And my hate of Hamish was the powder keg. Something inside me burst.

I yelled and jumped towards Hamish. The gun went off again but he missed completely this time. I smacked it out of his hand, grabbed him by the throat and squeezed. He kicked me in the knee and ran when I went down.

The knee hurt. But it was nothing compared to the anger. The anger was everywhere. I ran after him, roaring like a lion. Like a panther.

By the time I'd made it out the basement steps of Charlie Bursar's, Hamish was all the way down the alley, running towards the entrance to the Exhibition grounds that was across the street. I chased him.

The street was packed with tourists in fine clothes and parasols running away from the Exhibition. They screamed and hurried, pointing over their shoulders to the smoke that was growing from the Exhibition like storm clouds.

Before he'd left us at the Exhibition grounds, Rutheim had said the revolution would start here. His men would set cars on fire and tear the place to pieces. They'd use the chaos to seize the Government Pavilion and take the Prince and his consort captive.

'We'll strike right at the head,' he had said, and only now did I realize that Hamish had said almost exactly the same thing.

In the crowd Hamish got farther away from me. He'd run through the main gate of the grounds. I pushed through the scared, wide-eyed people trying to escape the Exhibition and chased after him. In the distance, inside the Exhibition, I could hear a low roar, like the ocean at Coney. It was the roar of angry men. You could feel it in your bones like thunder.

The west entrance to the grounds was right next to the Hall of America. I lost Hamish for moment in the crowds that were pouring out of the Hall, but he paused for a moment at the door, looking for me, I guess, and I spotted him.

I jumped a turnstile to make it into the Hall. Inside was a huge open area that could have held two or three football fields. There were booths everywhere and displays of American history and culture. Right in front of me was a diorama of two settlers shaking hands with a British soldier. Their smiles were so big you could see the teeth that had been carved into their mouths. Draped over the soldier's arm was the Jack and Stripes flag. I heard screams and shouts in the distance. Someone yelled, 'He's got a gun!' in a frightened voice. I took off running again.

I saw Hamish next to the American beef display at the same time he saw me. He was standing right in front of a giant billboard that had all the edible parts of a cow drawn out in dashed lines over a smiling Bessie. People were scattering away from him. I guess they thought he was one of the rioters, come to shoot the place up.

'Buggering 'ell,' I heard him say.

Hamish took aim at me and fired. The bullet pinged off the steel strut that was just to my right. I ducked under a demonstration table as he fired again. Anybody who hadn't been screaming before was screaming now.

I started running for him, using displays and booths to stay hard to hit. He took one more shot at me; I heard someone behind me cry out in pain and somehow got even more angry with him. This was my Hall. These were my people! Who the hell was he? I cut through a booth advertising some shimmery, flexible fabric and came out right in front of the big cow sign.

Hamish was gone.

I looked around. He was halfway across the Hall and heading for the far door.

I ran out the door and had to stop just for the horror of it all. On this side of the Hall of America there were fires everywhere. Buildings burned, windows were broken. Here and there the black and red flags I'd seen the picketers carrying earlier in the day hung from trees or lampposts. Most eerily, there wasn't a person to be seen. This area was empty of rioters, tourists, or police. Hamish stood out like a shadow running through the flames. I started running again.

I chased Hamish past the burning Pavilion of Australia and the Empire Stadium, which was strangely untouched. Between the buildings, as we ran I could see the great lake that only this morning had reflected the coloured lantern lights so prettily. Now it glowed a deep, ugly red, the colour of hellfire and smoke. All around me the buildings I had mooned over that morning were burning: Burma's sandy walls, Malaya's coconuts, Shonaland's standing drums. All of it was being eaten by the fire that moved like an animal from building to building.

I covered my face with my hands and ran past the flames that tortured the Shonaland Pavilion. Beyond it everything was different. Here were the men. They were everywhere: angry, yelling, shaking their fists and pushing against each other. Some waved New York provincial flags. Some waved the red and black flags of the anarchists. Some threw bottles of spirits lit on fire that exploded when they struck. Some had bats or clubs. All were pressing against a line of Queens coppers arrayed in front of the British Government Pavilion. I knew what it was because behind the coppers stood six great stone lions, guarding the entrance to the Empire itself, I guess.

It was loud and frightening, and smoke stung my nostrils and made my eyes water. Hamish had stopped about fifty feet ahead and was shouting at a cluster of policemen and pointing back at me. They either didn't know who he was or were too worried about the mob to deal with me. They ignored him. Hamish swore something I couldn't hear and took off running again. I ran after him.

He made his mistake by trying to get through the coppers. They pushed him back, thinking he was another of Rutheim's men. He turned left and tried to run around the crowd. He ran into the gardens that were next to the India Pavilion. I cut through a rose bed. Hamish was there, waiting with his gun up.

'You're a fuckin' disappointment, you mick—'

I leapt off a bench and brought him down, growling with rage, as his bullet went past my ear. I seized his coat and pulled him up; I think a part of me was about to bite him like an animal. He kicked my parts and scrambled away while I was down on the ground huffing and cursing.

I looked up in time to see him run in a side door of the great white Palace of the Rajahs. I limped after him.

Inside there were pockets of frightened tourists in their

fancy coats and pretty dresses. They huddled in alcoves, the men trying to look brave, the ladies grasping each others' hands. They stared at me in fright and, as bruised and soot-covered as I was, I couldn't blame them.

Thinking about the gun, I walked more carefully through the Pavilion. There were displays of spices, and different teas, and great murals of the British forts in Bombay, and a full-sized stuffed elephant that took up a whole room.

In the centre of the Pavilion was a big domed room. There were balconies on the floors above where you could look down upon a giant map of the British Empire that was painted on shaped plaster on the floor. India was in gold and red, and there were little plaster forests, mountains and rivers. America was just a little sliver off on the left side of the big map, small and tiny compared to everything else. Looking down at it, in the building with the paintings of elephants and rajahs, with weird forests all around me, I could almost imagine I really was Mowgli, running through the trees with Bagheera. My eyes started to water. I cried a little and then the tears came like a waterfall. I didn't care about Hamish anymore. I didn't care about Rutheim. I just so wished Carlo coulda seen it all. Seen it all with me.

An explosion rocked the building. Screams from hiding tourists came out of all the halls and rooms. There was another explosion and suddenly people were running everywhere, pouring out of every room and heading for the exit behind me. I could smell smoke and feel heat. Rutheim's men were still at work. I just stood there and let the people move around me. What use was running? There was no escaping the fire.

But then I saw Hamish. He was moving with the people, trying to get out of the burning building whilst looking around for me. He didn't see me, probably because of the smoke and craziness. He came within a few feet of me and all I had to do was reach out and grab him. It was that simple.

He grunted as I tossed him over the red felt barrier that circled the map. He landed hard on India and immediate turned over, desperately trying to crawl away. I was on top of him in a second. Hamish kicked me away and pulled the gun out of his coat.

I hit his arm and sent the gun flying, then grabbed him by the throat and banged his head into the plaster of the map. It cracked beneath his skull. He cried out.

Everything was red, I was so angry again. I was screaming things at Hamish but I didn't even know what I was saying. Everyone was gone. We were alone in the hall. The fire grew. Another explosion sent a blast of heat over us, like a tidal wave of smoke and flames.

'We'll die in here,' Hamish gasped.

I didn't care. I grabbed his throat and squeezed. He hit at my face and arms with his fists but they pelted off me like raindrops. I was crying so hard I could hardly breathe, could barely see him, and the snot was dripping over my lips and down my chin. I can remember the salty taste of it. Hamish's struggling slowed and he began to make sick gurgling noises.

That was almost the end of it then. Almost.

Some sound at the edge of the world caught my attention. It was screaming, a woman screaming. I took only a moment to look back over my shoulder.

The Indian Princess stood on one of the balconies overlooking the map, wreathed in smoke and flame, and screaming.

'Oh,' I whispered. It was her, from that morning. I looked at the beautiful brown woman, her coloured scarves dancing in the fire's wind. I looked at Hamish, bug-eyed and dying. I looked at the murals on the walls, the paint on them blistering and peeling away like old memories.

That's when I threw it all away. That moment. Carlo, Hamish, Rutheim, the future; another choice and it was all thrown away.

I left Hamish on the map and dashed for the balcony. I was there in a moment, it seemed, but it was already almost too late. I leapt for the railings and they tore loose under my weight.

'Jump!' I yelled up to her. It wasn't so far but she was too scared to move.

I leapt again and grabbed a ledge of white marble that was nearby. It was hard and I was tired, but I pulled myself up. The skin on my hands was raw and red with the heat of the flames.

The brown woman shrunk away from me. She must have thought I was one of the rioters, the ones who'd started all this. I suppose I had started all this. But there was no time. I could feel flames in the floorboards beneath our feet. I ran for her. She screamed and batted at me with her hands. I grabbed both in mine and tucked her under my arm. I looked below. Hamish was gone. The map was already starting to smoke and smoulder in the heat.

I jumped.

The floor, ten or fifteen feet down, hit me like a truck. My legs screamed. I lost my grip on the princess, who crashed to the floor next to me. I could barely see her in all the smoke.

'Are you okay?' I shouted. I had to yell over the roar of the fire. Even in the smoke and flame she was the most beautiful thing I had ever seen. Her brown eyes were surrounded by wide pools of frightened white. 'It's okay! I'll protect you!'

She slapped me and ran.

In a moment she was gone in the smoke. I was too surprised to do anything but watch.

It was only a few seconds and then the fire drove me out, coughing and gasping onto the grounds in front of the Pavilion. That morning I'd stood there, on that very spot, and watched the Indian Princess wave to me, and smile, and laugh. She was gone now. All I could see now was the flames and the smoke, and the rioters chanting and yelling and destroying.

There was another sound underneath the rumble of the fire now, popping and banging. I looked up. A group of soldiers emerged from a cloud of smoke and strode in a line towards the rioters, firing as they went. I watched in horror as ten or twenty men went down screaming and clutching at the bullet holes in their chests. The remaining rioters scattered like birds from a cat, disappearing into columns of smoke.

I stood and watched, too horrified to move. All the pavilions were on fire now. The Empire Exhibition was destroyed. It was a storm of fire and smoke, and in a daze I watched as it spread beyond the Exhibition to the buildings on the other side of the street. The fire danced and ran like the people who had fled before it. I ran too.

❋   ❋   ❋

You asked how it happened, and that's how. I never saw the Indian Princess again. Well, I see her sometimes in my dreams. I see Carlo sometimes too, smiling. I know he's not mad at me. Mostly I just see the fire, roaring and smoking. It burned up most of Queens, new and shiny as it was. Jumped the river in a couple places too. Rutheim's people tried their hardest, I guess. It took provincial guards three days to put down the riots, and it took another four days after that for the fires to burn out. They don't know how many died by bullets or flame but in the end thousands were dead. They say King George himself ordered that the fire crews let Queens burn, but I don't believe that. There was no putting out that fire.

The day the fire started I packed my mum into the truck and we headed north out of the city and then west. A newsboy in Helena showed me a paper and said that Rutheim had been arrested in Newark for high treason. They took him back to Manhattan and hanged him outside City Hall along with a bunch of men I didn't know. They didn't let him have any last words.

In the newspaper photo you could see Hamish next to the gallows. His back was to the camera but I could see his pipe, leaking smoke and ashes. I guess in the end Hamish got what he wanted. The Red Hunts started soon after that, and no one seemed to mind that folks were getting pulled out of their beds in the middle of the night. Nobody wanted another Queens. You didn't hear much tell of independence after that.

I don't know what Rutheim thought would happen, but he's dead and America's still a dominion of the crown, still a part of the Empire. I think about it a lot, at night, when I wake up from the dreams. I wonder what choices coulda been different. I still can't figure it out.

Rutheim said I had to bring the spark of fire back to the jungle. He said I had to do that if we wanted to be free. But I didn't set anybody free with the fire. I just burned the jungle down around me.

Here Grow No Flowers
by Alexander Zelenyj

"Truth, Duty, Valour."

—Motto, Royal Military College
Kingston, Ontario (Est. 1876)

I.

2 October 1934

My sweet girl,

I must be quick. The night is cold on this stretch of front, trembling the hands and making writing difficult, and I want only to say:
I love you, Rachel.
And I am strong for you, fighting this good fight for the Lady Britannia. We shall persevere! Me and the boys, we shall win you a war!
Your scent of lilacs lingers with me always,
And I am yours, always,

Kindred B. Green

❀   ❀   ❀

The sky here spits Jack Jeffersons like rainwater.
I'll never be the same again after this weather. It's ours and

it's ever-present, this constant din of man-made thunderheads crashing in the distance, the lightning-bright brilliance of shells dropping from the clouds and blanketing the infinite country ahead. I hear the wailing clamour as they fall from the clouds and wreak havoc on the invisible Polish lines and the rural Bohemian country beyond.

And with every clap that rattles my helmet and heart, sending cold dirt clods sliding over me along the walls of this trench and its myriad companions, with every concussive blow landed in this soil so distant from my home and heart—I think of her.

Only minutes ago, I'd snuck the briefest of glances while huddled in my trench-hole, like a sip from some magical, energy-laden canteen: her slim wrists and small hands encased in white gloves, a filthy apron tied around her waist, her coveralls drab and grainy photograph-grey in the picture she'd sent me and which arrived three weeks ago to the day. Our Motherland's flag marks her breast, a neat little patch sewn into the fabric of her uniform and making her look heroic. Safety goggles pulled up and resting atop her head, her dark hair tied back neatly, revealing her high, glistening arch of forehead. Her round cheeks grease-besmirched, housing dimples that have been the envy of Kingston boys since her final days in elementary school.

My girl, Rachel, shell-maker on the back-home front, gentle as a butterfly and devoted untiringly to such important and honourable labour. I pine for her, and my heart swells with overwhelming love and pride when I consider her efforts and her steadfast faith in the Motherland. My only means of escape, my girl, my transcendental sliver of hope in all of this mess every single time I conjure her image to mind.

Here it is a life of vastly opposing states: the first, one of eternal waiting, anxious and torturous, during which time elongates queerly and the mind is plagued with fears and uncertainties that tremble the very core of who you are; the second, one of becoming overwhelmed with the shock of action, violent and merciless, and there is no recourse left but for you to act the part of the soldier you claim to be and thrust yourself as if fearless into the heart of the fray. Days and nights endlessly spent pretending we are steady men, sure of our duty and our courage. Until the re-organised enemy lines hold their ground staunchly, undaunted by our superior numbers and weapons. Until the shells reach their high-shriek crescendo about our ears and our comrades and friends begin to fall around us like haversacks weighted down with a months-long accumulation of rain and filth.

I think of her during moments like these, racing frantically over the uneven ground of No Man's Land, my ears numbed with the ringing of terror in my head. The ceaseless buzzing that obliterates the world about me while the bullets fly past invisibly, cutting holes in our ragged formations. The sight of butchered boys at my feet gives me cause to conjure her in my thoughts every time, spell-like, a saving element amid the roar and frenzy of action. A comrade flying upwards in pieces as the land mine sends him skyward. An enemy infantryman cut down with his own gun still sputtering, his features contorted with fear or rage or pain or all of these. The perpetual fog of smoke and gas fumes shrouding the lines and blotting out the sky over our heads so that every day is more hazy and uncertain than the one before.

Rumours have abounded for weeks: our campaign is foolhardily ambitious, our appetite needlessly voracious. We have dug our trenches too deep and they will serve as our future graves, waiting for each of us to intern ourselves and be claimed forever along with the worms and fossilised layers of sediment and bomb shrapnel hidden in the earth. The reports fly about our heads like enemy flak: Germany is racing to offer aid to the beleaguered Czechs of Bohemia, because who are we to molest so young and militaristically weak a nation? The Poles' ranks will be fortified, and thus their courage and determination renewed. What almighty nation are we to wish to swallow all others into our ever-growing mouth and breathe our will upon this magnificently grand and diverse continent?

How has Great Britain become the great villain in all of this? Perhaps we've been wrong to incur the wrath of this larger German power. Will we pay the price of our lives for the transgression? Will the Germans continue uniting with the smaller nations and with the Russians threaten our stalwart island with the greatest *Blitzkrieg* ever launched? Is the flexing of the ever-growing German military machine just cause for the Motherland's swift reciprocal invasion tactics, merciless and unequivocal? The seed had been sown, after all, where the newspapers and generals tell us—deep in colonial African soil, when British settlers met their doom hardly more than a year ago at German hands, those greedy sons capturing the land's resources for their own, the diamond mines at New Birmingham in Shonaland falling to German guns and not a single child of the Motherland surviving to tell the tale. Then the Slaughter of Harristown, merciless and senseless, the true spark that birthed this great conflict of empires—a small village located several miles from the quarries, where entire English families had been decimated for no purpose other than to display the German military might, where children were left mauled and broken in the streets, bloodied under the hot sun. The massacre that captured national sympathy and allowed for our fury and outrage to burn like hatred, validated and just. The resultant fears of similar threats to Australia, where German and Spanish ships had been caught lingering darkly off the Arnhem Coast.

But has Lady Britannia's retaliation for such trespasses been too severe still, too crushing in her military might, swooping across borders of aggressors and peaceful nations alike? Ignoring long-standing treaties and morally-decreed laws of war in rabid reciprocity for the crimes committed against her children? Have we awakened and angered a lion too fleet and powerful to tame, and now her jaws seek our collective throat?

These whispers make the rounds among the trenches and camps as we push forward toward the Bohemian-Polish border, like anxious curses fluttering in the darkness and chilling us more than the nipping wind ever could. I sneak a final glance at her before replacing the picture inside my bag, and with her eyes of faith and courage filling my thoughts, I settle down for another sleepless wait for dawn-light.

✳   ✳   ✳

A day of endless marching is behind us. We continue our plan to follow the miles and miles of trench-line border until we reach Poland to the north.

Rodney passes me the time-yellowed clipping while I deposit my gear on the hard earth of our newest makeshift camp. I stare at the grainy image, the black man with gloved fists pumped high into the air, his skin cast with a heavy sheen of sweat visible despite the rough quality of the photograph. His features contorted in an exultation of triumph, nostrils flared and eyes piercingly severe, almost malign. The image of victory, Jack Jefferson post-match twenty years past, having successfully defended his Imperial Heavyweight title for the final time. A symbol, here in the trenches, of past victories that history can't ignore and of their tenacious spirit lingering blessedly until the present. Those shells with their coal-black smoke and incredible might have been named for the colour of the champion's skin and the awesome might of his left hooks.

'We got ourselves a champion here with us, eh, Green? Yes we do. He's still a goddamned champion, all these years later. Underdog ring-dancer fighting his way to one two three four world titles, not the first black fighter but hats down the best of them all, eh? Just listen to him out there. He's just pounding those Czechs and Poles. It'll be a first-round KO, pal, I bet you anything. What a *champion!*'

We listen together, and the clap of shell-bursts beyond the ragged country of No Man's Land chills me. I tremble, and the clipping is nearly stolen from my fingers by the ravenous wind. We listen and they go on and on, long wailing cries as the invisible planes overhead unload their cargoes of death, the deep sound of finality as they plague this land with their explosions and an aftermath veil of impenetrable black smoke.

A voice of sandpaper scratches from the murk, McCall disdainful and annoyed. 'Shut your yappin', Nancy-boys. The enemy's listening.'

Perturbed by the vindictive timbre of the interruption, by

the lurking threat inherent in its meaning, Rodney makes his voice a whisper. 'And you know what? You're one too, Green. Good night, Champ. Good night, pal.'

'Good night, Rodney,' I whisper, and I settle into my bag as if I believe that sleep will come to me this night and mercifully take me away.

❈   ❈   ❈

20 October 1934

My dearest Rachel,

I hope that all is well with you. Is the famous Kingston fall lingering and keeping the dreaded Old Man Winter at bay? I hope so, and hope also that your family is doing well–you might give your parents my regards and convey to your mother how much I yearn for the taste of her dessert brownies. (A soldier's rations are not of the delicious variety, and there are those of our company who not infrequently liken them to the scraps left over for those our staunchest friends in this world, our affable canine counterparts.)

I miss you dearly, my love, and long for the touch of your skin: the softest touch this soldier has ever known. I keep all of your letters with me at all times, secreted inside my pack, and when I am able I revel secretly in their lovely perfume–the smell of you blesses each page, and I cherish them all dearly. (I must confess, though, my dear, that I couldn't resist sharing your lovely aroma of lilacs and garden bouquets with a comrade of mine. His name is Rodney, and he is also a son of Ontario, a Windsor boy born and bred, and a good soldier and a great pal to me as well. He agrees, of course, and has said that my darling carries the scent of a flower kingdom with her, and that the scent is very, very lovely. When this is all over and we've won these battles for the Motherland, I made Rodney a promise of dinner at our future Kingston home. I think you'd quite like him a lot–he's the joker of this outfit, and he would have your sides splitting in no time.)

How goes the factory work? I received the pictures you sent only days ago, and I must say how beautiful you look captured on film. You wear your emblems well, my darling, and I wish you to know that your efforts are always greatly appreciated among our outfit here. You make us proud. No librarian you, with your goggles so spryly positioned atop your perfect head— you've the look of a pilot about you, I dare say, but mostly for the fearlessness in your eyes. We'd better not let Leonard spot this picture—he might begin sending you flowers across the ocean in the hope of wooing you! I recall often our early days of romance with the Effort, the mere idea of it thrilling us so. You and I sitting up late together in your porch swing long after your parents had gone to bed, reading in whispers the information in the campaign pamphlets—like poetry the words had been to our ears. The glory of the British Empire expanding across the great face of Europe, and our chance to serve those efforts abroad and at home.

Be brave, my sweet girl, and remember that we fight this struggle together, albeit on different continents. No ocean can keep us apart, my heart remains with you always. Listen carefully, and you will hear it keeping rhythm with you at all times.

Be well, my love, and we will be together soon.

Your Kindred

❊   ❊   ❊

The day has been endless.

My legs tremble still from slogging through the mud and slime. My ears buzz with electricity from the clappings of shell-bursts all around. My eyes are heavy and my spine seems bent and malformed from the painfully precarious dance of crawling then crouching then running over and over again, an interminable cycle enacted countless times while the sky rained its usual cargo of death and cacophony around our ears.

The Czechs have been defeated, just outside Prague in this day's short-lived battle. Bohemia is nearly ours. Their army had been weak and was obliterated as expected, easily and with few casualties to our boys. I shot a few men myself today. My final hit for the day stays with me, though, a ghost I wish I'd left behind in the field. He'd been my age, or thereabouts, clean-shaven and with large eyes of terror as I cut him down with my Stensa gun only several feet from where I walked, hunched, through the grass. The frenetic movements of his limbs as he stood in place a moment after the rounds found his chest, a final paroxysm of spastic pain as of a marionette lurching on its strings, and then he'd toppled like a sack of wheat to the ground. And I the puppet master, striding past with my comrades' murmured approvals setting secret suns of shame burning in my cheeks.

I cower into my bag in our newest dugout, avoiding the eyes of my companions eating from rations tins down the trench line. The pencil in my hand trembles on the air, scribbling a nerve-jangled invisible scrawl that reveals my teetering façade of courage.

I open the notebook in my hands to a new page. By the muted light of a cloud-veiled moon, I scratch once more at the rice paper, envisioning the exquisite eyes of an exquisite girl an entire ocean away yet hammering behind my chest every moment of this tenure in Hell.

And magically, I am there by her side.

※　　　※　　　※

24 October 1934

My Dear Rachel,

Let us, pretend, my sweet girl...

We are dancing in sunlight upon the lush sward of your parents' backyard lawn. The day is fresh and the heat on our skin fills us with an easy languor. You're laughing as I point out the plump bumblebee trailing our dance: his interest has been piqued by the brilliant, childlike scheme of your striped summer dress fluttering through his air space. Yellow and black and like a magnificent bumblebee queen yourself, you dance your daring aerial dance.

A veritable pilot you are, taking my hands and twirling me along. Lifting from the deep emerald grass your dainty feet, and taking me with you onto the soaring heights, we fly free of the earth, leaving your rows and clusters of roots-grounded children, but only briefly—we will return to your flowers once our air dance is done.

I look and I spy him: our tenacious bumblebee escort, drifting upwards in pursuit of your golden brilliance. But he only trails us briefly, my dear, for his is the power and design of a lazy striped dirigible, and our flight one of magic.

Together, we sail into the clear blue, in search of the sun.

Thank you, Rachel, for taking me away. Yours is ever the sweetest respite from this world when this world no longer makes sense.

Your Kindred

❀   ❀   ❀

The wailing begins anew just before dawn breaks.

I wake to it chilled to the bone from the ice wind, numb and with a spasm of contorted muscles aching my calves. There is a light dusting of snow covering me, and I crisp and crunch as I stretch my limbs. I've curled my body so that I'm able to reach my legs; I'm kneading them softly when Rodney's frightened child's voice flutters from the pitch beside me.

'They sound like babies,' he murmurs, softly, softly, a sound of fluttering moth's wings so ephemeral that I find myself craning neck and back in order to seek him out in the shadows so that I might confirm his existence in the unreality of this nightmare moment. I find him after a time, my eyes adjusted to the murky greylight of pre-dawn: his long, emaciated frame huddled into his sleeping bag, head reclined against his haversack, eyes wide, pale orbs illumined queerly from beneath his helmet. The gaunt, haunted look of him, a skeleton speaking to me from this shovels-sculpted scar in the icy earth, unnerves me, and I'm unable to find my tongue before he goes on in his rattling way.

'The bombs. Babies. The long wailing sound of them coming down way out there, or so close by. Like babies crying in the nighttime. I always think of giant babies out there in the fields, on the lines. In No Man's Land, just sitting up or crawling around over all the bodies and chewed-up ground. Giant babies with the loudest cries. I... I hate that sound. I hate it. I say that they're like Jack Jefferson out there, but I'm lying every time.'

We listen together a while and I hear and understand: the

mournful note in the descending shells, the funereal finality as they pound down into the world. The sound of something crying, innocent and forlorn. The sound of sorrow in the fields.

My friend the skeleton murmurs once more before turning inside of his bag and hiding his skull from the chill air. 'I hate it. I hate it so much.'

A shell strikes startlingly close at hand, and in its aftermath I think I hear the high mewling sound of a wounded Czech soldier from the trench network adjacent to ours. I picture him lying there, no more than one hundred feet distant, legless or armless or faceless, his comrades scurrying about in the earth, a platoon of agitated rodents scampering for their survival during these nightmarish wee AM hours. And I'm cold. His cries go on for several minutes, frantic and pitiful, and then cease abruptly. Maybe he's left this place of violent children forever. Maybe he flies higher than planes or airships or cloud fronts.

I listen and I hear the legions of mud-slimy infants crying in the cold morning dawn. And turning into my coat collar, I close my eyes and weep secretly for them all, and for all us soldiers throwing down the wailing din as though we still understood why.

✻ ✻ ✻

In Hell, even the earth becomes our enemy.

We lost one of our party to a sink-hole that opened up beneath his feet while he relieved himself twenty feet to the side of our camp. Perkins, with his pink cheeks and stubble-less child's face of wonder, peering up at us with an expression of quizzical terror while his hands frantically sought purchase along the slippery mouth of the hole. Mud flying through the air as we leaned in as close as we dared, one of our number lobbing hopefully the stout loop of rope, another reaching forward futilely along the wet earth with a wooden plank. Our efforts were short-lived and for naught: a curt, high-note shriek and Perkins lost his grasp, disappearing into the fissure in the earth. We stood staring wordlessly for several minutes, as though hoping madly that the earth might relinquish its hold on our comrade and vomit him back into our battle-thinned ranks. But though the deadly hole gurgled and hissed and oozed wetly like some hideous mouth, our friend remained within its dark maw, taken from us forever.

We spend the better part of the afternoon slogging through an artillery-blasted field as big as the world. No signs of life greet us but for occasional crows like black boomerangs arcing down out of the sky to pillage the charred landscape of soldiers' corpses strewn everywhere. There is the dog, too, the skeletal black dog that appears seemingly from nowhere, lost and sending its forlorn cries into the sky, searching fruitlessly along the barren steppes for the unit to which it belongs. I call to the animal but it won't have any of it, only watches me kneeling expectantly in the earth until it grows suspicious and lopes off into the mists. It's Rodney who sums it up so perfectly, the joker surprising us with his jarring poeticism, silencing us all for the remainder of our trek. 'This must be Hell, boys. Where else do dead bodies grow like goddamned weeds?'

It is indeed no garden through which we wander these days.

❁   ❁   ❁

'You got a girl back home, don't you Green?' Rodney's voice is small, anxious, floating there in the murk of recent dusk.

'Yes,' I tell him. 'I've got a girl.'

'Yeah. Me too. Me too. Say, what's her name again, your girl?'

I pause, deliberating, sensing that something is amiss, and I understand only as her name leaves my lips, the softness of its sound floating there before us: 'Rachel.' Her name should not be uttered in this kind of place, of filth and carnage and endless fear and shame. That perfect sound, those dual syllables which have always held all my hope for the future.

'I remember her picture. She's good-looking.'

I think of my darling girl the way I remember her most clearly: at home in her garden of flower-children. Her babies, she'd always called them with a twinkle in her eyes that only ever meant she was secretly content. I think of her large blue eyes, bright in backyard sunlight. Her red hair flaming in that kind of light, deep and lush and warm when I nestle my face there and breathe her fragrance of earth and hybrid flower species. Her splendid nose as she leans among a row of dahlias and inhales their heady perfume. Her supple neck, like a magnet pulling my lips there, puckered and ready to pepper her with kisses. Her round cheeks, rosy remnants from childhood pictures, the adorable girl of baby fat infamy, dashing about unhindered by her round sausage arms and legs. My girl's small shoulders, ideal to rest my weary thoughts and wait for her comforting words to arrive and soothe as they always do.

I think of the day we met, at the carb fountain: the door thrown wide to the balmy June afternoon, the crispness in the air as youthful summer tested the stuffy interior of the room, filling its corners and making everything new and energised. I saw her the moment I'd entered, mid-spin on her stool, playing the role of young girl with her two friends but fooling no one. Her eyes catching the sunlight spilling through the doorway and stopping me short while my friends and hers laughed at our silent display, forgetting any thoughts of sundaes or ice cream cones.

'Yeah,' I tell my comrade. 'She looks good. Every time I think of her. How about your girl?'

Rodney laughs softly, and somehow I like the sound of it floating in the darkness of our trench. 'Yeah, Green Man. She looks great, my girl. She looks just so great.'

The wistful note in his words causes me to frown, though, and a moment later the terrible song of the shells slips through my barrier of awareness once more. To this most awful of symphonies I might eventually succumb to fitful sleep, and if I dream, as ever, the dream will be forgotten by dawn.

II.

31 October 1934

My dearest Kindred,

I think of you always. I miss you dearly.

I hope all is well with you. Where are you stationed now? I fear you may have been moved from the Bohemian border and into Poland, where everybody says the fighting is very bad. The newspapers are full of stories saying this or that—nobody's sure what to believe nowadays. Did you receive my last letter? I hope so. All is well with me. My mother sends her regards, and Donna, too. (I'm now convinced—her first crush is also my very own brave darling!) Yes, she talks of you to all of her friends. You are her favourite hero. She shared this secret with me only last night. You've taken Perseus's special place, and I believe she's even pencilled in your very own entry at the back of her book of mythological heroes!

The factory goes well, and I work on untiringly. I have been relocated from small arms ammunition manufacturing and into the Big Room. The hours are long, but then so is the war, no? To think that I am even one small part of the struggle in Europe, well, let me just say how happy I am to be able to help at all.

I have been tending my flowers less and less of late, but thank you for asking, my love. The factory keeps me busy, and when I return home I seek only my bed before another shift begins. I still smell their fragrance, though, through the window which I leave ajar every night. They smell wonderful, my love, and cause me to think of you. If only it wouldn't wither on its way, I might send you a white rose for you to wear in your lapel, my fashionable soldier poet!

Oh, Kindred, my poet, my darling, I long for your words again soon. Be well, and may angels watch your every step.

I am yours,
Rachel

❋   ❋   ❋

The wind and rain are awful this morning but still I make my usual detour. It's become my secret ritual, and even before I arrive at the spot I know that my cheeks are red and the guilt is heavy in me. I turn down the grassy alley between houses, liking the feeling of aloneness as I walk underneath the trees. They make a roof over me as I walk down the lane with my hat pulled low over my head. No one can see me here. No factory workers. No mothers or fathers. No friends, and no soldiers.

I reach the cul-de-sac, holding a hand over my face at the stink of the garbage dump. I walk past the abandoned couch, looking all wet and heavy in the early morning drizzle, and I step past some rubbish that someone had been too lazy to place into the large, galvanised dustbin. There are tufts of wild grass poking up everywhere, rustling in the wind, and the sound makes me a little nervous.

I step into the small space between the dustbin and the wooden slats of the backyard fence bordering the alley. I look and, as ever, it's there. I stare at it while the drizzle touches me everywhere, while the grass is frightening-sounding around me. The paint is still bright against the wooden utility pole, a deep red. The rain hasn't faded it at all. A single bloody letter above and a short bunch of stacked words running down the length of the wooden pole beneath:

> *R*
> *Resist!*
> *Resist the*
> *Far-Away*
> *King!*

I've never seen another soul walking in this alley before. But I wonder who I'll meet if I keep coming back. I wonder what she or he or all of them will look like, and I wonder what they might say to me about their artwork if I ask. I wonder who they are, and if they guess that I wander here all the time. I wonder if they have kind eyes, or if they're evil-looking, mean like the war notices show the Germans and Spanish to be, exaggerated and scowling and scheming.

A small, mangy cat pokes its head out at me from behind the rubbish. Its grey fur makes me sad. It looks too much like the morning sky, overcast and depressing. Its ears prickle in the rain. Its eyes are cautious and its tiny pink nose twitches in my direction. It watches me a while and then disappears back behind the garbage bins a moment later, like a signal for me to start my day as always.

I leave the secret alley. The rain is pounding down now but I don't care. There are worse things falling from the sky elsewhere.

※　　※　　※

I look down the line and sigh. I wonder if I'm strong enough to make it through another day here. The heat covers me with sweat beneath this uniform, and the noise is frightful. My arms ache in the joints from yesterday's work, and my fingers are still swollen and tender.

Ours is the largest weapons manufacturing factory in all of Ontario. Our specialties are Bounce-Top shells, Ear-Boxer shells, Grand Slams, Thunder-Clappers and Jack Jeffersons—we make them and they send them over to Europe, where our boys drop them on the enemy in the name of the King. It's long work, and hard work, and very tiring work and we do what we have to do. I wonder sometimes at what exactly *they* do, these big shells, so sleek and deadly-looking. The damage they can do. How loud they are when they hit, and what would be left of a building, or a tank, or a person if they were hit dead on. It gives me the shakes and shivers sometimes, this work, but I tell myself to be brave and grown-up and to remember our boys in the dug-outs before I whimper about the heat and noise here.

The radio is on and we listen as we work. We hear sing-a-long songs by Noltan Nellie and Jenny Monroe and we sing with them, too, thinking about our boys. Every thirty minutes there's a news segment telling us things we knew or feared about the war. This is the time when we all talk loudly and quickly and nervously. Talking helps us deal with our husbands and brothers and friends and lovers being overseas. Talking helps time tick away when otherwise we'd be picturing them running through fields with bullets flying all around, or lying on a stretcher with bloody bandages covering them. We listen and hear how bad the Germans are for siding with the Poles, and how bad the Poles are for fighting back and sending our boys to Heaven. We hear about the weak Bohemian Army and the low character of the Czechs and how we made mince meat out of them, and how victories like this only serve to hearten other nations to unite against the Motherland, once neutral countries taking up arms and adding their numbers to the growing German machine.

We hear about the Spanish. Local news items help us to remember that the war has come home to us these days just as it rages over the ocean. We hear more and more stories of those sniping creepers, those night-ghosting killers, the Spanish paramilitary unit who call themselves *Los Fantasmas de la Noche*, elite saboteurs so proficient at infiltrating enemy territory that they're the talk of this Ontarian town just like they make the rounds of our boys' conversations overseas. 'Watch out, boys and girls,' we warn our younger sisters and brothers. 'Make certain to be indoors before dusk has fallen, because *Los Fantasmas de la Noche* creep in the dark, and haven't you heard the news reports and read the papers? The radio's saying that they're already here, bundled up inside of crabapple bushes and hanging upside down like bats from apple trees and skulking on rooftops in the moonlight. They'll find you, they will, they find everyone that they hunt for. And no soldier on guard can see them, no radar can detect them, no binoculars can pick them out from grass or hill or tree or where they swim in Saint Lawrence waters, until it's too late and the bullets have flown, and the bullets of the *fantasmas*, children, are always, always sure.'

On more than one occasion the radio gives another long list of names of newly dead British soldiers and it sends one of our girls home early from work, crying and screaming for a lost son or husband or boyfriend. And we shake our heads and pat each other on the back and stretch our sore arms and get back to work. The steel rattles and the sparks shoot. The conveyor belt moves quickly and we scamper to keep up despite our aching bodies. We're frightened all over again and a little bit more confused than we were at the beginning of the shift, when more of our boys were still alive.

But then, as always, I consider this assembly line and the front lines where my darling battles each day and night. And then I really, *really* put my shoulder into my work, and I even earn a 'good work' from the foreman, and I feel a little confident that I'm doing something right.

❋   ❋   ❋

10 November 1934

Dearest Kindred,

I spent some time in the garden this afternoon, though I fear my efforts now come too late. The roses sag like old men, and the orchids' petals are wrinkled too. The chill in the air is frightful, and I think that the days are numbered for my poor garden children. November has arrived, and I can only imagine what it must be like for you wherever you are tonight.

Mother and father send their love, and of course Donna, too.

I love you, my dear. Fair Kingston and I wait for you always.

Take care of yourself, and may all your steps be blessed, wherever you walk.

Your bumblebee girl,
Rachel

❋   ❋   ❋

I'm staring at the bloody words again this morning.

There's no rain today, but the wind is fierce. It's as though I'm not wearing a coat at all. My knees quiver in the icy air. My stomach hurts faintly. I have nearly thirty minutes before my shift begins and so I take my time examining the words. Their long neat letters. As though the writer of the words had taken his or her time. As if he or she had wanted to make sure that they got it right.

The bold look of them in the dark, wet wood of the utility pole chills me, or maybe it's still only the wind causing that. I feel the sad-looking cat before I see it; it's rubbing up against my legs. I let him sniff my hand where it hangs at my side, and I pet it behind its ears awhile until it grows bored with me and disappears behind the dustbin.

155

I stare a moment longer at the words, soaking up their vivid look. Then I turn and walk down the alley, into the wind. I think I notice someone in a window of one of the houses overlooking the lane, but I might be wrong. The curtains are moving or it's just my agitated imagination. My nerves are all jangled in my secret place, as always.

I reach the street and turn for one final look: the alley is empty, but not really. It's almost as though I can see myself standing there still, as if I never left the place at all.

Only yesterday I told Estelle, my favourite line-mate, all about him. My darling, a poet and a soldier and a nice fellow who used to frequent the carb fountain with his pals, and lucky me because I frequented that place too. A graduate from the Royal Military College right in our hometown.

'A homegrown hero,' Estelle had said, making me blush with pride.

Scenes from the RMC campus keep returning to me. The day my father and I visited. Graduation Day, and we waved to my beloved Kindred when we spotted him among his fellow soldiers in the parade. The drums pounding and the band marching in front and behind the troops. Their bright red uniforms and the blue summer sky. The sharp, clean smell of the Saint Lawrence River in the air, and the campus grounds all around, lush and green and beautiful. Everyone cheering and pointing out their son or lover in the ranks. A proud day for everyone. The ceremonial rifle barrage at the end put tears in all of our eyes.

I gouge at the wood with the pocket knife and the scratching sound makes my stomach queasy. It brings me back to the reality of this morning in the cold and the rain in the secret alley. I hold my breath and try to think clearly. I aim carefully and my writing is messier than I'd like as I chisel away with both hands upon the knife handle. The arrival of this moment has tortured me for weeks, months. Days of torment while I weighed my ever-changing feelings about things, my love of country versus my love of my darling. The risk to him and to his friends, and for what and for whom? Not for he and I is all I know for certain.

I think of my family, and my friends, and my little sister.

But mostly I think of my dear Kindred as I chisel the words into the wood of the utility pole. My sweet boy with all of his big courage and love for the Motherland, sitting in a trench and dodging bullets for the King.

But the message is clear, in spite of my nervous, shaking hand and the tears ruining my vision. Below the familiar red words, it's my own little poem or message:

I'm with you.
R.

And I turn and walk very quickly back down the alley, faster than I've ever walked there before. My darling weighs on my thoughts. I long for him beside me in these streets again. And I wonder what I've just done. I wonder if I've just changed the world one small or very huge bit.

❋　　❋　　❋

III.

I don my black mask and look about me. We are a horde of gargoyles, our transformation is complete.

We are demons that will hurdle through the noxious mists and stop the lingering Czechs's hearts beating inside their chests. Monsters we, descending on this small town's collection of orchards and narrow paved lanes, while about us descends the poison gas cloud that is our awful harbinger.

A child screams somewhere and a shadow scampers and falls close by, writhing horribly in its place. We march onwards, grimly, bayonets stabbing the death-air before us. I feel monstrous, a devil in weak human clothing. My booted toe nudges something stiff yet somewhat pliable—I look and through the fog see white eyes like moons as the dying girl stares terrified at the evil thing that is me lurching over her. The legions of Hell have risen from Below for her; I can see this knowledge in those beautiful eyes. Hell is swarming over her home, choking it and her family and friends out of existence. I watch her asphyxiate and I'm happy that she can't see my eyes through this dark mask.

'Let the Germans come,' is our war cry this dark dawn.

Let the Germans come and taste the Hell of our flame throwers and the poison breath of our gas assault. Let them fall back and be taught a lesson: no nation's power will threaten our Mighty Island with force and remain unanswered. No nation will bring their weapons to bear upon our distant colonies and leave our children ravaged in the streets. Let this dawn be the final night for those who oppose Lady Britannia and her taste for fair rule and expansion. Let these fallen Czechs and Poles serve as warning and example that our King commands an almighty empire, and that his empire grows with each rising dawn.

I march onwards and my boots weigh a tonne, and each shaking step feels as though the weight of the world is mine alone to carry into this foggy battle where the lines are so difficult to see.

❋　　❋　　❋

The day of fire and poison air is done.

In the darkness of my trench-crevice I cower, cold with mud and snow and slime, with my watery vomit stinking in a puddle beside me. I watch the clouds with unseeing eyes. In this quagmire, I cry and I cry. Another spot of inclement weather, another deluge of salty water.

Through my blurred eyes I stare out over the rim of my trench-hole. In the uncertain mists of No Man's Land I see the figure: immensely tall, lithely making its way through the upturned earth. I blink water from my eyes, amazed, a cry of alarm caught in my throat. The figure is stark naked, its skin a deep, obscene red in the moonlight. Bloody and appalling. Raw and vivid. I stare aghast and catch sight of a curling movement upon the air, and in a moment I realise that this is the thing's stout tail undulating like a python from its buttocks. It's the Devil that stalks through the ravaged field before me, crimson and proud. His black eyes find me and look through me piercingly, and a tremor quakes my body through and through. He raises a hand upon the air and in His palm stirs a black flame. He makes an 'O' of his mouth, and with His black tongue darting between swollen lips, blows the flame in my direction. It leaves His hand and drifts westward over the field towards me, quivering in my hole.

I drop from view and cower like a child in the water and mud of the trench. I clasp my hands together as if in prayer but I'm too chilled with terror and cold to articulate any such thoughts. Time passes: minutes, hours, I can't be certain. Eventually, I crack open the notebook and lift the shaking pen to the bare page. And I write, uncertain of my words and their meaning.

My darling girl,

> *Onwards, my comrades and I march*
> *We shall persevere, for home and country*
> *And for you, my dear*
> *I am strong*

Your Kindred

✳   ✳   ✳

We're comparing our girls and I know it just like all the other boys know it about their girls, too: I win hands down.

My girl, she's pretty as sunshine and more pleasant than a summer day in Kingston. She's tough too, working in the factory back home. She sends me pictures, and every once in a while, if I'm lucky, I even get them delivered to me out here in this mess. This latest snapshot was taken by her mother, who's caught my darling leaning back into the patio swing, her sandals kicked off out of the picture somewhere, her small bare feet dangling in the air. Her hair is down, wild-looking where it spills past her shoulders, dark where it frames her round cheeks and sad eyes. I'm a lucky dog, Rivers affirms it, and I tell him that he's one too, for sure, with a girl like his, all blonde hair and long legs. He's a good fellow, Rivers, another Kingston boy aching for the fresh air and balmy summer. It's because of him and me and two other Kingston boys, Blok and

Emerson, all together in one platoon, that we've called ourselves the Kingston Brigade. We brag about our school days at RMC, where Willy Bishop learned all the things that would help him fly like no other. 'Truth, Duty, Valour.' We often proclaim our former school's motto in the trenches, and the way we say it is filled with pride, as though we don't question its old meaning regularly in these new days of uncertainty.

Rodney jokes and it gets us all laughing: 'Hey there, Green Man, I wouldn't leave that picture of your sweetheart lying around. I seen McCall eyeballin' her, and he might want to borrow her next time he visits the latrine.' We all know McCall's sense of humour disappeared weeks back, somewhere on the Polish steppes, sometime in the middle of that firefight where he murdered the family begging on their hands and knees to be left alone. We're familiar with his distant eyes nowadays, and his surly moods, but still we get uncomfortable in our holes when his voice cuts the early evening murk like a knife, another little bomb-drop when all we want is a break from it all.

'You're a funny fella, Rodney. You must laugh it up while you're givin' it to that cow of yours back in Windsor.'

Silence descends in our trench. Only wind whips through the quiet, stirring our coats and reaching a high-note banshee squeal where it slips through the thin, meandering outlet branches of tunnels snaking off about us. Then the sound of Rodney scraping his way to a standing posture, and we tense and prepare to leap between him and the blasphemer, Murderer McCall, with his foul mouth and dead humour. But Rodney only makes his way silently through our hunkered-down ranks and disappears down the trench-line.

I follow soon after and hear the sound of his weeping before I pick him out in the darkness of the night. He's seated on an outcropping of rock, in plain view of any enemy soldier out for a midnight break of sniping, but he doesn't care in the least. He's clutching something to his breast and I know that it's the photograph of his girl that he'd passed around our circle minutes before. I clamber up beside him, and the sensation of open air whipping in from across the vastness of the fields goose-pimples my skin along the back of my neck. I feel reckless, I feel brave. I'm a solider fighting in a war whose meaning became lost many miles back.

I ask him if I can see the picture again. Rodney passes me the photograph without hesitation. By the wan lunar light I hold it close to my nose and see: the girl in it is round and wearing a surly expression. Her thick carb bottle glasses and forward-thrusting chin are to what she owes her troll-like appearance, despite her gentle eyes and soft spill of fair hair. I notice the dimples in her cheeks and wonder if they might have been more pronounced if she wore a smile rather than a scowl in the picture. I say, 'Those dimples are exquisite, Rodney. Truly. The cutest dimples I ever saw.' And I pass the picture back to him and the somewhat pleased look in my comrade's moonlit face makes the chill air and the rats scampering in the snowy trenches below tolerable, if only for the moment.

※　　※　　※

Rivers rolls the pair of dusty dice over the large flat-topped stone wedged in the mud between us. We wait for their tumbling to cease with vapid expressions while pinwheels of flame from the bonfire sputter down to touch our boots.

'Perfect twelve beats your six. I win again.'

His tone is dejected, weary, a small voice of victory from this hollow-cheeked young man with lost eyes. Only another soldier like the walking dead. I remember him the day we'd met, sparkle-eyed and gregarious back in the Kingston RMC days, and I wonder where that boy has gone away to. I wonder whether my old self and his are still the friends they were on that first day of greetings and introductions or whether they're even closer than before. Then again, I find myself pondering, perhaps they've faded away altogether, these two almost unimaginable people, and we're only spiritless shells wandering through these uncertain days.

The village around us is in ruins. Houses roofless, walls collapsed into rubble blocking the unpaved streets. Fences mashed by shell-fire, gardens decimated, never to host bounties of vegetable in any conceivable future day. The fire before us crackles lividly with its fuel of wooden timbers, tree branches and floorboards from the destroyed homes everywhere. It envelops these pieces of people's former lives, warming us only very little in the chill afternoon.

A shadow looms over us suddenly, drowning out the firelight, and McCall seats himself across from us. He's loaded with gear as ever, haversack bulging to capacity, bandoliers of shells making a crooked 'X' across his mammoth chest. He clinks and he clanks, he rattles and he fumes, even in his heavy silence intruding upon us in our futile game of escape. We feel his eyes search our faces through the sparks wheeling on the air. We sit in overwhelmingly loud silence a moment, until Rivers palms his blackened dice and tramps off wordlessly down the line.

I don't look at McCall but hear the familiar sounds as he disassembles his Stensa gun in preparation for its regular cleaning, placing its component pieces beside him in methodical, practised fashion. Clicks and clacks, curt and purposeful and somehow menacing in the broken serenity of this bonfire moment.

I rashly mistake him for another human being when I volunteer the information. 'I just want to go home. I want this to end so I can do that. That's all I want.' I wince when I hear his scoffing spit into the dirt at his feet, curse myself for revealing so much of my frailty to the emotionless creature loading cartridges into his gun. I consider leaving him to his solitude and searching for Rivers and another game of dice, yet something keeps me lingering in my place. Maybe it's the distinct personality of his presence, overwhelming and huge, like a dare for me to live down, like a test of my mettle no battle or dawn skirmish could provide.

His voice is like a boot dragging through gravel, coarse and jarring in the crackling calm of the fire's presence. 'War don't end, pal. Don't you know nothin'? War goes on and on, and then it goes on after that. This place? Right here and now? Hell, pal, this moment right now will last forever. Don't you know nothing', pal? We're takin' this moment with us when we break camp, just like all the other moments you ain't going to ever forget.'

His words birth a surge of anger in me and, beneath it, the old feeling of desperation that's been my haunter these past weeks.

I can't help myself, perhaps stepping into the trap of his argument, perhaps falling into some deeper snare of his that I'm too overcome with emotion to discern. 'What happened to you, McCall?' I wonder aloud. 'How can you say these things?'

His voice is even but emphatic, his mouth a snarl of yellow-brown teeth as he speaks through the fire, delivering his full attention from the weapon cradled in his arms to me watching him, incredulous, through the flames.

'What do you care, cry-baby? What do you care about how I started out? Maybe I speared the man on the cross on Golgotha. Maybe this is my fate. Maybe I'm here to fight, and I'll fight until the end of the goddamned world, or until I'm forgiven, and maybe then I'll shoot the bastard that forgives me, because there ain't no one can stand up to the wrathchild with a gun in his hands. Maybe I see things clearer than you ever could. Maybe I'm the strong kind of this Earth, and you're nothing against me. Maybe you're dead with a mortar ripping you into a hundred pieces come morning, while I'm going to live forever, and meet your girl one year, two years, three years down the road, and woo her easy as pie, and then she'll be mine while you watch from Heaven without a voice to tell her a damn word of warning. Maybe it don't matter, because maybe I don't matter at all. Maybe none of us matter a single goddamned bit. Hell, pal, maybe I'm you. Maybe you're me.'

He turns his eyes from me to the weapon he holds, their livid cast immediately relenting to a gentle sheen as he strokes the barrel, fingers the smooth-worn trigger. His voice is soft when he speaks now, calm. 'Maybe this right here is good enough, pal. Maybe the eyes of the enemy are always watching, and this child right here's good enough.'

And he hefts the Stensa to his shoulder and lets loose a brief volley of fire that startles me and scatters a flock of crows from the sunken rooftops and into the ashen sky. I watch them wheel there, despising myself for the tears that bead down my cheeks, obscuring their flight, revealing my weak spirit to the monster seated across the smouldering fire heap.

'Little cry-baby,' and McCall rises from his splintered wooden beam and turns from me. He's wading through the slop of muddy earth and debris, shaking his head disdainfully.

I stop his progress with my trembling words. 'I don't know what made you, McCall, but it didn't make me. I pity you. And you're no pal of mine.' I spit into the mud at my feet, a thick globule of acidic phlegm that feels as though it contains all of my fury and disgust. It makes a loud plunking sound into the depths of the mud-pool and I feel my features contort into a grimacing mask as I stew in my place atop the felled tree.

The Murderer stands in the mud, gripping his gun, holding his silence. He remains this way for what feels like an eternity. I stare at him until the tears have dried on my cheeks, until no more sobs wrack me. I watch him with determination, not exactly willing him to turn about and face me once more, but wishing at least that my words continue to bite him, to rankle and twist inside of him. Like shrapnel left too long and infecting the softness of the flesh in which it is embedded. Like a knife blade parting flesh and etching its design inside of him, this timeless, wandering killer, leaving my message scribbled there for him to decipher every day, a text for him to be haunted by from now until the end of time.

A hundred thousand years pass and finally the Murderer continues on his way. His gait is slower though, I notice, and less certain. His sodden boots step less surely through the muck and the mire. His shoulders slump beneath the weight of his haversack, as though he's at last tired from the weight of the days. As though he's perhaps suffered a wound and must nurse his limbs as he progresses through the butchered landscape, gingerly gliding through mud pools, carefully stepping over fallen houses and men and women.

I scan the sky and find them a moment later.

The murder of crows, making arcs in the vastness of the overcast heavens. They glide there a while, beautiful and bold, overlooking the smoking country all around. A 'V' plunging headlong into the iron cumulus, bravely, surely, swallowed by the grey immensity until they circle there no more.

✳   ✳   ✳

12 November 1934

Rachel, my love,

I stare at her name, looking small and frail on the rice paper before me, and a chill wracks me, a body-shiver covering me everywhere. My hand falters and my pencil quivers in the night.

Sometimes writing fairytale verse is impossible in the fields and trenches. Sometimes, when the mud is too much like a dark ocean swirling onwards as far as the eye can discern, when the screams of dying men grow too much to bear, when the report of rifles and the shaking of the earth itself during yet another bomb-storm make their way like sniping infiltrators into the deepest crevices of you, gunning for your peace and serenity. And sometimes they get you good, and you must put away your old tools of escape and face the darkness brewing on the horizon before you.

'Goodnight, my love.'

I whisper the words and wish them an ocean away, into the dreams of the girl I love and yearn for and from whom I hide with shame my new faltering belief in this whole muddy, muddled campaign.

And I tear the page from my notebook, crumple it in my filthy hand. I drop it in the trench mud, watch it drift a moment in the thin trickle of water and urine, then sink in the mire like my trembling will.

✳   ✳   ✳

Leonard Spencer strides among our ragged ranks, his cheeks round and the smile he wears confident, strong. No war can wipe its strength away. No soldier's bullet and no burnt village and no limping, wailing dog without a platoon-family, wandering the bomb-ravaged ranges with a forlorn note in its yips and cries.

We're stationed at a temporary headquarters located

several miles to the east of the trench-lines, sculpted out of the abandoned remnants of a Polish village whose name no one seems to recall. Several battle-beleaguered platoons have convened here as respite from the fighting while others take our places on the lines. His presence here is a surprise, although we've all heard tales of his visitations to scattered platoons resting up at just such impermanent makeshift stations. Boosting morale with his mighty entourage and words of rally. Offering encouragement and thanks for the efforts of every man and boy, no matter his role or his title.

I sit in the rear of our group, marvelling at the raucous cheers with which the great man's words are greeted. I listen to him and try to make sense of the words he gives us.

'We shall go on to the end, my friends. We shall fight in Poland, in Germany, we shall fight on the seas and oceans, we shall fight with growing confidence and growing strength in the air. We shall defend our island, whatever the cost may be, and spread our might further and further across the lands. We shall fight on the beaches, we shall fight on the landing grounds. We shall fight in the fields and in the streets. We shall fight in the hills. We shall never surrender. And even if—which I do not for a moment believe—our bountiful island or a large part of it were subjugated and starving, then our Empire beyond the seas, armed and guarded by the British Fleet, would carry on the struggle until, in God's good time, the New World, with all its power and might, steps forth to the rescue and the liberation of the Old. We shall fight on to the end, my friends. Over sea and ground. I say again: we shall *never* surrender!'

The roar of the platoons is overwhelming. The cheers are for the man before them, for the battles they've won and lost, and for the fighting yet to come. They cheer for their loved ones an ocean away, for their dead friends left unburied in the smoking fields, and for the fact that there is someone reminding them that what they do every day in the field is just and valiant, the way they'd believed it would be at the beginning of this endless campaign.

I hear the words and I hear the answering roar of the troops resounding throughout the tented area and surrounding compound. But I wonder: what if there is no end? What if you want more and more, General Spencer? What if we, your Kingston Brigade alone, put all of Europe in your pocket and then conquer you all of Africa, too, and the rest of Asia after that? Will the outlying islands without names be ripe for the picking, so that you might wear the plumage of exotic birds upon your shoulder or lapel? Will the peoples who dwell there be subject to your insatiable appetite for foreign land, to be served with your tea? And will you reach your flag towards the moon one day, too, once the paltry lands of this Earth belong in your hands, and with the flag flapping far overhead obscure her sad lunar light from reaching us down here and thereby kill all the romance that is left to us in this noisy, confused world?

In the exultant roar of my comrades I feel insect-small and tired and make no effort to join in among the jubilation.

＊　　　＊　　　＊

30 November 1934

My darling Rachel,

I hope all is very well with you. Though the hour is late, and my body fatigued from a week of long marches and occasional skirmishes, yet I feel the infectious sting of the writing bug that ever urges me to set down my thoughts for you.

General Spencer visited our camp this afternoon. No word of a lie, my dear, General Leonard Spencer himself strode these battlements and addressed our weary platoon, the First Lord of the Admiralty. His presence was inspiring and his words we took to heart as ever we have in the past. We shall fight on, my love, and never surrender ourselves to the rigours of battle. We shall free others from the tyranny of their governments, the weak institutions that seek to condemn them to a life less beneficial and hopeful than that promised by our honourable Lady Britannia. I hope the fact of his appearance among your love's company will in some manner inspire you as well, darling, to know the great worth of your noble efforts.

It is as Spencer himself said this very day: this Great War is a war on many fronts, overseas as well as upon our Homesoil. Only victory can come to the Motherland and her children colonies. The New Year bodes well.

Be well, dearest Rachel, and know that my heart longs for you.

Yours as ever,
Kindred

✻   ✻   ✻

Another village burnt to its foundations. By way of example, by way of orders.

His words brim with boastful scorn: 'Fighting these villagers is like fighting little girls! Eh, Green? Little goddamned *girls*.'

I watch McCall torch the remnants of the villagers before us, one short plume bursting from the tip of his flamethrower and consuming the ashen corpses in the road.

And he steps with heavy booted feet over the hill of carcasses, climbing to their summit like a king ascending a grisly throne. I grimace at the spectacle but watch as though entranced. I wonder, had these villagers, in the midst of their daily routines of garden- and crops-tending, of sharing suppers with their children, enjoying the bounty yielded by their hard farmers' work, had these burning men and women and children had much to do with the planting of the seeds of unrest into Colonial African soil? Had they filched glittering diamonds from the dead hands of British miners and thus earned their fates at the weapons of our Murdering Platoon on this day? Or did these events seem almost too distant, too unreal to these people of peace living off the land, as though the stories had never been true in the first place, only some unbelievable fiction crafted by those with minds better suited to scheming for political and geographic conquest rather than tilling any stretch of soil?

She comes to mind suddenly. I'd seen her once during a brief sojourn in New York City: the Lady Britannia, with her Corinthian helmet and robes, brandishing the three-pronged trident of Poseidon as a symbol of the Motherland's great naval power, and her oval Greek hoplon shield, too. At her feet crouched an iron griffin, a mighty creature no matter where in the world it is transplanted.

I watch McCall scramble simian-like over the hill of bodies. Once at their summit, he lets his submachine gun speak the rest of his words, firing off a long volley that chills us all into motionlessness, an awed group of hapless spectators watching our possessed comrade. A monarch atop his bloody meat hill, and I suddenly wish our beloved Spencer was here with his valiant soldiers to witness this skewed moment of triumph.

Truth, Duty, and Valour, all buried beneath smoking, ragged, ever-growing hills of death.

❄   ❄   ❄

IV.

20 December 1934

Dear Kindred,

I hope this letter finds you well. Is the European winter as angry an old man as he is here? I hope not, dearest, and that you're warm wherever you are. Christmas comes soon, but it won't be the same without you by my side, listening together to Noltan Nellie crooning 'Christmas Time is Here Again'. We received some snow only last night, only flurries, but the radio says we're due for a big storm in the coming week. The factory is cold when I arrive for work every morning, but once I've been on the line for no time at all I don't even notice it, that's how hot it gets. That's good, eh? Having summer indoors while Old Man Kingston Winter blows and blows outdoors isn't so bad.

Not very much is new here. Mostly only the same old winter and the same old worries, of spies everywhere and too much fighting overseas. What else? Do you remember Mikey McBride? That awful little freckled monster that terrorises the schoolyard? Well, believe it or not, the little fiend has taken a liking to Donna, who spends most of her break time fleeing him and hiding in the girls' toilets. Ha ha. Poor girl. I suppose only some girls are as lucky as I, no?

Becky and Annabelle visit me on weekends, although I've begun working these days as well. I get to see them every so often once we've finished our shifts, though, and our time together is always fun. Friends for life, us girls, and that's a vow we'll keep. Mostly we spend our time talking about our loves. (Becky's boy is fighting overseas too, a Kingston boy named Danny, who is currently stationed in Austria). I tell Becky that maybe you'll bump into each other one day, on some brave adventure in one place or another. We always said that it's a small world, didn't we?

I look forward to seeing you, very soon, I hope. I pray for you every night. Be well, my darling, and may angels guide your steps each day and night.

Ever yours,
Rachel

❈　　❈　　❈

It's always raining these days, making the snow disappear in ugly grey puddles. I'm tired of this weather. Where is the sun? It seems that I forget the feel of its touch on my skin, it's been so long since sunny days.

My grey cat friend is nowhere to be seen. The sofa is grotesque-looking. Rain puddles sink its cushions more than usual and a crow chose the seat as its place to die. It looks stiff and not very real lying there. It makes me anxious, like the sound of the grass rustling in this place. I think of mother and father at home at the breakfast table, wondering why I've left for work so early once again. Their eyes are worried nowadays, as though they think I'm getting into trouble.

I see the words on the utility pole and I'm shivering. Their words, my words. Theirs in red, bright on the black wood. Mine a jagged poem slashed crudely into the pole. I'm shivering and the wind isn't as terrible as it was yesterday or the day before. My stomach is queasy again, like most mornings but even worse because I'm so nervous. I'm a little dizzy too, and I think I might throw up. I feel suddenly un-alone and look again for the cat but it's still not there.

I turn around and the alley behind me is filled. They're a

whole gang, and I can't see their eyes and I'm frightened. They're wearing woollen caps and toques pulled down low over their faces and their baggy winter coats and gloves make them look big and scary, like monsters blocking the way to freedom. But then I remember something about them and tell myself that I can be brave now. It almost works, and I think I have enough bravery in me to say hello. I try but realise my mistake when I open my mouth and look foolish, shaking quietly in the rain.

A moment passes and one of the gang steps forward. He's tall and thin, and he says simply, 'Welcome. We are R.'

I answer, 'So am I.'

He looks up and I see his face. The expression in the man's eyes softens. It says the same as his words: it says 'welcome'.

❋   ❋   ❋

16 March 1935

Dearest Kindred,

I have good news: my children have returned!

I know it sounds too magical to be true, but I swear to you, my dear, that I speak no word of a lie.

I found the first batch only this afternoon and of course I thought of you. The first small white buds of my lilies look beautiful in the grass. Early bloomers! I wish you could see them. Like magic during this dismal stretch of cold rainy days. I have a feeling you will see them soon, darling. Soon, we'll be together again, and we can enjoy their perfume every afternoon.

Magic! Sheer, splendid magic!

Waiting for her final beautiful flower to come home,

Your Rachel

❋   ❋   ❋

It is with a different feeling that I watch the clock on the factory wall this afternoon. I breathe easier today. A weight has

171

been lifted from me.

When my darling comes home from the fighting, I'll tell him. I can't tell him in letters because I don't have the words. He loves me, more than anything. He'll understand. I'll be brave and I'll make him see and understand everything. I'll take him to the end of the grassy alley and show him how beautiful the words look upon the wood. He'll see the beauty and share in its meaning. He's a poet and he'll see beauty in those words and their meaning. It can be our secret. We will have new friends. Everything will be fine. We'll fight the same struggle, only differently. Everything will be fine.

Estelle eyes the clock herself and tells me, 'You know Willy Bishop? He went to school here, did you know? At the Royal Military College. Willy *Bishop*. That's right. The legend himself. Your boy's keeping some good company, eh? Hero company.'

We smile at each other. I like Estelle. She's kind and always says something cheerful when I need to hear it most. She's my sunshine during these grey days.

The bell rings like an alarm and a great sigh fills the Big Room. The girls can go home and cuddle in front of their fireplaces and sleep. We can offer prayers for our boys and wish them on their way home faster than ever. The ringing sounds louder than even the noise of banging metal and explosions of shooting sparks. The noise crackles my ears, and I feel it too, the relief at that sound, and I sigh deeply like the others.

And I head towards the locker room, and feel more free than I can ever remember feeling before.

V.

24 January 1935

Dearest Rachel,

Do you remember the carb fountain?

A silly question, I know, my dear. Of course you remember. A place of origins it is, after all. I propose a plan, let me know what you think...

After the fighting, and after we are married, what say we start our very own carb fountain? Just like Mr Weir's old place, the same spinning seats and candy-striped table-tops and long glass displays. The same girls and boys wandering in and out in the summer months, making eyes at each other over the table-tops, enjoying the fragrance of flowers where you've hung bouquets of your specimens here and there throughout our Carb Fountain Kingdom. The Bumblebee Bouquet. Rachel's Sundaes & Lilacs.

What do you say, Rachel Dearest, my sweet girl of botany and beauty?

A place of sweet origins, and wonderful days to come...

I love you. And I miss you dearly.

Your Kindred

＊　　＊　　＊

I stumble into the atrocity in the inky light of near-dawn. It jolts me instantly awake, alert, and numbs my mouth so that words are impossible in the awfulness of the moment.

Murderer McCall straddling the corpse of an inert village girl, shoulders hunched as he leans over her in rapt observance of the grisly work of his hands. A scratching sound disturbs the stillness of the morning, meaty and revolting. A butcher's sound in the muffled hollowness of the trench.

A moment passes and I watch as though spellbound by the terrible spectacle. Soon McCall leans back, cocking his head from west to east in scrutiny of his work. The knife in his fist gleams wetly, crimson. Brown-red streaks his hand too, glistens among the hair of his forearm where his filthy shirt sleeve is rolled high.

I'm calm as I pull my Tolta pistol from its holster at my hip. My hand is steady as I raise the weapon and aim precisely along its scope into the centre of the back of his head. My eyes clear as I release the weapon's safety. I hear no sounds as I sight along the barrel and consider the logic of the moment, questions that arrive unerringly in my mind as I prepare to kill a supposed comrade. Where had he found her? Had she been alive and filched like a loaf of bread from one of the outlying villages in our vicinity? What had been her crime in the madman's mind? Had she shown fear in her eyes when he'd surprised her in the fields, an unallowable emotion in this harsh time and place? Did she go only unwillingly with the burly soldier guiding her by the neck with a knife pressed to the softness of her throat? Or had she been a victim of the Empire's guns, some shrapnel finding her and bringing her to the ground of her parents' property until the soldier loomed out of the darkness and stole her away into the AM like some demented abductor of the dead?

He turns his head a slight degree to the northeast. Smelling my sweat or loathing or fear, sensing my intent if not seeing the weapon trembling in my hand, McCall murmurs, 'There's ice in this air, pal. Ice. Cold as Hell. Freezes a soldier's fingers right up. Makes his work hard. But we do what we do, eh? We do what we can. Eh?'

He says these things and only turns to me a moment afterwards, when my silence has grown protracted. His eyes startle me. Their soft sheen gentle and mellow. A tranquil gaze examining my rattled presence in the trench. And I squint, blinking lingering sleep or trench dirt from my eyes, but still the subtle gleam lives in that stare. Like a small fire burning in the holes of his irises, a darkly crimson blemish smouldering there in contrast to his otherwise soft expression.

'I could do you right now, McCall. Bullet in your face. I could do this.' I tell him these things, knowing as well as he that they are lies. Maybe he sees the trembling commotion of the Tolta on the air as my nerves rattle and quake my hand. Perhaps he sees my eyes in the murkiness and glimpses my terror of the world and the things that are allowed to transpire in it without constant and vigilant guardians overseeing the innocent.

He stands, and the serenity in his gaze of a moment before has passed. Shark-eyes watch me once more, and in his features I catch a suggestion of something persecuting. A contemptuous curling of his lips, a mockery of the eyes as he looks me up and down in calculatedly patient fashion. I'm weak beneath that stare, beneath the unrelenting barrage of that war visage.

He gestures to the dead girl in the mud and shrugs his shoulders to the sky as if to tell me something. I miss the meaning in the gesture. I can't seem to find it within the blood of this moment, and I can only watch him as he turns his back on me and makes his way slowly down the winding length of the trench. I imagine how it might feel to take a steadier aim and plug him good, one dead-sure shot in the centre of his back. A coward's shot, to fell a ruined shell where once there may have lived a man.

But no pistol-crack startles the morning. No demon corpse haunts this trench. I only let my hand fall to my side and turn numbly to the corpse before me. I inch closer, wincing, biting my lower lip anxiously at the mud-streaked limbs thrown akimbo. A large birthmark adorns her cheek, a deeper brown peering through the mud and blood, a chestnut geography like some secret continent mapped out against the grey landscape of her face. Her eyes are gone. Only deep, blood-rimmed caverns of gaping black haunt her wan features. Scooped out with a jack-knife, perhaps, or the frantic work of a madman's fingers while a gibbous moon guided his early morning blasphemy.

A single word haunts the girl's soft-looking flesh, a series of black-scarlet jabs etched recklessly into her skin, violently raked across her frail chest:

ENEMY

I shake my head because I must deny this. The sight of her. The notion scratched into her. The ruined girl and the wrongful message marking her so inappropriately.

This I know: there is someone in this world who loves her. A mother or a father or brother or sister, sleepless with worry and seeking comfort in their hope that the sweet girl they know and love will be returned to their care come morning. Or a lover perhaps, searching madly for his sweetheart through the ruins of a village to the east, or picking among the dead littering the adjacent crop fields with a deep, scrambling terror needling his heart.

I shake my head and deny the desecrated beauty in the mud but, of course, this doesn't bring her back. She still lays silently, unmoving, sad and horrible the sight of her. Another ruined meadow in this strange place where some men live with malignant spirits stirring inside of them.

I surprise myself when I raise my pistol and send its message into the silent sky. A single shot to awaken soldiers everywhere, all down the line. Awaken, comrades and enemies alike, and the blurred men who walk the precarious trench-line separating one from the other. Awaken, and welcome another dawn, another endless day in our senseless existence together. Or perhaps my morning bullet is more simple than this, a song for a Murdering man, a serenade of warning scarring the morning quiet so that its roar might reach the ears of a single kind of man or monster, reminding him that he walks in a world alongside those who dare to damn him and the deeds he commits.

❄   ❄   ❄

Our lieutenant hollers for roll call as the milky half-light of dawn seeps into the sky along this area of Polish-Bohemian front near the village of Smolenska, fading the few stars and bringing into relief the lingering ghosts of bomb- and vapour-trails criss-crossing the heavens. We call our names in return as best as we can muster, voices hoarse from fatigue and the past days of constant screaming over the cacophony of the guns. In this way we learn that one of our company is missing. Burns, his cot empty, he and his gear nowhere to be found.

'What, did a German steal him in the night?' some fool calls, and the lieutenant's rebuke is swift and merciless. Rivers, Irving, and Spellman had taken turn at guard, had noted no disturbances during the wee hours. I look to Burns's place in the trench, see the abandoned cot, filthy and worn, and the faded British emblem sewn into its threadbare fabric, and I wonder. I wonder at the strength of his allegiance or fortitude, and I wonder which stretch of front he scampers across now, or whether he's stowed away inside the empty hold of a supply truck headed far away, and fast.

And I'm overcome with a sudden urge to wheel upon my heel, a showy pirouette in the muck of the trench, and send a salute after him, vigorous and genuine. Instead, I only turn my eyes towards the east, where the sun is clearing the crooked horizon, looking for the all the world as though it's setting its touch to this land and cleansing it with fire.

❋   ❋   ❋

Stumbling on the place is like discovering paradise.

I walk with weary steps through the meadow like an oasis in the destroyed desert of Bohemia. My knees quiver and the feel of grass upon my heels is like silk. We'd removed our boots several minutes ago and revel in this nearly-forgotten feeling.

Flowers stir in the breeze: white rose buds grow wild, a scattering of virgin moths moving in all directions. Round-topped trees surround us, and apples bob in their leafy reaches like glistening holiday ornaments. We scamper about, silent in our stunned revelry in case of snipers sitting among branches, and munch on fruit as we skulk forward. I sniff and it's there, the faint tinge of smoke drifting into this place from some distant burning village or knocked-out jeep or tank husk. I forget about its cancerous presence soon enough and begin to enjoy once more the impossibly pleasant air on my cheeks and the luxurious feel of the verdant carpet beneath my feet. I crunch into my apple and reach for another as I pass beneath the overhanging branches of a bountiful tree. Its juice is refreshing and delicious and I thirst for more.

I start at a rustling from above, snapping my Stensa into the air. I see them and relax, and let the smile settle upon my face— a pair of birds dancing upon a branch overhead, stirring the leaves. They're of a species I can't name; I've never seen their beautiful kind before, all vivid crimson and lush emerald, with a touch of silvery-blonde feathers around their necks like some glimmering royal headdress. They turn their small obsidian eyes upon me, cocking their small, rotund heads curiously. I learn that they are songbirds and their song is one that adequately accompanies their meadow-home, a soft and gentle warbling that soothes the ears after so many past days of guns and cannon fire.

I watch them awhile, mesmerised by their stirring music, and when they drop like small winged fruits from their branch and flutter off into the warm air currents I imagine that I see a sprinkling of glittering dust in their wake, enchanting and surreal. I turn to my companions spread out in formation around me and see McCall in rare form—rifle discarded on the grassy earth, smiling wondrously at the small creature he holds cupped in his palms. I approach quietly, not wishing to ruin the magic of the moment, and stare amazed at the animal with its chestnut fur, spotted with silver and magenta, its small, dark eyes blinking up at us fearlessly. 'It's just a baby,' McCall whispers, and the smile in his watery eyes is enough to make me smile too. The animal scoots nimbly along his forearm and upwards onto his shoulder, where it remains perched like some charming ornament or insignia upon McCall's filthy uniform. I watch and must blink several times to make certain that my eyes don't deceive me and yet still I'm unsure. Is it a brief but emphatic salute the creature delivers us, rearing upon its tiny hindquarters and lifting a small paw to the side of its head in so uncannily human a gesture? Then it leaps upwards, grasping for the low-hanging branches and scampering into the lush reaches over our heads, lost in the greenery and taking all of its mystery along with it. We've never seen anything like it, equal parts chipmunk and bush baby and some nameless creature we can't begin to guess at. And I wonder at the mysteries hidden in the cracks and folds of the world.

I step away from McCall and leave him to drift in his own daze of wonder. I swing my mud-sodden boots by their laces and whistle a tune softly. No war song this but a radio ditty that my girl and I often cuddled to while swinging on porch swings. A ballad of love, hopeful and frightened and forlorn. A pair of butterflies arrives suddenly, attracted perhaps by my serenade. Large and bright, they beat a silent flutter in the air with their purple wings like velvet, sparkling iridescently in the sunlight and falling in beside me as I walk onwards.

I remove my notebook from my shirt pocket and open to a fresh page. I think that I will scratch away a poem here for my girl, so that I can convey to her this figment of fairy tale surprise that

I've been fortunate enough to stumble upon. I feel the gentling touch of the air on my cheeks, rejoice in its caress. I must push onwards for the poem that I know lies within me, past its central theme and the sole, simple way my mind urges me to convey it, with the ineloquent and overt directness of, 'I love you, my darling, and I miss and long for you and our old togetherness like a bubble.' It's a challenge that I'm up for, what with the breeze and sunlight touching me, and the apples and flowers impossibly in bloom about me serving as unexpected muse during this extraordinary moment of respite.

And then my bootless foot brushes the cold landscape of the arm in the grass and a chill wracks my body as I look and see its pale blue colour embedded in the green. Suddenly the birdsong is silent about us, and a tinge of smoke-smell returns to haunt my nostrils. I turn my eyes upwards and look and find him in a moment, the owner of this stray arm, several feet from where I stand, now unmoving. The boy had been eight years old, perhaps, when the shrapnel found him. He is blue-grey and shrivelled, an old man's visage mocking his small number of years. He has but the one arm, and one leg is shorn at the knee as well, but I scan the immediate area and there is only the single appendage before me. Where his limbs might be, I do not know. Images of them tangled among the branches of one of the surrounding trees come to me unbidden, tiny fingers curling around budding leaf, and I shudder. This place of silence and serenity should bear no such awful fruit among its delicious apples and lush, lofty reaches.

I think of my darling girl back home in a Kingston so remote it may as well be a fragment of memory from prehistory's dawn. The taste of salt is in my mouth as tears trail down my soot-swathed face. I replace the notebook into the breast pocket of my soiled shirt and the pen inside my coat. I stand rooted where I am for a moment, beside the torso of the boy, and let my tears fall like sun-lit beads onto the grass.

I go on only when I feel the gentle hand on my back, Rodney's ginger, stealthy touch of comfort. Then, together, we walk onwards through the ruined meadow, like the shadows of once brave soldiers through a blasphemed fairy tale country.

*   *   *

I'm secluded in the aperture of the trench wall, urinating into a mud-pool when I spy him.

Like a vulture or sentry of stone he stands immobile atop the lip of the trench, among the ruined pillars of wood and flattened barbwire netting. His profile etched as though from granite, his expression stoic as he surveys the fields to the west. One leg is propped atop a crumbled wooden slat-board, giving the Murderer a heroic attitude as he scans the scene before him.

I finish and button up but remain where I am, secluded inside the earthen crevice. Murderer McCall doesn't see me in my nook inside the dirt wall. He doesn't know that I'm watching him as he raises a steady hand to his temple, performing a salute to the ravaged country of No Man's Land. He maintains this posture for fully one minute before climbing into the trench and slinking along its flooded path towards the south.

I clamber up the rough-hewn earthen wall and peer through the slats and steel wire into the fields. I steel myself, as though suspecting some awful vision to confront me. But no man stirs there. No soldier, enemy or comrade, nor any black skeleton dog roaming the eaten-up land in search of meat. No skulking *Fantasma de la Noche* like a chameleon married to the colour of the earth in his deceptive ruse, watching me through his sure telescopic eye.

I look and I look and then I see: the column of smoke.

Black and conspicuous, it's a viscous plume of jet rising from the mud a hundred yards in the distance. No shell has landed in this stretch of No Man's Land for many hours during this Time of Blessed Silence. No gunfire has echoed its din through these dismal reaches in quite some time. I stare at the black column, watch it pour into the overcast sky like some devious living thing, a serpentine stalactite creating a denser shroud over the landscape where it joins and colours the cumulus darker everywhere.

And beneath its pall, beneath its almost tangible weight, I clamber back into the trench and sag towards the north.

❄   ❄   ❄

I awake early, listening, and I hear the familiar song of my comrades drift to me like the ghostly sad vapour of smoke: 'We want home from these lines/The food stinks and we'd much prefer wine!/Someone fill our bellies!/Will someone fill our bellies!'

I crawl from my bag, numb everywhere with cold. I consider joining the group but linger in my place a moment, waiting for my sleep-befuddled eyes to grow accustomed to the milky light. Then, I hear him, and the sound of his voice and the things it says sends a crawling sensation along my arms and spine, as of a spider's legs scampering upon me, feather-light and awful.

'It was just like murdering children... little, weak children and old men and women...' I turn in my bag and see McCall squatting in the mud, shoulders hunched as he stares at nothing, his eyes glazed and far-away. Shark-eyes, killing-eyes, only now tinged with something like remorse and shame. He sputters on, a cold flame chilling me in the wee morning. 'And they just went up in flames, you know? Almost like they weren't even people at all... Until the screaming, right? Eh? The screaming, and *then* they were people. *Real* people... And the baby in the meadow. The baby animal, it was so small, so small...' And his sobs frighten me, their big, frightened sound on the AM air.

And, wishing to temper this land's population of monsters with that of men, I sit up and lay my hand upon his back, leave it there a moment, before walking off into the new day and leaving him with his newest mountain of guilt.

I claim my breakfast of tinned rations and hope my stomach will accept it. I chew mechanically and think of all the machines we've brought out here with us, the jeeps and transports, the tanks and half-tracks getting bogged down in mud and slime. I consider the enemy and realise once more the twisted nature of things. What, exactly, makes the boy-soldiers we fight every day and night my enemy? And what of the village and farm children, and their mothers and fathers? How are they an enemy to the Motherland's self-righteous claims of dominance?

I see Spencer's face in my mind and I hope, I hope dearly,

that he is truly a wiser man than this soldier, who sees less and less of noble acts during these interminable months in Hell.

Then, like magic or some unclear message of fate, the sky rains miniature flags.

A storm wrought by the Motherland's mighty propaganda machine, leaflets by the thousands and thousands descending as if from the heavens themselves, with their bold declarations, emblazoned with the familiar colours of patriotic crimson and blue.

'The British have won! Join the ranks of your King! Let him free you! The Lady Britannia shall protect you!'

We reach about us and snatch the sky-fallen magic in our cold-numb hands. Some of us are laughing, others only stare about mystified, confused. Still others only turn their eyes back to the stale food in their hands and force it down until their breakfast tins lie empty.

We stare about us long after the invisible planes have unloaded their cargo upon this ravaged land, silent, pensive, tired after another icy night of fitful slumber. And in the distance, not very far away at all, thunder booms in an anxious sky, and we know that a storm is brewing.

❋   ❋   ❋

The iron monsters scarring the horizon send a chill through our meagre ranks as we blink the residue of sleep from our dazed eyes. The hulking, massive look of them keeping their silent vigil, long steel snouts pointed into the milky sky. One of us whispers their name, awed, and we all tremble in our water-filled boots: *Löwen de Folder*, the lions of the fields. Heibenzer tanks like sentries watching our every move. Hell on Earth.

No one had foreseen resistance this deep inside Polish territory. We've been lulled into foolhardy confidence by our recent victories over the Czechs and Poles, and now our bodies are set to be churned up like raw beef halves by butchers' tools. No one had expected our worst fears to come alive in the early hours of dawn.

The German ground forces have arrived at last, their dark

myth has finally taken tangible form in the world of our war efforts. The way behind is sealed with corpses and barbwire and the vengeful neighbouring enemy. Only northward can we go, into the maw of the legions awaiting our march, and perhaps, if God is with us, we might slip through their horrific ranks and reach a quieter country.

When they unleash their fury they do so unequivocally. It is the roar of vengeance. It is Hell manifest and visiting upon us the wickedness we have dared to inflict upon those whose lands we have raped for these long war months. The lieutenant barks his senseless orders amid the roar and we rush forward as though our final vestiges of sanity have abandoned us at last. Our rifles are toys in our hands and I remember my backyard war games from when I was a child not so long ago, taking aim at pretend foreign enemies skulking behind the spruce tree, amid the shadowy skeleton of the garden furniture at night. Spaniards fell by my steady hand, and Germans too. By the tens of thousands I felled my enemies and here I fight now, teetering on the rim of sanity while all the fury of a wronged nation roars about my ears. The heavy knocking against my helmet is a rain of earthen debris.

Through this most inclement weather, I look and see him: Murderer McCall, rooted in the mud, arms spread apart helter skelter with his eyes wildly staring skywards. The look of rapture his face wears is frightening to behold, making his grin maniacal and distinctly removed from the pummelling reality of the moment, or else given up wholly to it. His mouth moves and although I can't make out his words from the din of shells pounding the earth all around us his posture is telling, and I watch his lips and I swear that they utter some words of challenge or invitation to the broiling sky over our heads.

Then, an explosion close at hand, flattening me into the earth, leaving me winded and disoriented and eating a mouthful of muddy water. I choke and sputter, vomiting grey liquid into my cupped hands like some worthwhile gift of the body delivered up into the chaos of the world. And then the transforming element of the smoke curls away and the alchemy wrought by the shell lies revealed.

He's crawling in the mud and slime before me.

The strangled cry is the Murderer writhing in the earth where shrapnel has found him and made a red ruin of his body and face. His legs have disappeared. He's dragging his amorphous mass of ruined body behind him, uncoiled intestines, prodigious tentacles of veins and muscle and shattered bone all unravelling as he inches forward through the mire, a morass of red and pink ruin like some hideous jellyfish slithering through the war field.

I watch aghast, frozen in my horror, as he edges closer to where I lay. When he's close his lips part and through their red-foamed ruin a sibilant sound issues, serpent-like and in no way human. This is McCall in some final form of transformation, irrevocable and preordained. The mad look lives in his stare still, a black fire malignant and vile, and I know that the Murderer crawls only to murder more.

I notice of a sudden that the tip of my Stensa is making a furrow deep into his blood-soaked cheek. The filthy barrel trembles as I quake in my terror. I consider the near-impossibility of pulling the trigger and ending his agony. His shark-stare fixes on my own, that old killing-stare, and within its wildness and ferocity I make my decision. I'm no judge of others. Neither am I executioner, except when that kind of decision will bring me closer to returning home.

I pull my weapon from the Murdering Wrathchild's face, holding his stare for a lingering moment, and then crawl on my way, into the thickening fray, leaving him behind me to discover his own fate.

The gigantic babies of the fields wail and wail. Their cries are full of fury and tinged with a melancholy timbre, deep and profoundly stirring. I wish to coddle them, to hush them with my small words and bring them back into silence and peace so that they may drowse in these filthy fields if exist here they must. But their fury only swells, rising like a storm on the ocean, and crashing like dirge after dirge on every side. Their fury is awesome to behold and within its clamour I feel myself shrinking despite my staunchest efforts to find sense among the enormity of the confusing, shaking Earth.

I think that I am still running forward over the crooked earth, my trusty Stensa thrust forward, head low to the ground in my stooped charge. I believe my progress is sure and swift as I circumvent the fallen boys and men around me, the smouldering craters in the soil where retaliatory artillery shells found their mark, the abandoned weapons and shredded pieces of flesh littering this terrain.

I think for a lingering moment that I am at the vanguard of the charge with the others, with sad Rodney and silent Rivers, with Irving of the soft eyes and Spellman, owner of the bellowing lieutenant's voice. Until my eyes focus beyond the haze of smoke and I realise that the shadows darting before me are those of low-flying German Zeiben-Adler III bombers huddled against the cloud cover, and then I know that I am lying motionless in the mud, upon my back, staring with bewildered gaze upwards at the frenzied motion of a grey sky spoiled with war. I watch the skittering movements of the German squadrons and their opponent Flying Adders, their erratic movements as their formations are pummelled by anti-aerocraft fire of both sides, sending some of their number flittering away like giant, wounded mechanical birds. A rain begins and I'm dimly aware of its ingredients: earth clods and stone, blood and pieces of men. A shrill screaming begins near to me, and turning my eyes slowly in their sockets I see through the crimson mist a legless soldier. It takes me a moment to realise that it's Rivers, howling awfully while working futilely at the muddy earth with his hands, seeking to pull himself along away from his incredible agony, knowing that he must leave the remains of his legs behind, wherever their pieces have come to rest.

I become aware slowly of the great pain engulfing my own arm and shoulder and sending shooting pain like a thousand needles stabbing into my neck and skull. Something burns in my flesh, a smoking heaviness, perhaps shrapnel embedded in muscles or sheathed in bone, perhaps only the great weight of guilt settling into my chest for the things that I have done which I had no right to do. I'm hit. I wish to tell the figures moving past me, hunched and with eyes staring vacuously ahead of them, but can't speak for the drowsy sensation overcoming my tongue, making it fat and awkward inside my dry cavern-mouth. And the numbness settling into the left side of my body, though I fear its quick progress, offers some small amount of comfort too. Wouldn't sleep, for even some portion of my weary body, be welcome at this point in the war, at this juncture in the endless day of running among bullets and dead men?

Staring upwards, I'm suddenly aware of them, silently amazed at their presence. When had they arrived in all of this chaos? For a brief moment only I see them there, a squadron of angels in virgin white filaments among the chaos of aerial movement! Their long eagle's wings are sleek, strong as they beat elegantly upon the air currents, weaving in high arcs among the zipping low-flying fighters and bombers. Somehow I can make out their faces, despite their high vantage, and they are beautiful: round and soft-looking, with a glimmer twinkling in each of their emerald eyes as they search among the charred landscape for the fallen waiting to be rescued. I reach a quivering hand skyward, hopefully, tears beading down my cheeks. Then a trailing stream of black smoke obscures their cherubic visages and the plane-filled sky of war is returned to mark the view of the heavens overhead.

I watch the chaos and hear its din all around me, and the epiphany is overwhelming as it arrives in my thoughts, clear and awful and awesome as a missile finding its mark. There you are, my sweet girl, flashing down on this pock-marked mudland, brilliant, fiery lights like flares, doing damage where it must be done. My darling girl, smoking down in coal-box and Jack Jefferson fashion, a murderous girl with the loudest and most mournful cries in the world.

I lay here, and the tears are rivers down my dirty cheeks while I wish for a bullet or shell to find me. This isn't the way I wanted it to be. My darling and I, our land was going to be fairytale pretty, and green. Among the dandelions and orchids we were to dance, hand-in-hand. Among the lilac and lily, chasing away the pesky aphid, an honourable enemy to the last. Beneath the candy-striped roof of a carb fountain as close to escape as we could build for ourselves.

The revelation overcomes me, and in its wake I'm numb with regret: our sole bond now, in this confused time and place, lies in the tumult of the bombs themselves raining down all around, sculpted by fair hands in fair homelands.

And I can only weep for what has happened to us.

I close my eyes to the war above and mouth the words silently, a final poem composed for her upon this foreign soil:

> *My sweet love, I am there with you now*
> *In garden serenity, sipping drinks, dappled in sunlight*
> *Your hand in mine as we stroll beneath the apple trees*
> *I am there with you in a day of flowers the way you love them best:*
> *Bright, in bloom, the murky lilac and the melancholy rose*
> *The cheerful dandelion and the everlasting juniper tree*
> *We are together again, and the world sings for us*
> *And the song is beautiful*

A shell pounds down close by and the earth quakes. I feel it in my bones, a rattle deep inside my skeleton. I'm afraid and clench my eyes shut to the horror of the din.

I think of them, all of her vivid children rooted in rich soil, free of tumult and death. Long rows nestled closely together, ranks bountiful and bright and belonging to no army but her peaceful garden family.

Here, in this mud and devastated earth, no such brightness lives.

Here grow no flowers.

Here is where bullets sizzle the air and erase my comrades from this awful and confused life we once leapt into hungrily and surely. Here I lay waiting for this same fate, with my heart bursting for you, my dear.

I dare to open my eyes.

I search the heavens for angels but find only war planes dancing there.

Then whiteness, blinding, and a quick descent into sudden blackness and no more.

❊　　❊　　❊

VI.

25 April 1935

My Dear Kindred,

Your love and friendship has taught me one thing over any other: the value in following one's heart. I have followed its beating when it loved you from the beginning. I followed it into this factory to toil for the Motherland.

It beats a new beat today, my darling, when it comes to all of this fighting. I promise to tell you all, and explain myself, when we are together again.

I love you, more than anything in all the world.

The thought of you returned to me brings with it all the joy that's filling me up today, in my chest and in my belly and in the deepest parts of me.

Waiting for you,
Your Rachel

❊　　❊　　❊

I posted the letter this morning and now I breathe easier. I've spent my shift trying to picture him reading my words weeks or months from now. I picture him crouching in a trench with his helmet on, reading my letter by torchlight. I picture him frowning at the mystery of the words and then smiling because it's his girl who wrote them, after all, and so he knows that he has nothing to worry about. And he blows me a kiss on the wind and off it goes across the Atlantic Ocean and through my bedroom window and right onto my cheek while I lay waiting to fall asleep.

I stow my dirty uniform inside my locker, close the door and snap the lock in place. Tonight, after dinner, I'll meet with my new friends. I'll tell mother and father another little fib and I'll meet the group at the house on Verona Road. I'll listen carefully to the things they talk about to make certain that I still feel that I belong there with them. I'll check to make certain that they still have kind eyes, not like the evil eyes the magazines give the Spaniards and Germans.

Outside, the sky has cleared. My heart nearly skips a beat at the sight of blue peeking between the clouds. The grass of the field is still wet from the morning rain but I don't care. I pick a handful of pale dandelions from the edge of the field. I have a small bouquet and the air is nice. I start off and think I'll get home slower than usual, because I'm going to enjoy the day. My stomach aches faintly, small pains that are somehow comforting as I walk, providing a gentle rhythm to my steps.

I squint at the running people in the distance. A large group of them, thirty or forty, maybe more. The Bandage Girls, running from the medical supplies factory. Running in lines like ants from an ant hill. I hear their shouts but can't make out their words at this distance. More and more of them are leaving through the open factory doors. I'm suddenly afraid and start walking more quickly in their direction. I want to understand what's going on, to learn why all the shouting and panic and running.

Then, I look upward and I see, and I understand.

If he were here, he'd see those plumes of curling black smoke and strike a chord in me with a moving line or two. My soldier is a poet too, after all. But what do I know of poetry? I know only of the fear squeezing my heart inside my chest and the shaking of my knees as I run from oncoming death.

I'm running along with the others now while the scream of shells roars overhead and the rattle of machine guns cuts up the air all around. I hear the cries of those around me, and they numb me with terror: 'Night Ghosts! This far inland! Oh dear God! The *Spanish* are here!'

I see a woman fall from the corner of my eye amid a cloud of dirt risen into the air. I run onwards, leaving her behind. The impact of bullets slicing the earth all around and another woman falls heavily to one side of me. Through the dust and flying bits of earth, I see the face of my darling. His is a sweet face, with kind eyes.

The moment is suddenly returned, I recall it as if it were only yesterday: the tall, thin boy framed in the carb fountain's sunlit doorway, eyes taking in the room with its sticky, colourful tabletops and lazy whirling ceiling fan, its summer flies and summer patrons, of which I was one. His eyes finding me right away and remaining upon me and only me among my whispering, giggling girlfriends. He watches me still, even as the image in my mind becomes another, the two of us strolling through the neighbourhood on a balmy night a little over two years ago while fireworks crackled among the July stars over our heads, what a show for young and old alike, and still his eyes watched me instead of the pretty explosions above. Then the stars are gone and we're kneeling in the dirt with flowers on all sides and I'm teaching him about their different names, the lilac and lily and rose and dahlia. His hazel eyes burn golden in the sunlight. The smell of flowers turns into the smell of popcorn and we're inside the Capitol Theatre in downtown Kingston. I'm letting him wrap his arm around my shoulders because the giant ape moving across the screen is scaring me frightfully with his terrible roars, crashing through the black-and-white jungles as a king of his land is wont to do. The trees and plants suddenly have their colour again, bright and green, and now we're under the moon on the farmer's field on the outskirts of town, close to where my darling grew up and it's the first time we kiss and his lips are on mine, the taste of warmth and bubblegum. My first kiss, from my first and only love.

Machine gun fire in the field, cutting up the grass and dirt, and my thoughts are torn away from my powerful daydreaming. Remorse fills me up like water inside my lungs. Remorse at not pulling away from it all sooner. Regret at not writing different words in all of my letters bound for Europe. Regret at not Resisting sooner.

I open my mouth: 'I am yours, my love.'

Until the end, my allegiance is to you, and to our union, and to no other.

His face is gone and in its place I see the cartoon eyes of the enemy as we've been shown them to look, narrowed and cruel. I wonder distantly whether this is in fact how they look or whether perhaps they wear more human faces, more like ours, masks of courage or pride or patriotism. I wonder vaguely whether they've been here for a very long time, these enemy soldiers and spies, blended in among us like chameleons or shape-changers the way the war notices always wanted us to believe. Watching us, studying us, just waiting for the ideal moment to strike and truly bring this war across the ocean and onto our continent the way we deserve or don't deserve.

I'm crying. A little girl running for home. My fingers tear at the insignia upon my uniform's breast. I feel it come free with some resistance, see it flutter on the air before me, a wash of crimson and white and blue on the air. I'm better rid of it. I hate it. And now noise again, and pain, and the field rushing up to meet me.

Through my eyes the world is awash with dust and light. The rain fluttering down around me baffles me at first, and then I realise: it's a flower-storm. Yellow petals fall around me. I'm still clutching remnants of the bouquet. Their scent is strong. Their smell is the strongest and most potent fragrance I've ever smelled. Wild flowers chewed up by the war that's finally found its way here to these gentle fields.

In the power of the flowers' smell I close my eyes to the noise all around. I'm content to sleep. A weight has been lifted from me. The thudding of guns persists. And machine gun rattling and roaring. There's a huge clapping and the earth shakes. At last. I know the sound of Jack Jeffersons exploding upon their targets.

Fire and pain.

And no more.

❋   ❋   ❋

VII.

3 May 1935

My dearest Rachel,

I'm coming home.

I write to you now from a mobile armoured surgical hospital in Svansk, Poland. Firstly, I want you to know that there is no need for you to worry about me: I'm regaining my strength and will be well soon, but I've also been wounded, in the arm. It's a bad injury, my dear, and I fear the sight of me thus marked by this war will cause you great pain. It happened during a battle near the Polish border; the Germans came at us but we came on stronger! We fought for the Motherland, my darling, but secretly, as ever, I fought only for you.

I've been brave for you, my darling, if not for this secretly foolish nation divided on two continents.

I'm coming home to you and your open arms—this is the news that brings me joy, boundless and wild! I will walk down our beloved Kingston streets and run once I reach your block of Randolph Avenue, where the spruces grow so lushly. I will run when I see you in your summer dress like a mirage of sunlight on the horizon. And then, together at last, all will be well once more.

I will crush you with hugs under the crabapple trees and blue Ontarian sky.

We will wait together on your porch every morning for the mail man to arrive with this very letter, and we will read it together, chuckling at my romantic words to you.

I love you, my dear.

Thank you, for without the promise of you the grey skies of this awful and stupid war would have crushed me too, like they've crushed so many others.

I'm coming home, my darling.

Rachel, Queen of Verdant Lands— I'm coming home to you.

Once a soldier, but eternally yours,

Kindred B. Green

Flag Day
by Adam Chamberlain

1 June 1963
New York, New York

Britannia's helm gleamed with a majestic golden hue in the late spring sunset as her namesake coursed through the foam at the mouth of the Hudson. She stood tall, resplendent and resolute, braced behind her Greek shield as though steeling herself to fend off any invading naval force that might challenge her. But who would dare stand against her, I thought as I gazed up at her awesome statue? Rising some two hundred or so feet high, the starburst of the Ensign of the British Empire emblazoned upon the escutcheon in her mighty grasp, here stood for me a welcome representation of home and all I'd left behind after the past ten days at sea, a proud and heart-warming presence. To others daring to enter her waters she would doubtless pose a more fearsome herald, her steely gaze a representation of the resolve that had built and defended the Empire through centuries past and to this day, whilst draped around her feet on the monolithic plinth crouched a predatory griffin, its tail frozen in a serpentine swirl and wings tensely poised, a steely gaze peering over its fierce, gaping raptor's beak.

Stood atop the decks of HMS *Britannia*, we saluted her and all she represented as we sailed past Victoria Island, even as my thoughts returned once again to the heart-wrenching decision that had brought me here. Nigh on a week at sea had taken its toll both physically and emotionally, but in this moment I couldn't help but feel optimistic. If the past days' voyage across seas that were so often wild and tempestuous had at times seemed bleak and

193

uninviting, to be greeted by this giant representation of a quintessential British icon cheered my soul with its familiarity. I'd not felt this good about my small part in this tour of duty since we'd left berth in Southampton amidst all the pomp and ceremony and the cheering, flag-waving crowds that only the reigning Sovereign's naval entourage could command.

❃   ❃   ❃

Even as the imposing New York skyline drew closer and we rounded into the harbour, I allowed my mind to wander back to other events of that day, as it had done on and off throughout our voyage. I'd never spent nearly so long at sea, or for that matter on any single journey, and it afforded me far too much time for reflection. And so my life, this secret other life of mine with another woman in London, seemed like a distant memory at times. Yet at other times thoughts of Janine were all that anchored me and reminded me that I had something other than my sworn duty to the Crown plus a nervous sense of the adventure to come. Here I was stripped of all personal life or background. I was simply Evelyn Wright, Liveried Helper to the Royal Household, just simple Eve to most who knew me and 'Evie' to those that fancied their chances, those that thought it would somehow flatter me to be talked down to so. The distance that I tried to maintain from them had led to me being labelled something of a curiosity amongst the all-male naval and military ranks, just about afforded a modicum of professional respect but for too many a focus of lewd jokes and behaviour, both to my face on frequent occasion and undoubtedly even moreso in my absence. Janine often railed on the injustice of life amidst this overwhelmingly male-dominated environment, mostly for the fact that we had to keep each other such a closely guarded secret. It was all I could do to keep her from exploding the details of our relationship just to prove a point at times. She was right, though. Being our true selves was confined to a secret life behind closed doors, and outside them we were often simply the playthings of the rutting men that surrounded us.

But at least here the need to keep things secret hadn't been so much of a problem, and I had found myself enjoying the relative simplicity of a more solitary life in the limbo of my mid-Atlantic cocoon. Had I but known that this glorious afternoon fell on the eve of the most terrifying day of my entire life and the epoch-making events to which I was to bear witness, then there would have been no solace in my arrival on a new continent. But no such knowledge of things that were yet to be tainted this moment, as is always the way with unexpected turns of events, and so here I was, dreamily drinking in the sight of the advancing New York skyline.

✷   ✷   ✷

The strains of the Royal New York Philharmonic began to reach us just then, breaking my reverie, and in that moment it finally coalesced for me that this voyage really was nearing its end and that my personal discovery of the American continent was about to begin. We were pulling alongside the pier and the skyline had now grown to fill my point of view, the spire of the Empire Tower standing out above all else. It was surreal to see with my own eyes a vista that was familiar to me only from black and white film footage or photos in newspapers and books.

The collected 'Fantasia on Sea Songs of the Great British Empire' struck another familiar, homely chord within me, and I risked the merest hint of a smile on that deck as the gentle breeze stroked my face with a warmth that hinted of summer just around the corner. It carried with it the characteristic smell of rope, tar and wood from the harbour that added substance to this journey's end. The sound of trumpet fanfares drifted across the bay and hung in the air like vague reminders of a far-off time and place. The dullness of the preceding days that had given way to an edge of nervous anticipation drifted away in the pure stateliness of this moment.

The orchestra sat in a semi-circle on the very end of the pier whilst to their side was a small audience of invited dignitaries and decorated war veterans in regimented rows. Beyond them in turn was a gaggle of journalists waiting to capture this historic moment that would appear in a host of publications across the

Empire and the rest of the world. A chorus of smiles, waves and celebrations that would appear in newspapers worldwide and prove only in retrospect to further underline the tragedy that was set to unfold so soon after this most auspicious of occasions.

Governor Lyman stood at the foot of a landing staircase accompanied by his wife, ready to receive the monarch by way of an official reception. Waiting nearby was his pristine Ben Bernard limousine, which was set then to whisk them away to Long Island Palace, his official residence in New York, for the night.

Tomorrow was the main event of the visit: a procession through the streets from the gates of the Palace all the way to the Empire Exhibition Memorial Centre in the heart of Queens. But the crowds were already here in force to see their Queen and her Royal yacht arrive back on British North American soil. From my vantage point they were a largely indistinct mass that stretched out beyond the barricades that lined the road from the dockside back into the heart of the city, but I could make out a sea of both Union and Jack and Stripes flags being waved aloft into the distance, and the cheers and applause of the onlookers underpinned the stirring sounds of the orchestra. It was almost like a mirror image of our departure from England, and if Westminster was often filled with dissident voices that spelled out the differences between the Royal subjects on either side of the Atlantic, it was so good to see that the average New Yorkers were here in such numbers to welcome us without reserve.

As we began to turn in order to berth at the dockside, the playful sounds of the 'Sea Songs' reached their climax with 'See, the Conquering Hero Comes'. That seemed somehow appropriate and was doubtless timed to precision as we drew up to the harbour with seemingly effortless grace. Moments later the orchestra resumed once more in grand style as the first stirring phrases of 'Rule Britannia' made themselves heard across the bay. I'd heard this a hundred times or more at any number of state occasions, but it felt like it had been written for this very moment.

❋   ❋   ❋

Queen Elizabeth herself appeared then, flanked by the Duke, and the deck shuddered beneath my feet as dozens of soldiers and sailors stamped to attention and offered their salute in response to the order barked by their commanding officers. I felt a little lost as a civilian spectator but found myself straightening my back too as I watched them pass and make a brief inspection of the troops. The Queen was as dignified and business-like as ever in a plain, three-quarter length yellow dress, matching hat and white, elbow-length gloves, whilst the Duke was clad in full dress uniform, his breast a farrago of medals, retaining the militaristic bearing that was still his trademark.

They descended the staircase to be greeted by the governor, and then as if also cued by the conductor of the New York Royal Philharmonic, a roar arose from the sky out in the bay and a Staverton bomber flanked by a pair of Flying Adders completed a low, thunderous flypast overhead, leaving a trail of red, white and blue smoke in their wake that hung momentarily and then slowly expanded out into the still, cloudless sky. The journalists got a brief photo opportunity with the Royal couple and the governor as they conducted a few more perfunctory greetings with the dignitaries, and then they were escorted into the waiting car and were gone. It was only as their car slowly drew out of sight that the mood on HMS *Britannia* started to relax once more.

❋   ❋   ❋

The fact that I had the opportunity even to be here at all was of course only down to the Queen's steadfastness. Here was a woman whose power, presence and resolve outranked all the males that surrounded her, and who as a Princess and heiress to the throne had famously bewitched and then tamed her husband the Duke. A war hero for leading a successful covert counter-attack against *Los Fantasmas de la Noche* across the length and breadth of his native British North America in 1935, Prince Harold was highly decorated and had a fierce reputation as a fearless soldier who suffered neither fools nor women lightly. He'd said himself quite publicly and openly that, as far as he was concerned, the latter were simply a subset of the former. Janine despised him, naturally.

The story went, though, that he was quite uncharacteristically besotted with Queen Elizabeth from the moment they first met, during her only previous visit to British North America in 1957 to mark the 350th anniversary of the founding of Jamestown. His war record had led to him being recognised as a full Cavalier of St George, the highest of all military honours, and he was only the tenth British North American to be accorded such a prestigious title. Princess Elizabeth, as she was then, was enchanted by his overtures and graciously accepted the many bountiful gifts he lavished upon her. Theirs was a whirlwind romance and they were wed the following summer, upon which he was afforded his official title as the Duke of Columbia. Their first child, Charles, was born the year after that. He had remained at home with his younger brother for the duration of this official Royal visit, accompanied at Buckingham Palace by the Royal nanny, with whom he had spent so much time in the few short years of his life.

Perhaps it was due to the War of Wars itself that the Queen and the Duke were so powerfully drawn together, and that the Queen had become such a representative figure of the steely resolve of an entire Empire even as a young Princess, often pictured helping out with the Royal Engineers during the war effort. Out of such bloody and devastating events, their future together had in a sense been forged.

It's not something that I'd ever experienced, and I envied the tale if it were true and not simply some media-spun fairytale: to be so sure of your destiny and your future partner that such decisions and events fall so perfectly into place. To many people I have known that would be a curse, to others simple naivety, but I always felt a need to see the road ahead clearly stretched out in front of me: straight, true and certain.

＊　　　＊　　　＊

There was to be a further example of Queen Elizabeth's strength of character—or, as some would have it, overbearing nature—in the weeks leading up to our departure. In the finely tuned detail of arrangements between Buckingham and Philadelphia Palaces, the governor had accorded that protocol dictated his very own Horse Guards should provide protection to the Royal party throughout their tour of British North America. The Queen, however, had other ideas and was insistent in wanting her own Guards alongside her. She could be so very headstrong in such matters, even moreso since the War of Wars and her wedding, as though she had drawn an inner strength from both victories.

Moreover and perhaps more importantly, certainly to my own part in this tale, she was insistent that it be her own prized horses that pull her and the Duke on the many processions through the streets and towns of British North America that were planned for the coming weeks and months. Meanwhile, in full knowledge of her love of all things equine, the governor had been lining up a showcase of many of the fine breeds that British North America had produced since the days of the frontier to present to the Queen on her travels: from the Ungava Saddlebred to the Sioux Cream Draft, the Appaloosa to the Montana Ranger. Whilst he knew well of her affection for horses, his major blunder was in his underestimation of quite how much pride she placed in her very own Windsor Greys and in her resolve to travel with them everywhere she went, even this far afield to another continent. A brief diplomatic impasse had then marred arrangements, but its resolution was never really in any doubt. Within a matter of days Queen Elizabeth II got her way and so here I was too, having been requested over Janine to join the entourage. That had seemed odd to me in itself, since she was more experienced than I, although the reason was to become clear soon enough.

Her Royal Highness was a regular visitor to the Mews, taking a genuine interest in the welfare of each and every one of her horses. By tradition she gave each one their name, also selecting the six that were to accompany us, each of them named for the Scottish islands of which she was so fond. Bruray and Housay were brothers, veterans to state occasions and her personal favourites, having been the same two horses that drew both the gold coronation coach in 1955 and Victoria's phaeton carriage on her wedding day. Scarba and Benbecula were their half-brothers, with their youngest relatives Faray and Westray here as reserves.

*   *   *

And so it was to the preparations for the procession to which I was to turn all my attention as soon as we docked. All six horses needed to be transported to the stables annexed to Long Island Palace, then groomed and exercised, something I could finally do properly now that I could take them ashore. A carefully choreographed schedule then had me up at 4AM tomorrow morning to prepare them for what was set to be the grandest single day of the entire tour.

Riding back on solid land was an odd experience for me at first as we made our way to the stables. I rode each horse personally rather than transport them by horsebox, even though this added time to the task; I was as keen to have them feel the ground beneath their feet again as I was myself. Maybe it was their own time at sea that had their first steps on American soil feel so tentative, so uncertain, or maybe they simply empathised with my own apprehension. It seemed to help the further we rode, especially since New Yorkers continued to stream to the dockside all evening, vying to see HMS *Britannia*. We were always a curiosity to tourists back in London, but here that was amplified manifold. Even Bruray was tense, and he was usually unshakeable.

*   *   *

Bruray and the others settled in their temporary home eventually, and I had been given accommodation in a spare flat directly above them. It was approaching midnight by the time I left the stables and I was just climbing the steps, eager for a few hours' rest, when I was rudely impeded. I had paused to take in the sight of the moon hanging dramatically in the sky beyond the silhouette of Britannia, still visible out in the bay from this vantage point, only to be interrupted by the shout of an all too familiar voice calling my name—or rather that version of my name that always got my back up.

'Evie! Wait! Wait a moment.'

If I let out an involuntary sigh then I think I concealed it well enough as I lowered my gaze and greeted the man with a bland smile.

'Major King. Good evening,' I responded politely from the stairs as he hurried across the courtyard towards me. He must have been following me, I thought. He had no legitimate business being here at this time of night. I was outwardly polite in my greeting at least, but the knowledge of his behaviour, both now and in the recent past, had me on my guard.

'How many times do I have to tell you? Call me John,' he said smarmily, breaking into what I'm sure he considered his winning smile, the one designed to make the ladies swoon. I wondered how long he had spent practising that one in the mirror. To be fair, he was an attractive man, I suppose: fit, broad, tall, with carefully coiffed brown hair and a square-set jaw. He knew both me and Janine—although not half as well as he thought he did—since our paths often crossed around the Mews. He was a member of the Scots Guards, who were also here at the Queen's behest.

'Good evening, John,' I offered wearily.

'I was wondering if you would like to walk with me awhile this evening, to explore the city a little together?' he ventured.

'No, I'm sorry,' I replied. 'I have to get some sleep now. I'm up again in four hours.'

He was undeterred. 'Hardly worth going to bed at all, then, is it?'

'Be that as it may, this is me going to bed right now.' I turned away from him and started climbing the remaining steps. But he wasn't going to give up so easily. He never did.

'Then we can skip the walk. Even better.' He made for the foot of the stairwell himself.

'I don't think so, Major.'

He stopped on the first step, cocked his head. He was brimming with a sinister arrogance that I despised. So being polite wasn't going to work.

'Come on, Evie. We're both a long way from home, both here alone. I know you want this. I've seen the way you look at me when you think I don't notice.'

'You're mistaken, Major.'

'I don't think so. I think I know what you want better than you know for yourself.' He made again to follow me up the steps. I shifted the tone of my voice at this point. I think it was half out of exasperation and half from fear, but my replies became more clipped.

'So what is this? We have a two minute innuendo-ridden conversation in the New York twilight and now you think you're somehow entitled to spend the night with me?'

'It's not like we've known each other only five minutes! We've been here before, Evie. You know where it's been leading between us. It was just a matter of time. It wasn't easy to make sure you came here, you know. A little gratitude wouldn't go amiss.' And there it was, the answer to the question as to why I was here at all; Major King was well connected for certain. He ventured up another step. I felt suddenly nauseous but there was no time to waver.

'We've been having the same conversation on and off for months, Major, always initiated by you, and it's never gone beyond that. Have you never wondered why that is? You don't know me at all.' I felt the tremor in my voice, hoped it wasn't too apparent.

'Well, you really are finding a little spirit, aren't you? I like that in a girl.' Still so sure of himself, but he paused in his ascent.

'Yes, well, there's a little too much testosterone around here for my liking.'

'Are you sure about that? I have plenty to offer.'

'Goodnight, Major.' I rolled my eyes, turned and strode away to the door to the flat, fumbling with the key in the lock. I wanted this door between me and the major now.

'Have it your own way, then.' His own tone had switched too, just like that, no longer charming, still full of arrogance but now with added venom as he shouted up at me from below. 'I think you're more into those horses' huge dicks than you are men's! Am I right? Turned on by the smell of horse shit too, I suppose, are you?'

I found the lock, turned the key, hurried inside and slammed the door shut behind me, all but blocking out his voice. I made sure I had locked it again quickly and leant myself up against it for a good minute or two. My heart was racing and for a few long moments I struggled to catch my breath. But I heard nothing more from outside; at least Major King had gone.

＊　　　＊　　　＊

I struggled to settle after that near miss of an encounter. I read for a short while in the claustrophobic seclusion of the flat before turning in, although the sonorous lines of celebrated poetry were to me at that time but formless words on a page. My mind was elsewhere.

The book had been Janine's parting gift to me: a rare first edition of W. C. Lumsden's *Exile of a Scandalised Bohemian*, a collection of 'lost' journal entries and poems. It was in almost mint condition and whilst she knew of my love for antique books in general and poetry in particular, I had to wonder if she'd not selected this particular collection due to the encroachingly weary turn of phrase with which the poet described his journeys across the American continent at the end of the last century. She was given to that, beguiling acts of kindness or generosity that veiled some more insidious message and which betrayed the vicissitudes of her personality. It seemed to me at times that nothing she did could ever be an entirely unselfish act. Her intent with this particular gift was clear to me: to make known her view that this tour of British North America would bring me nothing but disillusionment and loneliness. I had chosen to exile myself as far as she was concerned, to lose myself and ultimately to be forgotten. Forgotten by her, was she intimating? She could be so infuriatingly oblique at times, and that only inflamed my imagination.

As my mind wandered from the book and Janine's reasons for gifting it to me, I found myself musing on our first meeting. We got together only as chance brought us to work alongside one another as part of the livery staff at the Royal Mews. It was not something I had ever sought out for myself. If I had some pre-existing latent attraction to women, then it was something that had never even occurred to me until she later confronted me with it so directly. That's how I always understood it to myself, but then again I do remember her appearance quite vividly from the first time we laid eyes on one another. She was quite tall—around five foot eight or so—and imperial with it, bearing her height with confidence such that she seemed taller still. Her long, dark brown hair always hung loose with its natural curls as it fell around her broad shoulders and down her back. Her ample breasts were evident even beneath the constricting overalls she was wearing, but it was the classical bone structure, full lips and wide, brown eyes that I noticed and coveted first of all. She was beauty as I wished it for myself; I stood shorter than her by four or five inches, with more rounded facial features and coarse, black hair that took much more effort to style than I would have liked.

As we engaged with and came to know one another better, it was her tenacity as much as her physical beauty that came to win me over, a confidence that seemed to come effortlessly to her yet mixed for the most part with a charming humility. That we fell so deeply in love, though, seemed to come as much as a shock to her as it did to me. We revelled in one another and the time we spent together, both at work and then increasingly so away from it too. Our roles at the Mews dictated early starts, nearly always before dawn, and so the waning cover of night was so often an ally in our illicit affair. It was as well that our charges had no voice, as the Queen's horses witnessed more than a few moments of carnal passion as dawn broke over the Royal Mews. It never felt wrong or inappropriate but in the eyes of the law it was, leaving aside how it would have been received by the establishment given our proximity and servitude to the Royal family.

I still have that Lumsden first edition about the place somewhere but it's packed away in a box rather than on prominent display on the bookshelf as perhaps it deserves to be. It's just that I can barely bring myself to look at it even now, for all the associations it calls to mind and for the fact that Janine was to be proven so right in her intimations.

✳   ✳   ✳

This should have been an opportunity for my first spell of unbroken sleep for a week or more given the absence of the Atlantic swell, but instead I lay awake into the night thinking of Janine, the muffled sounds of occasional traffic, unfamiliar in recent days, skirting the periphery of my thoughts without ever distracting me from them entirely, as much as I would have welcomed the reprieve. I felt the slow passage of time.

I have always had this acute awareness of time, manifesting itself in an uncanny ability to guess the hour to the minute that perhaps owed as much to a vocation beholden to such very specific schedules as it did to any innate sense. But it also applied to the passage of time on a grander scale, to the chronology of my own life as I perceived it. I'd spent several years living in and based out of London, scratching around trying to find my place in the world, some peace of mind, before I met Janine. We'd been together almost a year when the opportunity to be here had arisen, and for all those weeks and months our relationship had changed in that one moment. Our lives veered down a new path on the day I dared to suggest to her that I would accept this tour of duty.

Overtly at least, her main objection was that I had been offered the role over her in spite of her superior experience and that this therefore constituted nothing less than a betrayal of her by me. But as bemused as I was to receive the offer in place of her at the time, I also knew that she always had something of a possessive streak to her such that the fact I had chosen for us to spend so long apart was a huge deal to her. It opened up all kinds of issues that perhaps were there all along, imperfections in our union that had been glossed over in the rush of a blooming love affair, then with the daily routines that grew out of that. In the moment a decision formed in my mind to accept the post and I subsequently articulated that to her, I set in motion a chain of events that would set us thousands of miles apart, and that ensured nothing would be the same ever again. I wonder in retrospect what prompted the choice I made. The remembrance of a desolate Janine accompanying me to Southampton only to beg me not to leave, behaviour so at odds with her usually self-assured nature, haunted me at nights still, and this night was to be no exception.

I continued to pore over these recent events and the choices that had brought me here, and it occurred to me that sometimes the longer you agonise over something, the blinder you become to the matter and the more likely you are to make the wrong decisions for everyone concerned. It was the kind of thought that lingers in the mind at such an hour and refuses to give itself over to reason, that in the cold light of morning can seem foolish and misguided. Regardless, in the early hours I finally drifted into a fitful sleep, haunted by dreams of our history together both as it stood and as it might otherwise have been.

✳   ✳   ✳

I can only have slept for an hour or so when my morning call came, rousing me into a fitful semi-wakefulness such that I was grateful to be able to leave the confines of my bed. There was much to do, many preparations to be made: harnesses to be waxed and polished, feeding, grooming and exercise for all the horses to ensure they were limbered up, and then to dress them ready for inspection at 7AM. Bruray and Housay were the first choices to pull the carriage, but if there was any doubt whatsoever about their fitness then I had to be certain that each of the others were ready to step in at a moment's notice. All six horses therefore had to be prepped as though they would be taking part in the procession.

It was almost twelve hours later that the procession itself would begin. The Queen and Duke were to set off at 3PM from the Governor's Palace, from there taking a slow route through the centre of town, pausing for an artillery salute in St George's Park and then on to the Exhibition Memorial Centre in Queens, arriving on the dot at 5PM for a drinks reception. That was to be followed by a dinner hosted by Governor Lyman, the Mayor and dozens of assembled politicians, dignitaries and honoured veterans of the War of Wars. There the evening would culminate in the presentation of the Order of the Americas to Her Majesty, commemorating this twenty-fourth anniversary to the day of the signing of the Treaty of Wurzburg.

It was a little after the hour of 7AM by the time I had Bruray and Housay groomed, harnessed up and ready to be inspected. The Crown Equerry and the Master of the Horse, Sir Roger Penry, along with one of the Royal Coachmen, were there at the Palace Mews impatiently waiting in the yard for the inspection. But the nerves that had set in as usual for me in the final preparations, exacerbated by the absence of Janine alongside me, dissolved into wonderment as I led the horses from the stables and caught my first sight of the carriage in which the Queen and Duke were to make the journey through the streets of New York.

I knew a little of the craft and legacy of the carriage-makers from Janine and more from recent newspaper coverage on the subject, but it took no such prior knowledge to recognise that this was a thing of exquisite craftsmanship. Officially titled the Columbian Landau and hereby presented as a gift to the Queen by the governor, it was an open-topped coach fashioned exquisitely from East Texan ash and sugar maples from Quebec. Pristine and gleaming, it was glazed in black, the Queen's crest taking centre place on the doors on either side and flanked in turn by the seal of British North America. Along each side of the carriage and at the rear were smaller and yet more intricate carvings, every one representing some defining image from each of the territories and provinces, and also gilded in gold: here a steelhead trout from Drakeland, there a Lakota bison alongside a polar bear from the Arctic Islands Territory. It was often said these days that the art of coach-making was dying out, but this was the work of master craftsmen who understood the legacy into which they were taking their place. The Columbian Landau was destined to travel back with us once the tour was completed and would take its place in the Mews alongside several others from across the Empire. From my first glance it certainly merited its place there; this was a thing of beauty, and it was just another detail that would seem to have promised an historic and glorious tour ahead of us.

Its most distinguishing and startling feature was, however, the carving mounted at the front of the carriage: a huge, gold-gilded figurehead of Columbia and Britannia, arm-in-arm, each with their free hand outstretched forwards as if beckoning in whatever lay before them. I was afforded a few moments, as the inspection took place, to view the Landau and appreciate these details, and it was here at the front that I lingered. Was it me or did I see something of Janine in the features of Britannia as she was depicted here, in the lines of the face or the way her hair fell from beneath her helmet? Did I even recognise a little of myself in the visage of Columbia? Either way, here was a moment of perfect unity frozen and enshrouded in gold.

If I linger on these details, to revel in the features of a carriage-maker's artistry or some other aspect of the finely tuned preparations for that day during the hours leading up to that terrible event for which it shall evermore be commemorated, then I do so only to prolong in my mind a time when the prospects of happy endings were still tangible, when the crowd's mood was nothing but celebratory and before history was to be written in such a cruel and irredeemable fashion.

❋　　❋　　❋

I recall, then, that I had still been a little concerned that Bruray was unsettled, but both Sir Roger and the Crown Equerry were pleased with the inspection and congratulated me on my work, so the two steeds were harnessed up to the Landau. Already there was a considerable crowd at the gates of the Mews, but my work was not done yet. I had to remain here on standby until just before the procession, taking care of all the horses up to the last minute. And so the next several hours passed nervously. At one point I spotted Major King in full dress uniform pass nearby on an Ungava Saddlebred as he set out to take his post along the route. I avoided the obvious, lingering gaze he threw down in my direction and managed to look busy until he had gone. Finally, without any cause for concern and with Sir Roger happy that Bruray and Housay were both fit for duty, I was relieved and was able to take a few hours off. I was to meet the Landau at the far end of the route once the Queen and Duke had disembarked, but for a while at least could just be one of the crowd and enjoy the procession.

Exhibition Avenue was lined with crowds six or seven deep by the time I had made my way there, just as the procession was due to commence from the Palace. The sun was high in a cloudless, deep blue sky, beaming down upon a sea of Union flags intermingled with almost as many Jack and Stripes. The mood was boisterous yet celebratory, everyone just excited for their imminent glimpse of Queen Elizabeth II and the Duke of Columbia on this historic day. At this point, every member of the Royal Guard that passed by from time to time drew applause and cheers from the masses as well as a flurry of waved flags. Here was a celebration of all that was good about the Empire, a reminder as to why I did what I did.

My heart sank then as I suddenly felt an authoritative hand grab my arm and pull me to one side. I knew right away who it was. Was I to be haunted by this man? Little did I guess how much.

'Evie, what are you doing all the way back here?'

'Major,' I acknowledged, but that was all. I pulled free from his grasp as politely yet firmly as I could.

'Can't stay away from me, can you?' he teased me, full of that would-be charm all over again. It appears he had chosen to forget his final words to me of last night. I had not.

'I'm sure you have your duties to attend to, Major. Duties that do not involve me.'

'That I do, Evie, that I do. But you should be at the front just in case your favourite boys need you, don't you think?'

'That's not necessary, Major.' But it was too late, as he had already set about ordering the crowd in front of me to make way and let me through, insisting that I was here by Royal command or some such. He took the opportunity of having to physically guide me through to the barrier to manhandle me in all kinds of places as much as he possibly could, knowing I was hardly in any position to protest here. I apologised and offered embarrassed smiles to those that were bustled out of the way to make room for me, although no-one seemed to mind. It was as though they felt honoured to be close to someone who was obviously so important to proceedings. I didn't feel that way at all. I felt even smaller and more insignificant here thanks to the unwarranted attention, surrounded by strangers who had no idea of who I was but now offered obsequious smiles. I tried to avoid eye contact.

The major was now stationed just a few yards to my right and in plain view from where I was stood. His position and role were, ultimately, the protection of the Queen at all costs, but really in this scenario it was more a case of crowd control and to guard an escape route for the procession just to his right, should it be needed. All along the prescribed route at regular intervals there were allocated side streets that had been secured and were guarded in case of any kind of incident. This was standard for any such event and the result of intricate planning on the part of the Royal Guard in conjunction with the New York Constabulary. If any threat to the Royal carriage or entourage were identified then the Major's directive would be to help secure that route and to evacuate the Queen and Duke to safety. I was very much already aware now, though, that his attention was continually distracted towards where I was stood. I considered moving—if only I had—but was pretty much hemmed in by row upon row of people behind me. I did my best to ignore his leering attention and tried instead to focus on the revelry, but it was clear that he had placed me right by the barrier here for his view more than for my own.

❉   ❉   ❉

Over the next hour or so, dignitaries began to pass by, each with their own police escorts, including the governor's limousine, and as the excitement level amongst the crowd slowly grew, it was clear that it was the Columbian Landau and its passengers that they were awaiting with such expectation. Cheers went up from all around us as the sounds of the gun salute carried from St Georges Park to our position. The mood was infectious, and I allowed myself to forget about the major, for a while at least. When I did think to cast him a glance and check whether he was still ogling me, it seemed he had become bored or perhaps even angry once again at my spurning of yet more unwanted—not to mention unwarranted—attention. I was relieved at that, for the moment.

I had also found myself increasingly distracted as I waited in the crowd, looking at other people around me and on the other side of the street, imagining myself with them and how I might be as different versions of myself. It was something I often found myself doing in public at this time of my life, as though I was unfinished somehow, as yet undefined. I used to feel anxiety about how I would recognise the right people to invite into my life, the right people to be my friends and lovers, those with whom I could be the very best person I could possibly be, the person I was supposed to be. I think about it less now, although I was equally unsure as to whether I ever found any satisfactory answers.

And then, as the time approached a quarter to the hour, the buzz from further up the street roused me from this transient daydream and denoted that, finally, the Royal party were about to pass our position.

❋   ❋   ❋

The Landau was preceded by a half dozen of the Royal Guard in full dress uniform, the red plumes that sprang from the top of their gold helms making them appear even taller than they were. Another flanked each side of the coach and a further four brought up the rear. This whole group seemed to be marching slower than everyone else, at the precise pace in which I had rehearsed all the horses so many times, that I knew as if it were a part of me. It also, of course, afforded the crowds a good view of their monarch, who waved nonchalantly and constantly bore a broad smile, the Duke occasionally joining in at her side. He was in the same military uniform as I'd seen him in the day before, whilst today she was in full regalia and looked stunning in an off-the-shoulder pearl dress, with the Orders of George V and VI pinned to a blue silk sash slung across her left shoulder. She also wore the crown and looked every inch the living icon that she was known as around the world, just as the crowd expected. No-one in the world did this as well as the British, I thought to myself.

At this sight of the approaching party, the crowd around me and on both sides of the street went wild with rapturous applause and cheers. Union and Jack and Stripes flags of all sizes were held aloft: huge, rippling emblems in crosses and stars swaying back and forth in grand, broad strokes amidst smaller ones shaken in a dizzying blur by raised hands. The crowd shimmered with them as a wave of red, white and blue followed the Queen and Duke's carriage up the street towards where I was stood. Bruray and Housay looked resplendent, and having taken in the awesome view of the whole party as they drew almost parallel with my position, I took a moment's personal pride in them both. I have a strong remembrance too of wishing that Janine could have been there to see this with me.

It was at this very moment that I became aware of some bustling activity behind me. The transfixed crowd had naturally become more animated as people struggled to get the best view they possibly could, but even then I had a sense that something else was going on. And then I first saw him: a middle-aged man in an expensive-looking suit striking his way purposefully through the rows of people behind me towards where I was stood. It was as though he was heading straight for me, and I remember vividly being locked by the fierce gaze of his startling grey eyes for what can only have been a split second but in my recollection now seems much longer. What set him apart from everyone else was that in spite of his efforts to forge a path through the crowd he wasn't craning to see the Royal party, as were others around me, but seemed only intent on getting to the front.

I looked towards Major King's position, hoping now to get his attention rather than avoid it, but still it seemed he was now looking everywhere but in my direction, surveying the crowd and keeping a watch on the side street. He was doing his job now, at least, to a fashion. Neither could I see as far as the next guard up the street in the other direction, whilst those on the opposite side of the street faced directly away from me, concerned with watching the crowds there. People continued to part behind me as I looked about, not even affording this stranger a moment's notice, all eyes on the Queen's carriage as it processed right in front of us. Within moments he was right behind me and as he squeezed through next to me again his gaze locked with mine. It was at once resolute and yet emotionless. Whether he recognised the growing fear in my eyes or not, with his left hand he violently shoved me to the right in order to reach the barrier and I stumbled as he did so. His right hand was reaching inside his jacket, and even before he drew it back out and took aim at the Royal carriage, I knew he had a gun.

As I stumbled I cried out to Major King, hoping to attract his attention or that of another guard, but my voice was lost amongst the sound of the crowd, which was now at fever pitch. As I struggled to regain my footing, my fall broken by the sheer proximity of those around me, I called out his name again as loudly as I could muster and finally caught the major's attention. His gaze lingered on me rather than perceiving the true threat of the man next to me, and perhaps that moment of undue attention was in itself a fatal error. But in truth I lost all sense of time in the moments that followed as before I had a chance to do anything a trio of deafening shots rang in my ears, drowning out all thought and perception of anything else.

And then, pandemonium.

✳   ✳   ✳

Thinking back to that moment now I can only recall snippets, fragments of the seconds and minutes that followed; I lost all of that innate awareness of time in a swirl of madness. I can vividly call to mind individual expressions on faces frozen in my mind, motions to escape, to intervene, or somewhere between the two. And the face of the gunman himself for that moment that I had held his gaze: a blank stare that was yet so resolute. The major belatedly drew his weapon and sought to pick out the assassin, but the crazed motion of the crowd itself meant there was no way he could get a clear shot. There were screams of shock and panic all around, but above them I remember there was a single strain with the power to cut through them all.

The Duke turned to his Queen as she slumped backward in her seat, her pristine dress now soaked with blood, and crouched over her for a moment as though in a vain attempt to protect her. Then he stood and let out a cry that was somewhere between a wail of utter despair and a scream of uncontrollable rage and that pierced through the tumult of the rising furore. As he did so he whirled towards the commotion taking place around me. The gunman was trying to force his way back through the ranks of Royal well-wishers, some of whom were panic-stricken, screaming and doing all they could to get out of his way, but many of whom were physically barring his escape despite the fact he was still brandishing a pistol. It seemed I was caught right in the middle of all this, buffeted this way and then the other. But as the jostling threw my point of view back towards the street, I saw the Duke focus upon the point of the crowd's attention, pull his dress sword from its scabbard and launch himself in a single leap from the Landau and towards us.

Bruray was the first to rear up in response, confusing Housay to his side, who began to dance back and forth on the spot. They were, of course, all trained to react neither to crowds nor the sound of gunfire, but no amount of training could have prepared them for such a distressing and incomprehensible turn of events as this. The Duke's sudden, forceful motion as he leapt from the carriage only unsettled them further, just as the beautifully crafted carriage began to topple onto its side and one of its wheels buckled under the strain with a sharp crack. As the Landau began to fall, both horses veered over with it, thrashing and whinnying as they hit the tarmac. I vividly recall a moment amongst the mayhem wherein my instinct was to run and tend to them, but there was no way I could have even got close and I was still at the mercy of the crowd that hemmed me in. The Landau itself was rent asunder with the force of the crash, its hardy ash and maple splintering under its own weight to its ruination.

The reaction of the Royal guard to the front and near side of the carriage was at this point to protect the Duke, and it took three of them to wrestle him to the ground as he thrashed wildly to be allowed to wreak his revenge on the gunman. Eventually he allowed himself to succumb and to be led back to where the other guardsmen were tending to the fallen Queen, whose motionless figure was now sprawled unceremoniously in the street, just about still visible between the other guards that had dismounted and rushed to surround her.

Meanwhile, the gunman himself was being overpowered by the crowd as he struggled to break back through their ranks. The gun sounded again one last time into the air before he disappeared beneath several of them who wrestled him to the ground. I still knew where he was from the hail of fists and kicks that they rained down on him. Major King, now dismounted and accompanied by two other Royal Guards, forged their own way into the crowd and eventually managed to clear a space around where he now lay facedown and motionless. They drew their own weapons as they shouted for people to step away. I was glad not to be able to see that face again, not least since it was clear that in this short time he had been severely battered and bloodied. Nevertheless the lingering smell of burnt gunpowder from the discharging of the pistol hung in the air around me and made me feel nauseous.

I heard the Duke's voice cry out once more then and, even before I turned back again to see him stood over his wife, I knew in my heart in this moment that Her Royal Highness Queen Elizabeth II was dead, murdered in cold blood on this most auspicious of days, right before my very eyes. This leader of an Empire, this representation of youth and vigour and the future, now lay lifeless in a New York street.

※   ※   ※

Perhaps the strangest thing of all was how quickly silence fell on the scene, the deafening cheers stilled into a stunned silence. The flags were all still now; they had disappeared from view as so many hands lolled at their sides in dumbfounded shock.

Despite this reaction, I still don't know how the Royal Guard and the New York Constabulary maintained order that afternoon. Some people went straight home, as though they expected the city itself to erupt in the wake of such terrible events, whilst many more followed the ambulance that bore the Queen to the Royal Infirmary and crowded outside awaiting the inevitable news. Still more just lingered in the streets, inconsolable and uncomprehending as yet of the magnitude of what they had just witnessed. A silent kind of collective shock and grief seemed to descend over the city as one.

❉   ❉   ❉

Major King found me amongst the crowd within a few minutes and came over whilst the other guardsmen covered the top of the fallen gunman's body with a discarded Jack and Stripes flag. The major's face was white, yet his concern seemed genuine enough for once.

'Eve, are you alright?' His voice was shaky and I could sense he was trying to sound calm for my benefit.

'I'm fine, Major,' I gasped in reply. My shoulder hurt from where I had fallen, and I was clutching it with my other hand, but I still wanted no attention from this man. I did have need of him for one thing, though. 'Can you get me out to see to the horses?'

'Of course.'

He escorted me through the barrier and out to where Bruray and Housay were still lying in the street, and I began to tend to them. They weren't badly wounded, just in shock and in need of being unharnessed before they could get to their feet. It took a good half-hour to untangle them, and as I did so I was able to survey the damaged Landau. The two nearside wheels were completed smashed and their axels torn in two. The carriage itself had been ripped apart in several places, the ragged texture of the wood revealed now underneath the polished surface. A small pool of blood still stained the tarmac where the Queen had fallen. But the image I remember most of all is that of the golden figurehead of Columbia and Britannia, which had broken in two along its weakest point: where their arms had been linked. They each lay separately on their backs now, one arm broken off entirely and the other outstretched towards the sky.

After Bruray and Housay were disentangled from the debris and I was able to get them to their feet and calm them down, I took them back to the Palace Mews and spent a good couple of hours making certain that they were settled. The major was distracted as I left and didn't see me go, and that suited me. I found my comfort back at the stables amongst the horses and the familiarity of my duties. This was my first and foremost concern in the aftermath of what had happened, but it was only a matter of hours later that Sir Roger Penry himself came and found me in the stables. I had been identified as a key witness and ordered to report to the New York Constabulary Headquarters immediately. I had no wish to relive the events of the afternoon, but this was to be an even less pleasant experience than I had feared.

✻   ✻   ✻

A short, plump and unkempt man that introduced himself as Detective Chief Inspector Bob Baldwin met me at the police station, which was an imposing and similarly grubby building just down the street from the Exhibition Centre. He proceeded to guide me through an office that seemed to me a musty, dark and seedy looking place with papers strewn in chaotic piles upon desks. Maybe I only imagined the cascade of double-takes and barely disguised leering looks up and down as I passed by all the other officers and detectives present, many of them nursing cigarettes that clouded the atmosphere yet further, but it was behaviour I had come to expect as much as I despised them for it.

In spite of the attention being cast in my direction, it was certainly a hive of activity too, with vocostyluses ringing constantly about the place, and I was grateful to be led into the quiet seclusion of an interview room. Here I was offered a cup of tea, which I cupped in my hands for security as I sat at a plain table and recounted as best I could the events that I had witnessed to the diminutive detective, who sat opposite me taking copious notes. It was hard at this point for me to recall specifics in anything like the detail I have recounted here, with the questions continually returning to the description and behaviour of the gunman himself.

All that came back to me was that hollow expression, those staring and determined grey eyes.

Finally, DCI Baldwin abruptly ceasing posing questions, flipped his notebook shut, and stood up.

'I know this is difficult, ma'am, but please bear with me awhile yet,' he half apologised. I hated being called ma'am almost as much as I hated people not using my given name. 'There are some other people who want to speak with you.'

'What other people?' I asked suspiciously.

'Please wait here a moment,' was his only response. 'They'll be right in to explain their interest themselves.' And with that he left me alone in the room.

A couple of minutes later the door opened again and two very officious men in dark suits entered, one of them carrying a file under his arm with something printed on the front that I couldn't quite make out. They took a seat without introducing themselves.

'Miss Eve Wright of the Royal Mews, Buckingham Palace?' the man on the left asked. He had dark hair that was slicked back, revealing facial features that were hard and imposing.

'Yes,' I replied a little more curtly than I had intended. 'And you are...?'

'We have a few more questions for you, ma'am, in respect of the assassination of Her Majesty Queen Elizabeth II.'

Assassination. The word hung in the air as I slowly grew to understand the enormity of what I had witnessed. A sovereign assassinated on her own Empire's soil. This was unprecedented.

'We represent Her Majesty's Security Services, Miss Wright,' said the other man. He had short, blonde hair and a more sympathetic air. He was merely confirming my suspicions at this point.

'You're MI3, aren't you?' I ventured. I'd had a fair few dealings with MI1 and MI2 during the course of my work, especially the former given their domestic remit, and there was some trademark presence about these people that made it easy enough for me to recognise their sort, especially given the context. MI3 were new to me but I knew their area of responsibility to be limited to British North America itself. I felt at once empowered to have guessed their identity and sick with nerves as to what it meant that they were talking to me.

'Section 3. That's right, ma'am,' came the plain response from the first man as he exchanged glances with his companion. 'Ma'am, given your proximity to the assassin, we would like to show you something.'

At this, the second man placed the file on the desk in front of him, opened it and began to sort through its contents. I recognised the Military Intelligence insignia and the word 'CLASSIFIED' on the cover as the second man continued.

'The gunman was pronounced dead at the scene, and his face was badly mutilated by the crowd, making identification a little... difficult. Nevertheless, we believe we may now know his identity and need to show you this so you can confirm our suspicions.'

At this a black-and-white photograph was pushed across the table squarely in front of me.

'Was this the gunman you witnessed today, Miss Wright?'

I looked down at the face in the photo: a posed portrait of an attractive man with a relaxed smile. I still felt sick, but I also felt a rising rush of adrenalin. He was perhaps a few years younger in this photo, smiling and devoid of that hollow gaze that was to haunt me, but nevertheless I recognised him instantly.

'That's him,' I said.

'You're sure, ma'am?'

'Absolutely,' I confirmed. Then, a little surprised by my own boldness, I asked, 'So who was he?'

There followed a few seconds' silence, during which the first man carefully retrieved the photograph, placed it back into the file and closed it.

'Who was he?' I repeated.

'I'm sorry, ma'am, but that information is...'

'Classified, I know,' I said, finishing the sentence for him. As I did so, though, I reached across the table and made to grab the file. I did it without forethought but I think perhaps there was a part of me that was so desperate to know more, to understand who this man was that had pushed me to the ground in order to gain a clear shot at Her Majesty, that I lost my senses. After the day I'd had, I wasn't going to let either of these or any other men stand in my way of that knowledge.

The first man went to pull the file out of my reach but as he did so I rose from my seat, lunged forwards and clumsily caught hold of a corner of it. It fell from his grasp and photographs and documents spilled out across the floor.

In a moment I followed where they fell and was on my hands and knees, grabbing those closest to me. I caught glimpses of names, addresses and dates plus more photos of the same man alongside other people. One name was common to nearly all of them.

'Kennedy,' I read, even as the particular sheet of paper I had picked up was yanked back out of my hand.

'Ma'am, please step away,' was the brusque response I received as the men set about retrieving the documents one by one, both from the floor and out of my hands.

'John Kennedy. Son of the former Member of Parliament Joseph Kennedy,' I read from another typewritten document before it was taken from my grasp. It looked like some kind of record of military service.

'Ma'am, we won't ask you again. Please step away.' The second man grabbed my arm and pushed me backwards, away from the remaining papers and photos still strewn across the tiled floor. I noticed his other hand was on a holster within his jacket and so finally I obeyed. Still, my curiosity was far from sated at this juncture.

'You already knew he did this, didn't you?' I quizzed, aware of the edge in my voice now and making no attempt to disguise it. 'You didn't need me to do anything but confirm what you already knew. You have a file on this man. You didn't just prepare that today. It must have taken months to gather all that information. And yet you still let him get close enough to kill the Queen?'

The two men did nothing but exchange glances as I ranted at them until eventually the blonde-haired man held up a hand and spoke again in a long sigh.

'Ma'am, we can't discuss this. We thank you for your assistance and we are sorry for your obvious state of distress. Now please sit down and try to calm down.'

My moment of anger-inspired courage started to subside as I realised I was not going to elicit any information from these men and I sat back down. They were used to dealing with people far more difficult and far more dangerous than me. The two men, who of course never gave me their names, asked me once again if I was sure as to the identification of the man I had seen from the photo, and I was asked to provide a formal statement to the police. As I recounted the details over again and they were placed on record, I could see that face in the crowd imprinted even more clearly in my mind's eye. I could put a name to the face now, at least. This man, John Kennedy, had assassinated the reigning sovereign of the British Empire under the very watchful eyes of the world. What brought someone to such a decision, I wondered? What could drive a man to do this?

※　　※　　※

These very same questions haunted my mind later as I made my way back to the Palace Mews that night under cover of darkness, as they would continue to do for months and years afterwards. The details of John Kennedy and his family, who all vanished from their Massachusetts home soon thereafter, were confirmed and made public, but the mystery of his motive died with him.

There was of course much speculation in the media, which slowly uncovered further details of the family's background. Kennedy Senior had indeed been one of the select few British North American Members of Parliament and was a very vocal objector to some of the Empire's strategies during the War of Wars. He had tried and failed to invoke the Waller Unity Act of 1802 as a means of limiting British North America's involvement and quit his political career as a result. His other son, John Kennedy's brother, was killed on the African Front during the war. John Kennedy was thought perhaps to have been spurred on by the fall from grace of his father and the death of his brother, both the fault of a domineering British regime in his mind. Some of the people who had known him came forward to speak of him as a visionary who believed he had a better dream for North America, one free from British rule. They painted him as a peaceful activist, although the *Times* went on to claim that Military Intelligence was investigating the family on suspicion of their involvement in some sort of a cabal with the same mission. A more popular view was that Kennedy acted alone, based upon personal motives. Ultimately no-one knew, just as I came to learn that no-one can ever truly know what is in the hearts and minds of even those closest to them.

For my part, as I walked alone back to the Palace, I witnessed one final image that remains with me forever from that fateful day, an image of deserted streets peppered with discarded miniature flags, many of them trodden into the dirt as the former revellers had deserted the streets of New York.

❋   ❋   ❋

Two days later saw another, more sombre procession through the streets of New York as the Duke led the cortège on its stately journey to the harbour. Scarba and Benbecula pulled the gun carriage on which it lay as I had asked that their half-brothers be allowed to rest. Once again crowds lined the streets, perhaps even deeper than before, but there were no flags on display now save that of the Queen's that draped her coffin, hiding it from view. Gone too was the excited background hum of expectant crowds, replaced now by a reverential silence broken by the occasional sob or shocked cry of grief.

Some threw bunches or garlands of flowers in the path of the procession, and they fell on the coffin or onto the road to be trampled by the horses. They were alike to a shower of tears, such that it seemed the Queen was now an island swimming amongst the floral tributes. Others merely bowed their heads as the cortège passed them by. It seemed to me that there was something of a sense of shame too, deep shame that such events should come to pass on the streets of their city and on what should have been such an auspicious occasion. The Duke was stoic throughout, his features frozen in a steely gaze that seemed distant or disconnected. I'm told that once back onboard HMS *Britannia*, he remained in his cabin and did not emerge or even speak until the ship arrived back at Southampton, but whilst in the public's gaze on this day he remained utterly unmoved. Later I imagined him in that most private of moments, deep within Buckingham Palace, a man racked with guilt explaining to the Prince Regent that his mother would never return from that distant continent. This tiny child who was now King-in-waiting, who would know no life other than that of duty, not even to grow up with his mother—extraordinary as she was—to witness it and to be there for him.

❊   ❊   ❊

My dreams of discovering British North America for myself in tatters, then, I went home to Janine, at least for a while. We tried to work things out, but we were too distant from one another by that point. I had learnt that time can do that to people sometimes. It can bring people closer, realise that they are stronger together than apart, or it can cause two people to drift from that togetherness and realise that they clung to something that never really existed in the first place, and that's how it was for us. Still, I also understood that it is not physical distance that unites people or drives them apart, but something much more internal, a psychic distance.

For his part, Major King resigned his commission, blaming himself for the assassination and that it should happen on his watch, right before his eyes. There were moments where I blamed my own distracting presence for his error, but then I quickly dispelled such thoughts whenever they occurred to me. He was overly harsh on himself, but he was always such a proud man given so wholly to his duty and so perhaps this response was inevitable. We stayed well clear of each other, each for our own reasons I suppose, and I never learnt what became of him after that.

Janine and I went our separate ways a few months later, Janine leaving the Royal Mews whilst I felt that I somehow honoured Queen Elizabeth II's memory by still tending to her legacy of Windsor Greys that continue to reside there and serve the Royal Family to this day. I never regret the time Janine and I had, and she taught me much. In many ways—socially for one—she was ahead of her time, and I wonder if things might not have been different for us had we met one another two decades later, by which time attitudes had become somewhat more liberal. It was too late for us, though, as events had conspired against us and we were destined to become strangers once more. Our lives, propelled forward by pain and contradictions, were set to career off in new and separate directions. Sometimes I wonder if we were to meet again now and fall in love all over again with the wisdom we each would have accrued in the intervening years, whether we might be more right for each other, better able to make a life together. Maybe our paths merely crossed at the wrong time for us. It's something I still question now from time to time when it comes to Janine and I. I wonder who we might be if we were together now, but then I usually tell myself it hardly matters anymore, whether or not I believe that to be true. I do know that I can trace my life back to this point as that when I ceased to look forwards as often as I looked backwards.

❈   ❈   ❈

This was my first and only trip to British North America; I could never bring myself to return to those shores. The streets of New York and by extension the entire continent had for me been forever tainted by the Royal blood that had been spilled onto them. A single moment that wrought tragedy from celebration, that tore the glorious heart from the Empire, occurring alongside events that on a smaller scale had changed the course of my own life in the process. In the weeks that followed, as it became clear to me where my relationship with Janine was headed, I had begun to question what life might become without the woman I loved at my side. Who would I now become? And what would the Empire now be without her Queen? My memory of the Americas will always be poisoned by three devastating gunshots that cut through the flag-waving and cheering crowds on a bright summer's day and changed everything.

One final memory that stays with me to this day came as we sailed back out from the harbour and emerged from behind Britannia's long shadow as cast by the evening sun. The Royal yacht forged out past her into the wild, unpredictable Atlantic swell and this time I saw beyond that half-familiar visage and was struck simply by her grand illusion of amaranthine protection. She stood against any and all invading forces but could not do so against the ideology and resolve of one man determined to make his mark upon the world in the only way he felt he still could.

The Sun Yet Sets
by Joe Tangari

16 September 1983
Hartford, Connecticut

I looked at the gun, then at Dirk, and back at the gun. No shot from that thing at this range could leave anyone less than dead.

If Dirk was thinking similar thoughts, he hid it well. 'You hired us to put this show on, and we did it. We expect to be paid for our work.' He jabbed a bony finger in the face of the club owner. 'You Unionist, Tory cocksuckers are all the same. Falling back on a gun when you've nothing to say for yourselves, and the bloody police will support you.'

The owner seemed unimpressed by Dirk's show. 'Listen to me, Joe Putrid, or whatever it is you call yourself on stage. I booked you for a show. With music! I don't know what you call all that slop, but music it ain't. And you've bloody well cost me a fortune tonight in damages, inciting the crowd like that and getting the police in here. I ought to shoot you purely on principle.'

Dirk backed off a bit and turned to me. 'What do you think of all this, Eliot?'

I was in no mood to spend another second in that club. The mixed smells of lager and blood were making the room spin and aside from that my hands and most of the rest of my body had gone numb the moment the gun appeared. 'I think,' I stammered, 'that he has a point, and a very big gun as well. I think we should be off to Buffalo.'

Dirk looked at me in disbelief and the owner laughed, his stomach shaking as he did.

'The others are waiting, Dirk,' I said over my shoulder as I made for the door.

'You'll be hearing from our solicitor,' I heard Dirk telling the owner as I paused by the door. Dirk also smashed something on his way out, but I couldn't see and didn't care what it was.

The next thing I knew, he was smacking me in the back of the head, calling me a useless traitor.

'We're the Setting Sun, Dirk. Treason is our business.'

Dirk, now at the van, only looked at me before stepping in.

I felt a keen nudge from my bladder, which had clenched on me quite thoroughly in the club under threat of violence, and urinated on the back of the club before getting into the van myself.

'That's right, mate! Hit 'em where it hurts!' Monk, ever a fan of doing one's business in the royal streets and alleys of the Empire, said to me in mock congratulation as I settled into the passenger seat.

'Just drive, Monk.'

The old roadie flicked a cigarette out the window and pulled away from the rear of the club. The streets of Hartford were deader than Henry VIII.

Dirk was explaining the club owner's refusal to pay the band to Ryan, the keyboardist, and Eel, the drummer, both of whom were camped in the far rear of the van. Dirk had the middle to himself. Our band mates seemed unperturbed by yet another non-payment, perhaps numbed by the frequency of the occurrence. 'Eliot did nothing, of course.'

'I suppose maybe he didn't want to get shot,' Eel said as he prepared to violate Connecticut's drink-driving laws.

Dirk turned his attention to me. 'El, was there nothing you could do in there to help a mate out?'

'Dirk, when the man is holding a gun and telling you you're not to be paid for a gig, commitment to saving one's own arse becomes more immediately important than commitment to the cause of dismantlement.'

'You could always die for the cause,' Monk interjected, head cocked sarcastically to the side.

'He's not the martyr type,' said Dirk, and he was right. 'I

can't believe the bastard wouldn't pay.'

'Perhaps,' I said, 'we'd be paid more often if you'd stop creating situations that lead to police interference.'

'What did I do tonight that was out of line, exactly?'

'You cracked that Unionist square in the forehead with your phragm, for one.'

'Yes, but what did I do that was out of line?'

It was useless. We'd been through this a dozen times—more, truthfully, but the count had long been lost. Every time Dirk created trouble at a club we were denied pay, and every time Eel and I made him promise to control his anti-imperial tirades at shows he brought them to a new level of vitriol. Ryan only encouraged him. If we hadn't sold so many t-shirts and records, we would've been considerably in the red for the tour. That the records weren't in the big chain shops due to the ban had helped us sell piles of them each night.

'Do you know, guys,' I asked the rest of the band, 'that Dirk threatened to have our solicitor call the club owner?'

This brought laughter spilling from Ryan, Eel and Monk. 'I suppose we'd better hire a solicitor, then,' said Ryan.

Dirk pressed his back to the door, stretched his legs across the bench seat and smiled the sweet smile that brought untold girls to his hotel rooms when we overnighted in our tourstop cities. 'I thought it was rather clever.'

We left Hartford on the A91 and drove north in silence with the heat on low. The year was just turning down the road to cool weather and the New England nights were growing teeth. New England. Why should we need a new England? One was more than enough.

I craned my neck to see my band mates. Their faces were revealed to me in rhythmic intervals by the street lights. Ryan was rapidly getting pissed as usual and I could hear the bottles rattling by his feet. Eel drummed at the air and Dirk sat sideways squinting at a notepad, writing in it as we passed through the pools of available light.

By 01:00 we were on the A90 bound for Buffalo and God knew what kind of reception. New England and the Maritimes were friendly territory for us, but even there Unionists had begun turning up in numbers at our shows, waiting for the kind of trouble they knew Dirk would oblige them and cause.

As no one was sleeping, Eel took it upon himself to find a review of the previous night's show in the *Providence Journal* and read it aloud to the rest of us. Flicking on the overhead light, he adopted a stodgy House of Lords tone and accent:

Setting Sun Stoke Anti-Royal Sentiment, Forget to Entertain
Gene Wharton
Providence Journal

Providence, 16 September, 1983 — Separatist beat music is merely the latest stain to afflict the North American pop chart, but few offenders are more egregious than the New York group the Setting Sun. If you're wondering why a beat group of four members has chosen a singular name for itself, you're scarcely alone, but to hear group leader Dirk Cunningham (aka Joe Putrid) tell it, the name is symbolic of the end of the Empire. 'One day, the sun will set on the British Empire,' Cunningham told a squealing crowd of teenagers and university students. 'We are proud to be the setting sun.'

Grandiosity aside, Cunningham can barely be bothered to sing when the band around him begins playing and seems to enjoy provoking the arm-banded Unionists who brave the crowds at his shows more than the art of performance. Last night's show at the Crystal Palace began with the first of the band's two banned singles, the abominable 'Anarchy in the UK', a song that, among other things, advocates burning down the Houses of Parliament and bombing 10 Downing Street. Keyboard player Ryan O'Halleran, who goes by the stage name Thomas Pain, seemed in his own world as drummer Gerry 'Eel' Pie struggled to keep the set together with his plodding beats.

Amidst this spectacle stood Eliot Washington, a fiddle player far too talented to be bothered with such nonsense. He has the unenviable task of providing backup vocals to Cunningham, though during last night's engagement he gave up during the second song as Cunningham forgot the words and launched into a diatribe praising the assassination of Royal family members.

The heavily separatist audience naturally lapped it up, bursting into rapturous applause at the opening fiddle fanfare of the group's other banned hit, 'God Save the King'. One wonders if the BBC and CBC miscalculated in announcing the ban of this song, as the resulting controversy seems responsible for its number one chart placement in a great many of the territories of the Empire, including Scotland, Wales and much of North America. Certainly, it didn't make that kind of sales showing on artistic merit.

Somewhat redeeming the evening was a spirited opening set by Kingston, Jamaica's Pocomaniacs, a group that understands how to leaven its pan-Africanist politics with the yeast of strong composition and engaging stage banter that eschews confrontation and calls to violence. If only all of this new breed of political groups were so musically grounded and level-headed.

'Did you hear that, El?' Dirk asked as Eel finished. 'You're far too talented to be bothered with this nonsense.'

'Aye, perhaps I should be playing music hall or whatever Wharton thinks is acceptable. Seriously, why is that man reviewing beat shows at all? He's a relic and a king's pawn, just like all the other writers at that paper. And 'Anarchy' does not advocate bombing Downing Street. You just added that line last night.'

'Separatist beat music is a stain on the pop charts. Cor.' Dirk grabbed the paper from Eel's hand and glanced at the review. 'Gene Wharton is a twat and a Unionist. It's redundant to say that, but it's true.'

'I'll drink to that,' said Eel, hoisting a beer to his mouth.

'We're coming to a layby,' said Monk, 'and I quite need to take a piss.'

'I'll drink to that as well,' said Eel.

At the layby, long-haul lorry drivers stood conversing outside the entrance, cups of coffee in their hands. They eyed us disdainfully as we trudged red-eyed past them. Dirk and Ryan sneered back at them, straightening their vests to make the anti-empire patches they'd sewn on more clearly visible. Ryan belched loudly. I avoided eye contact. Eel, on the other hand, cheerfully greeted them, slapping the largest on the arm, right on his Cross of St Andrew armband. He was offering them cigarettes when the door closed behind me.

I entered the loo to find Ryan spray-painting 'God Fuck the King' on the wall through one of the roll-up stencils he carried with him. Dirk had his stickers out and was placing them on the hand dryers and mirrors, where no one could possibly miss them. IDF: YOU CANNOT STOP US, FREE NORTH AMERICA, THE SUN WILL SET ON THE EMPIRE YET, and the anti-Jack, the orange, green and black Union Jack the Imperial Dismantlement Front had recently adopted for an emblem, were his old standards, but he had a new one this time as well. This one paired a black and white image of Prime Minister Fox in a red crosshair with the message GO FOX HUNTING.

As I entered the stall, he handed me an anti-Jack. 'Here, put one of these on the wall.'

As I removed the backing, I asked him where he'd picked up the Fox hunting stickers.

'You know that fan I had back to my room in Providence? She had them. Hundreds of them. I quite like the message.'

'You don't think advocating assassination is a bit much?'

'Absolutely not,' Ryan, now in the next stall over, said. 'Don't tell us you're going soft on the old Prime Minister, Eliot.'

'Hardly,' I said, kicking the handle for the flush. 'But if it doesn't have to come to revolution I'd sooner avoid one.'

'War is the answer,' said Dirk, who was standing by the sinks, admiring his handiwork. 'At the moment, the stage is our front line, but four hundred years of history tells me it's come to that. Everything else has failed.'

'Where do you get the soldiers?'

'You're looking at them every night, El.'

I'm looking at a fashion statement every night—revolution couture, I thought, but didn't say it, tired of arguing.

Ryan emerged without flushing. 'How many times can you two have this exact conversation?' He twisted the tap and pumped the borax dispenser.

The door swung open and we froze, fresh graffiti all around us. It was Monk. 'Wow,' he said, heading for the urinal. 'A fine job, mates. We'll be free of the crown in no time.'

Back in the van, Eel was poring over the Upper New York map. 'I'd say we've got another three or so hours on the road tonight.' He yawned. 'Better Monk driving than me.'

'With your intake of Sam Smith's it sure is,' I replied.

'I gather you spent all that time talking to those tossers by the door,' Dirk said to Eel.

'I engaged them in a civil discourse.'

'They ought to be knocked about,' Ryan said.

'Fucking Cross of St Andrew on their arms,' Dirk said in disgust. 'I suppose they like their taxes supporting Princess Ann's cocaine habit.'

'They were rather nice for a bunch of pro-Union tossers,' offered Eel. 'I even got one of them to take an IDF pamphlet.'

'See what happens when you engage them instead of shoving an anti-Jack in their faces?' I asked Dirk.

Dirk asked if the trucker had read the pamphlet.

Eel looked at his lap. 'Perhaps when he was away from the others.'

'Of course,' replied Dirk.

❋   ❋   ❋

The reporter was one of those who wanted you to know he was on your side, that he believed in what you were doing.

'Buffalo is pretty friendly overall to the cause of independence,' he was telling me as Dirk and Ryan milled about at the front of the stage, checking to see that all of the power cables were in order. 'But.' He leaned closer to me. 'I've heard that the local Unionists are planning to be here in big numbers.'

'Well, they'll have to get tickets,' I told him as he waved his pocket tape recorder at me. 'This is a sold-out show. We've sold them all out since they banned 'Anarchy in the UK' on the CBC. A few bad imperialist apples usually get in, but the audiences are mostly friendly.'

'Do you suppose that if Unionists do show up there'll be another incident like the one in Hartford last night or London, Ontario, two weeks ago?'

'I suppose there will,' Dirk said from somewhere over my shoulder. He glared at me when I turned to look at him. 'There should have to be, I think.'

'Why's that?' the reporter asked him.

Dirk hopped down from the stage. 'Well, if they're going to come to our shows, knowing where we stand, in support of a government that siphons taxes to a bunch of useless royals and smashes peaceful pro-independence demonstrations with clubs and guns, they bloody well deserve a good thrashing. We've got North American men fighting and dying over weather stations in Svalbard right now for the vanity of a pig-fat Parliament that patronises us with barely nominal representation. There are only fourteen representatives in the House of Commons for 268 million people living in North America, and that is a travesty.'

'What do you think of the Philadelphia Congress? Is that a step in the right direction?'

Dirk rolled his eyes and spoke directly into the reporter's recorder. 'The Philadelphia Congress is a bad joke, meant to divert attention from the fact that North America is still subject to a corrupt crown and a doddering government that considers its people cannon fodder for adventures in Borneo and the Himalayas. And fucking Svalbard! Is there a more useless piece of land in the world?'

The reporter tried to lighten the mood by responding, 'Well, there's always Franz Josef Land.'

'Ha!' Dirk turned away and climbed back onto the stage. 'Suppose we'll be skirmishing with Russians there, too, soon enough. Weather stations. Ugh.' Dirk threw his hands in the air.

The reporter turned back to me. 'So you have nine more dates on this tour. What's next after this?'

'Well, we have some new songs we should try to record and release, though I doubt any of the big companies will touch them after the last two. After that, we've thought we might tour England. Y'know, take it home to the Empire.' I paused and raised my voice so Dirk would hear the rest of my response. 'Of course, we've barely broken even on this tour because none of the venues seem willing to pay us for our work.'

'Have you spoken to the musicians' union about that?'

'They might care if we were members and it wasn't run by Unionists.'

'The Setting Sun are known for their separatist stance,' the reporter said, cribbing from notes he had jotted in a small pad. 'What is your vision for independence? What do you see in North America after a split with the Empire?'

'Well, independence is just the half of it, really. More than separatism, our cause is really dismantlement. Total destruction of the Empire. Independence for North America is well and good, but it's only a half-won battle if the English still rule Scotland, Wales and Ireland, and British troops still occupy Burma, parts of India, Jamaica, Malaysia, Ghana and all sorts of other parts of the world they have no business being in. As for North America, we foresee a true democracy, where representation is genuinely proportional, and not this nonsense Dirk—sorry, Joe Putrid—was talking about before.' I hated referring to Dirk by his stage name.

This seemed to satisfy the reporter and he left us to complete our sound check. The acoustics in the club were detestable, with a low, hard ceiling and rotten angles that made it intensely difficult to balance the monitors properly. It was tough to say whether hearing the monitors would've mattered by that point, as there were enough nuggets of truth sprinkled through Gene Wharton's assessment of our show to form a small ribbon of ore. Dirk seemed bored with his own lyrics and frequently eschewed verses for whatever vitriol was on his mind that night.

This was one reason I enjoyed sound check. With no audience to exhort or antagonise—we still didn't know which it would be that night—Dirk tended to engage with the songs more and we felt like a real band, just as we had in the beginning.

After about twenty minutes of taking the board operator's word for it that we sounded okay—Monk usually confirmed the sound man's story for us, but was presently sleeping in the van—Dirk and Ryan were ready to quit. 'You fellows fancy a beer across the street?' asked Ryan.

'Well, we've got a few hours 'til doors,' I said. 'Would you perhaps like to play for a while first? It's been ages since we had a proper jam.'

Eel seemed game, grabbing up his sticks, but the others wanted no part.

'I'd rather get a couple of beers in me,' said Ryan.

'Is there ever a time,' I asked him, 'when you don't have a couple of beers in you? You'll be pickled silly soon if you don't cut back.'

'Right, since when did you become a fan of temperance?'

'Christ, I don't mean stop altogether, but you should know when to give it a rest! You used to have a bit of fire in you, but now you're just buzzed all the time. All the ideals you were so adamant about have just become a base hatred for the Empire. It deserves to be hated, but you have to have some sort of vision for what happens after it comes crashing down, and I don't get that from either of you anymore,' I said, turning to Dirk.

For once, Dirk didn't seem to know what to say. He mulled his options for a moment, then asked, 'And is "having a proper jam", as you put it, supposed to solve any of this?'

'What the hell kind of question is that? We're a band. Bands play music together. At least in theory they do. We don't, however, or haven't since the spotlight hit us. How are we supposed to get better without playing together?'

'We're as good as we need to be to get out our message,' said Dirk, lifting his guitar slightly out of the stand and slamming it back down for emphasis.

'And what happens when the Empire dies? Pardon me for wanting to make something that outlasts the thing we set out to destroy.'

'And how is the Empire ever going to die if we spend our time diddling about, jamming and what—preparing for some kind of career in this? It's a vehicle, Eliot. A vehicle for our message, which you were just so politely explaining to the reporter not half an hour ago.' Dirk jumped down off the stage, followed by Ryan.

Sitting in a pub drinking your brain cells to an early grave isn't about to crack the crown any time soon either, I thought, but didn't bother saying it as they were already near the door. I looked at Eel, still holding his sticks. His small eyes peered out at me from his rosy round face with a certain sadness.

'Sorry, Eliot,' he said as he rose from his stool, gingerly positioning the sticks on his snare head so that they wouldn't roll off. 'I'd have been game.' He stopped in front of me, still holding my violin and bow, and put his hand on my shoulder. 'Are you going to hit the pub?'

'No, Eel, go on without me. I'll stay here. Wouldn't have been much a jam with just the two of us anyway.'

Eel tumbled off the stage and looked back at me as he exited the club. We waved to each other and then I put the bow to the strings. I played everything that came to me—jigs, reels, laments, snippets of popular songs—and it felt good to simply let my fingers do their thing absent of any heavier implied meaning or political statement. After a few minutes, I noticed that the sound man had come back into the room and was sitting at a table near the back of the room, just listening.

I played for forty minutes, and when I felt I was done I sat amongst the cables, amplifiers and other assorted gear on the stage trying to figure out a plan for the evening's show. Would Dirk play his guitar? Or would it just hang from his body as he abandoned the songs and shot from the hip? Would there be Unionists? Buffalo was full of separatists—it was home to the *Dismantler*, among the top two or three American separatist newspapers, but we'd heard rumours that the colonial government had bussed Unionist mobs to our shows in Portsmouth, Hartford and Halifax and a few were bound to show up.

We were at least on sympathetic ground that night. The club—the Americana—was owned by two members of the IDF and sported Anti-Jacks on its interior walls. The girl tending bar, who had recently arrived to get ready for the crowd, wore a 'Don't Tread On Me' t-shirt and it occurred to me then that one of the things that truly separated Americans from the English was our mastery of slogan. The ability to boil down a stance or a moral position to a pithy t-shirt was lost on imperialists, who preferred old-fashioned verbosity and bloviation.

As I set up the merchandise table with a couple of local IDF members who'd volunteered to sell for us, I worried that the friendly confines of this club would further embolden Dirk and his crowd baiting. Dirk always had a way of working crowds, ever since I had known him. When he arrived in my secondary school class in

New Brunswick, fresh off the boat from Scotland, the kids instantly knew that this was someone to follow. It had gone to his head then and it was again going to his head now. The way he talked, it was as though he thought that our songs alone could sweep Parliament into the Thames and leave us free of English dominion. He spoke of Scotland as the original English colony and claimed dual oppression as a son of both the Highlands and the Maritimes.

The band had begun as a lark—we were called the Beat Boys when we first got our guitars out during finishing school, and Dirk was content to sing about problems with money and women with that booming brogue of his. He had the type of singing voice that drops girls to the floor, and he brought on fainting spells when we made our first little tour through the Northeast. It wasn't until we met Ryan at university in Philadelphia that Dirk's nascent radicalism went full blossom and became inseparable from the music in his mind. We joined the IDF, changed the name of the band, found Eel beating skins for a fluffy group called the Beatles and were on our way to the blacklists of the Columbia and British Broadcasting Corporations.

We had to admire Ryan. He was older, wiser, head of the Separatist Students' Council and organiser of dismantlement rallies. It was the moment I saw him calmly accept a blow to the head from a policeman's baton during a non-violent rally that I became convinced he was among the separatist movement's great hopes. By that day in Buffalo, however, I was no longer impressed and Ryan had given up all pretence of non-violence. He was simply a drunk, in love with hating the Empire. One could hardly blame him, the way his family had been forced from Ireland during his childhood, but the ideas that drew us to him were dormant, hidden by a spirits-induced fog.

As it turned out, Eel's old group—the Beatles—themselves adopted a dismantlement stance soon after we did. Their 'Going to Japan', a song about defecting to the Empire's greatest rival, was banned around the same time as 'Anarchy in the UK'.

The rest of the band filed into the tiny, rank-smelling backstage room shortly after the Americana opened its doors. We sat in silence together, listening to the crowd gather in the club.

Dirk slapped a few stickers on the wall.

Shortly before our scheduled start time, I asked if there had been any sign of Unionists outside the club.

Eel must have sensed the nervousness in my voice, because he cut in before Dirk could answer. 'There was a bus out there, but it could've been anyone's. No armbands, bulldogs or Royal Boys' Club insignia or anything like that. It may be calmer tonight than last.'

'I'll wager they do show up,' said Dirk as Ryan wobbled in his chair. 'I hope they do. I'm in the mood for a little conflict.'

'Dirk,' I said. 'Have you read what the papers are saying about the separatist and dismantlement movements?' I held up a copy of the *Buffalo Sentinel* I had been reading while waiting for them to return. 'They think we're a bunch of hooligans. We have separatist academics and writers trying to distance themselves from the IDF because of things like our shows. Starting fights is starting to hurt us. I mean, look at these polls...' I flipped through the front section. 'They've got fifty-two percent of the American public favouring dismantlement and only thirty-three who approve of the IDF. Almost none of them favour civil conflict.'

'That's a poll in a conservative paper,' said Ryan.

'It's a poll conducted by the Separatist Students' Council of America, Ryan! Which you used to be a fairly important member of if I recall correctly.'

'So anyway, your point is?' Dirk asked impatiently.

'If Unionists do show up tonight—and I'm sure a few will—why not take the novel approach of ignoring them and not encouraging our audience to beat them up? All we get is bad press when Unionists catch hell at our shows. It makes the movement looks awful. Plus, avoiding a fight will frustrate the hell out of them.'

Dirk was no longer listening. He was peeking out the door at the gathering crowd. Eel looked at me and shrugged.

'My God, there are a lot of them,' said Dirk, not specifying whether he meant Unionists or just show-goers in general. He turned to us and reached into his pockets, pulling out four crumpled pieces of notepad paper. 'Here's the set list, then.'

I looked it over.

'CBC'
'Don't Tread on Me'
'Sons of Liberty'
'God Save the King'
'John Kennedy'
'Free James Madison'
'King of Nothing'
'Et Tu, Britannia'
'Anarchy in the UK'
'Crack in the Union Jack'

'Dirk,' I said, 'This is barely half an hour's worth of songs. And "Crack in the Union Jack"? What on earth is that?'

'It's something new I wrote this morning between load-in and sound check, just after I talked to our good-for-shit manager Liam, who will once again not be here for the show. He mentioned we'd been knocked from the number one spot by the English Gentlewomen's cover of "The Sun Will Never Set on My England".'

We all knew this song in its original version by Richard Cliff—it had been drilled into us like a second national anthem when we were kids by teachers toeing the colonialist line during the second Burma War—but I didn't get where Dirk was going with this. 'So?' I asked him.

'So it's sung to the tune of "The Sun Will Never Set on My England".' He sang the first verse:

> There's a great big crack in the Union Jack
> Do you think it's going to hold?
> If every rotten truth spilled out today
> You know it would fold.

'Clever,' said Eel. 'Is there more?'

'Yes, of course there's more. I parodied the whole song.'

'We can't play it, Dirk. We haven't even rehearsed it,' I said.

'I think you can handle it. You know the song.'

'Even so, this is too short a set.'

'Well, we shouldn't even need all of it. I saw a few sure-fire Unionists out there. They must have heard that the club wouldn't allow armbands in, but you can tell them straight off. They don't mingle with the crowd.'

I was about to protest when a club employee burst in and told us to take the stage.

We scrambled to our instruments and as we tuned up and got ready, I could see armbands coming out of pockets in the crowd. There were perhaps twenty Union Jacks sliding up onto biceps in the club, and those were merely the ones in my line of sight.

Dirk looked at me, then grabbed his diaphragmaphone.

'Good evening, ladies, gentlemen and Unionshits!'

The crowd roared with a mixture of appreciation and jeers.

'If I'd been born of a higher station,' he continued, 'I'd be in Windsor right now, snorting cocaine off Princess Ann's curvy bum.' This time the cheers drowned out the hearty boos of the Unionists. 'As I was not, I am here with you instead. This first one is for every Scot, American, Indian and Rhodesian fighting in Malaysia for the glory of the bloody throne. It's called "His Majesty's Royal Malaria". God save the King and Queen and all who sail upon them!'

'His Majesty's Royal Malaria' wasn't even on the scribbled set list Dirk had given us. Eel and I exchanged panicked glances as Ryan launched into a sloppy rendering of the opening keyboard figure at a much faster tempo than we wrote it at. Seconds later, we were flying by the seats of our pants through a song Dirk had insisted we stop playing two weeks ago when it failed to draw a radio ban. In the crowd, I watched the Unionists pushing forward toward the stage, shoving our boosters out of the way.

As the song came crashing to a close with no two band members stopping simultaneously, Dirk was already introducing 'CBC'.

'This next song is dedicated to the cunts who run the Columbia Broadcasting Corporation. We expect it will be banned by said corporation as soon as we manage to record it.'

The intro to this song was mine, and I kept the tempo back as best I could. The crowd flailed to it anyway. Unionists were huddled at the base of the stage, making sure we could see their armbands.

As 'CBC' clanged along, the monitor speakers went out one by one. The cords were being pulled by the Unionists, a hulking lot who looked ready to murder us but appeared to be waiting for proper provocation. Dirk gave it to them as the song ended.

Stepping between two of the monitors to within a foot of the stage's edge, he said, 'I see we have a few Unionists in the house tonight, dolled up in their cute little armbands. Very brave, boys. I fully encourage the rest of you lot to damage them.' With that, he reared back and kicked the largest one squarely in the mouth with his steel-toed work boot.

The man fell back into the crowd and in seconds it was all pandemonium. Over the crowd, I could see the two local blokes we had put in charge of our merchandise attempting to keep a group of men from tipping the table over. Dirk swung his guitar at an armbanded guy who had clambered onto the stage and caught him on the jaw. I turned to see Ryan wrestling with another.

I shoved my violin into its case, nearly forgetting to unplug the pickup cord, and retreated to the rear of the stage, where Eel was watching the action unfold. A full bottle of beer shattered on the wall behind us. Ryan, too drunk to fight, was having a terrible time against two opponents now, just feet from us, and he called out for help. His second assailant, a shaven-headed thug wielding a short baton—how he got it into the club I wasn't sure—followed Ryan's pleas to us and charged. Eel ran, but I was hemmed in by an amplifier and an equipment case. The Unionist swung the baton at me but missed, and as he tripped on a cable I brought my violin case down on his head, knocking him unconscious.

Ryan by this point had the assistance of a few crowd members. There were an incredible number of Unionists in the club—more than at any other show—but they were still outnumbered.

I caught sight of Eel near the rear exit, and he waved me

over. I bolted for the door, but before we had a chance to open it a flood of police officers in full riot regalia burst through it. Eel and I were shoved aside and I watched as an officer plainly approached a scrapping pair, patted the Unionist on the shoulder to move him out of the way and clocked the other club-goer full bore in the chest with his baton.

'My God, they're working together!' cried Eel, just as two officers grabbed him and dragged him out the rear exit.

I searched in vain for some way out of the melee and decided it might be best to simply head for the back door myself. An officer stopped me a few feet from it, screaming at me to stop and drop my weapon with truncheon raised. I couldn't fathom what he was talking about. It never occurred to me that my violin case was the weapon in question.

Instinctively I raised my hands. I saw his arm move somewhere to my left and then everything went black.

❄ ❄ ❄

I awoke in the alley with Monk bent over me. I could feel him pressing something cold against my temple.

'You took a nasty hit,' he said. He pulled his hand back from my head and I could see he was holding a blood-stained cloth.

'Hey, good to have you back!' It was Eel's voice, but I couldn't see him. Still lying down, I turned my head to the right and beyond a few crumpled leaflets, a beer bottle and pile of ash and butts from an emptied tray was Eel, sitting against the wall. We were a ways down the alley from the back of the club. In the middle distance, I could see flashing red and blue lights and figures running to and fro.

'What's going on?' was all I could think to ask.

'Well,' said Monk. 'All hell's broken loose in there. You got a crack in the noggin from a copper, Ryan has three broken ribs and is off to hospital and we're fairly certain Dirk has been arrested.'

'I got off rather lightly,' said Eel. 'They just dragged me outside and I ran away. They didn't even chase me. I found Monk here two blocks away with the van.'

'I could smell trouble,' said Monk, 'so I thought it best to move our most valuable asset away from the club.'

I sat up slowly and my head reeled from the dull pain around my temple. 'Where's my violin?'

Neither Monk nor Eel said anything.

'I must have dropped it when I got hit.'

'Let's worry about it after the situation cools a bit, eh?' said Monk. 'They're not letting anyone into the club at the moment.'

The three of us sat for an hour in the alley while I built up the ability to stand. By that point fewer police were around and, ignoring Monk and Eel's protestations, I went back inside. My violin was lying less than a foot from the door and I snatched it, ducking back outside as quickly as possible.

Monk, Eel and I spent the rest of the afternoon attempting to figure out where Ryan and Dirk were. We discovered Ryan at the second hospital we checked, where he showed us bandages beneath his shirt. 'I see you managed to get a souvenir as well,' he said to me. The fight seemed drained from him.

We wound up at the offices of the *Dismantler*, where we were interviewed about the night's events. I couldn't think of much to say to the pretty young girl who was assigned to me. I tried to remember the riot officer who hit me but I couldn't place his face. Was he wearing a mask? The girl—Tyla was her name—fetched me a carb-tea after a few minutes, and when she came back, the interview lapsed from pointed questioning into a more casual conversation.

A radio played softly somewhere, old sing-along songs from the 30s, and I remember thinking what an odd sensation it was to hear Noltan Nellie's voice floating through the office of a radical newspaper.

'It is somehow calming, though, isn't it?' Tyla replied when I mentioned it. I had to agree.

Around 03:00, one of their reporters informed us that Dirk was being held at a Buffalo Police Station pending bail.

We called Liam, who was supposed to be waiting for us in Erie with hotel rooms, but he had left the hotel and was apparently on his way to Buffalo, according to the front desk.

We had little choice but to wait as the money to get Dirk out of police custody was well beyond the means of the small group of us whiling away the night. No one seemed to possess a clue as to what to do and impotent silence engulfed us. Here we were, a group of radical journalists and three of the four loudest separatists in the Empire, and we hadn't a word to share among us.

After two hours, which Eel, Tyla, Monk and I spent playing a type of table football with a rolled-up ball of newsprint, the doors to the *Dismantler* were flung open and in walked Liam Nelson, the self-appointed 'Duke of Earl', in his sport coat and sunglasses with Dirk and two others in tow. Sunglasses in the middle of the night!

Dirk looked like hell re-heated after a freeze. His right eye was swollen shut, his vest was torn and his slogan patches had been ripped from it. He walked with a limp, leaning on one of the others, who we were told had been a cellmate. Liam had paid bail for both IDFers Dirk had shared quarters with at the jail.

Before extricating Dirk, Liam mentioned that he had been by the Americana and salvaged what gear of ours he could with the help of a few local IDF guys, loading it into a trailer he rented for the occasion. Most of the drums, one of Ryan's keyboards and an acoustic guitar were beyond hope.

'I'd just gotten that snare the way I liked it,' Eel said, looking at the floor.

Dirk led the man he was leaning on over to us. 'Christ, you've got your violin with you. I should have guessed,' he said to me. Then, to everyone, he introduced Jeff Davis. 'Jeff plays the guitar and he'll be joining the Setting Sun for the rest of the tour.'

The rest of us exchanged glances. Even Ryan seemed taken aback.

'You go to jail for a night and come out with a new band mate. Fantastic,' I said. 'I suppose you've told him we're losing money on this tour.'

'He understands,' Dirk continued. 'We had a lot of time to talk once the police were done going over me.' He tugged on his vest and stuck a finger through one of the patch holes. 'And his attitude convinced me that he's just what we need in this band.'

'Um, not to put too fine a point on it, but is there still anything left of this tour after tonight?' asked Monk, flicking the ball of newsprint clear off the table.

Liam responded quickly. 'Oh, yes, of course! No one has cancelled. And the ticket sales are out of this world! You guys lost a lot of equipment and merchandise tonight, but we'll get more in Erie tomorrow. You're intercontinental news now, even more so than after the banned singles, and you are going to sell big.'

That was Liam, always thinking of how much money could be made. He didn't care at all about dismantlement or separatism, but in a sense he was the most American of all of us. 'When opportunity knocks,' he liked to say, 'be the opportunist ready to take him for all he's worth.'

'Well, Jeff,' said Eel to our new arrival, 'I hope you like excitement. It seems to have a way of following us around.'

'I'm game for anything that shoves one up the king, if you know what I mean,' Jeff replied. He was in high spirits and undamaged, from what I could see. His whole body moved when he talked, and Dirk had to re-steady himself against the back of a chair.

How will this band work with him in it? Can he even play? I thought. I was too tired to raise the issue just then. It also lingered in my mind that this was one more person to split money with, and money was something we had little of.

'I'm glad everyone's okay,' said Liam, 'but this show must go on. Shall we head on to Erie or try to get some rest here first?'

Still a bit dazed but grateful to be in the state I was in, all things considered, I pushed aside strong thoughts of simply staying behind and calling it all off—not to mention strong thoughts of possibly attempting to catch some rest with Tyla—and agreed with the others that it would be best to leave Buffalo and go to Erie. We would have two nights to recuperate before the next show, at the Dengue Fever Beat Club on the lakeshore.

❄   ❄   ❄

'Rat-hole' would aptly describe the accommodations Liam had secured for us. He stayed half a mile away in a high-rise block of flats with a woman he had met that morning. At a conservative estimate, there may be around a hundred little illegitimate Liams running about the countryside.

We were three to a dilapidated room, and the factions couldn't have been more obvious. Jeff stayed with Ryan and Dirk while Eel, Monk and I took the other room. The wallpaper was faux-Victorian and cast the room in pink reflected light. Eel and Monk generously gave me the bed in consideration of my wound which, upon inspection in a mirror, I decided could have been a lot worse.

By 14:00 the following day we were all awake and the six of us, absent Liam, met in the car park next to the van. The ringing in my left ear was as voluble as the day before and I felt faint as I half-listened to Dirk outline his plan for going on as a five-piece band. Jeff was affable enough at first blush, but it became clear that he was less a musician than a provocateur in the mold of Dirk, whom he seemed to idolise.

'Dirk,' I finally said, stopping him with my hand, 'Let's you and I take a walk. Everyone else go to the hotel restaurant. We'll meet you there.'

There had been no discussion of the previous night, but I didn't even know where to begin. So I instead began by surprising myself.

'Dirk, I'm leaving the band,' I said.

Did I just say that? I thought.

He reacted as though I had spoken Russian.

It is a feat to render Dirk speechless, so I repeated myself.

'I... You... When did you decide this?'

I considered that for a moment. 'Just now, I suppose. It's a thought that's built over the last few days.'

'Is this because...' He couldn't word it. 'Why would you leave?'

'Dirk, we've been friends since we were quite young. I value that. We've shared a lot, and we still share the same basic goal. We know this Empire is just like all the others. It can't last. And it shouldn't. But your methods... my methods... There are things we no longer see the same way. The music is one of them, and I just can't do it anymore.'

'I can't fucking believe this. Eliot, this band has been ours for six years, before university, even. We are just now beginning to have an impact. How can you even think about leaving?' He was regaining his lather as he went on.

'It's not a positive impact!'

'Any impact that helps kill Britannia is a positive impact.' He was nearly shouting but his voice was even.

'Indulging your hatred won't kill it. Look at my head, Dirk.' I stopped in front of him and moved my left temple as close to his face as I could. His breath was warm on my cheek. 'Look at it. And look at yourself.'

His eye was starting to open but his face was still bruised the colour of an avocado and his vest was a rag.

'These are not badges of honour,' I said to him. 'They're badges of failure. No one's mind was changed in that carnage last night. And no one's mind will be changed by it. The band isn't going to help any cause if you go off kicking someone in the teeth every night. All you're doing is ceding the high ground the CBC and BBC gave us when they banned those singles.'

Dirk began moving forward again with his head down and I fell in slightly behind him.

We were walking along a four-lane motorway lined with rows of shops and hotels. The sun had stowed itself behind a low cloud deck and cars ripped by through the dreary mid-day light, the occupants shopping, consuming, living out an American Dream that hadn't fully ripened yet.

Dirk's feet drifted over the ground with uncharacteristic slowness. 'It must be strange for you,' he said. 'Being fully American. It's a funny thing to be fully American. You get all of this'—he waved his hand at the shops across the street—'and it's your culture. There's Britishness in it, you know? But it's not British—it's got all these other things in it. The English came here to spread Englishness and instead they erased themselves by building a melting pot for Europe and Africa and Asia.'

'It's an odd construction, this empire, isn't it? What holds it together? It seems tenuous enough that there should be a string to pull and unravel it. And yet there isn't, or doesn't seem to be.' I looked at Dirk, who had his hands shoved into his pockets, staring across the road where we had unconsciously come to a stop. He was watching people drive thru at the Royal Burger. 'It's not odd for me to be a true American. It's the only thing I know. Someday, within my lifetime— I can feel it—the map will reflect my identity. Maybe it will reflect it more precisely than that. Perhaps I'll be a Maritimer or an Acadian or something. But whatever it is, at least I won't be a subject.'

'I think what you don't understand, as an American,' said Dirk, still watching the Royal Burger, 'is the humiliation. Of being a Scot, or being Irish like Ryan. America, or Columbia, or North America, or whatever it is, was never a nation, but Scotland and Ireland were. I might as well be a Cherokee, coming from Dundee. You talk about non-violence and taking it slow, but every time you hear someone say that it's an American living inside an English system. I don't see it the way you do. I look back and see violence against my people and independence is a fight in my mind. I don't just want a new government with more local engagement. I want an empire in tatters and a chastened nation that will think twice about extending its reach beyond Hadrian's Wall or Land's End. I want Unionist blood on the floor.'

'And I want no part in that.'

At this point we allowed ourselves into a sort of trance, our gazes fixed upon the billions and billions being served at Royal Burger—it just seemed oddly appropriate at that moment to be watching a fat family of four tumbling toward their Bentley wagon with a birthday crown on the head of the daughter, oblivious to the double entendre of the restaurant's name. No one seemed to connect the phrase 'Royal Burger' with the fact that we had a man of German descent on the English throne.

'I can't stop you from leaving,' Dirk finally said. 'And I don't want to. I also can't lie and say you won't be missed, because you're ten times the musician I am. But do one last thing for me.'

It was a simple enough request. We crossed the road at a mad run, dodging the cars that swerved and honked at us. Inside the Royal Burger, we slowly approached the front counter, the soles of our shoes squeaking on the brown mop marks that covered the floor.

'Can I help you, sir?' asked the mouth-breathing teenager behind the register.

'Yes,' I said. 'It is my birthday, and I would like a few of those little paper crowns you're always handing out 'round here. Six of them.'

'Uh...' He looked at me for a moment. 'I think you have to buy something to get those.'

'Well, then.' I looked up at the menu and saw nothing appealing. 'I suppose I'd like a malt. A chocolate malt. And six of those crowns.'

'Wait. How do I know it's really your birthday?'

'I've told you it is. And as I understand it, the customer is always right at this establishment.'

Apparently feeling himself outsmarted, he got the malt and the crowns. 'Two pounds, six pence.'

I handed him the money and he pushed the crowns and malt toward me across the purple laminated counter. I handed off the crowns to Dirk. 'Here you are, your majesty. One for everybody.'

Dirk was laughing as we left.

✳   ✳   ✳

The bus station was drafty but Eel, Monk and I didn't have to wait long for the 1776 to Philadelphia. I was going alone, but they insisted on staying with me. There was little conversation. Eel sat adjusting his Royal Burger crown. His correct size was between two of the pre-cut notches.

'We'll look sporting in these on stage tomorrow,' he said, stirring the silence.

I though about it for a moment. 'What you really need to

do,' I told him and Monk, 'is get enough for everyone. Hand them out at the door at shows. Let everyone be a king or a queen for an evening.'

'We'd need thousands,' said Monk.

'Make it millions,' I said. 'One for everyone in the Empire. Hand them out to strangers on the street. Make them all kings.'

Eel liked both ideas. 'I'll bring it up with the others,' he said. 'After all, it hardly seems right that we'd be wearing them and our audience wouldn't.'

The bus was remarkably on time for a mass conveyance. I quickly shook hands with Monk and Eel.

'I hope Dirk doesn't cause trouble tomorrow.'

Eel held up crossed fingers.

The trip across Pennsylvania doesn't appear long on a map, especially next to the vast western territories of the Empire, grabbed from the Spanish and the Mexicans so long ago. It is in reality an interminable ride, especially with a hard violin case in one's lap.

In Philadelphia I caught a quick dinner at Musharaff's, picking at random from the Urdu menu, and then returned to the Setting Sun's shared flat in an old red brick row house. In my room I began to pack, not knowing where I'd be going. One of the first items my hand found was the very first Beat Boys single, which we'd released ourselves to a public of parents, friends and pity-takers. I ran my hands over the rough artwork Dirk and I had made by hand all those years prior and put it aside.

Later that evening I broke from packing for tea and played it. The sun had set outside and there was Dirk's voice, rolling around the room, singing a sweet melody with me behind him. Setting my tea on a table, I lay down on the sofa with the remote control and played it again and again.

The Last Day
of the Old World
by Brian A. Dixon

2 April 1994
Christmas, East Texas

They christened her *Étaín I*. It's an ancient Celtic myth, the story of a woman transformed into a beautiful butterfly and forced by the winds to the farthest corners of the Earth, cursed to live amongst the outcroppings of rocks in a tempestuous sea.

It goes without saying that she's more pleasing to the eye than the bus that first carried me into space over twenty years ago. *Blodeuwedd IV* was heavy, imposing, overly reinforced, both physically and conceptually the mother of all planes. *Étaín I* is, by contrast, sleek, elegant, downright sexy, a technological embodiment of the spirit that will boldly carry the British Empire to the Moon and into a blinding future.

And my son's going to fly her there.

Dylan is standing beside me, revelling in his first real glimpse of his destiny. We're walking in endless circles about the craft deep inside the mammoth hangar that serves as the Christmas Centre's Spaceplane Maintenance Facility. I seem to be doing all the talking. Dylan's literally speechless for a time, taking in the spaceplane's curves and angles with eyes so wide they seem as if they're primed to pop. Every so often he stops, looking over a glistening exhaust port or one of the clean tank link-ups, and I can see the tip of his tongue slipping out between his lips as he furrows his brow and concentrates. I can't help but smile. I haven't seen him do that since he was four years old.

I can remember being introduced to the *Blodeuwedd IV*

253

back in '73. All I wanted was to be alone with her, to send all the administrators and technicians away so that I could have a moment with her to myself. When I talk to Dylan I speak softly, as if wary of breaking the spell that's come over him. 'Blimey, ain't she a beautiful kite.'

He lets out a long, low hum. He's in love.

'She's prettier than the beast that carried me out there. Say, how many father-and-son teams can boast that their names will be printed side-by-side in the history books as heroes and pioneers?'

Dylan only grins, offers me a mischievous sideways glance, and then goes back to examining the contour of the broad wing before us. I don't think it's quite hit him yet. I'm not sure he's accepted that his boyhood fantasy—the fantasy of every boy the Empire over—is, very soon, going to be rendered a reality.

I ask him, 'You think you're ready for this?'

His retort is immediate and it echoes throughout the hangar. 'Too bloody right, I'm ready!'

＊　　　＊　　　＊

His mother shakes her head when I say it but Dylan was born to pilot *Etaín I*.

He was always a good boy, a bright boy, exceptional at all that he had a mind to do. At school he seemed gifted at maths. He was involved in the science clubs. He even took home a trophy at rugby. Despite such distractions, his mother's fears were realised soon enough. He wasn't happy with his feet on the ground. He'd inherited his father's calling. Dylan needed to fly.

From the day he was brought into this world, I'd always considered it a possibility. I'd always hoped it would be true. After all, when he was riding in a pram, his father was flying manoeuvres overhead. By the time that Dylan was old enough to ride a bicycle, he was watching me orbit the planet on the telly. He'd spent half his life on the edge of Royal Air Force research facilities, waking up each morning to the sounds of experimental aerocraft roaring past the flat. There was jet fuel in his blood.

It's the greatest blessing of my life that Dylan wanted wings of his own. In most men's lives there comes a day when he and his son part company, when a father loses his son to other interests and the world. Dylan's passion for flying meant that he never had to leave. I've had twenty-eight years with my son, flying side-by-side. After he makes his rendezvous with the Moon, I want him to fly that kite back to Earth as smoothly as possible. I'm looking forward to the next twenty-eight.

✳   ✳   ✳

I'm stood outside the Fox Memorial Amphitheatre listening to the muted commotion of the press corps when Sethna spies me from down the hallway and doubles his pace. It's time for the announcement. He's wearing a frown of disapproval. This doesn't surprise me. 'You're not wearing a tie,' he scolds.

They always wanted a famous face up front at these press conferences, a man who could capture and embody the public's glorified understanding of space exploration. They wanted a known hero. Of the first three to make Earth orbit, I was the only one still with the Ministry. They chose me as a sort of special press secretary. They should have picked someone like Sethna.

I just about shout at him. 'Dammit, Raj!' The muffled conversations of three dozen or so reporters situated on the other side of the door remind me that I should lower my voice. 'I'm here to tell them that by the fag-end of the season we're going to be walking on the bloody Moon. They're not going to give a damn whether or not I'm wearing a tie.'

Sethna, always the PR man, shakes his head. 'The Ministry's ordered ties at all briefings. You know that. Hell, I think they passed down the order *because* of you. I told you, all you have to do is keep one in your desk drawer.' Sethna sometimes plays the part of my mother better than she ever did.

I steal a glimpse at the crowd through the auditorium door's round window. 'All they're going to want to talk about is Myerscough's rant,' I mutter out of the side of my mouth. 'Did you listen to him last night? It's like watching Henriksen play Iago in *Othello*. That militaristic madman's going to get us all killed. If he had his way, we'd be sending three bombs instead of three space mariners!'

Sethna's nodding. 'Well, Myerscough's the PM. He can say what he likes and the Ministry answers to him, not vice versa. You just stick to the script and don't get pulled into any talk about the Japanese.'

'Right, right,' I reply with a sigh. 'Weather systems.'

I push my way through the swinging door and into the auditorium. Without even waiting for their conversations to die down, I call out to them. 'Ladies and gentlemen, good afternoon!'

It takes only a tick for silence to ensue. They've been waiting a long time for this, the press and their readers. *Étaín I* was built to carry three pilots, but it was also built to carry the hopes and dreams of an entire Empire. They listen patiently as I recite prepared remarks about the revised scheduling into the podium's phragm but I can see they're eager. Here, in a desert town called Christmas, the reporters have the look of children lined up to have their turn on Father Christmas's lap. The press adores the Moon. Don't we all?

I call for questions and their reaction is a unanimous roar, the sort of human roar I haven't heard since the hatch was cracked after *Blodeuwedd IV*'s triumphant return to Earth. They have questions and they're asking them all simultaneously. I recognise some of the faces in the crowd. Adele Whyte, Arthur Clarke, Kay Prior from the *Times*. Others I don't. I call on one of the strangers in the front row, a tall blonde woman from the CBC who asks her question with an unexpected and undiluted New England accent. 'Can you tell us, Mr Flemyng, in your own words, why we're seeing an acceleration of the Ministry's timetable for lunar exploration?' Some of the other reporters look surprised by the amateur query but they're all silent and eager with the anticipation of my reply. She reiterates the simple question before sitting down. 'Why, would you say, are we so eager to get there?'

I think of Prime Minister Myerscough, his thunderous words still ringing in my ears from yesterday's wireless broadcast. I can almost perceive the echoes of his remarks lingering in the thoughts of these overexcited journalists. Why? Why are we going?

Why is Britain ready and willing to claim the Moon? The answer is in the air, placed by propaganda at the tip of our tongues by a government that's at last learned to turn its greedy eyes toward the stars. The PM was blunt and his words well captured the fears of all the Empire's children. If we don't reach for the Moon, *they* might beat us to it. If we don't make the Moon our own, there will soon be Japanese eyes peering down upon the Empire from one dark crater or another, and the British people will come to fear the skies.

I pause for a moment, then I force myself to smile at that blonde reporter from the CBC. 'To be perfectly honest with you, the origins and driving purpose of Étaín are rather modest,' I explain, sounding every bit the scientist and nothing like an explorer. This is not the voice I speak to my son with. 'There are terrific advances to be achieved in the forecasting and analysis of weather systems, for instance, which is to say nothing of the technological achievements we've made in preparing for this mission. You'll find these reasons, of course, in your press pack.'

If the reporters were stunned by the obviousness of the question, they're predictably bored by the official reply. I cannot help but lower my eyes and look to the podium for a moment. I consider that Sethna may have been right. I should have worn the tie. I am, at this moment, nothing more than a mouthpiece for the Ministry of Spaceflight.

'Next question, please.'

❋　　❋　　❋

Above and to one side of my desk here at Christmas Centre hangs an antique map of the Moon drawn by the astronomer Sir Robert Simpson. Entitled simply 'Selene', it was first published in *Results of Astronomical Observations Made at Discovery Bay* in 1808. I've kept it as a reminder, the sort of reminder that anyone who values discovery must cling to in the midst of a numbing bureaucracy such as this.

The map is an elaborate, intricately detailed piece of work noting the placement and scope of various seas and beaches, naming the peaks of supposed mountain ranges and calculating the presumed density of assumed jungles. It supposes the existence of whole ecosystems on the surface of our only natural satellite. Clearly, Simpson's imagination was as admirable as his scientific curiosity. For all its inaccuracies, it is a romanticised portrait, a lovingly crafted depiction of a rich and potentially bountiful new world waiting to be claimed by the human race and the British Empire.

Our understanding of the surface of the moon has changed significantly during the past two hundred years. Our desires have not. The truth is that even now, as *Étaín I* is being prepped for her historic flight from British North America to the stars, we do not know precisely what to expect on that dusty globe that waits above. Centuries apart, Sir Robert Simpson and Major Dylan Flemyng share one certainty. In those many craters there may lay unexpected wonders or terrors uncalculated. Either way, that beautiful orb represents our destiny.

❉   ❉   ❉

I have Bill Tanner on the line from London and he's sighing an awful lot. Bill Tanner, the Parliamentary Under-Secretary of State for Spaceflight and Minister for Spaceflight Procurement, is mumbling and taking altogether too long to choose his words. It isn't like him. He's stalling, I can tell. He's hesitating. My coffee's going cold whilst I'm waiting for him to get to the point. There's something he's afraid to tell me.

Though nearly all of the Ministry of Spaceflight's research and development is carried out in British North America and its foremost launch facility is situated deep in the heart of East Texas, there isn't a decision made by astrophysicist or space mariner that's not considered, debated, and approved by the bureaucrats in London. They've got the rubber stamps to prove it. Out of all those shameless men in London Town, Bill Tanner may be the only one left that I have any respect for. It's the reason they always appoint him to handle the terrible Texan.

'Milt, there's been a meeting.'

'There have been a lot of meetings, Bill.'

Any given day the MoS holds a hundred highly consequential meetings, meetings of historical import and international consequence. Since I traded in my spaceplane for a desk I've spent a lifetime in conference rooms. But the meetings we hold here in East Texas don't worry me. It's the closed-door meetings that take place in Whitehall that I've come to fear. I put my cold cup of coffee down on the desk next to a half-eaten Scotch egg and I listen.

'Look, I don't have to tell you how the press is going to handle this occasion. This isn't just a boost for the Ministry, it's going to impact the world's perception of the British Empire,' he says, and still he's stalling. This is nothing but bureaucratic jiggery-pokery. 'They don't want any decision affecting the mission to be made indiscriminately. The PM and Jeffries sat down this morning to discuss what's going to happen when Étaín touches down at the lunar landing site.'

I tell him what I told the press corps yesterday afternoon and a cocky grin cracks across my face. 'Bill, we all know what's going to happen. When Étaín touches down on the surface of the Moon, my son and two of His Majesty's proudest space mariners will become the first human beings to march on the surface of another world.'

Tanner isn't stalling any longer. He nearly interrupts my proclamation of fatherly pride. 'Dylan isn't going,' he says, his bluntness severe.

Every muscle in my body suddenly tightens and, before I can properly register what he's just said to me, I find myself attempting a joke. 'Excuse me? There's got to be some static on this cross-Atlantic line.'

I'm wrong, of course; the cross-Atlantic vox connection is crystal clear. No doubt he can even hear my teeth grinding from four thousand miles away. Tanner's voice has gone up an octave and suddenly he's speaking far too quickly. 'I'm sorry, Milt, but I've been handed a new roster and I'm handing it down to you. Dylan isn't on it. He's not going to the Moon.'

When I next open my mouth Tanner might be able to hear

me from London without the benefit of a trans-Atlantic line. 'Bollocks! That is complete bollocks! If Dylan Flemyng's not going to the Moon then who the bloody hell is?'

'At the top of the new list is Thomas Avon. Major Thomas Avon.' Tanner's tripping over his explanation. 'He's a, uh, test pilot out of Cornwall. Exceptional training. Drafted for the Ministry back in '92. Rising star. They want him. Myerscough has said that he's to be the first one out of the spaceplane. They want Avon to be the first man on the Moon.'

I repeat the name over and over in my mind. I can't bring myself to unclench my jaw, so when it finally slips out of my lips it sounds as a sort of primal growl. 'Thomas Avon. Out of Cornwall.'

'Please, Milt, you've got to understand—'

I understand. 'He's English.'

I understand perfectly. And Tanner, the messenger, clearly doesn't.

There's no point in arguing. Bill Tanner was simply tasked with handling me. I've thrown down the vocostylus before he can even reply. I've thrown it down so hard that it doesn't quite land in its cradle and, as if to emphasise that harsh order from the Prime Minister, it takes down a family photograph sitting atop my desk before it has finished its clattering.

❋   ❋   ❋

Anyone who's flown in the cockpit of an aeroplane with their hands on the stick—or has been forced to live with an intolerable man of such distinction—knows there are two types of people in this world. There are pilots and there are non-pilots.

You can imagine, then, what it's like for those of us who've flown in space. When I registered for flight school as a nineteen-year-old boy, I could not have imagined that one day I'd be taking the most expensive bus that human hands had ever built to 300,000 feet for a once-around-the-planet. No doubt you've read the interviews with Baker and Goldman, or seen the BBC re-enactments in the twenty years since. We've all tried to describe it, to share what it is we experienced up there with the people who live their lives down here on *terra firma*. We're still trying.

Blodeuwedd IV was one hell of a plane. Keeping to their traditions, they named the program after an old Welsh fairytale, the story of a woman named Blodeuedd who is transformed by magic and forced to take the form of an owl, cursed to be the enemy of all other birds and to never again face the light of day. I don't think anyone could have dreamed up a more appropriate moniker for that kite.

She was shaped like an SP-17 cross-bred with a Christmas goose, coloured silver and white and red and blue—as if they'd draped the Union Jack across her back and let the colours bleed down across her wings—but she was sharp. She sometimes handled like a decommissioned Flying Adder piloted by a shaky old War of Wars veteran but she was the most reliable craft that the kingdom's engineering ever built and she took us where we wanted to go. She took us where everyone wants to go.

She took us to the stars.

At one hundred and fifteen thousand feet, moving at six miles per second, Johnny Baker started to howl in the seat next to me. The sound of it scared the wits out of the boys back at ground control. They couldn't tell whether he was laughing or screaming. Goldman and I knew better and we both grinned the rest of the way in spite of the extreme forces pulling against our faces.

Everyone knows that the men selected for the Blodeuwedd program—and the Puck program, and the Étaín program—were men with egos. We had to be. We were the men chosen to lead the Empire into space, to carry the hopes of the human race, to initiate a new era of exploration. What no one seems to properly appreciate is that the moment you find that you're in space, you have no ego.

After pulling five times the Earth's gravity, things suddenly seem to slow down. The spaceplane's still moving, as fast as she ever was, but in the span of a heartbeat you're seemingly motionless in a place that has no horizon, no definitions, no substance. Your body is painless and weightless, almost numb. The grey-out that's blinded you during takeoff fades away and you're left gaping like a newborn into the darkness of true infinity, unsure whether the brilliant points of light that are taking their places before you are faraway worlds to be conquered or simply bright gaps in your still fragile sense of perception. You're no longer a man of the Earth. You're no longer a Texan, or an American, or a Briton. You're a part of the universe. You *are* the universe.

And the moment when my notion of self finally returned to me? That moment when sense and sensation returned me to my body and reminded me that I was, in fact, a foolhardy Texan crammed into a flight suit bearing the proud emblem of the Ministry of Spaceflight? At that moment and during all those that followed, I dreamt of the day when I could bring my wife and my son with me to the stars, so that they could experience the same.

✱   ✱   ✱

I've cornered David Nagenda, our Chief Flight Director, in the Christmas Centre Mission Control Room. His black, podgy face is twisted with a scowl. I know that's not simply because he's frustrated with the modifications he's attempting to make to one of the tracking grid consoles. He's been expecting me.

'You knew about this?'

Nagenda sighs, takes a sip from a bottle of carb-tea, and actually pretends for a moment as if he's going to be able to carry on with his equipment checks and test simulations in a moment's time, as if it will only take a moment to diffuse my tantrum. Whether he realises it or not, he's only succeeded in angering me further. 'Tanner rang me just before he rang you,' he says, pausing to flick a pair of toggles. 'He had to give us some kind of warning. We all knew how you'd react.'

He gives me a sideways glance before returning to his numbers. I have to reach across the console and seize the clipboard in his hands to earn his undivided attention. 'Oi! Come on. This is entirely unreasonable, David.'

'Is it?'

'Two months before the mission? You know it is. And do you know what the only difference between Dylan Flemyng and Thomas Avon is? The single distinguishing factor? Dylan trained here in Christmas, Avon trained at Cornwall.'

Nagenda won't have it. 'What I know is that the PM and the Ministers are the upmost authority on Étaín, and this is their Ministry of Spaceflight, not yours.'

'Wrong. The Ministry of Spaceflight belongs to the people, David.'

'Look,' Nagenda sighs, and he's lowered his voice dramatically, watching cautiously as one of the few technicians present moves about on the other side of the control room. 'Dylan's one of the best. No one is questioning that, and no one's going to say otherwise. I know you're upset, Milt—'

'Too right, I'm upset!'

'But you have to gain some perspective! You want to whinge and lecture me about the people's rights? This isn't your Moon landing, Milton.' He sounds a bit like Sethna, assuming the role of an absent parent, offering the tired rhetoric of loyalty and responsibility. 'I'm beginning to think this press secretary position they've given you is going to your head. Don't forget who you are, Milt. We've got a job to do here. You leave the public relations decisions to the suits in Whitehall and concentrate on the mission.'

Isn't that the English way? Don't make a fuss. Don't dare stand out. Keep your eyes on your work and defer to the man above and ahead of you.

Nagenda is trying his toggles once again. I'm so enraged by the sight of him right now that, for a moment, I have to shut my eyes. This is not the way it's supposed to be. It's all changed. They've taken the whole bloody program right out from under us. They've chosen Thomas Avon from Cornwall. Bugger the colonies; history will continue to be embodied only by Englishmen.

'You and I know what goes on, David, and you know I'm right. This reassignment isn't indiscriminate, it's symptomatic. This is *our* program. If we hadn't fought for it back in the '60s they'd be launching Australian spaceplanes from sodding Woomera! This is a spaceflight initiative engineered by American minds, built by American hands, and controlled by bureaucratic English puppet masters, which is to say nothing of the singular Japanese genius those bastards have tucked into their back pocket! It's not Blighty's boffins that are extending the Kingdom to the

Moon, it's American blood, sweat, and tears—and the Prime Minister's decided that the people shouldn't be allowed to watch it on the telly unless they've got some bloody British flyboy to plant the Union Jack once he's posed for all the world to see!'

Nagenda is carelessly adamant when he tells me, 'None of that matters.'

Sometime during my breathless rant a young officer has entered the room. He's standing just to the side of the control room door, as if he's waiting for someone or something. Nagenda has been watching him nervously, glancing over in paranoia every moment or so.

'Of course it matters, David!' I press on. 'What would your father say of the British government they've established back home in Guyana? What of the unrecognised work of your brothers and sisters? How did you end up as the chief of this control room?'

'You know damn well I ended up as chief of this control room through hard work and sacrifice.'

'Precisely! And how do the Ministers reward you for all your contributions? You are nothing to these people. We're both tools of the Empire.'

'What would you have me do, in this ideal world of yours? Eh? You'd rather have me overseeing an independent Guyanese spaceflight program from the beaches of Kourou?'

'Don't take the piss.'

'Seriously,' he insists, and by now he's flustered enough to have forgotten about his work. His clipboard flashes by, dangerously close to my face, as he waves an arm. 'You'd rather see me in Guyana, with the English minding their own national borders? That's your ideal world, is it? Think about what you're saying. Can you imagine a world in which the Empire is forced to answer to its colonies? Do you think we'd be poised on the brink of lunar discovery if America, or Ireland, or Guyana were left to their own devices, to fend for themselves? Ridiculous.'

'David...'

'I know you love your son, as I love mine. I understand that, but get a hold of yourself, Milton.'

'You know what's happening here, David, if only you'd

allow yourself to accept it. This is bigger than Dylan, damn it! In a couple of month's time Avon will be marching on the Moon. What will you tell your own son of the Englishman's Empire once it's swallowed whole other worlds as well as the people of his heritage? Or have you taken to wearing one of those Union Jack armbands?'

Nagenda cocks his head to one side and suddenly the expression on his dark face changes. He's no longer frustrated. He's lost his patience. He's angry. The next word to cross his lips is a hissed warning. 'Careful.'

I wait a moment. I take a breath. I try to change my tone of voice. 'Do you think that Myerscough cares if anyone understands what we do here in Christmas? Do you think East or West Texas factor into his grand plans for the next century's Empire?' I have to shake my head. 'Hell, disregarding the American effort isn't the worst of it. You heard his speech the other day. He's telling them that the Japanese are poised to settle in lunar craters. Crikey! What would the citizens of this Empire have to say about this Moon shoot if they had even an inkling that Yoshioka was masterminding all of this from a bunker in Cardiff?'

Nagenda's eyes widen at the name and I know I've gone too far. 'Milton, you've always been a difficult bastard,' he whispers, though it's the harshest whisper I've ever heard, 'but don't be stupid. You know what's off limits. Don't make me recite the Official Secrets Act, and don't you *ever* give me a reason to report you.'

Then, just in case I hadn't been able to discern his hisses, he says it again, slowly and clearly: *'Don't be stupid.'*

A flash of shame warms my cheeks as I realise that Nagenda is right, but somehow this only makes me angrier. Out of the corner of my eye I can see that the curious young officer is still hovering, still waiting, probably listening to all he can of this private debate. I note that he's wearing the pins of a major and before I realise what I'm doing I'm spinning on my heels, redirecting a new flare of rage at this inquisitive layabout. 'What the hell do you want?'

He doesn't even flinch. 'Excuse me, sir,' he says quite flatly. 'I'm the bloody British flyboy. Captain Cregg said I'd find you here.' Then, with a smugness that could only be properly employed by an Englishman, he snaps to something resembling attention and looks me square in the eye. 'Major Thomas Avon reporting, sir.'

✳   ✳   ✳

The Countryside hero ballads tell it best. When the Continental war cry, 'To Alcibiades in Heaven', was heard atop Nuez Hill in the autumn of 1836 and the guns began their own lethal song, the legendary John Mark Morgan was at the forefront of the Continental Army's contingent and led the charge. In that historic moment his rank as captain was irrelevant. Morgan, a hot-tempered Acadien born in Pilotsville and raised in the steaming swamps and backwoods of darkest Delta, fought with the rest. He forced his way through a dozen waves of Texian turncoats that day. Morgan pushed his potential, pushed himself to be more than a soldier. He became a legend.

Somewhere far behind him, hiding in tents from the heat of the noonday sun, the clean-coated field marshals of the King's Army measured the progress of their planned invasion with maps and charts. The blood of Morgan's brothers and compatriots—North Americans all—was spilt to claim the mount. The Battle of Nuez Hill was won, for the glory and betterment of the Empire, with the brawn and the lifeblood of Columbia's own children. History was theirs and they seized it that day in Huntingdon on the Brazos. The citizens of the south owe them a debt.

Even as we look towards an exhilarating future, to new territories on unexplored worlds, we must not forget the past. The very history of East and West Texas, perhaps the proudest of the King's southern territories, speaks to the plight of our people. The foundation of the Christmas Centre was made possible a hundred years prior by those brave men battling for the common good. They fought for their children, giving of their own blood for each dusty patch of ground gained. What would brave men like John Mark Morgan say to learn that their descendents still sweat and bleed for the very fundamentals of life under the supervision of those untouchable masters overseas?

David Nagenda denies a simple fact, a fact that Morgan surely recognised atop Nuez Hill. It's up to us to change the world for our sons. I had thought that Dylan was going to change the course of history, as I once did. Maybe he still will. But my duty is not yet done, my usefulness not yet used up. The people regard me as a page in their history books long since turned. Maybe in my self-pity I've come to believe it, too. But perhaps it's never too late to push one's potential.

❄   ❄   ❄

Dylan has finished flying a run from Christmas to Waterloo and back in a BNA Eagle trainer jet. I'm there at the hangar to watch him as he brings it in for a beautiful landing. Arcing in from the northeast, he manages to make it look like he's drifting on the wind, transitioning from air to ground as gracefully as the mythical butterfly woman his lunar spaceplane was named for. It's a better landing than I have ever claimed. Some surely would say such observations are the product of watching him through a father's eyes. For this very reason my protests will never be heard by the Minister of Spaceflight in London.

Walking confidently to the hangar, his blue and red RAF helmet tucked under an arm, Dylan spies me waiting for him and the smile that flashes across his face is visible even twenty-five yards away. Try as I might, I can't return that smile. I almost have to turn away.

'How was that?' he asks, not cocky but genuine.

I tell him it was fine. He smiles and asks, 'You think it's going to be so easy touching down in that crater they've picked out for us? Or do you figure the tabloids are right, that we're going to be swallowed up by ten yards deep of moondust?'

For a moment I can only shake my head. 'I don't know,' I manage.

He can tell that something's wrong. He puts his helmet down on the hangar floor. Then his hand is on my shoulder, gloved fingers brushing the Ministry of Spaceflight emblem that his mother stitched to my jacket years ago.

'There's something I've got to tell you,' I say. 'It's bad news, very bad news. Bill Tanner called me this morning from London. If he had been standing in my office I probably would have struck him.'

He has an inkling, I can see it in his eyes, but he asks, 'What is it, pop?'

They're simple words, but these are the hardest I've ever had to say.

'Dylan, *Étaín I* is going to the Moon without you.'

And, bless his humble heart, he doesn't show half the hurt that I did. I can only imagine how I've wounded him, deep down.

❀   ❀   ❀

There are at least two names that shall be missing from any historical accounts of this truly exceptional endeavour, arrogantly erased by the Ministry of Spaceflight's official record of the events. In that sense, my son now shares something in common with Osamu Yoshioka.

I may have been overheard to say that Yoshioka possesses a singular genius, an intellect that is unequalled in any territories belonging to the British, and I mean that. That he has been so secluded by the British government expresses their ignorance and shame, the sort of narrow-mindedness now flaunted by an emboldened PM. It would be more appropriate to recognise this man as the envy of an Empire. I was allowed one sit-down with Yoshioka; I met him but briefly. His defection to the British Empire from the Empire of Japan took place in 1984. Three years later, for a short time, they transferred him to an undisclosed location right here in British North America. When the powers that be handed him the capital challenge of Étaín, the Ministry of Spaceflight permitted me to meet the secluded mastermind that had promised to deliver our space mariners to the Moon itself.

They sent a bulging 'Eyes Only' packet of his most recent research ahead of him. This was my introduction. For two hours I pored over the notes and blueprints that the Japanese aerospace engineer had spent months preparing. In the three years since his defection, robbed of social interaction and isolated from the world at large, he seemed to have accomplished the work of five men. His insight was invaluable, his inspiration incalculable.

Our meeting was short. He spoke little, responding to my thoughts and observations regarding the ambitious lunar landing program with nods or single-word replies. What's more, Yoshioka looked me in the eye only once.

I'd dismissed him and he was making his way towards the office door, ready to rejoin the ever-present military guard that was waiting for him in the hall. The question that had been nagging at my mind ever since his research packet had arrived needed to be asked. 'Wait,' I said.

Yoshioka paused at the door, his back to me, head still hanging in what seemed to be resignation. 'I've read every transcript but I'm still not sure I understand,' I told him. 'Tell me why you did it. Why did you defect?'

Yoshioka turned slowly. Through the heavy lenses of his glasses he looked me square in the eye and then, just for a fleeting instant, I thought I saw the flicker of a smile. He lifted his arm and answered by pointing toward that romantic antique map of the Moon sketched by Sir Robert Simpson.

'Why did I leave Japan?' he said after he had lowered his hand. 'I left my home because there is only one place I want to be. Understand, I have only my work. I care not about your politics, your military. My work is all that I am. I want what you want, Mr Flemyng. I want to go to the Moon. And this Empire has what we need to take us there.'

Osamu Yoshioka bowed one final time and he was gone. They carried him back into obscurity, desperate as ever to keep the Japanese mastermind behind the British Ministry of Spaceflight out of sight of the public eye, out of their minds, and out of the history books. He's been working there ever since.

❊　　❊　　❊

Bringing life to the spaceflight dreams of an Empire and rendering Celtic myths a reality, *Étaín I* settles down amidst the grey dust and rocks of the lunar landing site dubbed Avalon at just after 1900 on 14th June 1994. She's on target and on schedule.

From Philadelphia to Tokyo, the world is watching.

There are more bodies packed into the Mission Control Room than I've ever seen before. Lines of technicians are manning their stations, monitoring with unblinking eyes everything from the spaceplane's fuel supply to the vitals of the space mariners onboard. I'm watching *Étaín I* on the projector screen from the back of the room with Raj Sethna, legions of enraptured reporters crowded in behind us. 'All that way,' Sethna mutters. 'They've flown all that way and with a single footstep they'll be standing on the Moon. How many miles? And it comes down to a journey of a single footstep.'

'A footstep for Avon, perhaps,' I snort with a shake of my head. 'You ask the hangar full of hardworking engineers next door if it feels like a journey of a single footstep.'

There is electricity in the air. David Nagenda is front and centre but, while the many men and women present are showing a spectrum of emotions that runs from unrestrained joy to nervous trepidation, his is a dark, sweaty face carved in stone. Whilst we're caught up in the unfolding of history, the chief is rightfully running necessary shutdown checks with the flight crew. He is a raven-hued hummingbird, snapping his toggles and consulting his clipboard, a hand always at the stylus over his ear.

That all-business demeanour cracks when the certain voice of Major Thomas Avon is patched through the loud speakers for all to hear. Nagenda beams with joy at me and, in spite of myself, there's nothing I can do but flash a smile back.

'Control, this is Étaín I *at Avalon. We're ready to head out.'*

His crisp Home County accent is eerily clear, surprisingly uncorrupted by static or distortion during its travel between worlds. The press swoons. The BBC have already taken to affectionately referring to him as 'Major Tom', seizing upon an informal handle dreamt up by some infatuated commentator.

There is almost complete silence as Avon and his co-pilots crack the hatch above the serenely resting spaceplane's wing and internal atmosphere bursts forth in a flash of white. It seems as if no one in the control room is breathing. We can hear that Avon is doing enough breathing for all of us. His raspy, laboured breaths echo throughout his helmet and across worldwide broadcasts.

As he works to haul himself out of the spaceplane I am reminded of my offhand comment to Sethna and my smile of pride falters and fades. I'm thinking only of the labour of the American engineers who built that kite, of the sweat pouring off the brow of the American technicians monitoring Avon's heart rate, of the stress and pressures that accompanied Dylan through countless training flights.

Outside of the spaceplane, the low gravity grants the space mariners a sort of grace. The public relations men at the Ministry of Spaceflight must be relieved that their English hero can claim such a grand entrance into history. Ian Andrew Myerscough is, no doubt, thoroughly satisfied. He's surely shown the Japs.

Somewhere in nearby East Texan barracks, Dylan is watching all this on the telly.

All eyes are on Major Tom as he grapples with low gravity to plant a pole from which hangs the tall, proud banner that is the Union flag.

I hear one of the journalists behind me—Clarke, a fellow who writes science related columns for the *Daily Telegraph*—interrupt the silence. He sounds choked, as if stifling tears, as he whispers, 'This is the last day of the old world.'

❋   ❋   ❋

In London, the shining silver Moon has risen above Buckingham Palace in full view of the King. We are told that George VII is watching from the vast Bow Drawing Room windows on the garden front as the Ministry broadcasts his voice across 239,000 miles and the vast emptiness of space.

'I am gazing up at the Moon right now, gentlemen, and I know that you are looking down on us. I cannot imagine what it must be like, to see your Empire from such a vantage; to see not countryside, mountains and glens, dales and fells, villages and towns, but the globe as a whole. It is impossible not to be almost overwhelmed by a mixture of deep emotions—of

humility and reverence, of happiness and honour. Plant your banner proudly. Your effort has captured the imagination of the United Kingdom, the Empire, and the world. Never before have the people of this planet been so united in spirit. We offer awe and appreciation, together with the fervent prayer that you space mariners and your craft will have a safe return to British shores.'

His Majesty's words omit a new truth. The Moon belongs to Britain.

❈   ❈   ❈

The last day of the old world is drawing to its close.

In the Fox Memorial Amphitheatre I deliver the necessary updates and announcements. Major Tom and crew are safely back inside their spaceplane, resting up before embarking on a proper exploration of Avalon and the surrounding craters. The press is pleased to capture their final story of the day as one of the first men in space offers his polite commentary on the first man on the Moon. If it sounds scripted, that's because it is.

Afterwards, I'm followed to my office by Adele Whyte. Whyte writes for the CBC wire service. Ever since I assumed this awkward press secretary position we've developed something of a rapport. She's sharp, never misses a detail; she understands that being a reporter is in the listening, not the talking or the writing. More importantly, she trusts me and I trust her, and that's a rare thing in journalism.

Miss Whyte doesn't seem to have been satisfied by my briefing. One of the RAF guards tries to stop her from intruding as I'm opening my office door but I tell him to let her through. She follows me inside. She's a beautiful young woman but tonight she's wearing an expression of frustration or confusion, as if she's trying to solve a particularly complex maths problem in her head.

'Wonderful statement,' she tells me. 'Very poetic.'

'Thank you. Sethna wrote it.'

Whyte nods. There's an awkward moment of silence and she breaks with the formalities, her curiosity all but bursting forth. 'Milton, what the hell was that parting comment all about?'

I don't even blink. For a moment, I have to play dumb. I

have to be certain. 'Excuse me?'

'You know exactly what I mean,' she presses. 'For six weeks you've been dodging Mysercough's commentary about the conflict with Japan, systematically refusing to politicise the Ministry's efforts. You've recited the MoS party line almost word for word. Today, after Major Tom posts the Union Jack, you're telling us "the Moon is no longer beyond human reach, no longer simply a flower on a high peak," and you're praising "the minds of many nations that have carried us this far."'

'And?'

She shakes her head. She's got it. She's got it and she isn't going to let go. 'And I want to know why you're improvising on Raj Sethna's speech. Flower on a high peak; *takane no hana*. It's a Japanese reference, Milton, and I know that you're not half as dumb with words as you pretend to be. You put on your Texan drawl and talk like you're still fresh out of flight school. You can fool the tabloids and the Osage local news with that routine but you can't fool me. You went out there today with something you wanted to say, something the Ministry of Spaceflight would never allow you to say. Give it up.'

I stifle a smile and then, certain she's right, so does she.

Miss Whyte's giving me a bit too much credit. I was never a true master of words, certainly not skilful enough to rewrite history. I'm going to leave that responsibility to her. 'Adele, now that we've done it, do you suppose there's anyone out there interested in knowing precisely how the King has managed to put an Englishman on the Moon?'

She answers by reaching for her notepad and I have to stop her. The rest of the quotes—for my sake, for my son's sake—are off the record.

'Let's talk about a man named Osamu Yoshioka.'

The Twelfth Man
by Adam Chamberlain

7 August 2001
Boston, Massachusetts

The sweet crack of willow against pristine leather echoes around Fenway as the new ball skims its way through the outfield to the boundary for four. A ripple of applause from packed stands heralds a mere fifty on the board for England but then quickly dies away again, as if nervous of outstaying its welcome. It lingers in the air up here in the pavilion and I savour the moment.

I am alone on the dressing room balcony for the moment and so I take the time to drink in the vista of the entire ground from this privileged vantage point. The packed stands enshroud the impeccably kept pitch like an amphitheatre. Beneath me is the member's stand, filled with well-dressed gentry, politicians and members of the MCC all the way from north-west London's hallowed ground. Beyond that, on either side, are tiered seats for the many thousands of fans that always make a Test match a sold-out event. These are then topped by the plush executive boxes, where businessmen and celebrities look on from their mostly anonymous cubicles. Many in the stands have flags—Union Jacks or Jack and Stripes betraying their affiliation—and from here I can clearly see how segregated they are. That was a deliberate attempt by organisers and police to quell the troubles that have threatened to overshadow the play on the pitch in this series, inflamed by the political mood of recent months and years and seasoned in at least some cases by a few too many hours spent in the beer tents. The tension is palpable, but for now at least the focus of the assembled thirty thousand spectators is on the thirteen men in white out in the centre, locked in this most beautiful of games for the last of twenty-five days spent across five of the most majestic cricket grounds in British North America.

Forget the politics, forget the troubles. Today is all about which team will manage to seal a decisive result here on this piece of ground and whether England or New England stand to take the series as a result. It is all about cricket and nothing else, at least to me. It was a clear blue sky earlier this morning, but now a gentle breeze blows a band of white clouds into the sky above us, as though they too have come to bear witness to the unfolding drama below. The heavens combine with the ground to paint a beautiful picture, and it may be the last chance I get to pause and enjoy it at such a pure level. Who knows if I shall ever get to stand here and bear witness to such an occasion again? To witness it at least, even if not truly be a part of it.

※　　　※　　　※

The purity of that moment is interrupted by an enthusiastic voice from the radio perched atop the lockers in the centre of the dressing room behind me. Its familiar tone is one full of respect for the sport but somehow with an edge of cynicism that leaks in and collides with an often tacky style of presentation.

'Well, England have been made to fight for every run today, and that's probably the first shot that's been played with any sense of confidence in this innings thus far. Newbery's clearly trying to steady the ship out there in the middle, and that assured cover drive to close out the over was a clear statement of a captain's intent. New England have three cheap wickets under their belt, but this might yet turn into the dramatic showdown that this final Test so deserves to be. With the entire series resting on this result, you can be sure that both sides will be fighting it out 'til the very last ball of the final over. The crowd here are glued to their seats. They don't want to miss a single delivery. You can smell the tension in the air like gunpowder, so don't touch that dial! As if this wasn't the tensest summer's cricket we've seen in decades already.'

Hunting, a great bear of a man with a grizzled beard to

match his temperament, tuts loudly from his corner of the dressing room, hurls a glove at the radio, misses. He's all padded up ready, next in to bat, and clearly not at ease with the fact given how the innings is going. He talks to the room in general rather than to me or anyone in particular. Hunched in his seat and gesturing wildly with long, muscular arms that end in over-sized hands, he looks like he might maul anyone that dares pass within his reach. 'That'll rile them up. You can always rely on Ernie's Test Match Special commentary. Just what we need, eh? I just want to be able to go out there and play my game. Just to play the game. Is that too much to ask? It damn well feels like it is these days.' And I get the subtext of what he is saying, just as I catch the momentary sideways look at me.

We tend to leave the televid screen on mute in the dressing room and have the CBC Test Match Special commentary on, but they've had Ernie Thayer heading up the commentary team this summer, and I'm not a fan. Most people love him—he's knowledgeable and entertaining enough—but he's been scathing of anything and everything the English squad has done since we arrived such that he's just another voice seemingly set to bring us down.

Politics aside, the commentary is a fair reflection of where the match is at. We've been making heavy work of the run chase up until this point in the innings, and it's particularly frustrating to watch that happen when you can do little or nothing to change the course of the match yourself. Chasing anything less than 250 on this wicket in a fourth innings should be relatively easy; it's less than half of what we achieved in our first and it was quite an effort from our bowling attack to have restricted New England to anything less than 300 in their second. Ernie Thayer was out in the middle just prior to play this morning and, with a few colourful metaphors about 'pounding balls' and the 'tinder dry square', proclaimed the wicket still firmly to favour the batting side. I can't help but imagine him enjoying our struggle out there from the privacy of the commentary box.

Two early wickets had fallen in the final hour of play on the fourth day, though, a session characterised by the most ferocious bowling attack I think I have ever witnessed. Gardner was brought in as night-watchman, at least managing to do the job required of him: to ensure we conceded no further wickets in the last few overs.

Losing both him and our elegant left-handed opener Blake in a single over at the start of this morning's session as Riley hungrily eyed a hat-trick was a disastrous start to the final day's play. He was ultimately denied by a textbook forward defence from Newbery but his spell only served to hype this aggravated crowd yet further.

But listen to me. I say all this as though I'm a part of the team, getting carried away as I do. Yes, I'm here in the dressing room alongside the rest of the squad, but in reality I sit on the outside looking in, deprived of the chance to show my own mettle on the field with either bat or ball. Such is my lot, the ongoing curse of Joshua Exley, seemingly forever destined to be merely the twelfth man.

❋   ❋   ❋

Riley powers in for his first delivery of a new over from the Townhouse end, only then to whirl around after Winthorp fails to get bat on ball to scream an unholy 'Howzat!' at Umpire Hopper. His blood-curdling cry pulls me back out of my thoughts and into the match. Stoic as always, Hopper pauses for a moment's thought before dismissing the appeal with the slightest shake of his head. Watching the replay on the televid screen in the dressing room, that ball was going way down leg side, not a hope of LBW. Riley's just trying to spook Winthorp, but this rock of our middle order is not so easily shaken. He responds in kind, executing a perfect cover drive that dispatches the next ball for four runs, clattering unchallenged up against a Columbia Carb-Tea sign on the boundary.

The psychological battle between players can be fascinating to watch, operating on a level within that at play between the teams themselves, and that's never been more the case than with our respective captains. As Winthorp steals a single with an edge behind off the next ball, Anson—the New England skipper—then takes his time resetting the field for Newbery. Three slips, a gully, a short-leg poised to pounce... It's an aggressive piece of choreography, all designed to intimidate a batsman into giving away his wicket. Once Anson's done setting the stage, Riley thunders in and the next delivery beats the bat altogether as Newbery offers a solid forward defence that is nevertheless wide of the mark. Gasps and shouts from the crowd only heighten the tension.

'And I don't think Newbery even saw that one!' chimes in Ernie Thayer from the radio. 'Ninety-seven miles per hour—what a belter!' The roar of a car passing by at speed comes over the airwaves as Ernie offers his own sonic representation of the delivery. I hate it when he uses the sound effects; cricket commentary used to be classier than this.

Riley takes his time shining the ball and strutting back toward the pavilion before turning and starting on his next run-up, quarters of the crowd echoing his own crescendo in encouragement. That one's a full beamer and Newbery ducks as the ball whistles over his head. Hopper is quick to call the no ball, and he intercepts Riley as he turns to make that walk again to have a quiet word. There's been too many of those throughout the series from the New England attack if you ask me, and whilst they serve to incite the crowd yet further, there's no excuse. Riley takes the warning quietly whilst seeming to shrug it off, offers no apology and gets set for his next delivery, which is equally unplayable.

Ernie Thayer can't resist these moments of drama and gets carried away with himself in the commentary box once more, remarking, 'This over's rapidly turning into a full broadside from the good ship Riley against HMS *Newbery*,' and illustrating his point with a sound clip that I suppose is meant to represent a volley of cannonballs. I do my best to ignore it.

Last ball of the over and that one's slower and much straighter. Newbery plays at it, attempting his trademark off drive, but he does so too tentatively, gets a thick outside edge that I can hear from all the way up here and Stevens scoops up the ball from behind the wicket one-handed. With a single motion he rolls sideways, rights himself, rises to his feet, scoops the ball skyward and shouts his appeal, his voice soon joined by that of Riley and his teammates. With all eyes on him in an instant, Hopper barely hesitates this time and he raises his index finger, and that's it: John Newbery, caught behind for seven and we're reeling on fifty-seven for five and in real trouble here. Our captain doesn't even wait for the New English to start celebrating; he knows his part in the match is over and he walks even as the appeal is being made.

So much for the hope of a captain's innings to set us back on course. Hunting curses from the corner, picks up his bat belligerently and heads for the door as Newbery begins the long walk back to the dressing room from the opposite direction. The mood is pretty muted but I add my voice to those of a few other players and Chadwick, the team coach, to Hunting.

'Best of British,' I offer. 'Dig in out there and we'll get a result yet.'

And, perhaps predictably, Hunting singles me out for a venomous response. He pauses in the doorway, turns back and takes a couple of steps towards me, violently jabbing his gloved finger in my direction.

'"Best of British"?!' he repeats back to me scornfully. 'Don't you bloody dare! You don't get to use that phrase! I don't need you'—another fierce jab of the finger—'talking to me like that just as I'm about to walk out to the wicket. Just stay the hell out of my way, don't even speak to me!'

I recoil from him in muted deference but it's the Coach that intervenes. Chadwick rises from his seat and sets his equally tall but much slighter frame between us such that Hunting's outstretched finger is practically boring into this chest.

'Come on, Hunters,' he says with arms raised like he's surrendering to the man on a battlefield. 'Don't be working yourself up here. Save it for out there.'

Hunting opens his mouth to protest further but Chadwick interrupts him and promptly escorts him out of the room, launching into a final pep talk as he goes. He returns a minute or so later to find me still rooted to the spot whilst the rest of the room looks everywhere but at me. Chadwick throws me a sympathetic look with raised eyebrows before resuming his seat and I head back out onto the balcony.

Coach prefers to watch the game on the televid so he can study the techniques of both sides' batsmen and bowlers in vivid detail. Right now, though, that means he gets to follow the close-up of Newbery's long walk back to the pavilion, the self-disgust obvious in his face, as the stats on his curtailed innings roll across the bottom of the screen alongside the CBC's perennial circular logo of Columbia's smiling face in profile, framed by her flowing black locks of hair. Newbery yanks his gloves from his hands angrily and keeps his head down, his square-set jaw locked in a steely grimace. It's a look very uncharacteristic of him since he normally carries his lean six-foot frame with gentlemanly elegance.

They can keep the televid as far as I'm concerned. Me, I prefer to soak up the atmosphere from the balcony, given this is as close as I can get to being on the field, other than the occasional request to fetch a new pair of gloves, a replacement helmet or bat, maybe a jumper if the afternoon gets a little chilly or some drinks if it's too warm. I head back outside by myself, take a seat and let out a deep sigh.

*　　*　　*

For all my encouraging words to Hunting, at this rate we'll be lucky to bat this one out as far as the tea break, and the prospects for the match and the series are both looking increasingly grim for us. Still, I remind myself that I am glad to be here even in this frustrated, side-lined capacity for what is still a sporting highlight in the calendar: an England versus New England Test match. That sense of occasion is still very much with me and within me. If political tensions and a perceived increase in the threat of separatist acts of terrorism in recent months had provoked talk of cancelling the tour altogether, then it was thanks to the resolute campaigning of the MCC that we are here now in spite of all that, making a stand for unity amidst a troubled Empire that still holds true meaning to me. Sport can bring people together in a way that perhaps nothing else but war can, cricket in particular. Whenever

I'm inside a cricket ground I feel that shared sense of purpose, that we're all here for the same thing no matter which team we're on or our affiliations. You don't get that from all sports, but you do with this one. Right here and now cricket stands as an immovable tradition that transcends the uncertainties that face us off the field. Or at least it still tries to be.

If I sound overly analytical of this whole situation, then I guess that's just as a result of the fact that five days cooped up in a pavilion whilst such a sporting event as this unfolds around you, that you're part of in name but which lies just outside your active control, gives a man more time for reflection than he would wish. That and the fact that my presence is seen by some—Hunting for one, although he's by no means alone—as inciting the divisions and controversies over the tour yet further than they have been already. That thought is always with me, a constant and distracting companion.

Whether I deserve it or not, to the North Americans who make up about three quarters of the crowd here I am a traitor, disowning half of my inherited dual nationality to elect to play for an England side that is as despised on this shore of the Atlantic as are our politicians. What's worse is that the media only seem to be contributing to the problem. The day we got off the plane, the whole squad posed for photos in our pristine cricket whites crowned with scarlet team blazers embroidered with the three lions, all smiles and full of optimistic expectations for the series ahead. The next day the *Libertarian*—a particularly virulent anti-English tabloid here—saw fit to put us on their front page beneath the headline 'REDCOATS INVASION', and the name seems to have stuck. Other newspapers have been more sympathetic or, better still, just reported the sport for sport's sake, minus the attempts at political allegory. Maybe I'm being idealistic to have expected that to have happened across the board, especially given my selection for inclusion in the squad, but there you go.

❋　　❋　　❋

Newbery walks back into the dressing room to a chorus of

consolations. He's sportsmanlike as always in accepting them all but I can see from here as I crane around that, from the way he slumps on the bench and starts un-strapping his pads, he's simmering with disappointment at himself. I can hardly blame him under the circumstances. That kind of feeling can stay with a player for weeks, months, or even the rest of his career, especially if it proves to be pivotal to the final result, as seems increasingly likely here.

An unhelpful comment from Ernie Thayer prompts a release of tension in the dressing room.

'So, the Battle of the Captains comes to a decisive conclusion as Anson has Riley tempt Newbery to fall on his sword out there. I wonder if he just took the war too with that delivery?'

This has Newbery leap from the bench and slam the radio off. He grabs a carb-tea from the fridge and makes for the balcony, where he takes up residency next to me. I can sense the rest of the team exchanging glances across the dressing room in silence from here. I daren't even speak to John at this point. I just offer a wistful smile and we watch the game in silence together awhile.

✻   ✻   ✻

You can hardly blame Newbery for feeling the weight of responsibility so heavily. It's been a tough tour. We lost the First Test at Haverford, Pennsylvania, by an innings and sixty-eight runs and scraped a draw in the second—at Chestnut Hill, Massachusetts—by batting out the last day as defensively as we could and surviving with three wickets to spare. The Third Test, at Grand Bridge in Hartford, Connecticut, was heavily rain affected but we put in a great effort with both bat and ball and declared on the final morning, setting New England an all-but impossible 290 for victory. This time it was their turn to bat out the remaining overs, though, and the match fizzled out when they accepted an offer for bad light that effectively brought the match to a premature close just as we entered the final session.

It was only in the Fourth Test that things turned so ugly on the pitch, though. That was at St George's Cricket Ground in

Manhattan, where New England's opening attack of Riley and Stengel resorted to the worst display of bodyline bowling the game has seen for decades, since the England v Punjab series in England in the mid Forties. That made headlines worldwide for bringing the sport into disrepute at the time, but this time around it seemed almost expected, and some of the media used it to fire up yet more aggression both on and off the pitch. In spite of Anson's tactics, we took the test by four wickets by lunch on the fifth day, and that left the series square at one all going into this fifth and final confrontation.

Much of the media here has argued that there has been something nonchalantly arrogant about our approach to the series, much as they deem the same to apply to British rule and its place in British North America at this juncture. Some now even argue that the word 'British' should be dropped from the name altogether, that the country should simply be known as 'North America'. Whatever their affiliations, they have all agreed on one thing: this has undeniably been a captivating series. If anything— the more aggressive bowling strategies aside—the tensions have seemingly elevated our performances as sportsmen, given each of us a sense of added importance and meaning to the game. I've always thought that those people who make jokes about the pointlessness of cricket, who dismiss it for the fact that you can play for five days and emerge with nothing more than a draw, never really got the game for what it was at its heart, never appreciated its poetry or rhythm. They never understood the true meaning of cricket.

That meaning was always central to me and has been for as long as I can remember. Playing cricket in the back garden with my grandfather is my earliest memory. I love this sport and all I ever remember wanting to do from the time I first gripped a bat, from the first time I stretched my tiny fingers to hold a real cricket ball in my hand, was to play it, just for the sake of being on that field. My grandfather always said that cricket was far more important than just a game, and slowly I began to learn what he had meant. If my presence on this tour has proven controversial, then I would point out that my pedigree in the sport cannot be so readily called into question.

My grandfather was Henry Crenshaw, one of the heroes of the game back in the Forties, captaining England for seven glorious and trophy-laden years. Ironically, it was the arrival on the scene of my grandmother that is now seen as the death knell on his career. A fast-living singer and actress, he was drawn into her world, one that ultimately ended her own career in an untimely fashion in 1953. That year also heralded his final season, when we were whitewashed by both the Australians and New England on home soil, and he resigned the captaincy as a result. His own performance was as bad as his ability to lead the side that summer; he only made double figures with the bat twice in both series. Returning home in disgrace, he never played for his country again and sank back into the twilight of his career with a quiet, unremarkable presence confined to the county circuit.

Their daughter—my mother—Maggie Crenshaw met my father when he was on tour here himself with the Test team in the summer of 1968. It seems that successive generations have always been drawn to other cricketers, had their lives bound by the game. My father had enjoyed a blistering series with the bat that summer; Wallace Exley was the only player on the tour to score in excess of 1,000 runs and finished the summer with the coveted *Lillywhite's Scores and Bios* Batsman of the Year award. My pristine copy of that year's almanac, signed to me by my father, is amongst my most prized possessions.

Mother was working in the catering team at St George's Cricket Ground in New York that summer and was, so the story went, swept off her feet by the charm and grace of the man who flirted outrageously with her during every single day's lunch and tea intervals. His behaviour was deemed a little scandalous at the time. Nevertheless, she accepted his offer to return to England with him at the end of the tour, and they married a matter of weeks later.

I was born the following year, but even then the cracks in

their union were appearing. It was, they have both told me since, a passionate but short-lived love affair as it turned out and that, coupled with my father's touring schedule and an incorrigible roving eye, led to their marriage falling apart when I was just seven years old. Sometimes it feels like my very existence was an accident. Two irreconcilable people had a chance encounter and I was the outcome.

After the divorce my mother moved back here to British North America and, whilst I stayed on at boarding school in England, I spent most summers in New York with my mother and saw more of her in all than I did my father. Adding insult to injury, she took up with a townball player a couple of years later and is still with him, now well into his retirement from a coaching career after he packed in the game itself. And so it is I have both English and North American heritage coursing through my veins, without ever feeling wholly one or the other. Those summers in New York have even led me to develop an odd mid-Atlantic accent that sounds like nowhere in particular. It still draws raised eyebrows wherever I go, although it's become a habit for me to slip into one accent or the other depending upon my company. I've never been easy with that lack of a single identity and it has, of course, complicated and restricted my career, but at least I get to play. Above all—and perhaps standing as the only thing that has been consistent in my life—I have my cricket.

I can't stress enough how much I love cricket. If so much else in my life has been uncertain for as long as I can remember, so undefined, so prone to change, then I have often consoled myself that I have always had the game. And I really do mean 'The Game' as nothing else comes close for me.

I had come to learn even as a child to keep them separate, these increasingly contradictory parts of myself: the Englishman and the North American. I compartmentalised my sense of self—not just my accent but every aspect of being—into two distinct halves that seemingly could not be allowed to co-exist. It was a means of surviving, to partition my very self between two continents.

❊   ❊   ❊

I'm daydreaming again, but Hunting brings me back into the match by hooking the next ball for a huge six over square leg. I hear the splinter of wood from here and the crowd erupts at the sheer immensity of the stroke as the ball clears the stands. Newbery squirms in his seat as he cranes to follow its trajectory, but I know he's feeling a mixture of elation and dread. Elation for the two-fingered salute it gives to New England's bowling strategy, dread that Hunting might throw away his wicket by slogging just to make a point rather than bat himself in properly, no matter how good an eye for the ball he has.

Chadwick calls for me then and I swear under my breath, realising what he wants before he even says so.

'Exley! Hunters needs a new bat,' he explains. 'That shot just splintered his Salix. His sponsors will be happy. Take another out there to him, be a good lad.'

I instantly feel sick at the prospect, but I feel I have a genuine reason to object.

'Really? You think it's a good idea to send me out there? Are you forgetting how he spoke to me?!'

'Give me some credit, Exley,' returns Chadwick gently yet firmly, tapping his temple with an index finger. 'I know what's going on up here with him, I know what makes him click. You're the perfect man for the job. Still, that said... Sorry,' he winces, knowing what will greet me out there. 'Do me a favour, though,' he adds, 'and ask him to rein it in a little. We don't need his fireworks, we're not in a hurry. He just needs to stay in and punish the bad ball when it comes.'

I nod my agreement, grab a brand new Salix bat from amongst several in varying conditions in Hunting's kit bag and leave the dressing room for what I know is about to be a very long walk.

❊   ❊   ❊

As I make my way through the largely empty corridors and

rooms of the pavilion, knowing what awaits me, I allow—if not encourage—myself to be distracted by my surroundings. There's something of this building that calls to mind the pavilion at Lord's itself, that has my mind wander once again to thoughts of England. The Victorian architecture of Lord's really speaks of the history of the game, staking its place at the heart of the civilised world that cricket surely represents. The paintings that hang in the Long Room there are steeped in that history as generations of historical icons and locations of the game rub shoulders with one another.

There's a whole other sense of history here in this building, which is a place of notable historic interest on this side of the Atlantic Ocean. It was here, on this spot, well over two hundred years ago in what was then a Townhouse that, during a rare visit aimed at quieting dissident voices, Prime Minister Pitt had spoken. This was a part of his campaign for what would become the Columbia Compromise, allowing representation from these shores to sit alongside the heart of government and of the Empire itself in the Houses of Parliament back in London. I was taught all this in school, told that this was one of those quiet moments in history that was to prove pivotal in shaping the future of the Empire, its historical significance only appreciable in retrospect.

A decade after that, in 1776, a notable traitor was imprisoned here for a short time before being shipped back to England for trial and ultimately his execution over the *Common Sense* affair. The place just oozes history from every panel of its walls, and if you study the building of Fenway Cricket Ground it's almost as if it sprang up from its historical connections.

The centrepiece here is now the Courthouse Gallery, which is like a temple to the sport. The walls are lined with a number of definitive portraits of cricketing legends both past and present. As I stride through I glance about at them, and here is one that stands out: that of my grandfather, flanked by W.G. Grace on one side and Samuel Wright on the other. I afford myself just a moment to falter and appreciate it, recognising the sharp, almost feminine features set against swept back light brown hair that so closely mirror my own. And then, in the next moment, I am aware again that the entire Test match is now waiting for me to take to the ground. I take a deep breath and step outside, down past the members' enclosure.

Straightaway I feel heads turn towards me and cameras flash; the media enclosure is here. One reporter even dares proffer a diaphragmaphone to me, following me out to the edge of the pitch, and I recognise her right away. Penny Carter from the *Columbian*, not the tabloid that printed that infamous headline but not much better. She shouts a question at me.

'Joshua Exley, do you feel you've chosen the right side to play for today? Would you be as proud of a win for England as for New England?' I catch her eye but merely glare in response, heading out onto the grass and making for the middle. And then the crowd erupts. There are whistles mixed with jeers and boos, although I also hear a little applause from a small minority. I try to focus upon that and shut out the rest, but they are all but drowned out, and then I spy a huge 'REDCOATS GO HOME' banner in the crowd just to my left being waved for the benefit of both myself and, perhaps moreso, the televid lenses.

I break into a jog towards the square and look up to see Hunting leaning on his splintered bat, just patiently watching my approach. He's going to make me walk the whole distance rather than leaving the stumps, purely to prolong my humiliation for as long as possible. I will his damaged bat to give way beneath him and have him collapse on the spot. It doesn't.

I only slow my pace as I reach him out in the middle, having passed New England players who have done their best to ignore me completely, and am now more than a little out of breath. I proffer the new bat with my right hand and hold out my left for his damaged one. 'Here,' is all I gasp.

'Thanks,' is his similarly curt reply.

I almost forget to pass on Chadwick's words before catching myself as Hunting goes to turn his back on me.

'Oh, a word from the Coach.' Hunting stops and half-turns, an eyebrow raised from beneath his helmet. 'He says to slow it down, wait for the bad delivery, concentrate on staying at the crease.'

'Tell the Coach,' sneers back Hunting, 'he can shove it up

his arse.' He turns away again but adds as a parting shot, 'As, by the way, can you.'

Right. That was to be expected. At least I passed on the message, and I'm not convinced that Chadwick knew what he was doing sending me out here after all. I take another deep breath and turn back for the pavilion when I first make out the chant from the far end of the ground, only then to hear it slowly grow as various other portions of the crowd join the fray. It's taken from a song I know I've heard, here just reduced to a guttural, raw monotone, but unmistakeable nonetheless as the crowd repeat it over and over.

'You're all out of time and your rules are a joke. You're all out of time and your rules are a joke. You're all out of time and your rules are a joke...'

If this is just the home crowd trying to maintain the momentum for their team and snatch a victory having spent too long in the beer tents during the lunch break then I would have expected something a little less barbed. It soon seems to surround me, and suddenly the protection of the pavilion seems farther and farther away. I am conscious that I must stop short of breaking into a full run and giving the impression that I am fleeing the ground, but I pick up into a jog again to make my exit.

Another of my detractors, William Randolph, is at long mid off, virtually on the boundary himself, and as I look up to seek out the gate back into the pavilion I catch a self-satisfied sneer that he unmistakably sends in my direction. I fancy he might even have joined the chant himself. I meet his cold gaze and return it with my own. And then I pass the media again with a hail of camera flashes and another attempt by Penny Carter, flanked by a couple of her competitors, to get a comment from me on record. Right now they wouldn't be allowed to publish what I might have to say, but I just look the other way.

This means that the last thing I see before I re-enter the sanctuary of the pavilion is Randolph again, a huge advertising board on the side of the stand bearing his face with open mouth hungrily advancing towards some mutated sandwich. The slogan— 'Real men don't bail on the Stump!'—reminds me of his tacky celebrity endorsements. This one is for a sandwich of sorts filled with one each of pork, venison and Cumberland sausages lined up and wrapped in a bun to fit around them that Feltman's have been marketing over here this summer. These hybrid monsters will be on sale at any number of their outlets behind the stands, and quite apart from how bad they probably taste (I've never tried one and have no intention of so doing) it sickens me that such brash commercialism finds its place here. If it's not Randolph and the Stump then it's our own Holliston advertising that Hi-Amp footwear enhances his bowling performance or some such nonsense. It's rampant on both sides of the Atlantic but I hate it.

These thoughts are at least another distraction as I return through the pavilion to the dressing room and the sounds of baying crowds subside behind me. As I re-enter the dressing room itself, I note that Ernie Thayer is droning on in the background once more. I may simply be paranoid but I have to wonder who turned the radio back on, when and why. I'm quite happy at least to have missed his commentary on that little intermission. I make for the balcony but Chadwick intercepts me.

'Thanks for doing that,' he says quite genuinely. 'I know it may not seem like it, but that will have evened him out and help him to focus him on the task in hand.'

I'm not convinced but I mutter that it was no problem and take up a spot in the farthest corner from the radio, not so keen to venture back outside for a while. I sit and watch the televid screen in silence for fifteen minutes or so and everyone does well to leave me be.

All this time Newbery's out on the balcony by himself, whilst out on the pitch Chadwick's being proved right as Hunting starts taking a little more care to bat himself in. We're at seventy-five for five now. Stengel's come back into the attack whilst Riley continues from the Townhouse End, New England's strike bowlers bombarding both Hunting and Russell Winthorp, that other stalwart of our middle order, from both ends of the ground. Still the occasional bouncers and beamers come, but both batsmen are by now well versed at evading them. I'm getting restless in here and so I get up and tentatively edge up to the open door, peer round the edge onto the balcony. John Newbery is seated but leaning forward over the railing, as though he's using sheer willpower to keep our batsmen out in the middle still in the game.

I chance my luck and step through the doorway out onto the balcony, then gesture at the empty seat next to him.

'Mind if I join you, skipper?' I ask, sounding slightly more meek about it than I had intended.

'Be my guest,' he says, and I can tell he means it. He's very much an open book that way, always seems so genuine. It's one of the reasons he's reassuring to have as a captain. 'It's still a free country here,' he goes on, looking up at me. He then proffers a wry smile as he adds, 'Well, last time I checked it was, anyway.'

We sit in silence for another few overs before I venture any further comment. The score is slowly climbing towards the hundred mark; it feels like at last the innings is stabilising.

'We can still make the target here so long as these two stay at the crease,' I suggest. Newbery pauses to see the result of the next delivery before responding. It's Stengel from the Boylston End and Winthorp fends that one off with a backward defence, right up close to the stumps.

'Sure we can. We've plenty of time yet, and wickets to spare.' Ever the optimist, Newbery, keen to ensure team morale recovers in spite of his own shortcomings out in the middle. 'Just not my day out there today. Anson seems to have told his attack to rain down fire and brimstone on us at every opportunity. It's just not cricket as I know the game, but what can you do.'

'I agree,' I offer, feeling somehow inadequate. 'There's so much on display here that just isn't the game I wanted to be a part of.'

I mean it, too. Cricket is all about codes of conduct and standards of behaviour. This modern era of the game is losing all of that. It's come a long way from *Gentlemen and Players*, although I have to wonder how many people related to the nostalgia of that classic film even back when it was first shown in the Eighties, in spite of all the accolades.

My last comment draws a look from Newbery but his attention is diverted back to the pitch as Stengel comes in again with another ferocious delivery. It's a full toss and Winthorp pauses for a moment, seemingly uncertain whether or not to play at it. It's a fatal split-second moment of indecision as the ball takes out his middle stump and it turns somersaults in the air as it's skittled down the pitch for about twenty yards. Winthorp strikes his bat in vain at the air before tucking it under his arm and starting the long walk. He made twenty-eight but it's unlikely to be enough and we're still eight short of the century mark with six wickets down. Newbery curses and slams a fist on the balcony railing and I wish I hadn't opened my mouth now. I stay put, though, and we just sit in silence.

The crowd's applause subsides and is overshadowed by chants and jeers from the home supporters. It's as though the applause came from the pure fans of the sport, and now the less desirable elements get to make themselves heard. Meanwhile, John Spalding has set out for the stumps. He's really in the side for his superior spin bowling—he took three wickets in the first innings for just fifty-two runs that helped to clean up the middle and lower order—but he can be useful with the bat too. I don't dare say as much out loud at this moment, though. And then, thankfully, Newbery breaks the silence. He talks as though both batsmen can hear him, through gritted teeth.

'Come on, lads. It can't end like this. We've come too far and fought too hard for it to end like this. There's too much riding on today.'

❋   ❋   ❋

He's right. The way this Test has played out thus far is as though playing here in British North America, and at Fenway in particular, with everything riding on this result, our squad feels like we have more of a point to make than the home side. Likewise, however, it is as though New England feel they have to deprive us of the glory. The historical baggage of so many Test series between our teams is constantly with us and is only yet further fired up by the attitudes of the crowd.

It seems to me that if you were so minded you could trace

the fall of civilised relations between Britain and North America in our cricket. With each season fewer and fewer players are rising through the ranks to this level, and fewer still are learning the game anew. Townball's seen as a cruder, inferior sport, but more and more kids seem to prefer it, on this continent in particular. More than any sport, though, judging from the headlines, they would rather be holding a gun than a cricket ball, rather a knife than a cricket bat. Tensions have risen here to such a level that mortal danger never seems far from the city streets. Shootings and stabbings are on the rise, and they often seem to be politically motivated. Being here this summer I feel that there is some outbreak of violence waiting to hit this country unlike anything the world has seen since the War of Wars. How can something as pure and gentlemanly as cricket hope to survive days such as these?

They even stopped King George coming here to watch the final Test in spite of his protests. I can sort-of understand it given the current climate, but sometimes I think they still treat him with the same kid gloves that they did for all those years after his mother's assassination. When he was the newfound Prince Regent after the Queen's death, there was a whole decade where it seemed they barely let him leave Buckingham Palace.

I don't claim to know or understand what's happened, really, and have never had too tight a hold on politics in spite of myself, but it's become almost impossible to separate the tensions of the Parliaments of Westminster and Philadelphia from those between these two teams, locked into twenty-five days of media-hyped sporting endeavour.

I thought this was a time when countries were meant to be uniting, with leaders the world over talking of common purpose. But it seemed the opposite was set to be true within the Empire itself. Even back in Britain, there was talk of the Union cracking at the seams, of Scotland, for one, considering seeking independence. Still, I've never claimed to be a politician. All I wanted was to be out on that field playing an honest game of cricket to the best of my ability, but as I saw it politics had robbed me even of that, and with no good reason. Whatever the result, history was set to be made here today, the culmination of a series set to be recorded forever in *Scores and Bios*. I just so want to be a real part of determining whether or not we retained the Byrd Diaries and got to take them back to England with us.

❈   ❈   ❈

Cricket lives and breathes history, and maybe that's best exemplified by the fact that any Test series between England and New England has earned itself the title of 'The Byrd Custodian' series. The title dates back to the earliest literary reference to cricket having been played on the North American continent, as recorded in *The Secret Diary of William Byrd of Westover*, to have taken place on his estate in Virginia in 1709. The diaries were only discovered at the beginning of the nineteenth century by Byrd's descendants. They were later bought at auction by the Patterson family of Philadelphia, themselves a historically significant cricketing family who have produced some of the finest players from this side of the Atlantic.

And so it was that in a bout of bravado prior to the commencement of the first ever Test series between England and New England back in 1888, New England's captain George Patterson was so certain of his team's superiority that he wagered with his opposite number that should the touring England side win the series, he would hand over the original bound copies of the diaries that had been in his family for over fifty years.

It was a wager he was to come to regret by the end of that summer, when England took the series by two matches to one, sealed with a five wicket victory at his home ground of Haverford. But, true to his word, he relinquished the journals and they left American shores for the first of what would become several occasions over the decades. It soon became tradition that the winner of any Test series between the two sides would retain custody of Byrd's original diaries, and the moniker was born from that. History passed from one side of the Atlantic to the other and back again as the years went by. They've travelled with us on the tour from ground to ground, and right now they sit on display in a glass case downstairs in the gallery for all players, dignitaries and club members to glimpse.

✳   ✳   ✳

See, there's so much history in cricket that to me, cricket *is* history. It's this living, breathing pantheon of tradition into which I am still trying to stake my place. And so long as I have the strength in my arms and legs I will keep playing this game: for myself, for my father, my grandfather and the entire legacy of this game I hold so dear. I only wish I could divorce it from the politics, because I know I'm as good as any man out there on the ground today. I know I deserved a cap on this tour.

It's as though Newbery is reading my thoughts as he turns and addresses me.

'You okay there? You always seem to be lost somewhere inside your head these days.'

'I'm fine,' is all I can muster in response, my gaze still fixed on the game.

'You'll have to do better than that.' He turns and faces me, forcing me to return his stare. It takes me a few moments, even so.

'Where do you think this is all headed, skip?' I ask. 'I mean... We've never had to play in conditions like this before.'

Newbery lets out a long, deep sigh, as though I've spoken of something that has been weighing heavily on him also. 'I don't know, Joshua. I just don't know.' I can feel his eyes surveying my features, gauging me as he might an advancing bowler. 'It's hard for you, isn't it? Harder than for most of the rest of the team, I mean. Given your background.'

'I suppose.' I don't really want to talk about this openly, not even with John, whom I trust implicitly. 'It's hard for the whole team, though.'

'That it is.' Another pause. 'But I wish you'd made the team. We could've really used you out there this summer. We talked about it, but we just can't afford to have you in the final eleven.'

It takes a moment for what he just said to sink in, but when it does I turn to face him.

'Excuse me?' I ask with some intent, and now it's his turn to look uncomfortable.

'I was... discouraged from picking you by the selectors,' he admits with a pained expression. 'I got you into the squad, 'cause like I say you deserve to be here. But there were... elements that felt it was best not to put you into the final team. And look at the crowd here today; they did have a point. Twelfth man was the best I could muster. And, let's face it,' as he disguises his discomfort with a grin and slaps my shoulder, 'You're the safest pair of hands we have in the field when we've needed you out there. That catch you took at Haverford to take out Randolph in the second innings was nothing short of spectacular. "Like a resolute lion pouncing to take out its prey," Ernie said, I think.'

That was indeed a great moment, one that even got the crowd fleetingly on my side when every other time the ball had come to me in the field that day it had been accompanied by jeers and boos, cries of 'Traitor', 'Redcoat', 'Turncoat' and much, much worse besides. It had been as thought the match ball carried a curse with it every time it was within my grasp. But I'd had too many moments like that and too few chances at glory and this was the first open admission from Newbery as to his part in that being the case. A moment's flattery wasn't going to cut it.

'Just how hard did you try, then? You told me you'd put your own captaincy on the line to get me here. Did you really, or did you just roll over and have them pay lip service to me?' I'm angry now; I'd never talk to my captain like this normally. He keeps his cool, though.

'Listen, Joshua, I did everything I could. Really.' I refuse to respond and so he fills the silence. 'You shouldn't take any notice of the crowd. It's just a few ignorant people.'

'That's not what I'm talking about. Forget the bloody crowd! You're the skipper! Your job is to get your best players out in the middle and then get the best out of each of them. And now you're telling me you've let the bloody MCC walk all over you?'

I go to get up but he puts a firm hand on my shoulder and pulls me back down into my seat. 'I did what I could, Joshua. I'm sorry, really I am, but I have to think of the whole team. And I'm sorry, but having you here is inflammatory and that's not good for the squad. Come on, you must see that?'

He's right, I suppose, but it does little to quell my sense of betrayal. It's funny that I never got this impression from him before, but then I know as well as anyone how we can think one thing and yet say another, intentionally or otherwise, how true thoughts and feelings so often go unsaid in our day-to-day lives, no matter who we are or what our situation.

I stay put and we watch a tentative Spalding block his first couple of deliveries with a solid forward defensive. The crowd are still volatile and mark each shot with a loud response.

'What do you make of all this, then?' I ask after a couple more minutes of uneasy silence. 'Of the mood, of the climate here?'

Newbery pauses again, considering his response carefully.

'I don't know what to make of it, to be honest. Just a minority of fanatics, bringing their cause along to the ground. I think most of the population are quite happy with the British. I don't think there's any real cause for alarm. We just have to be a little careful is all.'

I simply nod my agreement. Secretly, I am not convinced. I feel like I understand the mood at play here better than most, that there's something here that runs much deeper and stronger than most British people would credit. There's a tendency to always think things will continue the same, moreover that we're all destined for some happy ending. That's not been my experience of life so far.

We continue to watch in silence but I at least feel like we've broken the tension between us, that we understand each other a little better. Things continue to pick up on the pitch, too, and Hunting and Spalding see out the rest of the session and bring the total to 129 by lunch, halting the collapse that had seemed to be inevitable only an hour or so earlier.

There's still some tension in the air over the lunch break. I try to congratulate both batsmen on their return and we then all head down the corridor to the pavilion dining room, but Hunting still doesn't want to know and fails to even feign interest in what I have to say for the sake of common decency. Newbery takes them both to one side and gives them a pep talk and they seem to lighten up a little. Chadwick joins them as they take lunch together on their own table. I wonder what they're saying, although the tactics should be clear enough. We still have plenty of overs left in the next two sessions to make the remaining hundred or so runs required. The key is not to lose any more cheap wickets and not to be intimidated by the New England bowling attack and their unsporting tactics.

I take my lunch with the rest of the team, one eye always on their table. There's Maine lobster on the menu again, as there has been each day of the Test, but I have no stomach for it today. I pick at my food in silence for a while before prematurely taking my leave of the table, going unnoticed by my teammates as I do.

As I reach the door to the corridor back to the dressing room, a few of the New England team are only just making it in to eat. I step aside to let them through and am greeted by William Randolph leading them in.

He sneers through a smile at me. 'Lost your appetite?'

'Just getting yours back?' I counter. I'm done taking crap from the likes of Randolph. He's still bitter at losing his wicket to me in the third Test, but it's more than that. We've hardly come across each other save for that day a few weeks back, but it's as though it's given birth to some kind of rivalry between us. It happens, as much as I don't like it, and I'm not going to let him get the better of me. I make to pass him but he blocks my exit with his tall, stocky frame.

'Don't worry, I'm sure we'll all be able to go home early,' he says right into my face, to the audible amusement of his teammates. 'Remind me, where exactly is that for you?'

'Get lost, Randolph.' I'm on a short fuse after our last meeting and in no mood for his taunts, and I'm surprised at myself as to how firmly I try to front him out. 'Try filling that face of yours with that crappy dog food you're so fond of advertising if it'll shut you up.'

That's all it takes to incite Randolph to violence and I don't even see his fist before it connects with my jaw. I reel back into the dining room before composing myself to retaliate, but before I can do so Blake and Darling are at either side of me, holding me back and barking at Randolph to back off. The likes of Stevens and Barrows do the same with Randolph and they drag him off to find an empty table.

Newbery jumps up to join Blake and Darling whilst I wrestle free of their grip. I have to spend a few moments assuring them I'm fine and that I don't want any formal complaint to be lodged, as they start insisting should be, then return to the dressing room, which I have to myself for a few minutes before the rest of the team start back themselves, several of them checking that I'm okay. I shrug them all off and distract myself by listening to the Test Match Special, where Ernie's thankfully turned his attention away from events on the pitch and is thanking the Boston Women's Institute for delivering a Victoria sponge cake that he and the rest of the production crew are tucking into up in the commentary box.

❉　　❉　　❉

Play resumes with military-like precision at two o'clock on the dot and thankfully we pick up where they left off, Hunting dispatching two fours in the first over. Somehow, he always finds the time to play his strokes even against the fastest, most formidable bowling, but at least he's now selecting with more care which balls deserve to be punished. His eye for the ball is animalistic, instinctive in its coordination; he dismisses it from the crease with panache and provenance. For most players the New England bowling attack is a terrifying prospect, especially when wielding the added firepower of the new ball. But Hunting has now successfully turned those tables and put the bowlers on the defensive.

He is quite ably assisted by Winthorp at the other end, and the two seem to be bedding themselves in for a fruitful partnership, seeing out Riley and Stengel's spell with the new ball. Within a half-hour we're past the hundred and fifty mark and the match seems very finely poised indeed. I feel restless and spend my time between the balcony and the dressing room, as do many of the rest of the team. I don't have cause or opportunity to speak with Newbery again, as much as I'd like to. Thankfully, though, neither do I have cause to head out onto the pitch for a while. The cloud cover has extended to blot out the sun completely, so neither batsman calls for drinks.

There's a palpable sense of expectation in the dressing room, though, and also amongst the crowd, as our innings builds yet further and a victory slowly seems an ever more realistic possibility. Hunting's the first to reach his fifty off virtually as many balls and still retains his fluid form from the previous innings, which the crowd appears to appreciate. The edge seems to have gone out of the New England attack now, with our batsmen firmly on the resurgence. Less bouncers and beamers are delivered and Anson goes back to the textbook, seemingly urging his bowlers to concentrate on line and length and setting the field to restrict the chances for a single. Resolute, Spalding reaches his fifty with a square cut a while after Hunting's, notching up two hundred on the board at the same time. Just thirty-two needed for victory now, four wickets still in hand, and even Ernie Thayer's cutting back on the cynicism and begrudgingly granting England some credit for turning their fortunes around.

It's a new over and Anson brings Don Martin back into the fray from the Townhouse End. His medium pace hasn't been all that successful in the match thus far, but his first ball beats Hunting and earns a nervous, expectant gasp from the crowd. His timing is perfect with the next delivery, though, as he steps up the wicket to the ball and skies it for a huge six into the stands to our right.

It takes a few minutes for play to resume as the lively crowd are slow to return the ball and Spalding meets Hunting in the centre of the square, clapping a glove on his shoulder by way of congratulations as they exchange a few words. Hunting then tries to drive the next ball but doesn't connect with this one as well as he might have. Still, he optimistically calls for a single anyway and Spalding sets off from the other end. He's badly misjudged the pace he got on that one off the bat as the ball goes straight to Barrows at mid-off with too little pace behind it. He runs in, scoops it up and takes aim at the wicket at the Pavilion End as Hunting scurries to make the last few yards. Martin's already there backing up, but he doesn't need to be as it's a direct hit and the bails are knocked clean off. Hunting was running his bat in and there can only have been inches in it, so Umpire Rice reluctantly has to call up to the third umpire for a decision as Martin leads the appeal.

There's an excruciating moment then as the whole ground holds its breath, and then the replay is shown on the huge vid screens that flank the pavilion, as well as on our own here in the dressing room, around which we are all by this point crowded. Frame by frame it advances, but it soon becomes apparent that Hunting didn't make it. The word 'OUT' shouts across the screen above a repeating animation of a forlorn cricketer walking from the square, trailing his bat and hanging his head. The crowd erupts outside. Hunting made eighty runs that could well prove to be the innings that wins us the Test and the series, but with the score now at 206 for seven, once again there's everything to play for. Hunting will not be happy at all with being dismissed like that but he does at least remove his helmet and acknowledge the crowd with raised bat as he holds his head high and completes the walk back here to the dressing room.

Ernie Thayer, of course, has something to say on the subject. This time he's talking about the slight gradient in the ground that slows the ball when it's hit towards the Townhouse End. The Townhouse itself was built on a slight hill, by all accounts, and that's what's put pay to Hunting's day at the stumps this time around, or so Ernie would have us believe. 'Is it all downhill for England from this point on?' he postulates to another of his excruciating little jingles.

It's true that there is certainly something about cricket that is unique to each ground, to its pitch, slight variations in gradient, size, speed and even the atmosphere that inhabits it during play, but I always find myself focussing more upon that which is in common to each ground, the familiar. I look out from the balcony and find myself focussing on the square at its heart with this perfect green landscape radiating from its centre, and even in this tense moment of the match it inspires something of a pastoral, timeless sense of England, an arena within which two teams of eleven men play out the dance of this most beautiful game. Right now it is that feeling—the call of England—that comes to me, even as this series reaches its climax. It is in moments like these, moments of high emotion and drama, that I come to know myself better.

✳   ✳   ✳

My grandfather used to speak at length of how Test cricket is, at its heart, pure theatre: a drama in four acts within which we, the actors, explore the nature of each other through the language of this intricate sport. You could even read it in a similar way: if you know how to read a scorecard, he said, how to really read in it how an innings had unfolded, it was as if you could understand the drama through the numbers on the page. And the audience will always come to see that drama unfold, with the benefit being that this play is written and directed by the actors as you watch. It is always different from the time before. And so they come time and again to see their heroes in action, to see each act take shape in this or some other setting steeped in the history of past encounters, to be reminded of the ongoing legacy, of this connection between past and present that cricket provides.

He used to talk like that a lot, and moreso after the death of his wife, usually with a hefty glass of brandy in his hand. To run with his metaphor for a moment longer, though, there is a definite mystique to a venue such as this one, or Lord's, that I think only the most dedicated players can truly appreciate. It's as though it reveals itself through the Test as it plays out; it's another character all of its own, perhaps the most important one of all in shaping the result of the drama to which it bears witness. And who knows, but just maybe, in this moment, Fenway lent its character to the outcome of the entire series.

❋ ❋ ❋

By now Stockton's at the crease and marking middle stump for himself, preparing for his first delivery. These last thirty runs seem at once a relatively modest target and a huge task. Cricket can turn within a single over in one or other team's favour, and this could be one of those moments. The crowd swell in their support for the home side as Martin comes in for his next delivery, but Stockton catches it on the half-volley and fends it off solidly enough.

A tense few overs follow but the score creeps up past 210, and Stockton even manages a boundary with a lucky edge that just evades fine leg. Spalding passes his own fifty but then falls to Riley as Anson himself jubilantly picks up a simple enough catch in the slips. Just fourteen needed for victory now and the entire crowd, Ernie Thayer and our own dressing room included, are on tenterhooks. We only have two wickets to spare now and New England have worked well into our lower order. This could still go either way.

Frank Deford is new at the crease and sees off the last ball of the over, although it beats his bat completely, and now it's Spalding back on strike. Stengel's next over would have been a maiden save for a single bye, with both batsmen's performances now clearly suffering from frayed nerves. Then it's Riley again from the Townhouse End with Spalding on the receiving end of New England's return to a more aggressive bowling attack. By the fourth delivery he's clearly had enough of playing around. Riley lets loose another beamer and rather than duck out of the way of this one, Stockton decides to play it and strikes the ball at head height with a pure agricultural shot that nearly clears the boundary over mid wicket. As it turns out, it bounces once just this side of the rope and goes instead for four. That's just ten runs required now with two wickets standing, and the tension in the air is electric.

In spite of that and in what seems like a moment of lunacy to me, Riley tries the same with his next delivery, and this time Stockton's not so lucky. The crowd gasps as he attempts the same stroke again, misses, and the ball strikes the face guard of his helmet. He's stunned for a few moments and we're glued to the screen as he manages to remove the helmet and shakes his head. From the close-ups on the televid screen it looks like he's escaped with nothing more than a cut lip. He signals as such up to the pavilion but then motions to his helmet.

It looks like the face guard has been left pretty mangled, so he'll need a replacement. Chadwick turns to me, goes to speak and then seems to think better of it. He singles out Blake.

'Blake, take him a new helmet out, would...'

'It's okay,' I interrupt. 'I'll go.' It's the first time I've spoken for a while and I realise how much my jaw still hurts. Chadwick looks uncertain.

'You sure you want to do that?'

'I'm sure. It's fine.' I know what to expect but that only makes me more resolute to face the crowd, to be undaunted. It has to get easier each time, I tell myself. And so, spare helmet and a damp towel in hand, I set off again for the pitch. Newbery claps me on the shoulder and gives me a silent nod to wish me on my way.

I pause once more in the Courthouse Gallery to look up at the image of my grandfather, frozen in time, affording myself just a moment to falter and appreciate it. I can't hang around, though, and so I walk on past the glass display case holding the Byrd Diaries, surrounded on all sides by a set of Surveillance System cameras. Again I pause to consider whether they'll be coming home with us after today and it's then that I am caught squarely on the shoulder by a groundsman with a large, empty backpack slung over one shoulder crossing my path from the other end of the gallery.

He almost knocks me off balance, which wouldn't have been so odd had I not been stationary at the time and the gallery otherwise so empty, so I shout after him to watch where he's going. He turns and glowers at me, his head cocked on one side, a stocky brute of a man in the regulation blue overalls and wellies. He holds my stare just long enough for me to be unnerved, offers not so much as a word in reply—let alone an apology—before continuing on his way out of the gallery in the direction of the car park. Was he then so unaware of my presence or was he really just that obvious in his disdain as to strike me on purpose? I don't really have time to mull this over further just now, aware again that the entire Test match is now waiting for me to take to the ground, so I take another deep breath and step outside and down past the members' enclosure, this time jogging past the volley of looming journalists.

The jeers and chants start up again almost immediately. I wouldn't have said it was possible but the crowd seem to be baying even moreso this time around, perhaps spurred on by the almost unbearable tension in the match at this point. I break into a jog towards the square and am pleased to see Stockton heading back in my direction. He's a good man, one of my stalwart supporters in the team, and he'll be no more comfortable with this than I. He's almost in the outfield when he meets me with a clap on the shoulder and offers a grim smile.

'Thanks, Josh,' he says. I return his expression as he takes the new helmet, hands me the ruined one and uses the towel to wipe the blood from his lip before returning it. 'This damn crowd, eh? Let me get back to the crease, end this and get out of here.'

'You do that,' I reply. 'And don't be hanging around when you do. Find another boundary for the winner and then run for it. If we actually come through here, I've no idea how this lot will react.'

He nods, gives me a broad smile, puts on the pristine helmet with the air of some modern day Crusader, turns and heads back to the crease. I turn back and instantly catch sight once again of Randolph, still at long mid off out towards the boundary, the sole fielder between me and the pavilion. At this point I'm wondering if he requested the fielding position just to afford himself more opportunity to wind me up. As I approach him this time he just shakes his head at me and mouths something offensive that I can't make out; I wish I could return that punch to the face from earlier. The din seems to get louder still, the home crowd now perhaps trying to lift their team to take those last two wickets and snatch a late victory.

And then, the next moment, a whole different wave of sound fills my ears, drowning out the crowd in an instant, as I see as if in slow motion at least half of the first floor of the pavilion burst outwards with the force of a huge explosion. In the next moment I am flung backwards with tremendous force, the helmet spinning away from me as both it and the towel are torn from my grip.

As I keel over backwards, my senses struggle with the scene before me. Masonry, glass, bodies and a billowing fireball all burst out from the source of the blast, spilling debris onto the members' enclosure below and out onto the pitch. I catch sight of Randolph falling forward with the force of the explosion from behind before a dark cloud of smoke and dust engulfs him. Moments later that same cloud envelops me, too. I am pushed flat onto my back into the turf and everything goes black.

❋   ❋   ❋

I am not sure how long I am unconscious, but as I come round I feel my lungs burning from the smoke, my head is swimming and I have a surreal awareness of people screaming and running in all directions around me, of feet stamping past within inches of where I lay. It takes me a few moments to remember what I just witnessed and that I must've been knocked out by the force of the explosion, and when I do I lay on the ground for what seems like only seconds but could be much longer. It's only after I feel my senses return to normal that I begin to drag myself slowly and painfully to my feet. I wince and falter as I realise I've sprained an ankle or something, and so I hobble a step or two as I do my best to take in my surroundings.

As far as I can make out, players, spectators and ground staff alike are all haphazardly attempting to make for the exits, although from where I stand now I can't see properly for more than ten yards or so. The hateful chants have been replaced by a hideous din of screams, cries and groans that is underpinned by a rising chorus of wailing sirens both distant and close by. I put enough weight on my ankle to start walking in the direction of what I believe to be a way out at the end of the Avon stand to my right. Within moments someone slams into me as they rush past. I just about make out the outline of a man in full cricket whites before he disappears again into the dust cloud. I think that he may have been carrying a cricket bat. Stockton? Deford?

I stop again and simply do my best to remain standing, unable to move, dazed, stunned and almost toppling over as I strain not to put too much pressure on this right foot. Instinct dictates I should be making my way as best I can in the opposite direction, as most others seem to be, but in fact I find I've been hobbling towards the source of the explosion, as though some invisible force is drawing me towards it even as it has blown so much debris outwards.

As I approach, the smoke and dust begins to clear a little and I can see what remains of the pavilion in front of me. It seems now to be fashioned from clay and that some giant hand has reached in, scooped out its heart and dashed it to smithereens on the stand and the edge of the pitch in front of it. The balcony and dressing room where I have spent much of the last five days are a hideous void and I cannot believe that Newbery or any other member of the team can have escaped alive. Even in the midst of this chaos I am struck by how I was sat there with them all just a matter of minutes ago on a balcony that has now been obliterated. I remember too that had I not interceded with Chadwick's attempt to protect me from the baying crowd then I would still have been there when the blast went off, that I would have perished with them.

The coach, our captain, my friends, almost the entire team, just... gone. There's nothing left, surely no hope that they might still be alive, no sign of them save for the fragmented structure of the back wall of the dressing room, which is still partly standing. Everything in front of it has simply disappeared, the members' stand below and in front of them a burning, unstable mass of rubble, from which I can now see bloodied limbs protruding in places. None of them appear to be moving from within their smoking pyre. A violent sickness rises in my stomach.

Neither the scene of abject horror nor the stench of smoke and dust that grows stronger with every step is enough to daunt me and I find myself hobbling yet closer to the ruined facade of the pavilion itself. In the gloom I almost fall over a piece of advertising hoarding that has been rent from the boundary in front of the pavilion, flung onto the pitch, now embedded in the outfield. It's a Hi-Amp advert with an image of the lanky Sam Holliston sprinting through mid-air. I stare at the euphoric look on his face in the photo and can think of nothing but the fact that he is surely lying dead somewhere in the rubble mere yards in front of me. Maybe it's this sense of proximity or maybe it's the image of my grandfather's portrait that is still fresh in my mind's eye that drives me on, but I stumble forward yet closer.

It's clear that I'll never get to set foot into the pavilion itself again, though. From the white picket fence gate that marks the boundary and walkway into the gallery, I can see that the far half of the ceiling has collapsed under the force of the explosion or weight of the debris, whilst the half nearest to me is on fire. Dark, acrid smoke punctuated by licks of flames—the heat from which I can feel searing my skin from here—billow outwards and both the wood panels and the historic paintings that hang upon them are ablaze. I can make out the shape of my grandfather's portrait even as it burns, one of many priceless historical artefacts melting away before my eyes. The podium housing the Byrd diaries is a smouldering heap of debris.

Without even being aware of it I find I have fallen to my knees in front of the gate and I am sobbing. I am aware of an instinctive voice telling me to flee but nevertheless I find myself rooted to the spot, drawn to the ruination before me, to the devastating fire that may yet engulf me too. I wish it to do so.

❋   ❋   ❋

Wracked with emotion though I am, an entirely rational train of thought enters my head as to the nature of what has happened here. A bomb, then, an act of terrorism seemingly set to target the England team or perhaps the MCC members that were sat directly in front of the pavilion. Separatists undoubtedly targeting what they see as the colonial Imperialists of the English cricketing establishment or some such nonsense. So much history destroyed by this act even as it inevitably opens a devastating new chapter.

It's then I remember the man that I presumed to be a groundsman who collided with me a matter of minutes ago in the gallery. Did the bomber—or at least one of the conspirators' number, for surely there must have been more than one—walk right by me on his way out from planting the device? Would the SS cameras have captured images of him, or were they sure to have been destroyed by the blast? Did the man work here all along, or was he maybe an impostor of some kind? Who was he? What can he possibly hope to achieve by this? Worst of all, perhaps, did he purposefully collide with me as some statement of intent? Was I a primary target, given who I am and what people would have me stand for?

I retch now as this further realisation hits me and finally I turn away from the devastation of the building before me. Smoke wafts across the ground as if over a battlefield. Fewer people are on the pitch itself now, so far as I can see at least, but there are still many spectators in the stands, fighting past each other for a way down and out to safety. The Avon stand's huge structure to my left creaks ominously, causing a fresh wave of panic and screams.

Surveying almost the entire ground from here, or as much of it as is possible through the gloom, I think once again now of those who may have survived and search the figures that I can make out on the pitch for anyone else in cricket whites. I can see none. The pain in my right leg and ankle seems yet more severe as I stumble forwards again towards the square and, whilst it may be all in vain, I feel a need to find a fellow player alive amidst this horror.

Smoke and dust still drift about such that visibility remains sparse but I blunder through clouds of it almost blindly at times. I continue in spite of the continuing pain, although within moments I falter once again. At first I think my foot is giving way again before realising that something or someone lies prone on the ground in front of me. A bloodied hand reaches up towards me and a voice groans weakly for help. I look down.

It's Randolph, though I'm not sure he even recognises me. One side of his face is covered with blood. His hair is matted with it, his whites drenched deep red. His neck is kinked at an unnatural angle, his head rolled back too far. It clearly causes him great pain to speak at all but he manages to utter a few words.

'Please. Help me up,' he manages to rasp. He tries to move his head upwards and, as he does, I see that one cheek has been all but ripped off by some shrapnel, leaving the eye socket exposed.

I look down at him, a pathetic figure now far from the arrogant, sneering adversary that has spent the summer taunting me in public or private at every opportunity. There is no look of recognition in his face; in fact, there's barely any expression of note that I can detect at all. Randolph is never one to conceal his emotions, whatever they may be, but he is now barely capable of expressing any sentiment at all, save perhaps an implied sense of fear and pain.

I stare back down at him. I offer no words, comforting or otherwise. I simply loom over him and survey this prone, wounded creature. Calmly, I look about me; there are no doctors or nurses on the scene to be called upon as yet, only lost souls consumed with their own primal need to escape the ground. He speaks again.

'Please, get me out of here.' I turn my gaze back down upon him. 'Can't feel my legs.' He tries to look back up at me but struggles to do so. 'Can't lift my head.' I can see now that he is only talking out of the right side of his mouth. Here lies half a man, at most.

I am not aware that I even consider my next reaction. I am not mindful of lording any power of life or death over William Randolph, although perhaps, were anyone surveying the scene, I might appear in my cricket whites as some lonely angel contemplating the fate of the soul of a fallen comrade. There is no conscious decision, no inner conflict, but only one course of action that seems to even offer itself to me. I look up from the twisted figure that lies before me, identify the rough direction of the exit on the other side of the pavilion from the still creaking Avon stand, and I walk away.

I hear no further sound from him as I turn my back and I wonder if he is unable to speak further or if there might have been some recognition there after all, now at least. I wonder if he has any awareness of who has left him to his fate, of how easy it was to do so in a moment that was thoughtless in the literal sense of the word.

The heat from the pavilion burns my entire right side as I pass it so close, yet I limp on within inches of the rubble even as I dare not look in its direction again, finding my way eventually through another missing section of the boundary. I have no idea how long this takes me. I seem to be finding it harder and harder still to walk.

I pick my way through the rubble, stumbling once or twice, and find an exit alongside an edge of the members' stand. There's no-one else about here, everyone that could seemingly evacuated from this part of the ground, but more bodies clearly lie half-buried to my right, most of them lying face down where they have been thrown forward by the blast. Somehow I feel unaffected by the sight of them now, numb.

❋   ❋   ❋

As I emerge from behind the stand I find I am in the public courtyard area that encircles the ground, next to the Fenway souvenir shop. There are many more people about here: the walking wounded, the dazed, the lost and many more on stretchers being attended to by medics. Sirens rage beyond the perimeter wall with ambulance, fire and police crews beginning to arrive in significant numbers and racing about amidst the chaos. Those that are uninjured are being marshalled out through the open ticket gates, fire crews are just starting to be escorted in and the paramedics that are already here are doing their best to attend to the injured.

I know I need medical attention myself, but all I want now is out of this place. I make for the lines of hundreds of spectators being directed through the gates by police. I am hoping to blend into the crowd without being recognised, hoping that everyone else is too intent on their own escape to afford me—this object of so much hate what seems only a matter of moments ago—a second glance.

But I don't make it that far. Each step is more laboured than the last, my progress painfully slow, and then I feel fingers grab my arm. I turn and raise a hand to dismiss what I presume to be a paramedic only then to find myself staring into the cold reflective glance of a televid camera.

If I am taken by surprise then I instantly feel foolish to have been so. Of course the media will want to transmit this live, to beam the final act of this tragedy across the Empire. News crews are doubtless jostling for space on the other side of the wall to the ground now; I feel that there is no escape, not really, not for me.

I return the televid lens' blank expression and only after a few moments catch sight of Penny Carter, stood to its right and still clutching that phragm. I'm taken aback to even see her, surprised she survived the bomb at all given where she would have been standing, but, through some devilish turn of luck, here she is. Her face is bloodied, her hair matted with dust, but she's still determined to ply her trade. She looks for all the world like a war correspondent reporting from some burnt and dusty village in Sabah.

'Joshua Exley!' she shouts above the furore that surrounds us. 'Mr Exley, are you injured? Have you seen any of your team-mates? What did you witness from the field itself? Mr Exley?'

I feel a swell of hate and anger, but for all that I am weak and can barely speak. I hold up a hand in front of the camera and I shake my head. 'No,' I manage to say weakly. 'Not now. Not here. Not me.' Her eyes meet mine and something in my face makes her back off. I stagger away, until I am out of sight of the cameras, onwards towards the exit. Alone and separate, as the mayhem continues around me. I turn back and look at the ground from where I stand as ambulances and police cars swarm into and around it in ever increasing numbers. A sense of detachment comes over me.

The day has come, then. This has really come to pass. Newbery was wrong; there are men in this land who are to be feared, whose intent is deadly serious. He was wrong, and it has cost him his life to discover that truth. The union of Great Britain and British North American has surely been dealt a deep blow here on this day, one that will resound for many months and years to come. The sky grows yet darker with smoke and ash that swirls about me. My head swims and I feel faint.

Even then, in that moment, I imagine England's green fields under blue skies and days when I was less heavy of heart. But here, in British North America, in Fenway Cricket Ground, both the sport that has brought me such joy and the country that gave birth to half of who I am is dying here today before my very eyes. Stood surveying the devastation, I see no way back. How can I ever now hope to place myself once more in this treacherous terrain? I see no future in this land.

I now know that I am not of North America. Maybe I was once, but there is nothing that represents who I am and nothing of Britain to be found here anymore. This is not my world. I simply want to go home. With that thought foremost in my mind, everything fades to black once more.

I feel myself fall.

Appendix A
Timeline

14 September 1766   Prime Minister William Pitt proposes the Columbia Compromise, establishing a framework for North American representation in Parliament. Pitt's imperial vision serves to unify Britain and her colonies and establishes a centralised governing body for British North America. The British North American Parliament initially meets in a different city for each of its annual three-month sessions.

23 May 1768   In an historic election, fourteen American representatives are selected by the British North American Parliament to serve in the House of Commons of the 13th Parliament of Great Britain following the 1707 merger of the Parliament of England and the Parliament of Scotland.

26 August 1772   The Parliament of Great Britain votes to cease sending convicts to penal colonies in Georgia following sustained campaigning by politicians in both British North America and Westminster, where the primary concern was the potential danger that the country become a home for dissidents. This results in thousands of prisoners instead being shipped to other colonies, chiefly Australia.

3 January 1776   Thomas Paine publishes his incendiary political pamphlet *Common Sense*. The text, denouncing British rule, is immediately banned in all British territories. In the colonies, thousands of copies are burned before reaching readers.

14 July 1777	Construction begins on the Palace of Philadelphia as the city is officially established as the fixed seat of government in British North America.
10 March 1780	American insurrectionist John Adams is hanged at the Tower of London alongside traitors Richard Henry Lee and Edward Loomis.
7 June 1783	In Sautersburg, Kentucky, Archibald Pilling instigates the Breckinridge Rebellion, the first of many armed regional revolts against colonial tax codes.
23 February 1790	The British and Irish Parliaments pass the Union Act, officially merging the Kingdom of Ireland and the Kingdom of Great Britain. A secondary provision grants voting rights to land-owning Catholics but non-Anglicans are not allowed to run for office in Ireland until 1839.
15 January 1804	A minor incident of mid-Atlantic piracy—in which the *Gonzaga*, a ship of Spanish registry, seizes the goods of the British clipper *Argonaut*—sparks a naval conflict between Spain and the British Empire. The Spanish attempt to retake Florida from the British Empire but are ultimately driven back, losing the whole of Spanish Louisiana to Britain in the Treaty of Lausanne, signed on 10 September 1804. Unaware of the treaty, the Spanish Fifth Fleet is destroyed when it engages a superior combined British and Dutch fleet north of Grand Bahama on 12 September.
16 April 1806	Andrew Hathaway begins an expedition across North America to reach the Pacific and chart the Oregon Territory. His work bolsters British claims to the territory, which is officially annexed to the Empire in 1838. Hathaway later writes of his journey, 'It is a most magnificent place, the

West. I can only hope that in traveling to this Arcadian Eden, we've not precipitated its defilement at the hands of men motivated by profit, nor caused its native peoples future distress.'

3 August 1813   A division of American conscripts leaves Newport News, Virginia, bound for Europe. The unit becomes the first Continental Army division to fight in Europe, participating in the Peninsular Campaign in Central Italy, battling a combined Spanish and Austrian Habsburg force on the plain below Assisi. The victorious effort brings new respect from the King's Army for the Continental Army.

26 May 1829   War correspondent Matthew Handy—born in Pittsville, Erie—becomes the first to photograph wartime operations during the Franco-British campaign against the Ottoman Empire for control of the Suez and Sinai, the first joint military action by Britain and France. The three-month conflict expels the Ottomans permanently from Egypt and enables the construction of a shipping canal through the Suez.

23 August 1833   The Slavery Abolition Act is passed by Parliament, outlawing slavery in the British colonies. Within one year, all slaves in the British Empire are emancipated.

5 September 1833   In response to the abolition of slavery, citizens across southeastern British North America revolt, organising into militias with a hierarchy similar to the Continental Army's. The rebellion is crushed over the course of four years in a brutal, destructive and costly military campaign.

28 August 1836   The Republic of Texas, independent since splitting from Mexico in 1828 and heavily populated by settlers from British North

America, is invaded by the King's Army and Continental forces in retaliation for providing material and financial support to southeastern rebels. Texas is officially annexed on 30 October 1839 and split into the separate territories of West Texas, East Texas and Osage.

9 April 1839   In response to complaints from British settlers who have moved into northern Mexican territories, Britain launches a war of conquest designed to open a path to the Pacific Ocean, ultimately seizing a third of Mexican land, including the northern ports of San Francisco (renamed St Francis) and Los Angeles.

2 April 1842   The consolidation of the King's Army and Continental Army is completed. Units are still organised regionally but all serve under the same aegis. Barriers to American advancement in the King's Army are lifted.

13 June 1846   The British Empire, claiming infiltration by Mexican raiders along the southern border of its North American territory, declares war on Mexico. After a series of military victories, Britain offers to end the war in exchange for the territory of Baja California. The embattled Mexican government, on the verge of collapse, assents to the demand.

26 May 1847   The Crown India Act liquidates the British East India Company, nationalising its holdings under the auspices of Her Majesty Victoria of the United Kingdom.

16 September 1852   Philip Farnsworth completes the laying of the first trans-Atlantic telegraph cable.

1-30 June 1856   The massive failure of successive potato crops across Europe hits Ireland especially hard. Though hundreds of thousands of impoverished

Irish families face starvation, the British government continues to export food from Ireland to England, Scotland and Europe. The situation spurs mass emigration from Ireland to the American West as well as an Irish Nationalist uprising in 1859. A military crackdown and reorganised land policies end the revolt in early 1860.

1-31 May 1869   In the month of May, the governments of Britain and France, independently sensing that they've fallen behind the Dutch and Portuguese in their efforts to establish colonies and expand trade around the world, embark on campaigns of territorial expansion in Africa and Asia. The competitive nature of the campaigns is labelled the Scramble for Empire and leaves much of Africa in the hands of the two powers by 1888.

9 March 1877   Britain allies with Persia, Poland, Finland, Sweden, Bukhara, Khiva (now Turkestan), Japan, China and Romania against Russia in the Great Northern War to curb Russian territorial ambitions in Central Asia and Eastern Europe. The results of the war include: the territorial expansion of Poland, Persia, Japan, Romania and Finland; the transfer of Alaska to the British Empire; the restored independence of Lithuania, Bukhara and Khiva; and the creation of independent Tuva, Buryatia, Mongolia, Armenia and Livonia.

15 June 1881   David Mason becomes the first person to successfully record sound at his laboratory in Colwell, Michigan.

29 August 1886   The British Mosquito Coast Company acquires a charter to build a canal across the Isthmus in Central America. A strip of land is leased from the governments of Gran Columbia and Costa Rica for building. The project, expected to take

six months, takes twelve years. The Canal Zone is subsequently annexed by the British Empire in 1899, leading to the defeat of Costa Rica and Gran Columbia in the Thirty Days' War and the permanent acquisition of the Canal Zone by Britain in exchange for financial considerations and special trade status for the two nations.

18 February 1888   The last remnants of the Sioux Nation formally surrender to American forces at Blaineville, New Cambria. The so-called Red Indian Wars draw to a close.

13 July 1892   The Town Hall of Gateway, Missouri, is bombed by American separatists, initiating a series of attacks against prominent government buildings in Midwestern British North America—notably in the cities of Osage and Plains territories—attributed to the separatist and anti-British groups growing in influence in the new western territories. Prime Minister Arthur Martlew Dunbobbin deploys 15,000 British troops to the Midwest to keep the peace.

13 March 1899   Sir Rudyard Kipling publishes *The Empire Stories*, a popular collection of short fiction inspired by his travels in India and America.

31 December 1899   With separatist violence on the decline in the American Midwest, the British peacekeeping force known as 'Dunbobbin's Army' is withdrawn. The announcement is timed to coincide with various celebrations held to ring in the new century.

19 August 1910   Chinese Republican forces depose the last Emperor of the Qing Dynasty, establishing the Republic of China. The new government's first foreign policy act is to initiate trade talks with the powers of Europe, leading to the establishment of European trade zones on the Chinese coast.

7 August 1919	*La Purga* begins in Spain. Catalonian anarcho-syndicalists assassinate Alfonso XIII and overthrow the government, seizing power.
17 November 1921	The American Parliament enacts a law prohibiting the manufacture of liquor in British North America. Imported British spirits become the only legal alcohol in the American territories for nearly a decade.
23 April 1924	The British Empire Exhibition, the largest event of its kind ever held, opens in Flushing Meadows, Queens, New York.
15 August 1924	The Great Queens Fire begins with rioting at the British Empire Exhibition. Over the next four days, fluke winds drive the fire west toward Manhattan, destroying much of Queens and Brooklyn.
23 December 1924	John Rutheim—American agitator and leader of the western anarcho-syndicalist movement—is publicly executed alongside five of his associates outside Manhattan City Hall for the crime of high treason. Called 'Christmas for King George' by the papers, the hangings mark the beginnings of the anti-socialist movement in the British dominions. The Red Hunts last for two years and ruin thousands of lives.
23 June 1928	Austria and Hungary dissolve their union, becoming separate states. In the coming months Austria cements a union with Bavaria and is immediately attacked by Prussian Germany. In the ensuing three-month conflict, Britain and France intervene on the side of Austria. Unable to fight on two fronts, Germany abandons its war effort, reverting the Alsace region to France and removing Luxemburg from Prussian suzerainty. Baden-Wurttemberg joins the German federation, completing the unification of

Germany. British forces remain in Bavaria and Austria at the request of the government, despite German objections. The Czech regions of Bohemia and Moravia become the independent Republic of Bohemia, which is quickly reduced to a client state of Germany and Poland.

12 March 1933   A Southwest Africa-based German military unit under the command of feared General Josef Heichller attacks New Birmingham, a diamond-mining town in British Shonaland. Many historians cite the attack as the true beginning of the War of Wars. The offensive begins a campaign to expand German territorial holdings and access to resources in southern Africa. German forces seize Harristown days later and begin a drive toward Zimbabwe, the capital.

1 June 1933   Ignoring Polish warnings, British and Austrian forces invade Bohemia at Kralova, inciting Poland and Germany to declare war. British forces advance swiftly through eastern Bohemia, reaching the Polish border. Slovakia and Hungary join the war on the side of Britain and Austria on 9 June.

21 August 1933   The first major British offensive of the War of Wars outside Bohemia is launched against Polish and German forces in Moysche, Poland. In the Battle of Moysche Fields, British forces break the Polish-German lines in a matter of days, moving deeper into Poland.

18 November 1933   The Royal Navy begins a blockade of the Baltic Sea.

25 November 1933   British troops near Krasnostaw, Poland, are the first to use gas in a large-scale military offensive, resulting in the death of some 3,000 Polish defenders. The British advance grinds to a halt outside Kholm and both sides dig in for a long, bitter winter stalemate.

12 April 1934   A Polish attempt to dislodge the British at Kholm
                     fails and the War of Wars stalemate continues.

1 July 1934   Vocal sensation Jenny Monroe reaches the top of
                     the British North American hit parade with
                     'Thinking of My Soldier Boy'. The song comes to
                     be regarded as Summer 1934's most popular and
                     anthemic single and remains in the chart's top
                     slots for nearly one full year.

30 August 1934   After limited involvement in the War of Wars,
                     most significantly in areas of covert operations
                     and espionage, Spain joins Germany and its allies
                     in their efforts to expel the British from Europe.
                     During August and September, Spanish troop
                     transports run the British blockade. Despite
                     heavy losses, over 15,000 Spanish troops reach
                     Germany. The deployment of 10,000 Spanish
                     troops to the front at Kholm breaks the British
                     line, pushing the front fifty miles southward
                     toward the Bohemian border.

15 November 1934   Crooner Noltan Nellie overtakes radio with his
                     hit song 'Christmas Time is Here Again'. The
                     song remains at the top of the hit parade
                     throughout the holiday season and well into the
                     new year.

26 December 1934   *Los Fantasmas de la Noche*, an elite Spanish military
                     unit led by Fernando Corte Marquez, crosses into
                     British North America from Mexico. Over the
                     following year, the unit is responsible for
                     numerous acts of sabotage, assassination and
                     communications disruption.

19 February 1935   The Bohemian Legion, overtaken by British
                     troops at Prachdischa, suffers its greatest defeat
                     of the War of Wars. The Bohemian Legion's
                     estimated losses reach 6,000 during the three-
                     week British offensive.

19 March 1935   British forces in south-central Africa recapture Harristown, Shonaland, from German forces. The city is renamed New Harristown and completely rebuilt upon the site of its predecessor. It becomes the base of a strengthened British military garrison. A municipal dedication ceremony includes the unveiling of a monument memorialising Harristown residents killed during the German attack and occupation. New Harristown grows quickly, reaching a non-military population of over 10,000 within five years.

22 March 1935   France joins the War of Wars on the side of the British, striking through the Alsace into Baden-Wurttemberg. In late April, French forces cross the Pyrenees and unite with Basque rebels on Spanish soil. The French invasion bogs down in the hills south of Navarre and the Spanish Front settles into a pattern of trench warfare similar to that seen on the Polish Front.

25 April 1935   The largest offensive action of the War of Wars on British North American soil takes place when a detachment of *Los Fantasmas de la Noche* attacks the Trumble and McCain Industrial factories in Kingston, Ontario, with light artillery stolen from a nearby Royal Army supply depot. The assault is launched in conjunction with several smaller bombings in the territory, most notably at factories in Sarnia and Windsor, both mid-sized cities significant for their arms manufacturing efforts, and the power station at Niagara. This date comes to be known as the Day of Darkness and results in the establishment of major military installations throughout British North America's key industrial centres. This 'home-guarding' is observed for the remainder of the War of Wars.

12 June 1935   French forces reach the Rhine River at Mainz but are driven back five miles in the following week.

The sides settle into a stalemate by mid-July.

16 July 1935   Russia officially enters the War of Wars on the side of Germany and Poland but does not commit combat troops.

29 November 1935   A British expeditionary force sets out from New Harristown and drives deep into German Southwest Africa. On 24 December, the force reaches the territorial capital of Kruger. The German colonial force, severely weakened by the recall of most of its soldiers to Europe, capitulates on Christmas Day 1935, effectively ending the German colonial presence in Africa.

7 January 1936   Relentlessly pursued since the Day of Darkness, a heavily depleted *Fantasmas de la Noche* force makes it over the Mexican border. Of the unit's 500 men, only 38 survive.

23 August 1936   General Fernando Corte Marquez, the military tactician who led *Los Fantasmas de le Noche*, is assassinated by American spy Adam Hardesy at his home in Spain.

14 January 1937   After months of winter stalemate, the government of neutral United Netherlands invites emissaries from the warring nations to Maastricht for negotiations. A tenuous peace is agreed upon. Troops from all sides are moved toward pre-war borders in Europe on various fronts but no nation executes the full draw-down of forces called for in the agreement. A tense truce sets in.

28 April 1937   The Royal Military College of Kingston, Ontario, celebrates the efforts of its many esteemed alumni in the War of Wars, both those who died in the line of duty as well as those still serving Britain overseas. The event plants the seeds for an Empire-wide military holiday.

17 May 1939

Three flights of German strategic bombers totalling 450 aerocraft hit manufacturing sites in London, Coventry and Birmingham. German ground forces cross into Bavaria and strike France through Luxembourg while Polish forces launch an offensive in Slovakia. The offensives are blunted after twenty-four days of fierce fighting.

15 June 1939

The Republic of China, a careful and impartial observer throughout the early years of the War of Wars, allies itself with Britain. Serving the United Kingdom's effort in a crucial capacity, the country devotes a great deal of its labour power to the manufacturing of arms. The government of the Empire of Japan strenuously objects to the alliance, withdrawing its ambassador from London. Japan, however, has officially been at war with Russia since 1931 and remains on the sideline in the War of Wars, unwilling to join an effort against the British that includes the Russian Empire. It is the low-level, opportunistic naval action of Japan that prevents Russia from being able to focus fully on the European Front. Many historians point to China's involvement at this stage as a key turning point of the War in favour of Britain.

9 August 1939

The British Royal Air Force launches its first major air attack on a city, carpet-bombing the German aerocraft manufacturing centre of Frankfurt. French bombers simultaneously raid Essen.

14 February 1940

Russian and German forces drive into the Balkans from southern Poland, overrunning Romania. Germany's Heibenzer tank divisions and coordinated offensive strategy quickly secure large swathes of territory in an attempt to create a new front and relieve pressure on Poland and the German homeland.

29 June 1940	A large-scale British operation in the Balkans dubbed *Operation Icarus*, particularly targeted toward Russo-German ally Serbia, is thwarted largely by the Heibenzer divisions. Manufactured primarily in Russia, the Heibenzer tank proves to be the single deadliest machine of ground warfare used during the War of Wars and, despite Britain's efforts to match it, the Heibenzer is not equalled for mobility and destructive power. The Balkan Front remains fluid for the duration of the war, with German and Russian forces ultimately contained in Romania, Serbia and Bulgaria by British, Hungarian, Bulgarian, Greek and Ottoman forces. The Balkan Campaign is largely regarded as the key strategic mistake of the war on the part of Germany and Russia, distracting energy and resources away from the front in Germany and Poland.
6 July 1940	French forces take Barcelona. Hours later, the anarcho-syndicalist government of Spain is deposed by disgruntled veterans of the War of Wars, leading to two decades of military rule in Spain. Spain sues France for peace and most of its soldiers in Northern Europe, suddenly on the wrong side of the lines, become prisoners of war in Germany, Poland and Russia. The regions of Navarre and Catalonia become effectively independent under the terms of the deal.
2 November 1941	The Great Battle of Dresden concludes as British and Colonial troops overtake the German city after a ten-month siege. An estimated 250,000 men and civilians perish on either side of the lines during nearly a year of fighting. Leipzig, to the northwest, falls soon afterward, leading to the surrender of thousands of German soldiers.
5 August 1942	French and British Colonial forces cross the Rhine south of Frankfurt. They meet British and

Austrian forces at Augsburg in southern Bavaria days later. Late in the month, Japanese forces seize Vladivostock and land on Sakhalin, forcing Russia to transfer soldiers eastward.

11 October 1942   A large Russian force crosses northern Poland to relieve the German defenders of Berlin. The arrival of Russian reinforcements halts the British offensive in eastern Germany. The Battle of Berlin concludes with the retreat of British troops well south of the city's limits. A six-month stalemate known as the Long Wait ensues, eventually leading to an armistice between Britain and Germany.

2 June 1943   The Treaty of Wurzburg officially brings the War of Wars to a close, revising the national borders of Europe. The provisions of the treaty include the Federation of Poland with Lithuania; the restoration of the pre-war boundaries of Bohemia, Germany, Romania, Bulgaria, Serbia and Slovakia; international recognition for independent Navarre and Catalonia; the independence of Dalmatia; and the repatriation of Spanish soldiers to Spain.

1 April 1944   An agreement is reached between the signers of the Treaty of Wurzburg to negate debts stemming from the War of Wars.

11 September 1952   Parliament orders the racial integration of all units of the Royal Army, Navy and Air Force.

24 January 1957   The Japanese Imperial Navy completes the first successful test of a nuclear weapon on a coral shoal in the mid-Pacific Ocean.

27 April 1958   The British government successfully tests a nuclear weapon in the desert of western Australia.

2 June 1963 — Queen Elizabeth II is assassinated by an American separatist during an historic visit to New York City.

12 May 1964 — The Ministry of Spaceflight (MoS)—a government department responsible for overseeing all military and civilian aerospace research in the British Empire—is established as a response to escalating aerospace competition from the Empire of Japan.

15 October 1964 — The Empire of Japan launches the satellite *Yamato*. It remains aloft and in orbit for two months.

16 August 1968 — The Empire of Japan positions nuclear missiles in the far western Aleutian Islands. British Prime Minister John David Hitchcock decries the action as a provocation and threatens to take the western Aleutians by force if the missiles are not removed. Four British ballistic missile submarines take up positions just outside Japanese territorial waters. The crisis is resolved peacefully after a week of intense diplomacy.

30 September 1973 — The spaceplane *Blodeuwedd IV* is launched from Christmas, East Texas. Its crew—Major John Baker, Major Milton Flemyng and Captain Daniel Goldman—become the first men to orbit the Earth.

18 May 1980 — Mount St Helens, an active stratovolcano in Arcadia, erupts. Sixty-four people are killed. It is the deadliest and most destructive volcanic eruption in British North American history.

17 January 1981 — A renegade unit of the Russian Army, acting independently of orders from Moscow, seizes British, Swedish and Norwegian weather stations in Svalbard and occupies Spitsbergen. In the ensuing nineteen-month conflict, British and

Scandinavian troops brave difficult climatic conditions to slowly kill or capture the invaders. The Russian government, facing deep financial difficulties and growing armed rebellions in its Caucasian and Central Asian territories, offers no assistance to its soldiers in the northern archipelago. The conflict claims the lives of 350 Russians, 14 Norwegians, 12 Swedes and 83 Britons, most from British North America.

30 March 1982   H. P. Abendsen publishes *The Eagle and the Lion*, a controversial work of alternate history championed by advocates of American independence. It is widely considered the definitive separatist novel. The work earns Abendsen the distinguished Darlington Prize for Books.

12 December 1983   Prime Minister Harold Fox signs the Strategic Missile Reduction Treaty between the United Kingdom and Japan.

14 June 1994   Major Thomas Avon of the spaceplane *Étaín I* becomes the first man to walk on the surface of the Moon, planting the Union flag at a landing site dubbed Avalon.

7 August 2001   An act of domestic terrorism kills 248 spectators and sportsmen during a Test match at Fenway Cricket Ground in Boston, Massachusetts.

Appendix B
Biographies

Aguirre de Córdoba, Susanne Arrieta (22 October 1748–12 June 1791) was the daughter of Spanish Baron Miguel Arrieta Arroyo. Born in Córdoba, she was educated at Tarragona before travelling to England and then North America, where she was linked to an ill-fated revolutionary movement. She died in solitary confinement at Potomac River Commonwealth Prison at the age of 42.

Avon, Thomas (19 June 1964–) is an English test pilot. An aviator of proven skill considered to be one of the Royal Air Force's most promising flyers, Avon was selected by the Ministry of Spaceflight to lead the legendary *Étain I* mission and became the first human being to set foot on the Moon.

Chung, Chi-Ki (9 July 1881–10 March 1954) was the third President of the Republic of China. He was responsible for declaring China's official alliance with Britain during the War of Wars, stipulating that the country would serve strictly in an arms manufacturing capacity. As part of the agreement, he also closed the German coastal trading zone and allowed the British to trade within it. In 1947, Chung brokered a compromise that ended a long-festering border conflict between the Empire of Japan and the Republic of China. Though widely criticised for ceding territory in Manchuria and on the Korean Peninsula to Japan, he was generally lauded for deftly guiding China's growth into a major manufacturing nation and capitalist engine.

Cowryluch, Bogdan (17 December 1888–12 May 1959) was a decorated general of the Polish Federal Army who rose to the Premiership in 1933. In the period between the Austro-Hungarian split and the beginning of the War of Wars, he was active in attempting to affect the exit of the British from central Europe. Cowryluch was responsible for signing the 1933 Königsberg

Agreement, cementing the country's alliance with Germany. Though he held on to his office throughout the War of Wars, he failed to secure a seat in the Parliament of the newly created Federation of Poland and Lithuania after the war and retired from public service.

Cunningham, Dirk (14 May 1960–) is a singer and activist who performed in the influential Beat groups the Beat Boys and the Setting Sun, the latter of which was heavily associated with the Imperial Dismantlement Front. Cunningham dropped his 'Joe Putrid' stage name after the dissolution of the Setting Sun in 1986 and took up a solo career that lasted until 1991, when he abandoned music for a career in visual art. Much of his music and art explicitly reflects his anti-Imperial, anti-monarchy stances. Cunningham was arrested several times during the 1980s for inciting violence, disturbing the peace, assault, profanity and subversion and was known to write songs with the stated intent of having them banned by the British and Columbian broadcasting systems.

Custer, George Armstrong (6 December 1839–26 June 1878), born in rural Erie Territory, was an American cavalry commander in the Southern and Red Indian Wars. He is reputed to have been involved in the rise of the North American Separatist Movement. Though this has never been proven, recently uncovered documents reveal the extent to which British Intelligence considered him a threat, along with several proposals for his assassination, none of which are thought to have been attempted prior to his death.

Denton, Richard Lewis (1 August 1889–15 May 1954) was a Brigadier General in the Royal Army. He commanded and directed the development of weaponised chlorine gas and Dichlorodiethyl Sulphide 'Yellow Cloud' gas. He was on hand for the first tactical use of gas in the War of Wars on 25 November 1933.

Dudley, Nevill Maskelyne (13 December 1833–6 January 1895) was a leading military figure in British Imperial India, and then later British North America, where he gained charge of the campaign against American Nationalist insurgencies. In July 1892, he was present at the bombing of the Gateway City Hall, where he sustained injuries from which he never fully recovered.

Dunbobbin, Arthur Martlew (22 April 1812–4 September 1901) was a British Liberal Whig Party statesman who served as Prime Minister of the United Kingdom beginning in 1870. His legacy in British North America was 'Dunbobbin's Army', a peacekeeping force of 15,000 British Army troops deployed to suppress separatist violence in the Midwest.

Elizabeth II (Elizabeth Mary Alice; 10 March 1926–2 June 1963) was Queen of Great Britain and the British Empire and one of the most popular monarchs ever to have reigned. She owed much of her early popularity to the active role she took in supporting the troops and war effort during the War of Wars, where she volunteered her services to work in munitions factories and regularly visited the wounded in British hospitals. After the end of the War her popularity was further enhanced by the media hype surrounding her whirlwind romance and subsequent wedding to Prince Harold, who was afforded the title Duke of Columbia upon her ascent to the throne. She was assassinated in New York during a state visit in 1963 and it is estimated that three million people lined the streets of Westminster for her state funeral, the largest assembly ever recorded for a single event during peacetime to date. In addition to the Duke, she was survived by her sister, Princess Margaret, and one son, Charles George, who went on to become King George VII.

Fuller, John (30 September 1878–22 January 1966) was a British military theorist. He introduced the philosophy of *coordinated offensive action* in his 1932 book *Lightning Tactics*. The philosophy called for the coordinated deployment of infantry, artillery and air power in high-speed offensive action, though at the time of his writing military aerocraft, armour and communications were not yet up to the task of realising his strategy. During the War of Wars, it was the German military that came closest to perfecting the technique, terming it *Blitzkrieg*. Though it ensured the German military several victorious campaigns, the tactic was ultimately not enough to decide the war in favour of Germany and its allies.

Flemyng, Milton (13 June 1943–), a pioneering pilot and early space mariner, was one of the first men sent into outer space. In 1973, Flemyng and fellow space mariners John Baker and Daniel Goldman rode the spaceplane *Blodeuwedd IV* into low Earth orbit in the first successful manned spaceflight. Flemyng remained with the Ministry of Spaceflight for more than two decades following the historic mission, overseeing various projects and sometimes serving as the department's spokesman.

Fox, Harold (9 March 1921–30 May 1991) was a British Tory politician from Newcastle-Upon-Tyne who served as Prime Minister of the United Kingdom from 1979 to 1986.

George V (George Frederick Ernest Albert; 3 June 1865–8 March 1913) was King of Great Britain and the British Empire, second son and successor of Victoria. At the age of twelve he commenced a naval career which ended with the 1892 death of his elder brother, the Duke of Clarence, making him eventual heir to the throne. George V took a very public hard line against colonial notions of independence, although this policy has been attributed to his wife, Mary. Despite ruinous health in his later years, George V refused to abdicate the throne to his eldest son, Edward–whom he considered a failure–and died, as King, of heart failure.

George VII (Charles George Harold; 14 November 1958–) is King of Great Britain and the British Empire. He was officially crowned at a coronation that coincided with his eighteenth birthday on 14 November 1976, with Princess Margaret fulfilling his duties throughout his childhood as Prince Regent following his mother's death. A withdrawn and largely private figure, his style of reign is in stark contrast to that of his mother and predecessor, Elizabeth II, but he has for the most part retained his popularity with the public due to the wave of sympathy sparked by the tragic circumstances that led to his ascent to the throne. He is believed to have spent a troubled and over-protected childhood largely behind closed doors in Buckingham Palace, away from the media's gaze. Publicly he remains civil with his father, Prince Harold, Duke of Columbia, but it is widely rumoured that theirs is a strained relationship following the death of his mother and that the Duke believes him to be a weak and ineffectual successor.

Grey, Cynthia (19 June 1880?–10 April 1953), originally from Cartier in West Quebec, became the commoner mistress of King Edward VII just after his accession in 1913, causing a major scandal. As a divorcee, Grey was prohibited from the Court, and Edward nearly abdicated rather than end his affair. Ultimately, a compromise was reached allowing Edward to retain the throne so long as he never married Grey and produced no children by her. The couple produced two sons in defiance of the compromise, neither of whom received a title, and Edward died heirless after a prolonged bout with acute pancreatitis in 1918, passing the throne to his brother, who became King George VI. Grey spent the rest of her life in Paris, becoming a notable patron of the arts.

Harrington, Kimberley Horace IV (23 October 1772–19 July 1834) was a major hero of the Mediterranean campaign against the Berber corsairs. Harrington, then a lieutenant, etched himself in the British consciousness by raising the sword of his fallen commander and urging his men on in their successful assault on a major fort at Tripoli. Wounded twice in the battle, he became a celebrity in Britain. Given command of a New World expeditionary force during the post-emancipation revolt of the 1830s, Harrington's use of traditional battlefield tactics against an insurgency met with little success and he was killed by his own men in a mutiny.

Hathaway, Andrew (1783–24 October 1886) was an explorer and naturalist. Born just five miles from Land's End in England, he left home for the New World at the age of sixteen and settled on the banks of the Mississippi, deep inside the Indian Reserve. Adept at communicating and building trust with the Native peoples of North America, he was chosen by Prime Minister Honus Peakman to traverse North America in 1806. Hathaway became the first explorer to chart the Oregon Territory (modern-day Oregon, Arcadia and Alberta), bolstering British claims of sovereignty there. Later, he travelled much of the world and in 1857 was the first European to reach Lake Victoria in Africa. He famously navigated the full length of the White Nile and Nile. In his travels, he noted similarities and differences among local fauna, amassing a huge collection of specimens. During his late-life career as a professor emeritus of biology at Oxford, he caused controversy by suggesting that all life, including human beings, was related and arrived at its current state through a process of gradual differentiation, later termed evolution by his student Ramsey L. Barkley.

Hawkins, Stephen Dwyer (26 June 1763–28 August 1834) was a decorated, fastidious member of the King's Army Officer Corps for most of his life, nicknamed 'Old Fussy' by many of the men who fought for him in the early nineteenth century. He was promoted to the rank of Brigadier General for his role in securing Mobile Bay for the British Empire during a Spanish attempt to re-capture Florida in 1804. He was later killed under suspicious circumstances during a failed campaign in the southern Appalachian Mountains against rebelling citizens of the southeastern provinces and territories.

Heichller, Josef (12 March 1885–21 November 1950) was a general in the German Imperial Army and a military advisor to the Kaiser. He was a fervent colonialist and believed that Germany had failed to capitalise on opportunities for empire in Asia and Africa. He developed a fearsome reputation for his brutal repression of the local population of German Southwest Africa (modern-day Itenge).

In 1933, he successfully assaulted and captured the town of New Birmingham in British Shonaland, Africa, slaughtering most of the citizens and capturing the diamond mines located there. He followed this victory with similar actions in Harristown, Ham Chapel and New Westershire. He was recalled to Germany during the middle phases of the War of Wars and was wounded by a bomb during the siege of Dresden.

Henriksen, Lance (5 May 1940–), actor and director, is esteemed by many as one of the greatest actors of the twentieth century. Henriksen is perhaps best known for his Shakespearean performances in London's West End and for his high-profile film adaptations of Shakespeare's plays, most notably *Lance Henriksen's Hamlet* (1976), *Othello* (1979), and *The Tempest* (1992).

Holmes, Orval and Harold (8 August 1871–9 September 1947; 9 September 1873–6 June 1926) are credited with developing the first powered aeroplane over the course of the years 1897 to 1899. Having inherited an automobile and wagon repair shop from their father in 1896, the sister and brother, who had shared a childhood passion for kites and balloons, set to work building an aerocraft. After several test runs in a fallow tobacco field in their hometown of Windsor Locks, Connecticut, they transported their craft to a flying exhibition on Staten Island, New York, where Orval astounded the crowd by skilfully piloting the plane over the grandstand. In June of 1926, the two set off in opposite directions from Wilmington, Delaware, in planes of their own design. Orval became the first pilot to fly solo across North America and Harold the first to fly solo across the Atlantic Ocean. The event was a sensation across the British Empire but ended tragically when Harold and his plane were lost in a storm off the Irish coast as he attempted a return flight. Devastated by the loss of her brother, Orval never flew again.

Larianov, Pavel (3 December 1890–10 February 1955) was the Russian Minister of War for the duration of the War of Wars and was the man most responsible for allying Russia with Germany.

Under his guidance, the Russian industrial base mobilised to produce a wide variety of arms for the German war effort. Russian engineers were particularly helpful in the design of large field weapons such as the Heibenzer tank and the Ruppreich anti-air cannon, while the nation's vast manufacturing capacity fuelled the Germano-Polish war machine.

Loomis, Edward (26 December 1736–10 March 1780) of Bedfordshire, a Whig, served as a member of the House of Commons starting in 1766. He was removed in 1776 after being imprisoned for high treason in the British province of Virginia. Loomis was hanged at the Tower of London in 1780 alongside insurrectionists Richard Henry Lee and John Adams.

Lumsden, William Charles (11 May 1849–?), a minor British aristocrat, gained notoriety and fugitive status in the 1880s through his involvement with a series of illegal London clubs. He fled to North America and his fate there is unknown. He is remembered primarily for inspiring the later trans-Atlantic voyages of several members of the British decadent movement. Enoch Soames's novella *The Western Cockaigne* (1899) offers a fictional version of Lumsden's life in America.

Lyman, Jonathan David (20 May 1904–7 September 1997) served as Governor of New York from 1959 to 1968. A veteran of the War of Wars who saw action in a number of European campaigns, he entered politics soon after the War was over and his service as governor marked the pinnacle of his career. In later life, following his retirement from active politics in 1968 at the end of his tenure, he championed the campaign for peaceful negotiations over the future of British North America and spoke out fervently against separatist acts of violence. Suspected to be as a result of this stance, he was targeted in an unsuccessful assassination plot in 1982 when a gunman opened fire on him whilst he was giving an after-dinner speech in Torridon, Pacifica. He was only slightly wounded in the attack whilst the gunman was never apprehended.

Marquez, Fernando Corte (23 August 1890–23 August 1936), a General in the Spanish Army and a widely respected military tactician, was instrumental in the formation of *Los Fantasmas de la Noche*. The paramilitary espionage unit was the most feared of its kind, operating with a high rate of success well inside enemy territory and boldly infiltrating British North America, which at the time was widely believed to be impregnable. Marquez was assassinated by Nova Scotia-born spy Adam Hardesy on 23 August 1936–the day of his forty-sixth birthday–in his country house outside Toledo, Spain.

Monroe, Jenny (*née* Agnes Stoolenheim; 28 February 1910–3 March 1955) was a music hall singer from Poughkeepsie, New York, who achieved lasting fame for her 1934 sing-along hit 'Thinking of My Soldier Boy'. The song, among the first written by Carnaby Street hitmakers Martin Kenney and Richard Smallwood, led the hit parade in both British North America and the British Isles for a record thirty-four weeks and was the definitive anthem of the War of Wars' early years. Monroe began a film career in 1935 and briefly married cricketer Henry Crenshaw. Monroe's career ebbed in the 1950s and in 1953 she was found sitting by her pool in a patio chair by debt collectors, dead of an apparent overdose of sleeping pills and alcohol. She received poor notices for her final film performance in *House of Rage and Sorrow* (1953).

Myerscough, Ian Andrew (27 November 1937–) is a Tory politician from West London who served as Prime Minister of the United Kingdom from 1992 to 1997.

Nagenda, David (8 March 1962–) is a senior official with the Ministry of Spaceflight, responsible for overseeing all lunar operations and exploration.

Negus, Sosimas (28 April 1811–25 November 1879) was a pivotal figure in the mid-nineteenth century African Consciousness movement and founder of Black Star University in Seneca Falls, New York, the first black university in the British Empire. In 1890,

Black Star's name was changed to Seneca University and became the Empire's first racially integrated university. Negus was a noted philosopher and a principle inspiration for the American Ethiopic Church, though he was not directly involved with its development after 1838.

Nellie, Noltan (1 January 1900–12 December 1971), the so-called Golden Throat of the Empire, was one of the most popular sing-along crooners of the mid-twentieth century, scoring a number of major hits. The native of Sheffield, England, was responsible for the highest-selling single in history, the perennial favourite 'Christmas Time is Here Again', a song that even gained popularity in Scandinavia. Toward the middle of his career, Nellie weathered a number of tabloid scandals related to his tumultuous marriages and spent time in minimum-security prison for tax evasion but came back in 1965 with the well-received compendium *Noltan Nellie Comes Out on Top*.

Paine, Thomas (29 January 1737–8 June 1809) was a radical pamphleteer who encouraged the idea of an American revolution through his writings, most notably in *Common Sense* (1776), an incendiary tract denouncing the Columbia Compromise and advocating independence from Great Britain. Paine's works were illegal in both Britain and America and were often burned. A proponent of liberalism and constitutional republican government, he later outlined his political philosophy in what may be his best-known work, *The Instruments of Injustice* (1789).

Pitt, William (15 November 1708–11 May 1778), the Earl of Chatham, remembered as 'the Great Commoner', was a British Whig statesman. He first rose to fame as War Minister during the Seven Years' War and later served as Prime Minister of Great Britain. During his term, Pitt proposed and Parliament passed the Columbia Compromise, a set of laws that resolved conflicts between Great Britain and her American colonies and ensured British North America's place in an expanding empire.

Rutheim, John (21 September 1871–23 December 1924), an American political agitator, was born to German immigrants in Chicago and fought as a young man in the Red Indian Wars. The horrors of that conflict led Rutheim to Spain, where he associated with a series of populist movements including the anarcho-syndicalists of Mauricio Aridjis. Upon Aridjis's assassination by more extreme rivals within the movement, Rutheim fled back to America where he started his own branch and brand of non-violent social activism. Rutheim was executed for his supposed involvement in the workers' riots that sparked the Great Queens Fire.

Spencer, Leonard (30 November 1874–20 February 1965) was a leading British general famous for the campaigns he led during the War of Wars. Well-known as a warrior and strategist, Spencer is often considered one of the most important military minds in the history of the British Empire for his daring and resourcefulness.

Thayer, Ernest Lawrence (14 August 1963–) is a former professional cricketer turned sports journalist. During his sporting career he was a stalwart all-rounder for Massachusetts and New England. His Test career ended abruptly and somewhat prematurely when, in the Byrd series of 1988, he scored only twelve runs in four Test match appearances, including three ducks. He never regained the form to be selected to represent New England again but soon found another niche leading the Test Match Special commentaries for the Columbia Broadcasting Corporation, transferring his trademark fervour and sharp wit from the cricket pitch to radio. Following the terrorist attack during the final Test of the Byrd series of 2001, he set up the Fenway Foundation to promote the staging of sports events as a unifying force for troubled or warring communities and territories.

Trask, Simeon (18 April 1742–3 April 1801) was an American lawyer and politician. After being educated at Harvard University, he spent some time practicing law before being appointed as Justice of the Peace for Virginia's King William County. In 1768 he was elected to the House of Burgesses, where he remained until 1780. A staunch loyalist, Trask's direct intervention on several separate occasions helped to defeat various upstart North American independence movements.

Turabian, Ariadne (19 October 1953–) is the first Beat singer born in England to top the chart in British North America and also the first female singer to top the chart in either the Home Islands or British North America with a self-penned song. A child motion picture star during the 1950s and 60s, Turabian became a popular Beat singer in the early 1980s. In the 1990s, she leveraged her fame as a singer and film performer into a second career as a spokeswoman for a broad range of environmental and social issues.

White, Karl Ellicott (aka Carlos the Eagle; 15 November, 1958–) founded the Imperial Dismantlement Front–a student organisation that publicly advocated the complete dismantlement of the British Empire and self-determination for each of its territories–in 1976 while studying graphic design at Philadelphia Polytechnic. He devised the organisation's anti-Jack logo, a negative image of the Union Jack in orange, green and black. The organisation's radical wing, the Black Jack Brigade, was tied to several car bombings and kidnappings, as well as illegal arms trading and forgery, though White himself was never directly implicated.

Wolcott, Henry (24 May 1819–31 December 1879) was the founder and leader of the Agrarianist Society, based in the town of Montford, DuSable. The society opposed the encroachment of the Industrial Revolution into Middle America and engaged in acts of industrial sabotage against ironworks in several cities in the Great Lakes region and Ohio Valley. Wolcott was arrested in June of 1856 for his involvement in several bombings and the assassination of wealthy industrialist Ernest Conroy and sentenced to death by hanging. However, his followers freed him moments before his execution, killing several officers of the law and legal authorities in the process. Wolcott and his family escaped to Mexico and lived out their years farming in the hills around Monterey.

Woether, Hermann (12 June 1894–4 January 1947) was a much-renowned German pilot of the War of Wars. His fighter of choice was the Zeiben-Adler I, though he later flew its successor, the Zeiben-Adler II, nicknamed the Hellbat by British pilots. Later, he turned his skills and knowledge of air war tactics to the converted Zeiben-Adler III, a flying fortress bomber used for bombing sorties against far-flung urban and industrial targets. During his time as a fighter pilot, he obtained the highest number of air victories in the War, with a total of 25.

Yoshioka, Osamu (11 January 1942–) is one of the leading figures in the development of spaceflight technologies for the United Kingdom. Born in Tokyo, Yoshioka trained as an aerospace engineer and was a member of the civilian-sponsored Space Sciences Society. In 1984 he defected to the United Kingdom and secretly joined the Ministry of Spaceflight. His contributions to the *Étaín I* Moon landing were revealed amid great controversy shortly after the historic mission.

Appendix C
List of British Monarchs

The British Royal Family stands as by far the most well-known constitutional monarchy in the world. The monarchy has maintained a singular level of executive authority across the Empire, although in practice that authority afforded over the Parliaments of Westminster, Philadelphia and beyond is rarely employed and the monarch's presence in such arenas is generally ceremonial only. Even so, and alongside a generally high level of popularity throughout imperial territories, the cultural and symbolic significance of the Royal Family has often rendered them targets of those with an axe to grind against the British Empire. Over the centuries some monarchs have been reviled whilst others have been cherished, some reigns celebrated for heralding huge success within the Empire whilst others have been marred by national or personal tragedy.

Anne	1707–1714
George I	1714–1727
George II	1727–1760
George III	1760–1820
George IV	1820–1830
William IV	1830–1837
Victoria	1837–1898
George V	1898–1913
Edward VII	1913–1918
George VI	1918–1951
Elizabeth II	1951–1963
George VII	1963–

Appendix D
List of Prime Ministers

The Prime Minister of the United Kingdom is the political leader of the country and head of the monarch's government. The position of Prime Minister evolved slowly, its origins traceable to the late seventeenth century when political power began to shift away from the sovereign. Some early Prime Ministers acknowledged neither the title nor the office but the position slowly grew in stature nonetheless. The British Parliament also increasingly sought to enact policies that affected the colonies, hence the ultimately successful campaigning by British North American politicians in particular for representation in Westminster, an act of appeasement on the part of the British government. The three dominant parties in British politics are the right-wing Conservative (or Tory) Party, the left-wing Workers Party and, to a lesser extent, the Liberal Party which occupies the middle ground between the two.

Name	Party	Term
Sir Robert Walpole	Whig	4 April 1721 – 11 February 1742
The Earl of Wilmington	Whig	16 February 1742 – 2 July 2743
Henry Pelham	Whig	August 1743 – 6 March 1754
The Duke of Newcastle	Whig	16 March 1754 – 16 November 1756
The Duke of Devonshire	Whig	16 November 1756 – 25 June 1757
		Government was essentially run by the Earl of Chatham, William Pitt.
The Duke of Newcastle (2nd term)	Whig	2 July 1757 – 26 May 1762
The Earl of Bute	Tory	26 May 1762 – 16 April 1763
George Grenville	Whig	16 April 1763 – 13 July 1765
Marquess of Rockingham	Whig	13 July 1765 – 30 July 1766
		Repealed the Stamp Act.
Earl of Chatham, William Pitt	Whig	30 July 1766 – 14 October 1768
		Brokered Columbia Compromise.
Duke of Grafton	Whig	14 October 1768 – 19 January 1778
The Earl of Shelburne	Whig	20 January 1778 – 14 August 1781
The Marquess of Dorset	Tory	17 August 1781 – 21 December 1790

The Earl of Shropshire, Abel Ransom	Tory	21 December 1790 – 4 November 1793
The Duke of York	Whig	4 November 1793 – 18 February 1795
The Earl of Norfolk	Whig	18 February 1795 – 16 January 1796
The Duke of York (2nd term)	Whig	20 January 1796 – 22 June 1801 *Assassinated by stockinger Archibald Kelly Clark.*
Honus Peakman	Whig	23 June 1801 – 6 September 1807
The Duke of Somerset	Tory	6 September 1807 – 29 February 1812
The Earl of Essex	Whig	29 February 1812 – 12 October 1820
The Viscount Dyson	Tory	14 October 1820 – 30 May 1823
The Earl of Chesterfield, Arthur Aubenden	Tory	30 May 1823 – 19 March 1827
Sir Godwin Ellery Pierce	Tory	19 March 1827 – 23 August 1830
John Effingham	Tory	23 August 1830 – 16 November 1830 *Died of a cerebral hemorrhage whilst in office.*
The Earl of Strathmore	Tory	23 November 1830 – 17 March 1842
The Marquess of Granby	L. Whig	18 March 1842 – 27 July 1846
The Duke of Fife, David Fisher	Tory	27 July 1846 – 27 July 1849
Sir Shawn Dunston	Tory	27 July 1849 – 15 December 1856 *Died in office after slipping on ice outside Number Ten and hitting his head on the curb.*
Humbert Upbridge	Tory	15 December 1856 – 3 April 1862
Lord Everley	Tory	3 April 1862 – 2 January 1870
Arthur Martlew Dunbobbin	L. Whig	2 January 1870 – 15 August 1882
The Duke of Northumberland	Tory	15 August 1882 – 13 November 1883
Sir Harold Nicely	L. Whig	18 November 1883 – 9 September 1886
Sir Thomas Pickering	L. Whig	9 September 1886 – 5 March 1889
The Duke of Northumberland, (2nd Term)	Tory	5 March 1889 – 10 August 1891
Ferdy Twillington	Tory	10 August 1891 – 11 October 1894
Eugene Brakeman Lewis	Liberal	14 October 1894 – 3 September 1899
Phillip Tellwood	Blue Coat	3 September 1899 – 20 January 1900 *Only Blue Coat party Prime Minister, ruled without a majority.*
Myron Goldsmith	Liberal	21 January 1900 – 16 September 1911 *Only Jewish Prime Minister.*
Sir Giles Tuptall	Liberal	16 September 1911 – 12 September 1916
Waring Scott	Liberal	12 September 1916 – 7 March 1918
Lord Gunther Horatio Semple Strumpett	Liberal	7 March 1918 – 24 May 1921 *Died in office of a pulmonary embolism.*
Declan MacDaniel	Liberal	24 May 1921 – 17 June 1924
Sir Edwin Waters	Tory	18 June 1924 – 26 November 1933
Anthony Hewlitt	Tory	26 November 1933 – 9 October 1940
Bryan Bilson	Liberal	9 October 1940 – 1 April 1950
Arlen Murray	Liberal	1 April 1950 – 6 June 1956
Franklin Stanshaw Pitt	Liberal	6 June 1956 – 13 May 1959
Malcolm Lindley-Leach	Liberal	13 May 1959 – 4 July 1964

Sir George Orwell Ford	Workers	4 July 1964 – 7 July 1965
John David Hitchcock	Tory	7 July 1965 – 22 August 1972
		Born to American migrant parents in Sheffield, South Yorkshire, England. First Prime Minister not born to parents from the British Isles.
Neville Markley	Tory	22 August 1972 – 8 January 1979
Harold Fox	Tory	8 January 1979 – 21 October 1986
Joshua Ulrich	Workers	21 October 1986 – 22 October 1992
Ian Andrew Myerscough	Tory	22 October 1992 – 10 September 1997
Marilyn Severin Smith	Workers	10 September 1997 – 8 June 2000
		First female Prime Minister.
Rupert Hawes	Tory	8 June 2000 –

Appendix E
Letters & Documents

THE COLUMBIA COMPROMISE

The eighteenth century was a time of growth and development for British colonies in North America but also a time of unrest. It was the Columbia Compromise, put forth by Prime Minister William Pitt in 1766, that served to unify the colonies and established the foundation of British North America. These laws not only repealed the Quartering Act of 1765 but, more significantly, provided for colonial parliamentary representation and called for a centralised ruling body in North America. On 23 May 1768, fourteen duly elected American Members of Parliament took their place in the House of Commons and British North America assumed its place in an ever-expanding British Empire.

The Compromise was not, however, celebrated by all citizens in the provinces of British North America. The legislative agreement was attacked most famously in *Common Sense*, Thomas Paine's anonymous monograph published on 3 January 1776. Paine's political argument demanded a revolution from these newly validated colonies, stipulating that any compromise short of independence was unacceptable. The text gained infamous notoriety in part because of the strict ban immediately placed upon its publication and distribution. It has been estimated that over 60,000 copies of the pamphlet were destroyed before reaching readers. The following selection from *Common Sense* offers specific references to Paine's grievances with the Columbia Compromise.

THOUGHTS ON THE PRESENT STATE OF AMERICAN AFFAIRS

In the following pages I offer nothing more than simple facts, plain arguments, and common sense; and have no other preliminaries to settle with the reader, than that he will divest himself of prejudice and prepossession, and suffer his reason and his feelings to determine for themselves; that he will put *on*, or rather that he will not put *off*, the true character of a man.

Volumes have been written on the subject of the relationship between England and America. Men of all ranks have embarked in the controversy, from different motives, and with various designs; but Mr Pitt hath deemed all arguments excepting his own to be immaterial and the period of debate hath been prematurely closed. Arms, as the last resource, must resurrect the debate and decide this dispute; the appeal was the choice of the king, and the continent must accept the challenge.

It hath been reported of Mr Galloway of Pennsylvania that on his being admitted to the House of Commons following that inequitable election he declared that *'the rights and liberties of America stand secured under our political union with the Mother State.'* Should a thought so grave and sinful possess the colonies at this time, the name of ancestors will be forever remembered by indentured future generations with detestation.

Fortune never championed a cause of greater worth. 'Tis not the affair of a city, a country, a province, or a kingdom, but of a continent—of at least one eighth part of the habitable globe. 'Tis not the concern of a day, a year, or an age; posterity are virtually involved in the contest, and will be more or less affected, even to the end of time, by the proceedings now. Now is the seed time of continental union, loyalty and honour. The least fracture now will be like a name engraved with the tip of a blade on the tender rind of a young oak; the wound will enlarge with the tree, and posterity read it in full grown characters.

By referring the matter from argument to arms, a new area for politics must be struck; a new method of thinking hath arisen. All plans, proposals, &c. prior to this day must be as the almanacks of the last year; which, though proper then, are superceded and useless now. Whatever was advanced by the advocates on either side of the question then, terminated in one and the same point, viz. a union with Great Britain; the only difference between the parties was the method of effecting it; the one proposing force, the other friendship; but it hath so far happened that the first hath failed, and the second hath been revealed as a perilous falsehood forced upon us.

As much hath been said of the advantages of this union, this compromise, which, like a pacifying dream, hath clouded our minds and left us as children, it is but right, that we should examine the contrary side of the argument, and inquire into some of the many material injuries which these colonies sustain, and always will sustain, by being connected with, and dependant on Great Britain. To examine that connexion and dependence, on the principles of nature and common sense, to see what we are to expect, if dependant.

I have heard it asserted by some, that as North America hath flourished under her connexion with Great Britain, that the same connexion is necessary towards her future happiness, and will always have the same effect. Nothing can be more fallacious than this kind of argument. We may as well assert, that because a suckling child hath thrived upon milk, that it is never to have meat; or that the first twenty years of our lives is to become a precedent for the next twenty. But even this is admitting more than is true, for I answer roundly, that America would have flourished as much, and probably much more, had no European power had any thing to do with her. The commerce by which she hath enriched herself are the necessaries of life, and will always have a market while eating is the custom of Europe.

But she hath protected us, say some. That she hath gripped us is true, and defended the continent at our expence as well as her own is admitted, and she would have defended Turkey from the same motive, viz. the sake of trade and dominion.

Alas, we have been long led away by ancient prejudices and made large sacrifices to superstition. We have boasted the protection of Great-Britain, without considering, that her motive was *interest* not *attachment*; that she did not protect us from *our enemies* on *our account*, but from *her enemies* on *her own account*, from those who had no quarrel with us on any *other account*, and who will always be our enemies on the *same account*. Let Britain wave her pretensions to the continent, or the continent throw off the compromise, and we should be at peace with France and Spain were they at war with Britain. The miseries of Hanover's last war ought to warn us against connexions and compromises.

THE POST-EMANCIPATION REVOLT

Following the Slavery Abolition Act, passed by Parliament in August 1833, a series of isolated revolts in slave-holding regions of British North America and the Caribbean grew into an outright war in eleven Crown colonies. All recently emancipated male slaves between the ages of fifteen and forty were required to complete a term of service in either the Continental Army or the Royal Army. The revolt was eventually suppressed.

This diary entry was written during the conflict by Fortune Jackson, former Private of the Royal Army, King's Negro Brigade, on 14 November 1834.

We've marched hard for two days and two nights now, with scarcely a moment of rest. I've no idea how many miles it is, but we've reached the northern borderland of Cherokee Country. Sosimas knows this ground from his fugitive years and, though I never thought I would say it, I'm glad to have him as a leader at this point in our journey. Because I took care to fill our packs with rations and ammunition for the rifles, we've not had a moment of hunger.

For the first time since leaving, we've chosen to make a kind of camp, in a hillside cave above the Chattanooga River. The cave has evidence that vagabonds and various other people with reasons for running have used it before, and it has good lines of sight into the valley should any pursuers come searching behind us. Our impression is that we have no pursuers. Hard to imagine that army successfully pursuing any men, let alone such a tiny group as us.

When we move, I attempt to walk alone at the back or between Solomon and Sosimas. They walk silently and with purpose. Kwame also walks silently, but it is a cold silence. He seems to be plotting something in his head that keeps him from speaking and has twice failed to acknowledge me when I spoke to him. Howell speaks constantly to me when I find myself next to him, of religion and Africa and all the other ideas Sosimas has put in his head. Strangely, Sosimas himself has gone mostly silent on the issue.

We will be on the move again soon. First, breakfast, and a hot, proper one at that. A possum and squirrel killed by Howell and Kwame last night. I wonder what we'll find when we reach the West, but as long as we can be truly free, this will be worth the journey.

THE BRITISH DECADENT MOVEMENT

The British Decadent movement arose in the late nineteenth century as a reaction to Victorian principles of morality and Puritanism. Most adherents of the movement travelled to British North America, especially the North American West, in the hope of fashioning a society less shackled to traditional social mores.

The following excerpt is taken from *Old World Exiles* by M. Gregory Jankowski of Liverpool University, written circa 1915 and unpublished. Neither a full version of Jankowski's manuscript nor the letters he refers to are known to exist.

...Through these few surviving journal entries [of William Charles Lumsden] we have been able, in some small way, to piece together a fairly vivid, if at times frustratingly fragmentary picture of that early westward path into America. We have seen how, for Lumsden, the romance of the new world wore so quickly thin as the real functionality and everydayness of the west was revealed to him. Undoubtedly with hindsight we can say that Lumsden had rather a naive view of what this virgin new world could provide him, and as such we are hardly sympathetic to many of his hardships. However, it is important for us to precisely understand the social climate of the era to better appreciate the massive pull 'the magnificent west' had on the rest of the empire in those years.

Lumsden himself features prominently in a number of letters sent from the London journalist Robert Galliano in the summer of 1887 to the writer Nigel Tourneur (then resident in Paris). They reveal much of the spirit of the age, under the spell of exotic America, and the stark contrast of some of its realities. (It should be remembered that although at this point a warrant had not yet been issued for the arrest of William Charles Lumsden, he was under investigations for the activities of his London clubs.)

From 30th July 1887:

The capital would seem to have degenerated into the vulgarist sort of spectacle these past weeks—all bugles, fireworks, gun-smoke, stars and war whoops—all red, white and blue and the promise of wide open skies—to which we level-headed sorts have only the power to turn up our noses, shake our heads in silent impotence, and choke on an avalanche of accumulative glitter and firework ash becoming thusly dislodged from the peaks of our bowlers. For all the rest, rejoice that Buffalo Bill's Wild West Show is in town (and appears to be in no real hurry to leave). Every wall of the city is plastered with his ostentatiously tasteless posters—filled with whooping Red Indians, runaway stagecoaches, sharp-shooting cowboys and cowgirls, the most ludicrous hats you ever saw—and also I feel moved to add, perplexingly, kangaroos (kangaroos?!) . It is all anyone is talking about wherever one goes, often affecting, in the process, a fashionable North American draaaaawl. A sort of brashness—a sort of wanton garishness has encroached upon... nay, has rampaged through our world.

Kingsley, with whom I often dine nowadays, is terribly philosophical about it. He dismisses the whole thing as just another in a long line of Imperial whims—ethnic patronisations, he calls them—and reminds me how, last season, it was all about Chinese tea and opium. It will as quickly go out of fashion, he tells me, though I am unconvinced.

In any event, this is what I am writing to tell you: we were both coming up through Burlington Wednesday last, around six, where to my horror I had noticed many of the outfitters now offering what they called the North American outfit displayed in their windows, replete with one of those ridiculous hats, when through the arches of some smoky building or other, and as ever surrounded by a dubious crowd, came that ghastly William Lumsden no less—'the most visible fugitive in Piccadilly,' Kingsley calls him. I have little doubt that were it not for the fact that every man in the district (and no fewer women besides) have something to fear in the prospect of his arrest and the possibility of their own peccadilloes could set to scrutiny in a court of law, it would not be in his interest to remain so 'visible'. A finger in every pie that one!

He beckoned to us. 'Share a glass of wine with me,' (oh! that strange, strangled, odd-pitched tone of his). Knowing sure enough that Kingsley for one dare not refuse him, we had little choice but to have that queer crowd bustle us out of the night air, through subterranean arcades and into the dusty and dubious back door of a little tavern which I do not know. 'It is called The North American,' said Lumsden, tapping at the sooty placard with the tip of his cane, 'but don't let that worry you; it has an ironical charm, you'll see! Come on!'

It was, in fact, a spectacularly dismal place, with lots of gloomy little alcoves, inhabited by sallow, silent, drunken faces hung piteously over the murky contents of their glasses. Lumsden's dubious entourage took to mingling. I did not at all see the charm of any of it, ironical or otherwise.

Lumsden ordered and poured for us copious glasses of a sweet cinnamon liqueur which he boasted he had had introduced to him by the Bohemian Prince Florizel during a recent London adventure. And quickly, as I'm sure was his intent, we were numbed into a sleepy kind of immobility, and so putty in his hands.

He had, it turned out, taken quite an interest himself in this current vogue for the new world, though from a typically off-centred perspective. I attempt here to recall, as best I am able, the gist of his observations: 'The first great lie which America presents is that it is able to reveal to us the extent of its sensations simply through a series of loud yells, bangs and general racket, such as a travelling gypsy circus might present similar clamour in an attempt to ensnare prospective runaways to the shabby workaday world behind its glossy façades. The second lie, however, is no less gross...' He let his head swivel about on his neck at this point, as if taking in a fine piece of music, or the scent of a perfume. 'This place I discovered not entirely by chance a matter of weeks ago...'

It had, he went on to explain at great length, been shortly after the time of Henry Rutherford's 'disappearance' following the riots at the opening of that 'obscene and traitorous' Kensington Jubilee Garden of his (I'm sure you don't need me to remind you of that particular outrage). Lumsden, who claimed to have been there at the less than ceremonious dismantling of the thing the following morning, set himself at once to the task of discovering the whereabouts of the architect, in whom he believed he had discovered a kindred spirit. And so, acting upon information that certain disappearances had a habit of remerging in the tavern in which we now sat, he had investigated.

'These sad, defeated, drunken wretches,' he went on (a little too loudly), 'were a different class of exile altogether. Take, for instance that gentleman yonder!' Clearly, the fellow to whom he referred had once been a gentleman, and a gentleman of means from the cut of his clothes; but they were all now frays and patches, and drink stains. He was blinking into an empty glass. Lumsden went on: 'He told me that night of how he once made a vast fortune from canal navigations in Scotland in a time before the railways appeared to pose any serious threat. And of how, naturally, being a man of his times, he would not simply be content to rest upon his laurels, or in a slightly less metaphorical sense, upon the immense mountains of

money he had amassed for himself. He turned his attentions to North America, and seeing no reason to believe that the geographic immensity of the new world wouldn't translate into yet more immense wealth, he sank just about the entire lot into the fledgling British North American Canal System. Poor thing! I understand you can still see them you know, like cardinal points on a map, shooting out of all the eastern cities and never meeting up. The railways went straight over them and there was nothing anyone could do. The money dried up before they even got wet... The second great lie of America, is that the mundane follies of a dreary old world commercialism can ever hope to get a foothold in the fresh new soil of North America. The fellow over there,' he went on, 'lost his fortune in Pacific shipping... and that one built dams in Michigan...' And he took us—figuratively—with him, around the room revealing the catalogue of costly fiasco which had bought every one of the denizens of this sorry place to their knees, and to here, bizarrely, in search of some glimmer of the wonderment they once experienced; a tavern called 'The North American'.

One of the last things Lumsden said to us: 'To have a brand new world at one's disposal—a new Eden even—and to waste the opportunity so foully, on such ordinariness... that is the lie. And this place is its irony!' He waved his arms.

I think I understood then. And furthermore, I understood precisely what he was asking of me. Lumsden must surely have known that Rutherford sailed for New York the week after the events at Kensington, and of our relationship. Without prompting, I wrote down for him the Manhattan hotel from which Rutherford's last letter had arrived. Then we left him and his crowd for the night air—left them to amuse themselves at the expenses of those squalid, drunken gentlemen down there. We did not wish them a good evening. We did not wish Lumsden a bon voyage.

In the smoke and noise of the streets, Kingsley and I went unsteadily in the direction of Shaftsbury Avenue. Kingsley hadn't said a word for some time. A volley of fireworks fizzed and banged somewhere off in the direction of St James Park.

'Bloody circus,' I told Kingsley.

'...compass points...' I heard him muttering '...all pointing west.' He was drunker than I had realised. But I was very drunk also.

Reprinted below are some extracts from *The Western Cockaigne* by Enoch Soames (London: Leonard Smithers, 1899). The character of the Exiled Count in this novella is clearly a romanticised version of William Charles Lumsden. By the last years of the nineteenth century, following his disappearance, he had developed into a sort of cult amongst the similarly exiled British decadent community. Like all of those involved in this movement, Enoch Soames is known never to have met William Charles Lumsden.

[From] Part 2: *Nishat Bagh*

Came the first feeble flush of dawn over the eastern parapets, and I awoke to myself looking dreamily out through the elaborate tracework of my chamber windows. An immense and undulating panorama opened out of the darkness before me; of rich emerald laurels and immaculate lawns, all flecked and folded in the ruby reds and azure of wild chrysanthemums; and from the singing silver waters of an enormous fountain at the centre of it all, stone effigies of the nine muses emerged magnificently into the cool light of the morn.

I would sleep no more, but reaching out for my morning clothes where last night I had laid them ready on the ottoman at the foot of the divan, I discovered them gone, and replaced, presumably by some stealthy servant of the Count under his instructions, with a set of the same queer, oriental garments as I had witnessed being worn at my initiation the previous night.

This angelic American creature went before me through the passageways, the loose obsidian curls of her hair spilling and cascading into the small of her back. Not a word did she speak, but I followed her; through chambers perfumed with myrrh and dappled in streams of morning sunshine, wild with exotic charms, perverse treasures of the east and of the west, of the archaic and of the contemporary side by side: a palace of earthly delights.

And at length, we came before a set of splendid doors, bound in filigree, and she turned once more to face me. Her eyes were black and wide as the heavens. She raised a single exquisitely willowy finger to her lips. I froze, dead! Then she pressed her palms against the doors, and as if they had been nothing they were cast effortlessly, and noiselessly wide open.

Again, I followed her, inside.

This was the vastest of all the chambers I had seen thus far, and though it would have seemed unfeasible, it was also the most lavish.

Cathedral-like, the vaulted ceiling ascended fathoms above us, and from which, on extended chains, were hung lanterns of an Arabic fashion along with feathery Red Indian charms and huge censers emitting a greenish smoke, resembling in aroma I fancied that of *cannabis saliva.* All the walls and pillars were aclamour of antique rugs and tapestries depicting legends of antiquity, amid which I thought I could glimpse the hidden entrances to dim, chapel-like antechambers, and the humanity therein, concealed from the world in its deeds.

We followed the mellifluous strings of a *sitar* then, the lovely creature and I, toward the centre of the chamber. And there, amid velvet cushions I beheld for the first time the person of the Exiled Count, puffing serenely at an enormous *hookah,* pondering over some leather-bound tome, while all about him lounged and dozed a perplexity of persons, such as the children of Pan.

I knew that I should not bother him now, so quietly I followed my guide still further, stepping carefully between those slothful folk and amongst their dishevelled limbs.

[From] Part 4: *East of Eden*

I returned from the pavilion with painted Wakcha. The Count was sat where I had seen him before, atop the sandstone outcrop overlooking the great prairie, but now the darkening sky seemed to press in all around him with a intense blue, the colour of lapis lazuli, or the waters of the Caribbean. Presently, he glanced towards us, and beckoned me by name. I climbed up and sat beside him, leaving Wakcha to her flowers.

Through the hard summer heat breathed the gentlest breeze, and the air was electrified by the crackle of cricketsong. The sphere of the world surrounded us, curving off into the deepening twilight. The Count spoke, but it was all morbid stuff. He spoke of the impermanence of things; of the nature of paradise as something bound to be lost and destroyed, just as Eden was lost to humanity, and so too even the great gardens of Jahangir and Shah Jehan fell into oblivion and nihil. Such, he said, are the flowers of the desert, which bloom with such heartbreakingly harsh profundity in the midst of desolation, and climb and stretch their faces to the sun, and burn and crumble to dust.

I could not grasp all that he told me, but I understood well enough that that thin plume of smoke which we had earlier witnessed wavering upon the eastern horizon had for the Count a more tragic and esoteric significance. For him, the trains represented the binding of the great continent, the cutting of distances into times, the folding of space. They perpetuated by clattering furlongs that most appalling state of being known as human civilisation. And by furlongs they had delivered the Exiled Count, in spirit, back into the wide cultivated world from which he had striven to free himself so completely. His new paradise seemed to him at that moment no more than a child's toy theatre: all *papier mache* and the sheen of too-thickly applied gloss paint.

Impermanent!

THE WAR OF WARS

Historians have long debated the true causes for the War of Wars and the motivations behind its participants. The war was fought mostly in central and eastern Europe but several minor peripheral theatres also saw fighting, including southern Africa, northern Borneo, Iberia, Italy, the western Rhine Valley and British North America. The naval war spanned the globe, with engagements in the North Sea, South Atlantic, Indian Ocean, Yellow Sea, Red Sea, Black Sea, Kara Sea, Caribbean Sea, and Mediterranean Sea. Major combatants included the United Kingdom and its allies France, Bayern-Austria, Slovakia, Greece, Hungary, the Ottoman Empire, China, Bulgaria, Romania, Portugal and the Republic of Italy, opposing Germany and its allies Russia, Poland, Bohemia, Spain, the Kingdom of Italy, Serbia and Albania.

The war was preceded by a major military buildup in central Europe and tensions were stoked by border disputes that remained unresolved after a brief 1933 war between Germany and Bayern-Austria, in which France and Britain intervened on the side of the Bavarians and Austrians.

The first true military action of the war occurred far from the main theatre, when German forces captured several towns in British Shonaland in the hope of obtaining better access to resources. The ensuing conflict caused widespread devastation in Europe. Early phases of the war in Europe were characterised by heavy trench fighting and prolonged artillery barrages. Improvements in technology during the war led to the first-time deployments of chemical weapons, mobile artillery, armoured vehicles, single-wing fighter aerocraft, strategic air bombardment and the mechanisation of infantry units.

❋   ❋   ❋

This brief letter from Kindred B. Green to Rodney E. Howard—dated 15 May 1935—was delivered at Svansk Mobile Hospital once Howard had awoken from a coma induced by a severe concussion incurred during the Great Blitz of Pavansch Ridge.

Rodney,

Good luck, my friend, and be well. It was good to know you.

Your pal,

Kindred

490 Christine Avenue
N9B 3A8
Kingston, Ontario

P.S. By the way, that picture of your girl? I'll never forget it, that's how beautiful she was. No wonder you survived the Blitzkrieg at Pavansch—you lucky dog.

✳   ✳   ✳

The following letter from William H. MacReady to Joel Emerson was delivered at Svansk Mobile Hospital while Emerson was recovering from his wounds and after MacReady had been released and re-stationed elsewhere.

Em,

We survived Pavansch! I'm told this is big news all over. You're a hero, Em, like I always told you! I don't remember much of it, how about you? Just mud and blood and thunder. Those Heibenzers—I don't ever want to see one of them again. But I don't remember much besides. I was pretty scared, just between us two pals.

You may have already heard by the time you're reading this, but some of our gang didn't make it through. That's a sorry shame, eh? We were quite the gang, weren't we? The Kingston Brigade, with some other wise-acres, too. And the Murderer. He didn't make it. I heard from some of the boys he was cut down in the early part of it, but I don't know. I keep thinking I'm going to see that sonofabitch again sometime, in some trench or village or banging a kettle over my head to wake me up for no good reason at some ungodly hour. Those fucking eyes he had, you know? But then again, there's Murderers all over, eh?

Anyways, when this is all over for good we'll have a laugh or two or three about it all. You'll be back on your feet in no time, pal. I hope to see you soon. I'll be near Warsaw in a few days, but I know we'll see each other soon.

Be well. God bless you, pal.

—Mac

✳   ✳   ✳

This newspaper article describes what has come to be known as the Great Blitz of Pavansch Ridge. It appeared in the 29 March 1935 edition of the Kingston Tribune.

A DARK DAY AT PAVANSCH
By Simon Garrison

British and Colonial forces suffered one of their most severe losses to date at the beginning of the month. On the first of March, several companies of our King's faithful soldiers came under a surprise assault by a massive German mechanised division.

The focused German attack, which commenced in the early morning hours on the ridge near Pavansch, Poland, included infantry supported by Heibenzer mobile artillery vehicles. The power of the focused assault forced British troops from their positions on the ridge.

It has since been discovered that several Winston kite balloons, sent for reconnaissance the evening prior, were brought down by heavy ground fire, contributing significantly to the element of surprise which so aided the subsequent German assault.

The battle remains particularly notable to local area residents for the fact that a peculiarly high number of Colonial soldiers involved were Kingston natives. The Royal Military College announced earlier in the week that those Kingston area survivors, as well as those deceased, will be honoured accordingly for the courage they displayed in the face of insurmountable odds. No date for ceremonies has yet been announced.

Pavansch Ridge, where the battle took place, was re-claimed by British and Colonial forces in heavy fighting during the week following the German assault. At the time of this writing, the ridge is fully in the hands of the Royal Army.

This transcript of a recording of a Czech military unit's communications represents what appears to be a variation on a traditional Czech war-era song. It was recorded on the evening of 28 November 1934, courtesy of British espionage Surveillance Unit #0466, stationed along the Treboshev-Kieshchiecha border, and translated from the Czech language. The lyrical content is notable for the curious addendum following its initial verse, which in most renditions of the song represents the piece in its entirety. The song's lyrics are reproduced here with the additional sequence presented in italicised font:

> The King's lines, we wish they would yield
> Let's hurry this up and get back home, boys
> We've ladies waiting, and bread and wine
> Let's break the King's lines, boys
> And get ourselves back home
>
> *But we see strange things dancing in the fields*
> *Neither Brit nor friendly Czech nor Pole*
> *With skin like blood and eyes like coal*
> *Oh, there's strange things dancing in the fields*
> Oh, how we wish we were home

❋   ❋   ❋

This propaganda pamphlet was produced in autumn of 1934 by a secret separatist group based in Kingston, Ontario. The pamphlet was distributed via post to random Kingston residences as well as left in various work venues and social halls. Similar literature was widespread throughout many other Ontario cities and towns during this period. The authors here are unknown.

R!

<u>Who</u> is Your King?

Who is your King? Who is he really?

Does he care for you and yours? Is his concern for your sons and daughters? Your husbands and lovers?

Or does His Righteousness preside over you with His Iron Will and Hand, and send your loved ones to fight and die in His Wars of Greed? Does His will command them to fall in foreign lands where they, and He, have no business at all? Is it worth their throwing down their lives, or leaving behind an arm or a leg? All for Him? All for whom?

Does your Hungry King care for them at all?

Is He even your King at all?

Resist!

Resist the Far-Away King!

And join those who see the injustice and tragedy in His dreams of Greed.

Peace is a better state, for all.

The world is a big enough place, for all.

—R

POPULAR MUSIC

Popular music in the British Empire changed gradually over the course of the nineteenth and early twentieth centuries. The expansion of the recording industry and the improvement of recording equipment combined with economic hardship to spark an explosion in styles in the decades following the War of Wars.

The first commercial recordings were made available to the public on 11" shellac discs played at 80.75 RPM in 1901. The 65 RPM 10" single was introduced during the War of Wars in 1935, followed in 1948 by the long-playing 21 RPM 12" compendium. In the 1970s, reel-to-reel cartridges were introduced by Stevens Imperial Sound Corp. but failed to catch on until the introduction of the mini-cartridge in 1987.

Songline Magazine began compiling sales charts for the whole of the British Empire, with sub-charts for local regions. For much of the early twentieth century, the Songline charts were dominated by white performers from Britain and North America. Prevalent styles included music hall, theatre songs, and sing-along songs.

Dozens of vigorous new styles developed outside of the mainstream in the late nineteenth and twentieth centuries. Improvisatory music, dubbed 'Cool' by its players, became popular in African-American communities across North America in the 1800s and grew in sophistication and diversity in the twentieth century. Folk styles, including predominantly white 'mountain music' and predominantly black 'blue songs' and 'jive songs', were gradually popularised from the 1910s through the 1940s.

The slow introduction of African, Middle Eastern and Indian sounds to British North America through migration and intra-Empire commerce created a melting pot of genres. By the mid-twentieth century, musicians had begun to hybridise popular styles and traditional music from across the Empire. The resulting profusion in styles led to the coining of dozens of new genre descriptors. In terms of sales and output, the most dominant sounds of the late twentieth century were Beat music, AfroSound, ElectroBeat, New Jive and an updated form of mountain music referred to variously as Western and Countryside.

✸　　✸　　✸

The best-remembered of Jenny Monroe's hit singles, 'Thinking of My Soldier Boy' dominated the British North American wireless bands as British and Colonial troops fought on the Polish Front during the War of Wars. It remained at the forefront of the hit parade for nearly a full year.

'Thinking of my Soldier Boy' by Jenny Monroe
(Music: M. Kenney/Lyrics: R. Smallwood)

My girls and I are going dancing
But my mind is somewhere else
My girlfriends wanna go dancing, dancing
But my rhythm's lost its step

I don't know if I can dance tonight
I don't know if I can dance no more

I'm thinking of my soldier boy
I miss him so and so
I'm thinking always of my soldier boy
I think I'll save this dance for him

My girls took me to a picture tonight
But oh, I missed it all
My girls liked the music, oh they did
But I don't feel it at all

I don't know if I can dance tonight
I don't know if I can dance no more

I'm thinking of my soldier boy
I miss him so and so
I'm waiting always for my soldier boy
So brave and strong

I'm saving this dance for him

[*repeat chorus*]

❋   ❋   ❋

'Christmas Time is Here Again' was the biggest of Noltan Nellie's many hits and remains a popular standard today. It is estimated that over 12,000 versions of the song have been recorded around the world, often with variations, including an alternate second verse and even a third verse added by Virginian mountain singer Thomas Puddle in his 1942 version. The song topped the hit parade for fourteen weeks in its original version. Nellie himself brought a second version to number two three years later. 'Christmas Time is Here Again' was heavily associated with the homefront effort during the War of Wars until it was given a much less sombre treatment and a verse about Santa Claus by glamour singer Alice Digby in 1945.

'Christmas Time is Here Again' by Noltan Nellie
(Music: I. Blok/Lyrics: R. Blok)

Christmas Time is here again
But what's new with the world?
Christmas Time is here again
But what is it that's different in the world?

Oh, there's fighting far away
And our sons are far from home
Holding the Flag high and proud
While we pine by garland-decked pines

Christmas Time is here again
But what's that something in the air?
Christmas Time is here again, friends
But everyone's wearing long faces

Oh, there's fighting going on in distant lands
It's our sons in the middle of it all
Being brave for our King and Land
While we wait with longing hearts

Christmas Time—we think of you
It's Christmas Time—our hearts with you
Christmas Time, boys—we're thinking of you
It's Christmas Time—come home soon

❄   ❄   ❄

Beat music, originally a hybridisation of many styles, including Celtic folk, Cool and Jive, developed in the 1960s and 70s and grew to become the most popular and malleable style of the late twentieth century. Beat groups began to electrify and diversify their music in the early 1980s. By the 1990s, Beat no longer referred to a particular style so much as a group of loosely related genres.

Among the most influential of the Beat era's bands was the Beat Boys, as indicated in the following *Underground Magazine Guide to Beat Music* (2000 edition) entry.

> The Beat Boys were among the most important bands of the early Beat period. Formed in 1978 by poet/vocalist Dirk Cunningham and classically trained violinist/guitarist Eliot Washington, the band was initially a rather ordinary contemporary romantic group. The band cycled through several members before settling on a rhythm section of Ross Marx on drums and Morris Gilbert on the standup bass.
>
> The Beat Boys gained a local following in Philadelphia and frequently toured New England and the Maritimes, building a fanatical base of followers over the first half of 1979. Cunningham was an uncommonly powerful singer and Washington's sense of composition placed them in a league above the average early Beat group. On 13 July 1979 the band finished a fourteen-date tour at the Trumbull Auditorium in New Britain, Connecticut. The night had been especially frustrating for the band as they had been unable to hear one another over the crowd.
>
> Over the following month, the band worked with engineer Thomas Whitney to develop a sound system that could cope with the noise and fill the larger venues they were playing. Washington and Whitney began experimenting with a solid-

bodied guitar, outfitting it with magnetic coils that comprised a makeshift onboard pickup. By the time of the band's next show, at the Palladium in Portsmouth, New Hampshire, they had become the first fully electrified Beat group and also the first group to play onstage with monitor speakers.

Volume Magazine founder Matthew Unger, then a writer for the *Portsmouth City News*, was shocked by the volume of the show but became one of the band's biggest boosters. 'They're the reason I founded *Volume*,' he was quoted as saying in 1994, when the band reconvened for a single show at the magazine's fifteenth anniversary celebration.

By mid-1980, thousands of Beat acts competed vigorously to see who could be the loudest and the Beat Boys were largely eclipsed by tougher, more amplified acts such as the Shangri-Las, the Motors and the Silver Machines. Gilbert left the band and was replaced by keyboard player Ryan O'Halleran, who performed under the stage name Thomas Pain in tribute to the revolutionary whose writings were suppressed in the late 1700s.

O'Halleran was a member of the Imperial Dismantlement Front, a student organisation that advocated the complete dismantlement of all remaining portions of the British Empire. Cunningham and Washington joined the group, but Marx was uncomfortable with the message and eager to finish his schooling and so left the band. The remaining trio poached drummer Gerry 'Eel' Pie, an IDF member, from a competing Beat group called the Beatles and revamped its sound system with the help of Whitney and former Silver Machines sound designer Robert Fulton.

By early 1981, confrontational, anti-imperial politics dominated the band's message and image, and the members had begun to intentionally simplify their playing. The raw, often droning music alienated many of the band's erstwhile followers but set them apart from virtually all of their peers. In order to place their message at the center of their image, the band re-named itself the Setting Sun, a reference to the oft-made boast that 'the sun never sets on the British Empire'.

The band's final single as the Beat Boys, 'Africa/Vision' b/w 'Don't Just Stand There', released in December 1980, points strongly toward the future direction of the Setting Sun.

(see entry for: The Setting Sun)

BEAT BOYS RECORDOGRAPHY

65rpm 10" Singles:

- ⊙ 'The Sting of Love'/'I Don't Want to Be in Love' (self-release, January 1979)
- ⊙ '40 Days & 40 Nights (You Still Don't Answer When I Call)'/'It's You' (Talent!, April 1979)
- ⊙ 'Running Out of Chances'/'Philadelphia Shake' (Talent!, August 1979)
- ⊙ 'Out West'/'A New World' (Talent!, November 1979)
- ⊙ 'Down and Out'/'It Wasn't Really Nothing' (Star Time, February 1980)
- ⊙ 'Electric Shake'/'Comanche (instrumental)' (Star Time, June 1980)
- ⊙ 'Africa/Vision'/'Don't Just Stand There' (IDF Entertainment, December 1980)

21rpm 12" Compendia:

Shake with the Beat Boys (Talent!, January 1980)

A   'The Sting of Love'
'I Guess I'm a Fool'
'Saturday Night, Alone'
'Busted and Beautiful'
'Leaving the Road'

B   'My Heart Belongs to No One (But Her)'
'Every Day I Try'
'I Can't Be Without You'
'Desolation (instrumental)'
'What Does It Take (To Win Your Love)'

❋   ❋   ❋

The Setting Sun's debut compendium, *All the World That's Fit to Burn*, was controversial in its day, widely panned in mainstream publications and embraced wholeheartedly by the underground. The second song on side one, 'Clang', gave its name to an entire sub-genre of Beat music. The following album review appeared in an edition of the *Hartford Courant* published in March of 1982.

THE SETTING SUN
All the World That's Fit to Burn
(IDF Entertainment, 12 March 1982)

After a string of five banned singles, the first compendium from Beat provocateurs comes as little surprise. The recording is profane, caustic, purposefully base, droning and at times nearly unlistenable. The band fails to include any of its singles, instead penning five murky, dissonant songs for Side A and devoting all of Side B to an interminable, noisy piece called 'Be Home Before Sundown'. Even violinist Eliot Washington, a former band member who now helms the interesting, highly musical ethnic Beat fusion group Empire of Sound, is dragged into the morass, appearing on three tracks as a salaried guest musician.

Vocalist Dirk Cunningham, aka Joe Putrid, broadens his range of confrontational, unconventional vocal tics, screaming and hissing about the Empire. 'Take me back to dear old England,' he sings in his best imitation of music hall star Michael Darbyshire—and an admittedly good one at that—before switching to a sneer to deliver the repugnant rejoinder, 'so I can ravage the Princess and tear the walls down.' This is on the title track, which otherwise sounds very much like an electric Beat group falling down the stairs.

It's hard to understand why musicians who've proven their musical talent in other concerns would resort to this. The band's greatest abomination yet is 'Be Home Before Sundown', a double entendre for the January curfew and the sun setting on the British Empire. It begins with a single held tone on the violin, to which are added other held tones at strange intervals. There are no drums—rather, percussionist Gerry 'Eel' Pie pounds sheets of metal with mallets like the slave driver on a rowing ship. Cunningham makes a noise of his own, ranting about the Empire and the police services.

This is a band that would do far better to leave the arguing to politicians and get back to making actual music. Beat is remarkable for its ability to break new ground, but this is ground that should have been left well alone.

—Merrill Dark

❋   ❋   ❋

Another opinion regarding *All the World That's Fit to Burn* is offered by critic Tunde Adewale, who penned the review reprinted below for *Underground Magazine* upon the compendium's release.

THE SETTING SUN
All the World That's Fit to Burn
(IDF Entertainment, 12 March 1982)

The Setting Sun's first compendium is a major statement for Beat music. No other group has yet been this bold in its attacks on authority, nor indeed so bold musically. These songs are caustic, frightening, and entirely bracing in their originality. Side B is dominated entirely by a nineteen-minute revolution in sound entitled 'Be Home Before Sundown'. Old mate Eliot Washington creates a squirming sculpture of sound for the band to build on and build they do, mimicking the sounds of industrial England by pounding on sheet metal and rising to a frenzy so intense and unexpected that most listeners will likely be reeling from it for years to come. Beat music has been a fun diversion since the mid-70s. It's recordings like this that make Beat music important, vital and exciting. —Tunde Adewale

❋   ❋   ❋

'CBC' was one of a string of anti-imperial songs to be banned by the British Broadcasting Corporation and the Columbia Broadcasting Corporation, the latter of which it takes its name from. Both the BBC and CBC banned all tracks from airplay. CBC host Donald Griswold was famously sacked for locking his engineer out of the studio and playing 'CBC' seven times in a row.

'CBC' by the Setting Sun
(Music: Eliot Washington/Lyrics: Dirk Cunningham)

I can't sing
And you can't stop me
You're all out of time and your rules are a joke

We can't sing
But we're all here anyway
Banded together, we're not blowing smoke

[*chorus*]
Empire is a waste of time
The shit always floats to the top
We only grow louder when you tell us to stop

Anyone can dance
If you give them a beat
The Nation of Rhythm will smash you in time

We won't march in your wars
And you can't make us
We'll never do your marching 'cause we're free in our minds

[*chorus*]

[*bridge*]
I need a new nation
I crave assassination
We've got the determination
To make it all come crashing down

[*chorus x2*]

THE ROYAL FAMILY

Much of the role played by the British Royal Family, especially in modern times, is ceremonial in nature. The diary of the monarchy is typically packed with a wide variety of duties, from the pomp of the annual State Opening of the British Parliament and Trooping the Colour to hosting state banquets for or audiences with foreign dignitaries, the bestowing of investitures of honours upon subjects from around the Empire, attendance to charitable events, hosting Garden Parties and many more such public appearances. Some merely represent the vestiges of a bygone age whilst others are more novel and bring the monarch into close contact with his or her subjects. Each and every one serves to define the role of the Royal Family in the eyes of the public.

A Royal visit to any town or city is usually cause for celebration and sees the streets lined with families and well-wishers by the thousand. A visit to British North American soil, or that of any of the colonies, is particularly prized and usually marked in style. For Queen Elizabeth II's fated tour of British North America in 1963, her first stop was New York. The governor, Jonathan Lyman, was set to host a banquet at the Exhibition Memorial Centre to be prepared by the finest chefs from only the finest ingredients that the east coast had to offer. As the banquet was to be attended by local politicians, gentry and war veterans, an invitation to the soiree was to be prized indeed. A copy of the invitation for what had been intended as a great celebratory occasion is reproduced here.

Jonathan D. Lyman,
Governor of New York,

cordially requests the pleasure of your company

in the
Great Hall of America
at the
Exhibition Memorial Centre

for pre-dinner drinks from 5pm
and a banquet to be served from 7pm

on the first day of June, nineteen hundred and sixty-three

in the presence and to the honour of

Her Royal Majesty
Queen Elizabeth the Second
of the
United Kingdom of
Great Britain and the British Empire

and culminating in the presentation to

Her Royal Majesty
of the
Order of the Americas

THE IMPERIAL PASTIME

Test cricket is the most elite format of a sport that England has carried with it to every corner of the Empire. Traditionally played by gentlemen but increasingly now the preserve of all, it is characterised by and equated with a sense of fair play and finesse. The modern game has its origins in the sixteenth century and is as popular at the county level in a number of different formats (3-day, 1-day and CricketMax). It first travelled to British North America in the mid seventeenth century. The popularity of the game there grew out of gentlemen's clubs on the east coast, with the American Cricket League—the ACL—proving extremely popular nationwide every summer. The Test team representing British North America retains the title New England, honouring the spiritual home of the sport in the country.

There remains something about the sport, however, that is forever enshrined with a sense of rural England. In the words of celebrated former player and cricket journalist Ernie Thayer, 'Cricket remains deeply rooted in the psyche alongside the utopian vision of the village cricket match. It equates with a romantic illusion of a simple way of life, a tranquil, gentlemanly and unchanging order in an age of bewildering flux.'

❋   ❋   ❋

Of all the rivalries in the sport, that between England and New England is the most fervent and the most celebrated. Whichever side of the Atlantic it is being played, the Byrd Test Match Series always captivates fans of the sport but also a much wider audience given its history and notoriety. The 2001 series, played out at five historic locations across the east coast of British North America, was destined to come to a tragic conclusion that changed the sport forever. The final Test was fated never to be decided, even as a packed ground sat enthralled on the fifth day as the match reached its climax. The scorecard when the match was abandoned was as presented below.

Fifth Test: New England v England
Fenway Cricket Ground, Boston

Match abandoned
Series drawn 1-1

New England won the toss and elected to bat.

NEW ENGLAND 1ST INNINGS			RUNS	BALLS	4S	6S
Cooney	c Gardner	b Holliston	24	37	4	0
Barrows	c Hunting	b Holliston	7	26	0	0
Anson*	c Hunting	b Holliston	15	32	3	0
Proto	c Holliston	b Stockton	132	102	21	0
Gutman	c Hunting	b Holliston	65	59	8	0
Kelly	hit wicket	b Gardner	65	141	8	0
Stevens+	c Hunting	b Spalding	19	36	2	1
Randolph	c Newbery	b Spalding	60	90	5	0
Martin		b Holliston	12	12	2	0
Stengel	st Hunting	b Spalding	50	69	8	0
Riley			0	2	0	0
EXTRAS	(1w, 3lb)		4			
TOTAL	(all out)		453	(100.5 overs)		

FALL OF WICKETS:	1-23 (Barrows), 2-42 (Cooney), 3-65 (Anson), 4-239 (Proto), 5-243 (Gutman), 6-283 (Stevens), 7-347 (Kelly), 8-366 (Martin), 9-452 (Stengel), 10-453 (Randolph)

BOWLING	O	M	R	W
Holliston	30	2	135	5
Stockton	18	0	129	1
Newbery	3	0	15	0
Deford	24	3	93	0
Gardner	8	0	25	1
Spalding	17.5	6	52	3

ENGLAND 1ST INNINGS			RUNS	BALLS	4S	6S
Blake	c Cooney	b	57	111	6	0
Hearst		b Kelly	92	160	7	0
Darling		b Martin	15	63	0	0

Hunting[+]	c Barrows	b Riley	181	301	22	0
Stockton	run out		45	93	1	2
Newbery*		b	35	44	4	0
Winthorp	c Gutman	b Riley	44	81	4	0
Spalding	lbw	b Riley	10	17	0	0
Gardner	lbw	b Riley	4	4	1	0
Deford	run out		4	6	0	0
Holliston	not out		3	5	0	0
EXTRAS	(4nb, 1w, 2b, 3lb)		15			
TOTAL	(all out)		505	(130.3 overs)		

FALL OF WICKETS: 1-84 (Blake), 2-138 (Darling), 3-194 (Hearst), 4-278 (Stockton), 5-381 (Newbery), 6-469 (Winthorp), 7-484 (Spalding), 8-489 (Gardner), 9-496 (Deford), 10-505 (Hunting)

BOWLING	O	M	R	W
Riley	29.3	1	140	4
Stengel	30	0	93	0
Randolph	32	0	115	2
Martin	24	6	82	1
Kelly	15	1	60	1

NEW ENGLAND 2ND INNINGS			RUNS	BALLS	4S	6S
Cooney	c Darling	b Newbery	39	88	5	0
Barrows	c Hunting	b Holliston	6	17	0	0
Anson*	c sub	b Holliston	54	112	7	0
Proto		b Holliston	14	28	2	0
Gutman	c Hunting	b Holliston	65	121	8	0
Kelly	lbw	b Gardner	47	102	2	0
Stevens[+]		b Deford	0	2	0	0
Randolph		b Holliston	5	24	0	0
Martin	c Winthorp	b Gardner	6	11	1	0
Stengel		b Holliston	18	11	1	0
Riley			7	41	0	0
EXTRAS	(2w, 7lb, 14b)		23			
TOTAL	(all out)		284	(92.5 overs)		

FALL OF WICKETS: 1-13 (Barrows), 2-88 (Cooney), 3-114 (Proto), 4-127 (Anson), 5-210 (Gutman), 6-210 (Stevens), 7-241 (Randolph),

8-250 (Martin), 9-253 (Kelly), 10-284 (Stengel)

BOWLING	O	M	R	W
Holliston	24.5	4	87	6
Stockton	4	1	19	0
Newbery	21	7	52	1
Deford	31	6	69	1
Gardner	7	2	18	2
Spalding	4	0	14	0
Darling	1	0	2	0

UMPIRES: G Rice, DW Hopper

NEW ENGLAND: Proto, Gutman, Anson*, Cooney, Barrows, Kelly, Stevens[+], Randolph, Martin, Stengel, Riley

ENGLAND: Blake, Hearst, Darling, Hunting[+], Newbery*, Winthorp, Spalding, Gardner, Deford, Stockton, Holliston

Appendix F
Maps & Diagrams

Fig. 1. The original thirteen British colonies: New Hampshire, Massachusetts, Rhode Island, Connecticut, New York, New Jersey, Pennsylvania, Delaware, Maryland, Virginia, North Carolina, South Carolina, and Georgia.

Fig. 2A. A map indicating territorial acquisitions of the British Empire in western North America. British expansion toward the Pacific Ocean proceeded through a blend of military conquest and negotiated settlement. The government in London encouraged subjects to settle in most of these territories, especially Oregon and Pacifica, long before their annexation.

Fig. 2B. A map indicating territorial acquisitions of the British Empire in eastern North America. British territorial control of the eastern half of the continent was largely settled in the eighteenth century.

Fig. 3A. The western territories of British North America. Borders in the western half of British North America reflect patterns of territorial acquisition and the outcomes of negotiations, including efforts to resettle native peoples. When independent Texas was annexed, it was divided into three territories to limit its potential influence.

Fig. 3B. The eastern territories of British North America. Modern boundaries primarily reflect settlement patterns and land grants from the sixteenth through eighteenth centuries. Ungava was separated from Quebec as a native people's land grant.

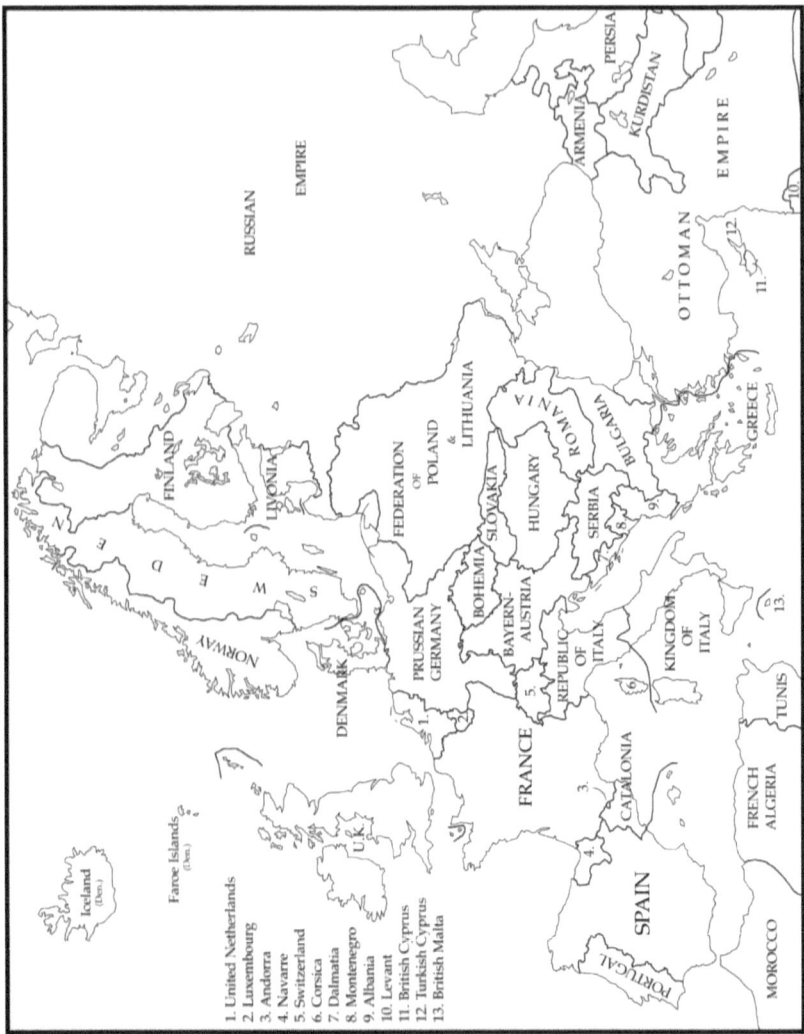

Fig. 4. The political geography of Europe. Europe's modern borders were shaped by centuries of warfare and royal alliance. Modern Europe is a hodgepodge of genuine nation-states, lingering empires and leftover unions created before a broad continental shift toward representative democracy. Borders have been largely stable since 1990, though separatist and irredentist movements persist across the continent.

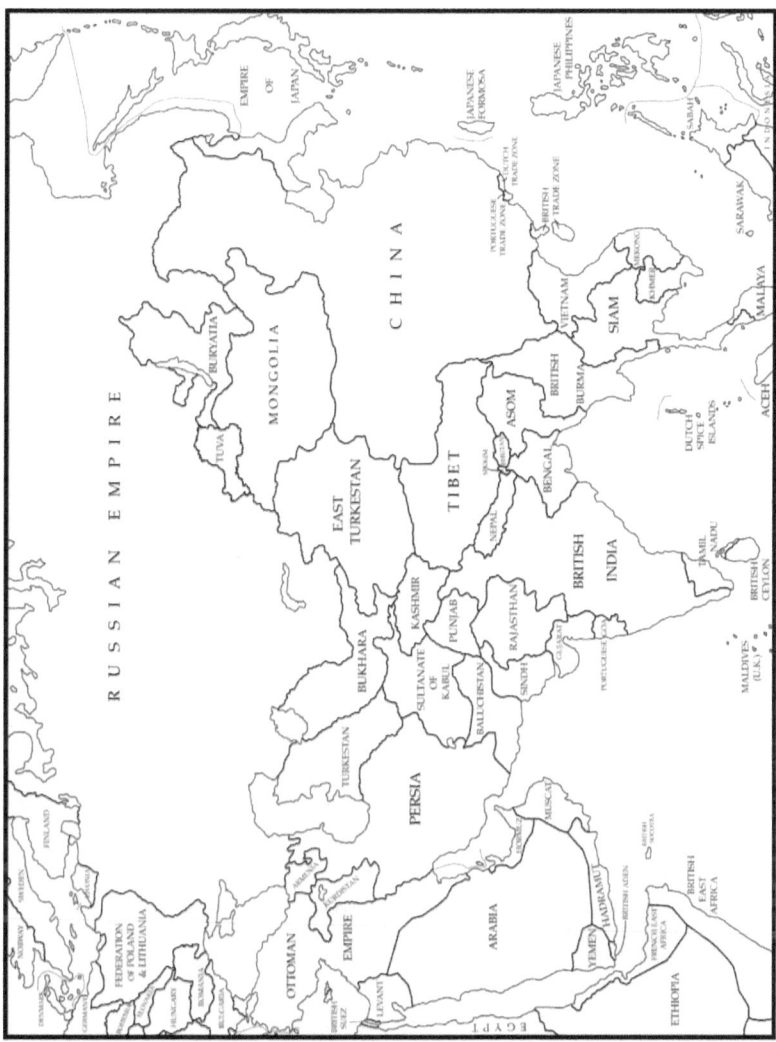

Fig. 5. The political geography of Asia. Modern Asia is moving toward greater home-rule and independence as the age of European colonialism fades. In India, a number of new states have emerged from the National System, in which nation-states ruled by the British Empire are organized and placed on independence tracks. The aging empires of Russia and China entered phases of decline in the mid-twentieth century.

Fig. 6. The political geography of Africa. Africa was nearly entirely colonized in the late nineteenth and early twentieth centuries by European powers—the Ethiopian Empire was the lone exception. Less than 100 years later, colonization had largely ended after a series of European wars weakened the occupying powers and a series of uprisings pushed them out. Some residual colonial presence remains, with plans for a peaceful transfer to independence for all remaining colonies by 2020.

Fig. 7. The political geography of Latin America. Apart from a few lingering British colonies and island possessions of European powers, Latin America largely shook off the colonial yolk by the end of the nineteenth century. Though borders have remained stable for decades, most nations in South America are particularly beset by sometimes violent nativist movements and drives to assign regional autonomy.

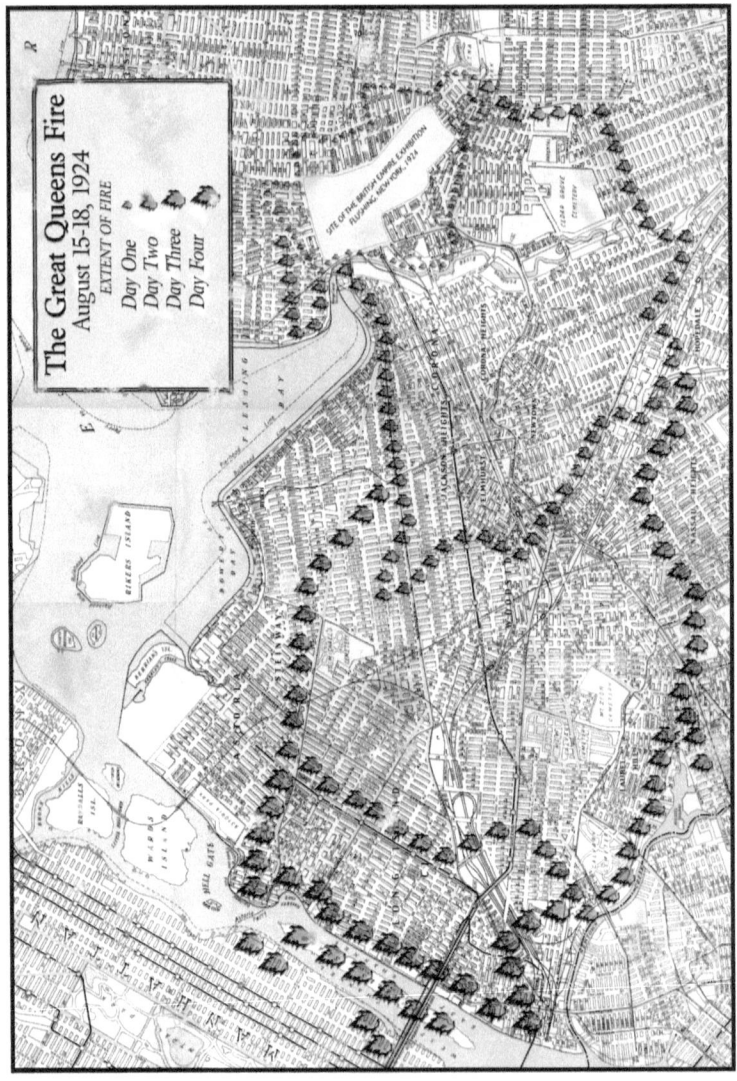

Fig. 8. A map of the damage caused by the Great Queens Fire, which began as a result of rioting at the site of the British Empire Exhibition in Flushing on 15 August 1924.

Fig. 9. Frederick Burr Opper political cartoon dated 23 December 1924. Originally drawn for the New York *Daily Mirror* on the day of the execution of six anarcho-syndicalist agitators blamed for the Great Queens Fire, the *Mirror* refused to publish the cartoon. Opper broke his relationship with the paper and eventually published the piece in the *Gotham Gazette and Register*. He is credited with coining the phrase 'Christmas for King George', by which the hangings are popularly known.

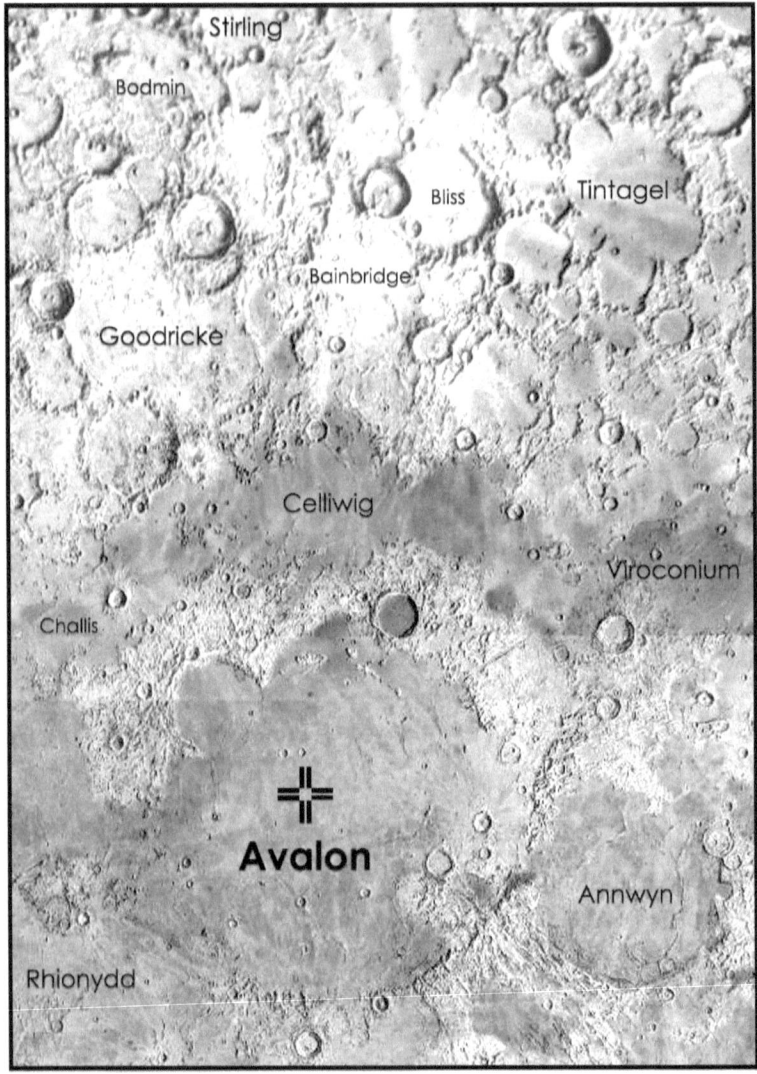

Fig. 10. Layered Ministry of Spaceflight photographs revealing the geography of the Moon, including Avalon—the landing site of the historic craft *Etaín I*—and its surrounding craters.

Index

Acadiens, 266
Adams, John, 316, 338
Africa, 41, 46, 52, 59, 89, 106, 167, 249, 319, 322, 324-25, 336, 354, 361, 371-72, 390
Alaska, 319
Alberta, 336
Alfonso XIII, 113, 321
American Dream, 248
Anarchism, 103, 113
Anarcho-syndicalism, 113-15, 129, 321, 341
'Anarchy in the UK', 230, 233, 238, 240
Anglicanism, 43, 52, 316
Anti-Jack, 232-33, 342
Appalachia, 39-41, 50
Appaloosas, 199
Arcadia, 329, 336
Arctic Islands Territory, 207
Aridjis, Mauricio, 125, 341
Arlington, Virginia, 295
Arnhem Land, Australia, 142
Asia, 167, 249, 319, 336, 389
Asr, 96
Atlantic Ocean, 22, 30-31, 188, 195-96, 205, 225, 259-60, 282, 286, 288, 291, 295, 316, 318, 337-38, 361, 378
Australia, 106-07, 131, 142, 263, 315, 328
Austria, 170, 321-22, 361-62
Avalon, 270, 272, 330, 394
Avon, Thomas, 260, 262-63, 266, 270-73, 330

Babel, 92
Baja California, 318
Baker, John, 260-61, 329, 334
Baltimore, Maryland, 20
Barbary Wars, 72
BBC, 230, 238, 248, 260, 270, 374
Beat Boys, The, 238, 251, 332, 370-72
Beat Music, 238, 246, 251, 332, 342, 368, 370, 371, 372, 373, 374
Beatles, The, 238, 371
Bedfordshire, England, 36, 338
Ben Bernard Motors, 196
Berlin, Battle of, 328
Bible of St Sosimas, 45-47, 52, 59, 75
Bishop, William Avery, 160, 172
Black Hills, 90
Black Jack Brigade, 342
Blodeuwedd Program, 253, 256, 261, 329, 334
Bohemia, 141, 145, 177, 321-22, 328, 361
Borneo, 234, 361
Boston Women's Institute, 300
Boston, Massachusetts, 47, 49, 58, 86, 275, 300, 330, 379
Brazos River, 266
Brighton, England, 78
Britain, 24, 30, 47, 83, 85, 141, 257, 272, 294, 314-19, 321-22, 325-28, 331, 333-35, 340, 352-53, 362, 367, 370, 377

Britannia, 34, 80, 139, 142, 158, 167-68, 182, 193, 201, 208, 216, 225, 240, 248

British Empire Exhibition, 106, 113, 135, 196, 321, 392

Brugge, United Netherlands, 83

Buckingham Palace, 198-99, 218, 223, 271, 294, 335

Buffalo Sentinel, 239

Buffalo, New York, 227, 229, 233, 237-39, 244-46, 356

Burma, 132, 235, 240

Burma War, 240

Byrd Diaries, 309

Byrd, William, 295, 305, 341, 378

Canada, 405

Cardiff, Wales, 265

Carter, Penny, 289-90, 313

Catalanists, 113

Cavalier of St George, 198

CBC, 230, 233, 240-42, 248, 256-57, 272, 277, 281, 341, 374-75

Charleston, South Carolina, 56, 71

Cherokee, 50, 64, 68, 71-72, 74, 249, 354

Chestnut Hill, Massachusetts, 283

China, 90, 319-20, 326, 331, 361, 389

Christ, 59, 124-25, 236, 245

Christmas, 169, 256, 261, 321, 323, 325, 340, 369-70, 393

'Christmas Time is Here Again', 169, 323, 340, 369-70

Christmas, East Texas, 253, 256-57, 262, 265-67, 329

Chung, Chi-Ki, 331

Clarke, Arthur, 256, 271

Claudian, 81, 92

Cliff, Richard, 240

Colonies, 20, 50, 80, 83, 87, 114, 158, 168, 238, 263-64, 315, 317, 319, 340, 347, 351-54, 376, 383, 390-91

Columbia, 19, 24, 29, 198, 208-09, 216, 238, 241, 249, 266, 278, 281, 288, 315, 319, 333, 335, 340-41, 347, 351, 374

Columbia Carb-Tea, 244, 262, 278, 283

Columbia Compromise, 19, 24, 29, 288, 315, 340, 347, 351

Columbian Landau, 207, 210

Columbian, The, 289, 332

Common Sense, 19, 24, 28, 34, 288, 315, 340, 351

Coney Island, 106, 130

Connecticut, 227-28, 283, 337, 370, 383, 405

Continental Army, 55, 68, 266, 317-18, 354

Cornwall, 260, 262-63

Countryside Music, 266, 368

Cowryluch, Bogdan, 331

Crenshaw, Henry, 285, 339

Crimean Tartars, 103

Crown, 20, 24, 36, 44, 109, 114, 136, 194, 207-08, 211, 232, 234, 236, 249-50, 318, 354

Cunningham, Dirk, 227-51, 332, 370-71, 373, 375

Custer, George Armstrong, 89-90, 332

Custerites, 114, 129

Dakota, 87, 89, 91, 103

Day of Darkness, 324-25

Delaware, 337, 383

Delta, 266

Democracy, 235, 388
Denton, Richard Lewis, 332
Derby Day, 80
Descartes, Rene, 58
Dismantlement, 228, 235, 238-39, 246, 342, 371
Dismantler, The, 237, 244-45
Don Quixote, 103
Drakeland, 207
Dresden, Great Battle of, 327, 337
Dudley, Nevill Maskelyne, 81, 333
Dunbobbin, Arthur Martlew, 320, 333, 348
DuSable, 342

Eagle and the Lion, The, 330
Earth, 59, 77, 96, 104, 146, 163, 167, 182, 184, 253, 255-56, 261, 329, 334
East Texas, 253, 258-59, 317, 329
El Dorado, 90
Elizabeth II, 196-99, 201, 206-07, 209-10, 214-16, 218, 222, 224, 329, 333, 335, 345, 376-77
Emancipation, 50, 54, 76, 335
Empire, 30, 34, 47, 70, 80-83, 89, 91, 102, 106-08, 112-13, 115, 122, 131-33, 135-36, 145, 158, 166, 174, 193, 195-96, 198, 207, 209, 215, 218, 221, 224, 228, 230-32, 234-36, 238, 245, 248-49, 251, 253-54, 256-59, 261, 264-66, 268-69, 271, 281, 288, 294, 313, 316-20, 325-26, 329, 331, 333-34, 336-37, 339-42, 345, 351, 355, 361, 367,
371, 373, 375-78, 384-85, 389-90
Empire Stories, The, 107, 122, 320
Empire Tower, 195
England, 19, 29, 34-35, 47, 78, 107, 196, 229, 234, 275-76, 281-82, 284-86, 288-89, 295, 301-03, 310, 314-15, 318, 331, 336, 340-42, 349, 352, 373-74, 378-79, 381, 405
English Gentlewomen, The, 240
Erie, 244, 246, 317, 332
Étaín Program, 253-73, 330-31, 343
Ethiopia, 40, 47, 60
Ethiopic Bible, 45-47, 52, 59, 75
Europe, 47, 145, 151, 153, 167, 190, 249, 317-20, 323, 325, 327,-28, 331, 353, 361-62, 388
Exile of a Scandalised Bohemian, 203
Exley, Wallace, 285

'Fantasia on Sea Songs...', 195-96
Fantasmas de la Noche, 154, 180, 189, 197, 323-25, 339
Feltman's, 291
Fenway Cricket Ground, 275, 288, 293, 304, 312, 314, 330, 341, 379
Florida, 41, 316, 336
Fox, Harold, 232, 255, 272, 330, 334, 349
France, 47, 317, 319, 321, 324, 326-27, 353, 361-62
Franz Josef Land, 234
Fuller, John, 333

Galloway, Joseph, 352

Gateway, Missouri, 77, 79, 86, 320, 333

Gentlemen and Players, 292

George V, 334, 345

George VI, 136, 321, 335, 345, 393

George VII, 271, 294, 333-45

Georgia, 46, 315, 383

Germany, 141, 166, 321-23, 325-28, 332, 334, 336-37, 361-62

Ghana, 46, 235

God, 39-40, 42, 44-45, 52, 57-59, 63, 72, 80, 102, 166, 183, 189, 229-31, 239-41, 243, 363

Goldman, Daniel, 260-61, 329, 334

Golgotha, 163

Grace, W.G., 288

Grand Bridge Cricket Ground, 283

Great Plains, 84, 87, 91, 100

Great Queens Fire, 127-36, 321, 341, 392-93

Greenwich Village, 102

Guyana, 264

Hadrian's Wall, 249

Halifax, Nova Scotia, 237

Harristown, Shonaland, 322, 324, 337

Hartford, Connecticut, 227-29, 233, 237, 283, 373

Hathaway Valley, 81, 88

Haverford, Pennsylvania, 283, 295, 297

Heaven, 19, 21, 38, 77, 99, 153, 163

Heichller, Josef, 322, 336

Helena, 136

Hell, 113, 118, 125, 128, 131, 146, 148-49, 157-58, 162-63, 174, 182-83, 236, 239, 243, 245, 255, 260-61, 265, 272, 280

Henriksen, Lance, 255, 337

Henry VIII, 228

Hi-Amp Footwear, 291, 309

Himalaya Range, 234

HMS *Britannia*, 193, 197, 200, 223

House of Burgesses, 22, 26, 34, 342

House of Commons, 24, 29, 36-37, 234, 315, 338, 351-52

House of Lords, 230

House of Rage and Sorrow, 339

Hudson, 193

Huntingdon, East Texas, 266

IDF Entertainment, 372-74

Imperial Dismantlement Front, 232-33, 237-39, 245, 332, 342, 371-74

India, 89, 108, 116, 132-33, 235, 318, 320, 333, 389

Instruments of Injustice, The, 340

Ireland, 235, 238, 249, 264, 316, 318

Islam, 51, 52

Jamaica, 231, 235

Jamestown, Virginia, 198

Japan, 238, 268-69, 273, 319, 326, 329-31

Jefferson, Jack, 139, 143, 147, 153, 186, 191

Jesus, 59, 110, 114, 124, 127, 129

Judaism, 348

Kentucky, 316

Kholm, Battle of, 322-23

King, 6, 19, 43, 45-47, 50, 68, 113, 115-16, 118, 123, 136, 152-53, 157-58, 168, 182, 190, 201-03, 208, 212-13, 215-16, 223, 230-31, 240-41, 246, 251, 266, 271, 273, 294, 317-18, 321, 333-36, 341, 352, 354, 364-66, 369, 393

Kingdom, 22, 34, 144, 261, 352

Kingston, Jamaica, 231

Kingston, Ontario, 139-40, 144, 155, 159, 161, 167, 169-70, 179, 190, 192, 324-25, 362-65

Kiowa, Great Plains, 78

Kipling, Rudyard, 320

Krasnostaw, Poland, 322

La Purga, 125, 321

Lake Victoria, 336

Lakota, 207

Land's End, 249, 336

Larianov, Pavel, 337-38

Lee, Richard Henry, 316, 338

Leipzig, Germany, 327

Libertarian, The, 282

Lillywhite's Scores and Bios, 285, 295

Locke, John, 59

London Paddington Station, 85

London Waterloo Station, 85

London, England, 21-22, 37, 80, 83-84, 194, 200, 205, 258, 260, 267-68, 271, 275, 288, 326, 337-39, 355, 357-58, 384, 405

London, Ontario, 233

Long Island Palace, 196, 200

Lord's Cricket Ground, 288, 303

Löwen de Folder, 182

Lumsden, William Charles, 77-104, 203-04, 338, 355-59

Lyman, John, 196, 206, 338, 376-77

Madison, James, 240

Maine, 299

Malaya, 132

Malaysia, 235, 241

Manhattan, New York, 102, 106-07, 136, 284, 321, 358

Marquez, Fernando Corte, 323, 325, 339

Maryland, 24, 46, 383

Marylebone Cricket Club, 275, 281, 297, 310

Massachusetts, 221, 275, 283, 330, 341, 383

MI1, 218

MI2, 218

MI3, 218

Michigan, 319, 358

Ministry of Spaceflight, 255-60, 262-63, 267-69, 271, 273, 329, 331, 334, 339, 343, 394

Mississippi, 68, 336

Missouri, 79, 320

Missouri River, 78

Monarchy, 332, 345, 375

Monroe, Jenny, 153, 323, 339, 368

Montana, 88-89, 91

Montana Rangers, 199

Moon, 23, 69-71, 76, 83, 93, 122, 146, 161, 167, 175, 190, 201, 253, 255-60, 263-73, 330-31, 339, 343, 394

Moravia, 321

Morgan, John Mark, 266

Mount St Helens, 329

Moysche Fields, Battle of, 322

Moysche, Poland, 322

Myerscough, Ian, 255-56, 260, 265, 271, 339, 349

Nellie, Noltan, 153, 169, 244, 323, 340, 369
Nelsonville, Florida, 40-41
New Birmingham, Shonaland, 142, 322, 337
New Brunswick, 238
New Cambria, 93, 320
New England, 229, 256, 276-77, 279, 281, 284-85, 287, 289, 291, 293, 295, 299-01, 304, 341, 370, 378-81, 405
New Hampshire, 371, 383
New Harristown, Shonaland, 324-25
New Hellfire Club, 80, 83
New Jersey, 383
New World, 86, 102, 166, 335-36, 355, 357-58, 372
New World Zionism, 86
New York, 79, 87, 105, 132, 168, 193-97, 200, 202, 207, 210, 215, 217, 222, 224, 230, 232, 285-86, 321, 329, 333, 337-39, 358, 376-77, 383, 393, 405
Newfound Gap, 39
Nine Men's Morris, 85
North Carolina, 383
Nova Scotia, 339
Nuez Hill, Battle of, 266-67

Official Secrets Act, 265
Ohio, 342
Ontario, 54, 56, 139, 144, 153-54, 192, 324-25, 362, 365, 405
Operation Icarus, 327
Order of George V, 211
Order of George VI, 211
Order of the Americas, 207, 377

Oregon, 84, 104, 316, 336, 384
Osage, 273, 317, 320
Ozark, 91

Pacific Ocean, 316, 318, 328, 358, 384
Pacifica, 338, 384
Paine, Thomas, 19-20, 24, 28-29, 315, 340, 351
Palace of Philadelphia, 199, 315
Parliament, 20-21, 24-25, 28-30, 50, 109, 220-21, 230, 234, 238, 288, 315, 317, 321, 328, 332, 340, 347, 351, 353, 376
Patterson, George, 295
Pennsylvania, 251, 283, 352, 383
Penry, Roger, 207, 217
Pernod, 84
Perseus, 151
Philadelphia Congress, 234
Philadelphia, Pennsylvania, 19, 28, 47, 199, 234, 238, 250-51, 270, 294-95, 342, 345, 370, 372
Pilotsville, Delta, 266
Pitt, William, 30, 288, 315, 347, 351
Pocomaniacs, 231
Poland, 143, 151, 166, 192, 319, 321-22, 325-28, 332, 361, 364
Pompeii, Kingdom of Italy, 84
Portsmouth, Rhode Island, 237, 371
Poseidon, 168
Prague, Bohemia, 145
Prince, 112, 115, 117, 130, 197, 223, 294, 333-34, 357
Princess, 108, 111, 134-36, 197-98, 233, 241, 333-34, 373
Prior, Kay, 256
Providence Journal, The, 230

Providence, Rhode Island, 230, 232
Puck Program, 261
Punjab, 284
Putrid, Joe, 227-51, 332, 370-71, 373, 375

Quebec, 207, 387
Queen, 80, 89, 113, 146, 192, 196-99, 201, 204, 206-07, 209-10, 212-16, 218, 220, 222, 224, 241, 251, 294, 329, 333, 376-77
Queen's Royal Lancers, 80
Queens, New York, 105, 132, 136, 196, 206, 321

Red Indian Wars, 121, 320, 332, 341
Revolution, 24, 125, 130, 232, 340, 351, 374
Rhode Island, 383
Richmond, Virginia, 17, 22, 27, 32-33, 36-37
Rocky Mountains, 94
Royal Air Force, 254, 267, 272, 326, 331
Royal Army, 39, 43-44, 46, 50-52, 54, 64, 68, 324, 328, 332, 354, 364
Royal Boys' Club, 239
Royal Burger, 249-50
Royal Military College, 139, 156, 160-61, 172, 325, 364
Royal New York Philharmonic, 195
'Rule Britannia', 84, 196
Russia, 47, 319, 325-27, 337, 361, 389
Rutheim, John, 115, 117-27, 129-30, 132-34, 136, 321, 341

Sabah, 313
Salix, 287
Samuel Smith's, 233
Sarnia, Ontario, 324
Satan, 25, 79, 86, 110, 157
Scotland, 231, 235, 238, 249, 294, 315, 318, 357
Scotland Yard, 84
Scots Guards, 201
'See, the Conquering Hero Comes', 196
Separatist Students' Council, 238-39
Setting Sun, The, 227-51, 332, 371-75
Seven Years' War, 22, 340
Shonaland, 132, 142, 322, 324, 337, 362
Simpson, Robert, 257-58, 269
Sioux Cream Drafts, 199
Sioux Nation, 320
Slaughter of Harristown, The, 142
Slavery, 41, 45, 59, 68, 317
Smolenska, Bohemia, 176
Soames, Enoch, 338, 358
South Carolina, 56, 62, 383
Southampton, England, 194, 206, 223
Spain, 17, 36, 113, 125, 316, 321, 323, 325, 327-28, 339, 341, 353, 361
Special Branch, 112-14, 116, 119, 124, 126-28
Spencer, Leonard, 165, 167, 169, 181, 341
St George's Park, 206
St Lawrence River, 154, 156
Staten Island, New York, 337
Stensa, 145, 162-63, 177, 184-85

'Sun Will Never Set on My England, The', 240
Svalbard, 234, 329
Svansk, Poland, 192, 362-63

Tanner, William, 258-60, 268
Terrorism, 281, 309, 330, 341
Texians, 266
Thames, 238
Thayer, Ernie, 277, 279, 283, 291, 301-02, 304, 378
'Thinking of My Soldier Boy', 323, 339, 368
Throne, 168, 197, 241, 249, 333-35
'To Alcibiades in Heaven', 266
Tokyo, Japan, 270, 343
Tolta, 173-74
Tories, 227, 334, 339, 347-49
Tourneur, Nigel, 355
Tower of London, 19, 316, 338
Treason, 29, 36-37, 136, 228, 321, 338
Treaty of Wurzburg, 207, 328
Tribal Council Bluffs, Missouri, 78, 80-81
Tripoli, 72, 335

Ungava, 387
Ungava Saddlebreds, 199, 208
Unger, Matthew, 371
Union Jack, 232, 240-41, 261, 264-65, 273, 275, 342
Unionists, 227, 229, 231, 233, 237, 241-43, 249

Victoria Island, 193
Victoria, Alexandrina, 113, 200, 318, 334, 345
Virginia, 17, 19, 21, 24, 26, 32, 35-37, 46, 295, 317, 338, 341, 383
Volume Magazine, 371

Wales, 112, 231, 235
Waller Unity Act, 221
War of Wars, 139-92, 198-99, 207, 221, 261, 294, 322-28, 331-34, 337-39, 341, 343, 361, 367-69
Waterloo, East Texas, 267
West Quebec, 335
West Texas, 265-66, 317
Western Cockaigne, The, 338, 358
Whitehall, 259, 263
Wilmington, Delaware, 337
Windsor, Berkshire, England, 241
Windsor, Ontario, 144, 160, 324
Windsor Greys, 199, 224
Windsor Locks, Connecticut, 337
Whyte, Adele, 256, 272-72
Woether, Hermann, 343
Wright, Samuel, 288
Wurzburg, Treaty of, 207, 328

Yoshioka, Osamu, 265, 268-69, 273, 343

Zimbabwe, Shonaland, 322

Mark Beech lives in Worcestershire, England, where he spends much of his time exploring Welsh border churches and experimenting with exotic European liqueurs. He has had articles appear, at rare occasions, in *Wormwood: Writings About Fantasy, Supernatural and Decadent Literature* and *The Third Alternative,* amongst other places.

Adam Chamberlain lives and works in London, drawing some of his inspiration there from the dramas that unfold on the stages of its theatres all the way to time spent in some of the quieter, leafier corners of the city. He is the Associate Publisher of Fourth Horseman Press and co-editor of a number of its publications.

Brian A. Dixon is a writer and educator and a resident of New England. His short fiction has appeared in the pages of such publications as *Connecticut Review, Weston Magazine, Dead Letters, Zahir* and *A Thousand Faces*. His drama has been seen on the stage of New York City's Sargent Theater. Dixon is also the creator and editor of *Revelation*, the magazine of apocalyptic art and literature.

C. Mitchell O'Neal writes in Southern California, where he lives with his beautiful wife and daughter. His work has appeared in *Paradox, Flashquake* and *Revelation*, among other venues.

Joe Tangari is an American music critic and fiction writer, raised in New England and currently residing in Arkansas. He has written news items, features and album reviews for the music web magazine Pitchfork since November 2000. His short fiction ranges from speculative fiction, sci-fi and supernatural explorations to humor, literary fiction and character study, sometimes all at once. His short fiction has been published in *Revelation*. He is currently seeking a publisher for his first novel.

Alexander Zelenyj's fiction has appeared in a wide variety of publications, including *Revelation, Front & Centre, Freefall, Cerebral Catalyst, Euphony Journal, Inscape, Underground Voices, The Windsor Review* and *The Rose & Thorn*. Zelenyj is the author of the short novel *Black Sunshine,* published by Fourth Horseman Press, and the short fiction collection *Experiments at 3 Billion A.M.*, published by Eibonvale Press. He lives in Windsor, Ontario, Canada.

www.ingramcontent.com/pod-product-compliance
Lightning Source LLC
Chambersburg PA
CBHW020507020726
47493CB00001B/224